CUTTING LOOSE IN PARADISE

MARY JANE RYALS

A LARUE PANTHER MYSTERY

Pineapple Press, Inc.
Sarasota, Florida

Pineapple Press, Inc.
P.O. Box 3889
Sarasota, Florida 34230
www.pineapplepress.com

Library of Congress Cataloging-in-Publication Data
Ryals, Mary Jane.
Cutting loose in paradise / Mary Jane Ryals. — First edition.
 pages ; cm
ISBN 978-1-56164-784-2 (pbk. : alk. paper)
I. Title.
PS3568.Y25C88 2015
813'.54—dc23
2015001120

First Edition
10 9 8 7 6 5 4 3 2 1
Design by Carol Lynne Knight
Printed in the United States

*This book is dedicated to
Barbie Ryals and Sue Cerulean.*

ACKNOWLEDGMENTS

Despite what we think, books need lots of people to get from the imagination to the page.

Most writers need writing groups, yours truly included. Thus, I'm grateful to the Black Dog Java Girls—Lynne Knight, Donna Decker, Laura Newton, and Melanie Rawls; also to the Horsewomen of the Apocalypse—Lynne Knight, Anne Meisenzahl, and Jane Terrell.

For assistance and inspiration from hair stylists, thank you Barbie Ryals and Michael Moncrief.

For the space, time, and solitude away from this noisy, fast world, I thank Hambidge Center and the Bowers House.

Most writers need employment. Thanks to institutions that pay me and allow me to interact with others about reading and writing all the time: the TCC Learning Commons and College of Communication and Humanities; Flagler College Tallahassee; and the FSU Business Communications Program.

Agent John Sibley Williams is a literary angel. Thank you.

Pineapple Press, the largest independent press in Florida, I thank you for publishing my work. June Cussen, thanks for your genius editing and encouragement. Jesse Rice, owner of Backwoods Bistro, thanks for your open and generous use of the restaurant for cover photos. Al Hall, thanks for the rad photos. Beauties Pam Ball and Sherece Campbell, thanks for modeling. Lynne Knight, thanks for the artful cover design and masterful layout.

I couldn't do this without my family—Dylan Ryals-Hamilton and Ariel Ryals-Trammell, my cool kids who as adults still teach me; my new Strauss family, in particular Susan and Katherine Strauss who, when I broke my foot, said I'd be writing a novel in bed. Such confidence galvanized me to continue.

And how grateful I am for my husband, Michael Trammell, ingenious writer, who encourages and reads my work, and who makes me laugh and loves me through everything.

CHAPTER 1

I STOOD IN FRONT of the closed double doors of the funeral parlor clutching the cut and style bag I carried for house calls. I pushed on the doors. They gave easily. When I reached the coffin of my friend Trina, I laughed aloud.

I know, my sense of humor is skewed. But Trina was one of us, a regular person who liked a glass of wine, and she could quote Darwin with scientific aplomb. Yet here, her arms were folded in prayer, she wore a high-cut Victorian blouse, and a green Gideon bible perched on her skirted stomach. This was not my irreverent friend. Neither had the news of her suicide fit her character. She'd shot herself in the chest, they said.

I went sober and glanced around to see if anyone had heard me laugh. In the wood-paneled room, I felt Trina's complete stillness now. Her stone china face was so silent, the certainty that I was alive, so terribly here.

I recovered. I had a job to do. A client, my friend, had died, and she'd requested long ago that I do her hair when the time came. People do have pride, even anticipating the casket.

And employment was in the dumps after the oil spill all over our Gulf, so on these St. Annes Islands I took work wherever I could get it. But as much as I needed the cash, I wouldn't take money from a dead client. This was Trina, substitute grandmother for my kids. I was bringing them up alone, and I needed all the help I could get. I should say Trina'd been a close friend, but I couldn't. She kept her life private. My kids knew her better than I had. Her body had been found on a foggy early November Monday night, driven to the funeral home on Tuesday, embalmed Wednesday, now time for the new updo today, funeral Friday.

I touched her cheek. Trina. Trina's pale cheek. Cold and hard. Not Trina.

We're brought into this world with nature's violence, with blood and ocean fluid, with pain. So why would we think dying might prove different? A flush of heat went to my cheeks, and I got to work.

Blonde-streaked Trina had doted on my kids. Her flaxy hair had lengthened an inch since I'd last seen her. The roots had grown in brown. I'd coaxed her into those blonde glints a year before. They lightened her face, making her look younger.

"Trina, I'm sorry," I said. "Fresh blonde color is out of the question." The crease between her eyebrows had relaxed. Instead of cutting, I decided to pull the hair all up at the crown of her head and then use a curling iron to soften the fringe around her face. I'd curl the strands that strayed.

Being a hairstylist in a small island community meant people told me stories they wouldn't tell their best friends. How they were plotting to run away from their husband and children as soon as they found a way off of these islands. The great affair they were having with the guy down the street, their best friend's boyfriend, the one with the new trailer hitch. How they really felt about the new town mayor. Who was running drugs now off their fishing boat, or trying to, due to the dry-up of money. Yet I'd never figured that Trina was troubled. I thought Trina was in the prime of her life, middle-aged, in control, traveling a lot. Living in a nice house up at Live Oak Key. You never know about people, the mystery in them.

But most people did tell me secrets deep as springs. And why? I attributed it to touch. I'd learned this majoring in psychology. A degree that got me jobs waiting tables in my youth.

Even though I had a monopoly in the hair business on St. Annes, the tourist part of our string of popular islands, winter seemed to slow business down in north Florida during the chilly months. Fog could get thick as cotton, wind could rasp and slap in from the ocean like huge cats howling. Rain might fly in sideways, pinging off the skin like ice shards sometimes. Tourists didn't take to such weather. But we were only easing into those cold blue nights. The sun still slanted sideways into our windows. We only now began to think about when to turn on the heat.

Last week had actually brought a warm wind from the south, when Trina Lutz, pronounced *lootz,* had still been alive. She'd been composed, a beloved fixture in our community, the best sort of accountant, unlike Enron and Lehman Brothers. She knew red from black and had the *cajones* to call the city commission out when they wanted to go into debt to build a new shopping center on the dock. She was also a woman who knew her county commission husband Fletcher Lutz tried to get everything he could lay his hands on, from women to boats to land. That other-women thing bothered Trina most, of course. Fletch caroused most every night in the bars, something we offered plenty of in a town mostly in the fishing and tourist business.

But Trina had always gone about her way with dignity. A loner who worked from home, she had a put-together character. She sported a tan slacks and black blouse style—uncommon for us islanders, who were as often as possible, casual. We were flannelled and long-jeaned in the winter and tank-topped and short-jeaned in summer while Trina always showed up tidy and crisp. She had nice hair, too—and a hair stylist does know. Even tousled, her pageboy never looked unruly.

When we'd moved back from Jacksonville, Trina had always asked after Taylor and Daisy, my kids. She'd given my sixteen-year-old Taylor a rebuilt computer she'd found on the web and paid for my eight-year-old Daisy's dance lessons. When the news broke about her suicide, the town of St. Annes went into utter shock. No one wanted to talk about it. At first, we'd run into each other at the post office or in the cafe, glance, shake our heads and say nothing. People spoke in small clumps, always in hushed tones, theorizing about her death.

Of course, the school counselor gave a lecture at the town hall on death the night after the suicide. I dragged my kids, and they slumped like beached manatees in the back, miserable. The bars filled, too, but without their usual back-slapping rowdiness, and without people standing on bar stools yelling and playing drinking games at tables. *Why?* was everybody's question. *Such a good woman.* Did Fletch's maneuvers with other women finally get to her? My kids had walked around those first days gloomy as crows over gray winter, both refusing to talk about it. Wednesday, Daisy knocked on Tay's door, and he whisked her inside. Half an hour later, they'd come out to dinner swollen-eyed. At least they could confide in each other.

Now I picked up Trina's stiff head to lift the back of her hair towards the crown. Her rigid neck freaked me out. This was only my second remembered encounter with death. I was six feet tall and could reach in and around, brushing her kitten-soft hair straight up with one hand, holding her head with the other. I gently lowered her neck down on the silken pillow. Next, I whooshed the sides and front up and back towards the crown. Easy enough to do with someone alive in the chair telling you about the new rich guy up the road restoring the old black church. Not so with your dead friend's hair in your hands.

I stepped away from the casket and wiped my hands on my hips—as if you could wipe away death. I glanced around the low-ceilinged room and searched in my bag for bobby pins. A sappy scent of pumpkin spice, like a waxy furniture polish or cheap candle, turned my stomach. Dark brown carpet covered the floor. The wood paneling was dark, too. Those cheesy, orange-yellow beach sunset paintings you see in motels were arranged on three walls without windows. Why do funeral homes always have an element of spook mixed with sap?

Trina's hair felt long and uneven. I put bobby pins in my mouth and began winding a rubber band tight around the hair I'd gathered. Sweat ran down my forehead like an oysterman in noon's sun as I pulled together loose strands and tried to half hide the pins anchoring the hair in place. Freed of the bobby pins, I unpursed my lips and breathed in gasps.

"Dang, Trina, aren't you hot?" I said. The egg-blue blouse had a collar buttoned up to the neck. "Too formal," I said shaking my head and plugging in the curling iron. "You look Victorian." I glanced out the door to see if the funeral home guy could see me. No, behind me through the doors, just the hallway and a blank wall.

This next part sounds insane. I undid the first button of the shirt to cool her off. Then I picked up the hot curling iron and brought it to the tendrils in front of her waxy face.

What I saw sent a burn soaring from my heart to my hand. I dropped the curling iron, which bounced to the floor. I looked again at her neck. A razor thin cut, raised and stitched up neat as a shirt hem. Slashed all the way across her neck, just above the collarbone. Though the cut was covered in makeup, I could see plastic stitches precise and black as moorhen feathers.

She was supposed to have shot herself in the heart. A clear case of suicide, the St. Annes *Chronicler* had said. My fingers shook. I laid the iron back into its metal rest and grasped the shirt's third button. I unbuttoned down to the base of her rib cage. Please forgive me, Trina, I said in my head. I opened her blouse and pulled up her beige stretchy bra. No blown-out chest, just a hard breast. I checked the right side. Nothing unusual.

Has she slashed her neck? I checked her wrists. White as bone and untouched. How could the paper have gotten it so very wrong? I glanced behind me to the door again.

Suddenly, my cell phone rang. I jumped at the high-pitched chirp, then grabbed it in hopes that the funeral home guy wouldn't hear it. I didn't want to be caught undressing a corpse.

"Hello?" I said, forgetting to use my business name, Cutting Loose. My fingers shook as I tried to button up Trina's blouse, the phone cradled awkwardly between my ear and shoulder.

"Mama, there's nothing to eat. Nothing in the 'frigerator." Daisy. Home from school, singing her anxious whine-song—the verse about wanting me in the apartment to list out the snack items. Children have a conservative streak in them. Mothers need to perform that job 24-7, kids seem to think. As my fingers somehow pushed the next button through its hole in Trina's blouse, I cleared my throat, swallowing sharp fear.

"Honey, yes there is," I said, low. "Potato chips." Guilt guilt guilt. Bribing children with junk food. Desperate measures. "Yogurt," I added.

"I hate yogurt," she whined. "And the peanut butter's gone. That pig Taylor probably ate it all." I wanted to scream. Kids wanted minutia at the worst times. And in a flash I knew I'd forgotten how to pluck life from the small pleasures like after-school snacks. But who could handle a lyrical life with a dead body beside them?

"Honey, there are grapes, cinnamon bread and butter, chocolate milk, something. I can't talk right now, but I'll be home soon."

"What's wrong?" she said, picking up on panicked, rapid-fire speech. At eight years old, she possessed a native shrewdness, emotional intelligence. Her brother had his own intuition, but he didn't pick up on voice strain.

"I'll tell you when I get home," I said, buttoning all but the top button. "Everything's okay. I'll see you soon. Bye." I pressed END on the phone just as she said, "But—" Cutting her off made me as queasy as the funeral home's fake-floral scent had.

The parlor director walked in. I could smell the beeswax and mineral oil of the old-school Brylcreem on his deep brown hair. He slicked it straight back like Cary Grant. He looked familiar, like a distant relative or somebody I'd seen year after year at one of the St. Annes art festivals. He wore glasses thicker and nerdier than Clark Kent's, square, dull black. But he had a clear complexion and a noble nose, kind of a refined face. Even in the black suit. He was the real *Mad Men* thing.

"How's it going?" he nodded.

"Oh, swell." I swallowed, grabbed the curling iron and wrapped a straight stray strip of Trina's hair to soften her stone china face. "I'm done with the cut—haircut—just curling this around the face. No need to worry." I gave him a smile, hoping he'd wander back out. He didn't. He stood a few feet away on the other side of the casket. His arms were folded in front of him.

"Strange request," he said, "wanting her hair done up. Most want it falling down around the shoulders. Women, I mean." He stared in the middle distance. He made me think of ice. Frost.

"Some people want to look good and composed regardless." I sounded too high-pitched and cheery. Swell? Had I really said swell? I loosened the updo, pulling the band out a little. It slowed me down, made me feel less scattered, reminded me to be deliberate about Trina's hair.

"Sad about the suicide," he said as if studying the floor's carpet. "Quite a lady." His eyes shifted to me, then darted away. He licked his lips, and his Adam's apple slid up and down hard. He paced slowly towards the lower end of the casket.

"You just never know, do you?" I glanced at him as I curled another wisp of hair around her face. Surely he knew—he'd read the newspaper and seen the body. The body told a different story. Was he hiding the scar with the button-down blouse? *Calm yourself,* I thought. Surely the slash was an autopsy scar. Or there'd been a mistake in the paper. I was no detective, no doctor, no funeral home director. Still, my mind couldn't switch off the speculating. Maybe her death had been more gritty than Fletch's family wanted others to know. But this funeral home guy wouldn't have left me alone with the body, would he have, with a cover-up? Yet why did the newspaper state such incorrect information?

Now the Clark Kent of funeral homes was pacing back and forth, staring down at the floor. His eyes never lit on Trina, and he held his arms tight across his chest. "Once, I had this lady whose medicine had given her bruises, all over, you know? And her husband had wanted to hide it." My stomach turned over and then over again. I wished he'd shut up. "Makeup can't cover everything, you know?" he said. "The bruises looked kind of green by the time I got finished. The green gal, I called her." He laughed half-heartedly as he combed his hand through that Cary Grant hair. Somehow, he seemed disturbed. Maybe because of it, cruel.

I gave the last curl on Trina's hair an extra twist, made sure the updo was secure by tugging it mildly. I unplugged the curling iron. Trina's top button still wasn't fastened. The blouse stood slightly agape, almost showing scar. I couldn't button it without his witnessing the move. I stood waiting for him to leave. He stood, arms still stiff, folded across his chest, waiting.

"Well, see you later—at the funeral, I suppose. Tomorrow." I packed up brush, pins, iron. He released his arms from his chest as though he were unfurling. He followed me to the exit. The fierce-angled winter sun stung my eyes as I stepped out the door.

CHAPTER 2

IN THE CAR, warmth washed over my skin. My spirits lifted like a sea-bird aloft over the morning wind currents. Dollar Store sunglasses helped with the glare. The twenty-minute drive home would offer time to consider what I'd seen and let it sink in. In this rural county, we had little traffic, some thousands of acres of national, state, and local forest and plenty of salty-dog road life. Sometimes the place bored me, but then a coral sunset in a winter sky would pull me back to gratefulness.

My master's in English had gotten me as far as an oyster boat without a motor. So when I left my marriage in Jacksonville and headed home, I'd studied for a hair stylist license. I set up shop in the town where my dad and his mother lived, where my blood was salted.

I drove past the now-empty canoe shop with its purple gorilla statue standing outside, frozen in a hello wave. On beyond the last pastureland with a few cows munching in the chill. Most cattle farms now were situated north of the city of Tallahassee, fifteen miles above Wellborn, and spilled into Georgia.

The phone rang. I was relieved for distraction. They say we are all in peril with phone jabber and driving now. When you live an hour from pharmacies, clothing stores, dentists, the accoutrements of our twenty-first century lives, the phone assists in the business of life. I felt around on the seat for the cell. As rural as the road was, we had no stoplights for ten miles. What locals worried about most was fishermen and tourists partying too much and veering around on roads from Cureall. The town of Cureall promised a hundred years ago to dip you in magical waters and heal you. Now, it served as a tiny commercial fishing port.

"Hello, this is LaRue Panther of Cutting Loose," I said into the phone. I had passed a boiled peanuts stand and eight cars lined up, rusting bumper to bumper, near the beat-up old railroad line that took lumber down to the Gulf a century ago.

"LaRue?"

"Mac?" I said, in a cracked voice. MacKenzie Duncan, who lived on the island part-time, my connection to the well-to-do Capitol gang up in Tallahassee. Mac was one of a kind, a barrel-chested lobbyist with a white head of hair, cowboy boots, and bolo. A booming voice. He was approaching retirement, and his family owned land from the Gulf back north to the farm land two counties up into Georgia. He helped me out like we locals did for each other.

Most lobbyists wore black or white versions of power suits. Mac didn't care about the suit. He owned the only condo hotel complex on the Gulf on St. Annes. He booked special events in a big reception hall with glass that overlooked the water. He introduced me to those who could help me make a living. I was the only hairstylist on St. Annes. My shop's name I'd decided on after I flew out of Jacksonville in the middle of the night with my kids. If their father had been awake, I'd never have gotten away. So I'd cut loose and in a hurry. Panther's my Indian name, my father's name. LaRue, my Christian name, came from my mother's French Canadian name. She died giving birth to me.

I passed the old whitewashed Bert Thomas Grocery and Gas Station and the Southern Spirits Lounge and Liquors, and headed toward the pine-, tupe-lo-, and bay-lined road that took me toward home—and turned my attention back to the phone.

"The wedding tomorrow evening is yours," Mac said. "They decided it best to wait and do the hair out at the island." When folks decided on an island-theme wedding, they went all out. Politicians who dined and dealt with Mac had big bucks to spend on their preciouses, what we out in rural north Florida called their children. A mixed blessing, I'd discovered, weddings and hair styling. Perfectionism pervades weddings, and the hairdresser catches it when things don't come out looking like heaven. Still, weddings paid well.

"Thanks a million, Mac. You're an amazing friend."

"Yeah," he agreed.

"Did you know about Trina Lutz?"

"Yeah," he said. "Terrible shame. Didn't expect her as a suicide type. Did you?"

"Well, everybody year-round here knows each other," I told him. I was avoiding answering the question. "When you have so few, it's not hard to get a sense of most folks. You see them in the yard, at the post office. But Trina was great to my kids. Didn't have any of her own." With seven hundred year-round residents, we all knew when anything went down. Tourists were another matter. They came and went like the tides.

"How old was she?" he asked.

"Oh, you know, about fifty-five. A young fifties, you know?" A couple of small herons flew past, distracting me. They reminded me that I had approached wading bird territory.

"Hmm. How'd she die again?"

Heart staccato in my chest, I said, "I heard it was a gun to the chest. Guess you never know about people. Say, did the *Tallahassee Times* report this?" I realized as I said it that I'd decided to keep the new information close. Maybe the city paper had gotten a more factual account.

"Shot herself, yeah? Sorry to hear it," Mac said. "Madonna let me know Trina'd done herself in as she passed by this morning. Let me check the paper here." I could hear paper rustling. "Shot herself. In the heart," he said. "A shame. Sometimes the lonely island life gets to people."

I bristled a little at his cliché. Trina wasn't lonely. At least I didn't think so. I also shuddered at the taste of folks sometimes. A huge tacky blow-up Santa sat in a mildewy boat on a junky front yard I was passing. Our Gulf people could be described as a bunch of crazy old beat-up Floridians. Another cliché? Still, they were my crazy old beat-up people.

"Right," I said, my mind elsewhere.

The island landscape did have a way, a gravity that pulled the locals backwards in time, possessing us with who we all used to be, dependent on the ocean and its terrain for survival. How would he know that? He was a loaded outsider. He had the bucks to hobnob with rich and infamous lawmakers. I headed through the light at the highway towards home.

"Well, Tiffany is helping me by closing a real estate deal out by the Indian mound there, so I need to run," Mac said. "I'll be talking to you about the details of the wedding tomorrow. Say, can I get a trim while you're over at the reception?"

"Of course. We'll celebrate being alive, okay? And your deal? And thanks, as always."

I wondered what he'd sold, out by the Indian mound. I didn't know he'd invested in the land near the river as it wound into the Gulf. Still, I was relieved. Winter wanted to be the slowest season in north Florida. Slump time, the cold and misty months when businesses either made it or not. Fall and spring pulled in tourists with cash to toss around on fishing, excursions, a spa, a fancy hotel, and incredible views. In the off-season, making a living on St. Annes Key was, like island life everywhere, a precarious enterprise.

I drove past the first island, Shell Island, which proudly announced itself as such, adding, "Welcome to a Golf Cart Community." The fishermen loved to sneer at the sign near the wetlands where the St. Annes River met the Gulf. As I reflected back on my conversation with Mac and the Shell Island deal, I figured he'd probably either done a state park deal or arranged something from a rich Midwesterner who'd always dreamed of living on the fringe of an Indian mound where the weather hovered in the soft ranges.

Then I wondered: Why had the paper gotten this cause of death so wrong? Had anybody else noticed it yet and complained?

Was the "haves and have-nots" situation worsening? Bad enough that Wall Street suckered working people out of bazillions, but this past summer, oil had burst up out of a deep hole in the sea bottom created by the mega-company BP, burst up and into our TV screens for us to gawk at. On the Islands, this spit of coastal pineland, folks broke their backs on shrimp boats and serving margaritas and broiled grouper to tourists.

And despite our country's brightest engineers, our massive machines, a wealthy world government, no one in this world could stop the oil gushing into our waters for months. Since shrimp are bottom feeders, and the oil was settling at the bottom, there could be no shrimp food. No water algae and plankton, and no shellfish. And without promise of sea-oated dunes, we had no tourists. The coast sat quiet, except for an occasional dead animal floating up to shore from Louisiana, the state that had seen the worst of the spill.

Images of the western Gulf of Mexico coast broadcast around the world for months. And in the water, death underneath. Maybe for decades, the biologists were saying. Some even said our entire Gulf could actually smother and die.

And like it or not, I needed steady money. I covered rent on the business and apartment in town. As well, I paid the mortgage on the family land back up on the St. Annes River near Newport where Dad and Grandma Happy lived. The twenty acres was about half paid off, but "half" does not equal "owning." Just this year, the local city bank had tanked, and Old Man Patterson next door to Dad had sunk into foreclosure on the ramshackle cabin he'd lived in for twenty-five years. He moved himself into a nursing home up in Wellborn. Word had it he sat in a wheelchair covered with a plaid blanket staring out the window at the parking lot. His heart wouldn't pump much longer.

All around the islands, strangeness and loss showed on fishermen's faces and on shop owners' rounded shoulders. Whoever decided to put those oil rigs out into waters had forgotten how those waters rocked us all to the rhythm of the ancient, feral heartbeat. I passed a flock of turkey buzzards hulked together in a tree. They waited for me to pass so they could return to feasting on the dead possum in the road. I wound my way through the tall woodsy lowlands and down into the swamps. Herons, yellow grasses, with blue-water sky overhead.

Laura, my news editor friend, had fallen in love with this place and never looked back after rocketing here out of south Florida. I myself had sworn never to return here, but the undertow had sucked me back. Laura did not get facts in the media wrong, but she'd gotten the cause of Trina's death incorrect. I punched in her number.

"Hey, you," said Laura Knight, who'd reported Trina's death. I'd wanted to try a new color on her thick, curling hair. As someone with straight hair, I was fascinated with curls. Maybe honey and ash blonde streaks to contrast, like a small boat wake in a sea of waves. "You're on for Saturday night?"

Occasionally, we tried to head to Tallahassee or somewhere for a movie, play, anything like culture on weekends. We made up the minority group on the island—those who didn't haunt the bars from sundown to closing. Nor did we wake Sundays at dawn's light to attend church.

"Hey," I said. "Can you meet me at the Rusty Rim Pub in ten minutes?"

"Ten minutes?"

"Really important," I said. "Check the info on Trina's death, will you?"

"What's wrong?" she said, her voice on alert. Even though Laura was from elsewhere, she was born with such earnest duty and a hard work ethic that she'd made her way to the trust of most locals.

"I really want to talk in person—can you be there?" I said.

"Sure," she said in her low-affect, count-on-me voice.

"I'll tell the guy with the camo and bandana to leave you alone," I promised. I was thinking of one of those barflies who drifted to our island from who knows where. This one came in and hit on her constantly. She chuckled.

"See you in ten," she said.

CHAPTER 3

I PASSED A STAND OF SLASH PINES and then a cluster of swamp chestnut. Then, the bald cypress, which clues you that you're in woods and swamps. The whisper of reeds and grass. At dusk or dawn, deer grazed alongside the road. An occasional bobcat might dash across. I always felt like a mermaid along this wettish road—half woman, half fish.

Next, the sandy swamps and natural canals of St. Annes Island. It's not an island, but a good river port, the confluence of the St. Annes River and the Gulf. A laughing gull gave a raucous call in the chilly fog overhead as I pulled into the parking lot that had served Posey's Bar. Posey's had taken countless fishermen, shrimpers, and oyster men in her wild arms and rocked away the weariness of that life through beer, jukebox, and pool.

Now Posey's sat on the St. Annes River, battered, windowless, and wrecked from floods. A dead bar made me think of Trina. I slammed the car door and walked away, towards the Rusty Rim Pub, a homely cube of a cement block building hanging on to the bank of the river right next to the shell of a wooden building that had been Posey's Oyster Bar before the last hurricane washed it out. The Rusty Rim had housed a fish storage in earlier days.

Brrr. This was the coldest winter we'd experienced in north Florida. Newscasters said it might snow next week. Whiffs of snow teased Tallahassee every five years or so, but the Gulf, no. Not in written history had it snowed on our Florida beach. It had gotten to the 30s, and the newsman told us it was headed for the 20s and teens.

I walked towards the pub holding my breath. Many brace themselves for the stink of the Rusty Rim Pub. No matter what, it always reeks like a wet dog. I walked across the concrete floor to the deck where there stood a skinny, leathery guy missing a few teeth. I'd stopped wondering where some of these folks blew in from. Many stray seagull types I knew, but other old birds flew in and out like dandelion seeds floating on a fierce Gulf wind. "Please do not Feed the Birds from Inside the Restaurant," reminded the sign overhead.

With relief, I spotted Laura sitting hunched over in her bright red sweater and down jacket. She was frowning into the booth. She glanced up through her huge red-framed glasses and waved, beckoned me to sit with her as she pointed to the round outdoor heater next to her.

"You are so from south Florida," I said, grinning as she huddled in her jacket, wrapping her scarf tightly around her neck.

"This isn't Florida." She shivered, pointing out the window at the Gulf.

Her mouth was twisted in a near smile. "It's the north Georgia mountains on the Gulf, and it's snow and ice in Atlanta right now." She then glanced at the weather news looming in the corner TV over our heads. Laura took our place at face value and dug in, reporting news of environmental betrayals and local infrastructure disasters. Now she covered the economic plunge the community was experiencing with the damage of the oil spill. Like most humans, she was full of contradictions. She did not go outdoors, was allergic to a laundry list of natural and manmade stuff, yet she had a passion for protecting all things tree, sky, earth, air, animal.

She'd most recently written an editorial that stated BP, the oil company across the Atlantic that made this mess in the Gulf, was made up of "a bunch of bankers and shysters." They knew how to suck oil from the Gulf but had no idea how to deal with a blowout or a spill that would pollute the waters for thousands of miles. TV and wire services picked up on it and had begun calling Laura about the situation on our Big Bend "Forgotten Florida" islands. I tapped her head in affection and sat down.

"Ash blonde," I said, smiling, reminding her of my plans for her hair's future.

"What's up?" she said, brow wrinkled beneath those square glasses. She called herself slightly Aspergers, but I thought of her as quirky-brilliant.

"A funeral and a wedding to work tomorrow." I sighed and looked around for a waiter. A plastic oversized crab and a seven-point stuffed deer head made up the décor on the wall before us, a stuffed mako shark to our right.

I leaned in to talk to her. "Very weird, Laura. Who told you Trina had shot herself?"

She shrugged, her green eyes puzzled. "The usual. The police report, of course." Now she leaned in. "Why?"

"Who fills that out?" I turned up the heater nearest us.

"Cooter," she said. Cooter Lutz. Local guy, ex-fisherman, brother-in-law to Trina, now cop. Bald as a potato at only thirty-two.

"Well, he's friggin' blind." I leaned deeper into the table, rested my elbow there, lowered my voice as I said it. "Or he's a big fat liar."

"Gossiping again, LaRue?" The voluptuous cinnamon-skinned Madonna stood over us, hip to one side, hand propped, and waiting. Exotic beauty, our friend Madonna from Cuban, African, and redneck heritage. Her curling dark locks washed across her shoulders. She had been born and raised in St. Annes.

Laura scooted over on the bench and made room for Madonna, who plopped down. In a bigger place, the three of us were an unlikely trio—a brainiac science type, an English-psych major who cut hair, a sexy tri-racial bartender. We wouldn't think of ourselves as friend material in a city. But on an island of under a thousand residents year-round, landscape is the common denominator.

I glanced at Laura. I had thought this would be a private conversation about newspapers and police reports. "I told Madonna to come over." Laura's eyes apologized. I shrugged. Madonna shivered. She was loyal and intrepid. Magically, as always happened when Madonna was around, a guy showed up, this time a new young server guy in a pink polo who appeared out of nowhere and came over. Madonna asked for a pitcher of Coors, the only beer Laura wasn't allergic to, and a platter of oysters. Laura filled Madonna in on the conversation. Perhaps Cooter was lying about a police report on Trina, I added.

"Okay, what do you mean, was lying?" Laura said.

"Okay, off the record, Laura, agreed?" I wanted to give her fair warning.

"Huh?" Laura frowned. "Of course." She shrugged. Madonna leaned in, amber eyes ablaze. We went quiet, leaned back as the waiter brought us three mugs and a translucent plastic pitcher. We poured a round while the young waiter hovered.

"Hey, Madonna," the guy grinned. Laura and I rolled our eyes. Men went gaga over our friend, who took it all in stride. She worked at the Hook Wreck Harbor down the street by the dock where all the action happened. She raked in more in tips as a bartender than Laura and I earned combined, even with our degrees.

" 'S up, Matthew?" she said. "How's the new truck?" They chatted, and then he wandered off to fetch our oysters.

"Damn, this is intense," Madonna said. She held up her glass and made us toast to keeping our mouths shut. She took life as it came, dissolved difficulty. I rarely saw her ruffled.

"Rue," Laura said, a little impatient. "What's the deal with the lying cop report?"

I conveyed what I'd discovered at the funeral home. The two stared in shock. A long silence ensued, and the jukebox clicked on and belted out "These old bars are all closed, and it's four in the morning." We sipped beer.

"Oh, my god," Madonna said under her breath. "Poor Trina. She was murdered?" The two of them glanced at each other and then back at me. Laura was shaking her head. She stood abruptly. Facts were like religion to Laura.

Unsure how to react to Trina's neck, she said, "I'm walking over to the office to check this out."

"What? Wait! The oysters are on the way!" Madonna said. Leave it to Madonna to stay in the body.

"It'll only take a minute," Laura said, and then she was out the door.

I turned to Madonna. "I don't know. Did Trina seem suicidal to you?" Matthew, with his quick smile, brought out the oysters on the half shell, watery and plump. "Never mind," I added. "We'll wait till Laura gets back." It was sacrilege here, but I'd hated oysters since I'd been sick on them as a child. They arrived on a big metal platter, the oysters on half their shells and bedded in the ice. Quartered lemons, horseradish, and tiny cups of red seafood sauce perched on the rims. Madonna rattled a pack of crackers and slid out two saltines.

She then stabbed a fork into a fat oyster, squeezed lemon on it, set it on a cracker, and took a big bite. I turned away to watch the weather channel overhead. As usual, the weather media was picking up on anything odd. That often meant Florida these days. This time, an expectation of snow in the Sunshine State.

Madonna was well into her third oyster, chasing it with beer, when Laura came back and slid into her side of the booth and took a long swig of beer.

"Mmmm, slimy, chewy, salty, babylicious!" Madonna said, mocking my disdain of the slimy, gritty raw shellfish. Then she got serious. "To answer your question about suicide, Trina was kind of preoccupied, you might say." Laura silently dug into the oysters on her side of the plate.

"What do you mean?" I took a good long slug of beer.

"Over the last month or so. Quieter. One day she'd come in to the Hook Wreck at about five to watch the sunset. Always sat by the window looking out on the water, you know? And ordered a scotch and soda. Just one. She didn't say much. A couple of times, she came in with Randy."

"Randy?" Laura and I said in unison. He was the local-boy-done-good, an attorney who'd moved back to the islands after his wife died. We'd dated in high school, but I'd dumped him to go to college a year before he graduated. Rangy, athletic with a now-weathered baby face. He usually wore hiking boots and cargo pants.

"Robbing the cradle?" Laura said, this time dipping the slimy mollusk into red sauce.

Madonna shook her head no. "I don't think so. They'd talk about serious stuff—some church trip one time."

"*Church* trip?" Randy was the preacher's kid who lived up to the name, getting into trouble and leaving the church for good in his rebellious youth.

Madonna went on. "And later last month, another time, she brought these pages and pages of reports. Lots of words and graphs. Randy met her there."

"Accounting?" I asked.

"I don't know," Madonna said. "Those two seemed pretty tight. And she seemed kinda withdrawn and focused on the papers. But not, you know, depressed."

We turned to Laura to see what the police report had said. Laura stuffed a second oyster into her mouth as she shook her head. "Clear as day, LaRue. The police report? No question. The report is specific—a shot in the heart with a thirty-eight revolver, six-nineteen p.m., found in her office at home. Says Fletch found her. No note, though. Strange . . ." Her eyes wandered off, and she stared at the mako for a minute, then a TV freak snow in Louisiana, headed for southern Alabama. She went on. "Cops usually carry thirty-eights. Smith and Wesson or Colt revolver. I wonder if Cooter was on a drunk and—"

"No. You know he doesn't drink on duty," I said. In a village, town, whatever you wanted to call St. Annes, you were lucky to get a police officer at all. And with half the town in the bars, an alcoholic not drinking while on duty was the right choice. In a village, people would never approve of a drunk cop dealing with drunks. Cooter knew this much.

"Cooter's not the sharpest hook in the tackle box, but he knows when not to drink," Madonna said. "He comes over to the Hook Wreck on duty and stares at the bottles behind me. Always gets coffee."

"Are we accusing the local cop?" I said. "I don't know. I'm just somebody who likes to read and ended up back in my hometown cutting hair. Got two kids to raise. And I need to get home soon. This is so not my—" I pulled long on my beer, then refilled. "I'm not a friggin' detective."

"Shit, LaRue, don't you know that's how everybody is?" Madonna ate her last oyster and pushed the plate to Laura. "School's where you learn a bunch of theories. Life is where you test them out to see how it really goes. A detective is someone who's nosey and doesn't believe any hype. And by the way, I called Daisy like you asked me to earlier. She said Taylor's home now, and they're making their own dinner." When I looked up at her, she grinned. "Don't worry so much."

"Okay, I'm gonna call Jackson," Laura said with resolve.

"Wait. Wait a minute. Jackson? What Jackson? Who's that? I'm not sure—" I said.

"He's an ex-crime journalist for the *Tallahassee Times*." She explained that when he started beating the cops at finding facts, information, somebody in state police hired him. Now he was working for the Florida Department of Law Enforcement as an investigator, usually for big scandals.

"I can't pay anybody," I said.

"He'll do it for me," she said.

"Is this guy honest?" I said.

"He's a babe," Madonna said, smirking. "He goes on 'The List.' " The List consisted of irresistible guys, cute with a heart, like a George Clooney or Daniel Day Lewis. Intense and funny like a Lawrence Fishburne. Then the real guys we knew, like the now mysterious Randy. Madonna amended her comment. "Well, he's not the babe Walter was."

"Walter's been off the radar for years," I said of my former husband.

"Fair enough," Madonna said. "I just meant—sorry."

"It's okay," I said. "I'm just a cynical divorced woman." They both moaned and said, "Oh, come on," pulling me out of that momentary sense of fate and bitterness.

"Okay for me to arrange a meeting for you two tomorrow? Then you have to promise that I break the story." Laura, always the media-savvy reporter. It's not why I loved her, but it was partly why I respected her. She didn't do emotional, and we needed her for analytical balance.

"I can't do tomorrow. I've got a funeral and then a big wedding, remember?" I said.

"How about Saturday?" she pushed, pouring herself the last of the beer.

The sun had slipped close to the horizon, and the sky would soon turn an orange-red, the color of a fire touching down on a lavender ocean. Headlights shone into the bar from the road. My animal instinct cued me to check on family. I paid my bill and bid good evening to my friends, who didn't have kids. The part of me that smelled wild ocean aroma wanted to stay all night. The better part of me was glad to have the heavy anchor of home.

CHAPTER 4

"**WHAT?**" Daisy answered the phone. I was headed out the bumpy county road to say hello to my dad before I came back to the apartment in St. Annes.

"What? What do you mean 'what'? It's your mom." You never know what you'll say when you become a mother.

"Duh," she said. She was hanging out with her older sibling, a sarcastic teen brother. I could hear a TV laugh track in the background.

"Where are your manners? Have you eaten?"

"Tay made me a banana and peanut butter," she said, ignoring the first question. "Where are you?" Now she sounded like a tiny version of me. I choked back a laugh.

"Going to check your granddad, if you all are doing okay." There was no answer, just the laugh track of a rerun of "That '70s Show." "Hello?"

"What, Mom?" she said, impatient. She could go from needing me to thinking I was a nuisance in nanoseconds. When would I learn to ride the Ferris wheel of motherhood?

"Nothing. Tay's with you, right?" I could picture the fluorescent-like TV flashes of colored light across their faces.

"Yeah. He says meat's bad for you. Why do you feed us meat?" she said.

"Oh, god, is he off on his vegetarian rant again?" I said. I kept it to myself that I'd once practiced vegetarianism. "We'll talk about it tomorrow. Keep the doors locked. I'll be home in about an hour, okay?" I hoped my son hadn't begun to choose the way of the culty environmental terrorists in response to a reactionary state. He was hanging out with the kids with dreads, cheek piercings, chains hanging from their pants. They discussed things like shutting down chicken farms with smeared blood. Friends they knew in Tallahassee had thrown homemade explosives into designer ham shops.

"Okay, love you, bye," Daisy said in one breath.

I hung up as the road got rougher, with tar patches. I called Dad. "I'm stopping by. Just for a minute. I need to get home. And I've got a wedding and funeral tomorrow."

"That's my girl," he chuckled. The connection to his landline was, as always, littered with static.

I turned off the county road onto the oyster shell drive with the homemade "Panther Pit" sign hung at the fence post. A stone pony sat on each side of the entrance. The shells chinked their music as the car's wheels rode over them. When the county had built the road, they'd dug out lime rock on the property.

This they used to lay the road, which left an ugly pit. But by some good fortune, road construction had hit a spring or the aquifer. The hole filled up with clear water, and now Dad owned the best twenty acres in the swamplands.

Dad had built the log cabin on the place with his own hands thirty years ago with the help of a plumber and an electrician. At eight, I'd helped out, hauling lumber and feeding nails to the bin after school, selecting the stone ponies. Now and again, we painted the pair. This year, I planned to put a black Santa on the right side pony and a pink Santa on the left. That would keep people thinking. I parked and slammed the car door shut. The wind smelled of night swimming.

"How's my baby?" Daddy was outside waiting for me and held out long arms. Tall, bony, and hook-nosed like you see on sculptures of Indians in Mexican museums. I looked like him. I'd come home when my husband died, as much to care for him after his stroke as to crash at home.

"Fine, Dad." I hugged him. Dusk. The curved blade of moon reflected in jags through the pond. "You need to come in for a hair trim. Your hair's circling over your ears. How's the garden?" I admired his broccoli and carrots, even oranges that he nurtured and covered. I wondered how he kept it all going when the cockamamie weather had us snowing next week.

He ignored the haircut remark. "You gonna go say hey to your grandma?"

"Okay," I said. Grandma Happy always had a lecture and a warning. Dad had moved her from the Rez ten years before when she turned eighty-four. She knew about medicine, well, natural medicine, and she was full of folk superstitions. She believed in the Little People who lived in the trees. Claimed she talked to them. Of course, Dad had told me this Indian lore—that these Little People in the trees could give you knowledge, but they could also cause mischief. It sounded like believing in fairies, which, in truth, appealed to me. Just because you can't see it doesn't mean it's not there. I gazed up into the pines as I walked to Grandma's trailer, looking for glimmers in trees.

"Grandma!" I hollered. She couldn't hear well. The screen door screeched open. She always made my heart stop—all four feet nine inches of her, a billowy turquoise Seminole skirt, the plaited knee-length hair piled carefully on her head, orange necklaces from her breasts up to her ears.

"Come in." She gave me a hug. She wore nine-plus decades of knowledge no one else much cared to hear about. "Now I got to give you a tonic." She always was abrupt like that. No sweet talk.

"Grandma, I don't need one." She scowled, the only evidence that she heard me. Here we go, another lecture on Indianness. She'd be all night making up a batch of something.

She beckoned me in and showed me a dark red tea she had going on her stove. The scents of her kitchen unfolded—coffee, chocolate, mint, and holy basil, dust. I had to admit, she knew the natural remedies for bug bites, coughs, and colds. Mostly they came from what you'd call yard weeds. She'd been around before cars, before TV, before movies, air conditioning, cell phones, before the big bombs. I couldn't fathom what she'd absorbed in her lifetime.

Indians didn't have the answer for bad teeth, though. She only had ten left—six on top, four on bottom, only four total in the front. She poured some of the red tea into a thermos and screwed the top on. "I been talking to them," she said. She meant the Little People. "You got opposites going tomorrow. You be careful." She wagged her bent brown finger at me, then put the potion in my hand.

"Dad told you," I said.

"A funeral and a wedding. Opposites. You need tonic."

I didn't argue. She was stubborn. "Thanks, Grandma. I have to get home to the kids now."

"And take this," she said. She placed a big gnarly root the size of a tennis ball in my other hand. "Ginger. Ordered it on-line from far away. Shave some off and put it in the kids' food. Keep their hearts good." I didn't ask how she got on-line, and I didn't want to know where ginger grew that big, so I nodded and thanked her, waving goodbye. "You young ones go too fast," she shouted in her old voice. She muttered some Seminole profanity on her way back into the house. She'd begun using this profanity more lately. We ignored it. Who's going to tell an Indian lady going on one hundred years old not to cuss like a redneck war veteran?

Dad handed me a battered basket filled with a just-picked batch of broccoli. We stood near my car, and the floodlight of his front porch shone down. A bat swooped down and past us.

"You think that Lutz thing's for real?" he said, speaking of Trina Lutz's death.

"What do you mean?" I said. The last thing he needed was to know and to worry. A hanging black branch swayed in the wind.

"Can't see that girl committing suicide." A whippoorwill called from across the pond. The world had shifted, and evening was giving in to night. It reminded me of growing up on the pond. Crickets, mourning doves, the wind in the treetops. I slipped my arms around his waist.

What would it have been like to slip an arm around my mother, had she lived? Suddenly, I missed Walter again. Not him, just the company. I hadn't had time to yearn for her in a long while. "Too many people dying of cancer around here these days," he said. "Nobody died of cancer thirty years ago." Cancer? I hadn't mentioned cancer.

"Well, Dad, Trina didn't die of cancer," I said. "And besides, you know — the bad food we eat, the plastic, the pollution in the water. And those fishermen — they never protect their skin."

"All those still births? That's not normal," he said. I just let his words call out like the whippoorwill, echoing across the pond.

"That Fletch." He shook his head as he spoke of Trina's husband. "I wouldn't put nothing past him." Dad squinted, staring across the pond. "He killed somebody once. They said it was accidental."

"Really?" I said. "What happened?" A barred owl started up in the woods, the sound echoing across the pond.

"Don't remember. But I do know it was a gun involved. Even if it weren't an accident, he's protected. All that family covering for each other. Like the mafia or something."

The weapon that killed Trina was a razor or a very finely sharpened knife. "Interesting," I said, then opened the car door, broccoli and tea in the other arm.

"Dad?" I said. "What's that got to do with cancer?"

He shrugged.

"Don't be a stranger," he hollered. "And send those grandkids around here sometime. I need Taylor to help me move chicken wire." I promised I wouldn't and that I would and rolled up the car window. This land, the pond, each other. It's what we had.

As I rolled back onto the county road and headed back to St. Annes, I thought as always about our fresh water underground. Thus, our clear water on the property. It always made me think about the waterway just below this surface.

A whole system of underground caves ran just feet below our car wheels, a groundwater system holding water from the metro area down to the Gulf. Like Grandma Happy's legend of Little People in the trees — you couldn't see it, but it was there.

CHAPTER 5

"HOW DEMORALIZING to live in a terminally quaint village on the confluence of rivers and the Gulf coast of Florida," Taylor said, swishing his shoulder-length, green-streaked hair. "Especially now, when the national psyche is totally depressed, and we live down the street from the gulf of poison." My tall bony son could sound like a Gen X film.

He had walked out of his room when he heard the screen door slam. Long blond hair and thin Indian face, eyes black as a quarter-moon night. Too smart for his own good. I wondered if the more intelligent the person, the more unhappy they could become. I hoped he'd outgrow teen gloom. I was learning to bite my tongue when he complained. He was, after all, seventeen. I hugged him and handed him the few staple groceries.

"What's the matter?" I said. A small, fat, toddler years ago, his eyes now looked down to meet mine.

"You can't even buy a decent video game at the arcade or video store now," he said, putting groceries away, talking about his afternoon. "The tourists last year bought up all the good stuff. I'd saved allowance to get good flicks, and inventory's down. New movies won't come in until—guess when—*next* tourist season, if we ever have another one after BP's bloody bollocks up." I was about to tell my son to please stop being so profane, even if it *was* British, but didn't. "And since the economy is so tied to—"

"Mama, I'm so hungry!" called Daisy, running down the hall to embrace me. Her eyes held the evening's amber light, and her hair was black as mine, only more orderly, shinier. She had her father's family's elegant noble-nosed looks. And at eight, she still loved her mother.

She hugged me, nearly knocking me down. "I got some Oreos." She jumped up and down, clapping her hands. The age difference in my kids alone kept me exhausted, not to mention their varying emotional needs. She had interrupted her brother's rant. He wasn't really talking about video games, but something deeper, closer, more personal. I took out the mac and cheese package, because I am Betty Crocker only on free days, which aren't many, and set water on the stove to boil pasta. I would drag out Dad's broccoli and throw that into the mix.

"Hey," I said to Taylor. "Come see." I pointed out the window. We lived at the corner of Riverside and Port St. Leon, looking out towards the old Spanish Fort at the confluence of two rivers and the Gulf. From our front balcony on the second story, you could see the few blinking lights from boats and buoys in the now-black winterish night. "This. This is still ours." I hoped he wouldn't lecture me on the sugar in Oreos.

"Cool," he said, hands on the railing, his body leaning out towards the view. Still, his black eyes looked doleful.

"How's school?"

"Terrible, as usual," he said. "Stupid, slow, boring. Have you been to high school lately? It sucks. Well-known fact."

I sighed. He couldn't make sense of the Trina ordeal, just as his father's death hadn't made sense to a young boy. He'd admired Trina's work with the environment. He knew the planet was in peril, and some teachers at school had warned me that he was way ahead of everyone—including teachers and administration, if you asked him. Still, I thought he needed to learn how to fit in. He'd dyed his hair cobalt blue at thirteen. After that, he'd grown his blond hair out to the middle of his back. People stared at him. A little conformity, I had learned, went a long way. He had sneered at my out-loud thoughts about all this.

"Oh," he said now, brightening. "I forgot. Madonna called." He pushed his hip out like Betty Boop and flicked his eyelashes. Even my son recognized that Madonna was a striking combo of Georgia farm girl and exotic African-Hispanic woman. She looked like a pin-up with a Southern accent that would melt tea china. And Madonna had that rare ability to really listen to everyone. It's why men would confess anything to her.

"Oh, stop it," I said, but was glad when he grinned and nudged me. We turned from the window, and walked back to the kitchen.

"She wanted you to call her right back. Hey, can I go out tonight? After dinner? After I clear the table?" I nodded and went for the phone. I had quit asking him if he'd done his homework. That always meant a big debate over busy work versus reality.

"Help your sister with Oreos and milk, will you?" I said. He nodded.

"Hook Wreck," Madonna said, somehow pulling four syllables out of the bar name. I could hear bar murmur in the background, the clink of glasses.

"So you made it to work. That St. Annes waiter didn't take you off into the sunset?" I said.

"He's too city for me. College boy. Still a baby, too," she said, pausing, taking a drag off a cigarette. She indulged while working. Said it alleviated stress. "Glad I only had two beers with oysters, though. Anyway, did you hear about our cop Cooter's wife, Mary?"

"No, what?" I admired Madonna's radar for juicy gossip. I poured the pasta into the boiling water as the kids set the table with clinks and whispered sibling disagreements.

"Well, the thought of Cooter leaving her on their date night to go over to Piney Point to do that police report on Trina Lutz just about did her in. She got drunk as a rabid yard dog at that bar up in Cureall Tuesday night, swearing Cooter was having an affair with Laura," Madonna said. One of the fishermen had told her this.

"Laura?! Our Laura? Knight?" I said. The drunk and early-balding half-cop with my eccentric and brilliant friend, Laura? Impossible. Mary, concocting paranoid stories.

"Our Laura," Madonna chuckled, and went on. I was fishing around in the refrigerator looking for butter. She went on about how one minute Mary was dancing drunk on one of the tables, threatening to strip. The next, one of the Greek spongers who was off the boat for some days from down Tarpon Springs way was trying to pull her down off the rickety table. Mary started swinging at him. He thought it was funny till she picked up a beer pitcher and nearly took out his left eye.

"Then she broke a glass and came at him. That's when the bartender called Mac. He was over at the Cureall Cafe by chance. Mac called the county cops and had her hauled off to the county jail, waiting for Cooter to get off work," Madonna said. Mac was the go-to guy when Cooter was out of pocket, or if it involved Mary. His money and influence gave him cop-clout.

"Mary creates her own bad reality TV, not poetry, like she claims." My kids sat down in front of the TV watching "The Simpsons."

"A bartender's job could go on prime-time reality TV sometimes," she said. "If it ain't a shrimper coming in after two weeks on the Gulf without a bath, it's the oystermen already drunk on some rot gut and just come in to pick a fight."

I pointed out that Laura lived out near St. Annes Key, not at Piney Point.

"Close enough for Mary," Madonna said. "I think she sees Laura reporting news while Cooter is doing police reports and puts two plus two together to equal thirteen."

"Damn, you ain't saying." I was falling into my Cracker accent and slang with Madonna. I'd flip from college English teacher talk to my home girl twang quick as the wind picks up on a sailboat without even realizing it. "The county jail?"

"Cooter could have stopped it, you know," Madonna said.

"Well, it's not like Mac had to call and have her drug off." Neither of them was the Mother Teresa, even if Mary was three-quarters crazy, I surmised. "Another day, another St. Annes drama." I was relieved to be talking about stupidity with my girlfriend. I threw the broccoli into the boiling pasta pot.

"How about giving me a haircut before the funeral?" she asked.

"Sure," I said. "But I just saw you, and unless somebody threw a bucket of paint in your hair, you don't need one."

"Please. I need a change. Then I can tell you the rest," she said. "Can't tell you on the phone."

"Hmm," I said." Okay, then."

I dumped the pasta water and mixed in the gooey cheese and got off the phone.

We decided to eat in front of the TV. The kids had settled. After our modest dinner, we began dipping Oreos into glasses of milk, even Tay.

Daisy came over to the sofa and cuddled up. "I love you, Mommy." She squeezed me, warm and soft against my side. We settled into watching old videos of "Dexter's Laboratory," our favorite cartoon. Taylor, revved up to go out, sat down across from us and began talking about how he'd learned, from his grandfather, tricks for seeing in the dark. I usually tuned out his explanations for camouflage clothing and stealth tactics. He lectured us on how you have to sit in complete darkness for one hour before your eyes adjust completely.

"Then you can rescue people," he said. I didn't like this rescue obsession, which had begun just after the divorce—guarding this, rescuing that, saving the other. He went through a "Dungeons and Dragons" phase that swallowed up his middle school days. Maybe it was a guy thing, as Madonna would say.

"Well, you be careful at the park," I said.

He let out an impatient breath. "*I will*," he said.

"Be home by ten. No later, hear? It's a school night," I said.

"Yeah, yeah," he said, standing up, hands in his pockets. He looked skinny and fragile to me. I held my arms out, and he gave me a quick hug.

"You doing okay?" I said. He nodded, not looking at me. He went out, shutting the door quietly. I could hear him skipping two steps at a time as he bounded down the steps. I went to the window to see him walk down the street into the vast night.

CHAPTER 6

THE NEXT MORNING, I was savoring one of few indulgences, Ethiopian coffee, when someone knocked on the door. "C'm in," I said. My cagey neighbor, Tiffany Parrish. A youngster, about twenty-one, who had come to town to do a community college internship. "Hey, what's up?" I put down the local *Chronicler,* hoping she'd say *Nothing.*

"Nothing," she said, sitting down, raising her eyebrows up quickly the way she did when nervous. Which meant *Something.* She had stringy hair with no personality. Taylor said hair can't have personality, but I said *Who's the hair authority in this house?* I could do something with that hair, I thought. "That funeral . . ." Tiffany said, then drifted off, flinging herself onto the sofa across from me, pulling up her legs.

"Yeah?" I said, putting my long clumsy feet under my long torso. "The funeral?"

"Do I have to go?" Up went the eyebrows.

"No," I said. I observed her youthful body, tight and expectant. Tiffany centered the talk in town these days. The men's topics, anyway. A new woman, young, good-looking. Why was someone like her here? and who would get her?—the underlying question. "Why do you think you have to go?" I said.

She shrugged. "I don't know. Everybody's going. I—Fletch wanted me to go, but I just feel—too weird, you know?" I was constantly amazed at her inability to articulate what she meant. I had the same problem at twenty-one. The reason for my inner hostility at her, a shrink might say.

I felt tired, which annoyed me. Just before this, the coffee had started to coax me into a good speedy mood. "Don't go then." I took in a deep breath through the nose and let it out, grabbed the remote and turned on TV news. CNN's image of the oil drilling platform going up in a big blast hovered on the screen again, like it had a thousand times on various channels over the past months. I turned the TV off. "Want some oatmeal?" She nodded, so I got up to make some.

She spent a lot of time out of her house in the evenings. When she first arrived in August, she'd come over to borrow a fan. She wasn't used to not having AC in a two-story building two blocks from the Gulf. The sun blasted into everything during the summer months. She'd shown gratitude for the extra old AC unit I'd loaned her to shove into a window to finish out the long summer. We all joked that we had two seasons—fall, and hot as hell. Not any more. Weather was changing. This week, we might have snow, or the drought that had plagued us recently could return.

Tiffany had offered very little about herself, except that she'd attended a two-year business college in Tampa and wanted to get her real estate license. Maybe her contractor's license, so she could build. Not a great time for either career choice. But she also wanted to save the environment, she'd told me. She was doing an internship for her lobbyist friend Mr. Mac Duncan. Nothing about parents or family.

"An internship for a construction and real estate lobbyist for someone interested in the environment? Is there such a thing?" Madonna had asked in September on a quiet Hook Wreck night where we'd met to watch "Ironman." Robert Downey Jr. was on The List.

"She got papers in the mail from the community college about it," I shrugged. "Seems like a decent goal." I played devil's advocate. "Apparently, the school is giving her a fellowship to work on a project towards Magnolia Springs. The huge development that started in the sixties. Magnolia Gardens. I think it covers her rent."

"I wish someone would give me a stipend to cover the house payments," Laura had said. "Magnolia Gardens. The homeowners are in a snit about their roads not being paved. And I know for certain there *are* serious problems with their septic. Safety issues."

"Maybe that's what she's working on. She's a self-starter," I said. "Says she's interested in protecting the fragile environment."

"Well, somebody better start," Madonna said. "Did you see that the Block's land is up for sale? All two hundred acres of it, mostly in the swamps surrounding the St. Annes River, Magnolia Springs and Magnolia River. Who's gonna want that but a builder with back-up investors?"

I wondered how they'd get a permit, since most of the land was wetlands.

"That property is too near Dad's place for me," I said.

"What I'm saying is, businesses get around this stuff somehow if a lot of people aren't raising hell against it like they did the bottling company in Jefferson County on the Wacissa River," Madonna had said, then clicked on "Iron Man" so we could put environmental concerns on hold for ninety minutes that September night.

Shortly after, Tiffany had begun avoiding my eyes. By then she had wandered around town finding out who was important. Fletch and Mac were important—big business. So was Randy, the lawyer, but he was a recluse. She asked about him, though. And Mrs. Fielding, who'd taken the senate seat for her deceased husband. I'd seen Tiffany having morning tea on Mrs. Fielding's Victorian porch more than once down on Main Street in St. Annes.

Tiffany brought me back, licking her spoon of the oatmeal. "That was yummy."

"Cinnamon and honey," I said as Taylor's alarm went off down the hall-way. He stomped out to the kitchen blinking. Since he made a habit of dressing for school the night before and sleeping in those clothes, they were wrinkled. He wore a black T-shirt with big orange lettering in front that said, "Help the World, Ban Country Music." On the back, a mask in orange glared a grin. Flames surrounded the mask.

"You could get yourself into a juicy fight wearing that," I said. After all, we lived in a county where more than half the population loved their handguns, the Dixie flag, and relished rolling on the floor in a pool game fight.

"Mom, get over it," Taylor said in a dismissive mutter.

"There's extra oatmeal in there if you—"

"You know I can't eat anything until noon," he snapped.

In spite of myself, I went on. "You need some sustenance if you're going to—"

"Mom, I can't! I'll be late!" He grabbed his backpack and flew out the door. Tiffany looked bemused.

"Teenagers," I said. "Tay!" I hollered. "You going to the funeral?"

He hesitated on the stairs. "I don't know yet—maybe." I figured he could walk the half mile from school to the cemetery.

"You'll need a note from me, won't you?" I said. More hesitation.

"Just call the school!"

"How do you ask?" I demanded, wanting him to say please. To remind him I was his mother, not some fool he could beat up on verbally.

"Please," he said, with only a slight mocking tone. Then he started up the '89 Dodge van I'd given him when I got the Saturn. Daisy came running down the hallway.

"I'm starved!" she announced. "Oh, hi, Tiffany." Tiffany waved.

I pointed to the oatmeal. "Just in time," I said.

"Guess I'd better get home," Tiffany said. "Maybe I will go to the funeral. What are you going to wear?"

"Oh, simple. I don't think black is necessary anymore. I just wouldn't go, you know, decked out," I said. Up went her eyebrows. "I'll probably wear this old dark purple dress, a wool one I've never had any use for until this year, with a black jacket, scarf, boots." Madonna had it right. Most of life isn't what you learn in school. It's how you improvise. "By the way, did you hear about Trina Lutz?" She raised her eyebrows again and swung her leg high. Then she cleared her throat and stood up.

"Yeah. Didn't know her," she said, and headed for the door. That had to be a lie. Tiffany worked in Mac's office. Trina and Fletch used Mac's copier for big runs.

Just before the door shut behind her, I said, "It's going to be cold." Then she was gone.

DAISY REAPPEARED "DRESSED" and ready for school. She wore red and white striped bell-bottoms with a green and gold plaid top. *Don't say anything. Let her wear what she wants.*

Taylor didn't like taking Daisy to school, because she moved slow as sludge most mornings. So I drove her to school over by Seventh Street where kids from K-12 landed every day unless they'd dropped out. Which they did. Often. The senior class ended up having about ten students every year. Boys dropped out to fish, oyster, clam, crab. The girls tended to get pregnant and learn that single momming wasn't easy. "Mama, what did Trina die of?" Daisy asked.

"Die of?" I said. "I'm not sure." Honest, if vague, I thought as we passed the Methodist Church on Third Street. We should have walked, but Daisy wasn't a walker.

"Do you think she hurt?" We were stopped at the corner where the oldest Indian mound stood facing the Gulf. I wondered how those mothers had talked to their children about murder.

"No, honey, I don't," I lied. I imagined someone reaching from behind, the knife at Trina's throat. We passed the Holy Roller church and headed up the hill, one massive Indian mound. The Gulf was choppy, and the sun didn't hold much promise for coming out. Still foggy.

"I don't want to die yet," she said. She'd half-discovered death at five when her cat died.

"Don't worry." I reached over and patted her leg. "You don't need to worry about that." We headed down the hill toward school. The leaves on the palms, cedars, and oaks still had a deep muted green of dragonfly wings in winter. I felt grateful to live around trees that thrived in winter. All the green life around us oozed in summer when we were languishing. I only hoped the oil spill wouldn't do the green any deep damage. The hard part was not knowing. There'd never been such a huge oil disaster in human history. All across the world, people saw visuals of the combusted rig, the oil spreading across miles of Gulf. They didn't see our town's small businesses quietly starting to close down months later.

Daisy kissed me goodbye with pooched-out lips. She pushed the car door open and tried a triple twirl, then a new tap step. Where I walked on the earth like Gumby, she flew like Tinkerbelle. There's an old cliché of a heart having wings. I can think of nothing that fits that cliché as well as when a daughter continues to dance as you're stewing over disasters. I waved goodbye and decided to take a walk on the beach.

CHAPTER 7

I VEERED OUT to Wakulla Key for a walk on the wide sandy beach. Wakulla Key adjoined the main town to the east and then turned south. The only real beach in the area, it stretched mostly east to west along the water. But at points, it arced back north, revealing the lights of town across the water. And what rich waters, where the St. Annes and Magnolia Rivers and the Gulf converged and mixed. As usual, the few winter tourists were finding out what good fishing meant along our coast with or without an oil spill. Three boats, which took tourists out to the islands, coasted on the gray water as the fog was lifting.

Wealthier homes had been built on the key in what now seemed like the extravagant seventies and eighties, and a small tar airstrip lay beyond. I passed Laura's house first. She'd already left for the paper, since her car wasn't sitting in the drive of her perky sixties A-Frame. After crossing the short canal bridge, I passed Randy's long, one-story California-style house on Wakulla Key. Already the FedEx guy was ringing his doorbell. I parked down the road and zipped my down jacket, then walked back up the beach I'd just driven past. The wind was blowing, and the sun sat low across the horizon. And still, no oil sloshing up on the beaches.

But anyone knew intuitively that that much oil, and the dispersant sprayed to dilute it, would affect life somewhere under the water. When would evidence wash up?

Evidence. Suddenly, I realized the obvious. Not about oil spills, but about Trina. I walked back to the car, picked up the cell, and circled back down to the beach, phone to my ear. Dang, I looked like a tourist, walking the beach with a cell phone. The waves broke hard against the sugar sand.

"Laura, it's Rue."

"Whoa, you're at it early," she said.

"Did they do an autopsy on Trina?" I was dodging seaweed as I talked.

"Right," she said. "I thought of that. I'm gonna see what I can find out."

"Did you know that Mary Lutz thinks you're having an affair with her husband?" I said. No working boats headed from the marina, since they had pulled out way before the sun rose. The fog had lifted enough on the island water that Sprangle Island was visible, hunkering down through the flats to the west. The lighthouse on Lighthouse Key jutted up east from where I stood.

"She what?" Laura said, her voice rising. I told her the story Madonna had conveyed to me. "That poor woman," Laura said. "She should drink less and think more. I wouldn't touch that man—I mean, his name is Cooter, for god sakes. No offense to all members of the class Reptilia, but he reminds me of his turtle namesake, a little bit wet, and fungus growing . . . never mind. Anyway, I'll see what I can find out. By the way, I called Jackson. He's eager to talk to you. He says what you told me is strange. Amongst the cop, the morgue, and the funeral director, something, someone should have caught this. This is a cover-up."

I didn't want to feel alarmed right now. I took in a deep breath. "I can't see him today," I said.

"I know. We'll meet you for a late breakfast tomorrow. Say eleven?"

"Sounds good," I said, guardedly, though Laura didn't always pick up on stuff like dread, shyness, new crushes, or even fear of jail time.

"See you at the funeral," she said and hung up.

I passed back by Randy's house. He stood on the deck with coffee, shirt flapping in the wind. My stomach made butterflies as I remembered the tender way he had kissed long ago. Full lipped, without expectation or aggression. He had healthy disheveled good looks, and a shy smile that warmed me in that all-over way so new back then. I waved. He waved back. No smile, no change of expression. I wondered if I should thank him for helping Tay out over the past few years. He had taken Tay out on his boat fishing almost every other weekend over the summer. Randy, alone and educated in this place, identified with a smart kid in a honky-tonk town. Or maybe Trina had badgered him to help with Tay.

At any rate, fishing is largely an excuse for men to get together and hang out. Tay and Randy had explored the island marshes of Sprangle Island, still full of alligators, bobcats, bald eagles, and big snapping turtles you'd rarely see on the mainland. And snakes and mosquitoes, of course. Randy showed Tay the old graveyard where Victorian villagers had been buried. Tilted and up-heaved gravestones stood as the only remains of the old town before the tidal wave of 1917 washed everything off the border island.

Now, Randy turned around, his stiff back to me, and walked inside. Okay, then, I thought. So much for a chat. You missed your chance of a lifetime, buddy, I thought. His wife had died, too. Maybe he was stinging. He'd been moody as a teen, but now he had the trait in spades. Tay and Randy both thought logically. They also shared computer websites and played outer space games together.

Taylor had told me Randy was astute about the natural world. I did appreciate what Randy could offer my son. Next, I did the one thing I could for Taylor—called the school to give him permission to go to the funeral.

Seven snowy plovers with their fat breasts stood together on a sandy stretch of beach, their feathers puffed in the wind. Good. Something stable, our winter birds, and not covered in oil.

IN THE SHOP DOWNSTAIRS FROM THE APARTMENT, I readied everything for the wedding party that would rev up after the funeral. Long day. I'd have to get back to work on that an hour after the funeral ended. Mac had invited folks from around the islands to attend the reception. This seemed strangely optimistic to me, to have well-to-do city folks mixing it up with fishermen and rednecks, especially when booze was involved. Maybe that was why it might work. Alcohol at parties could sometimes be a great leveler. Mac probably wanted a few dance partners. Islanders knew how to shake it.

Brushes and combs, scissors, blow dryer and curling iron, all into the black bag. Then loads of bobby pins, hair spray and mousse, the trick to taming hair into something a bride wanted. This bride would have the bridesmaids and flower girls all wearing pearl bands with orange ribbons trailing. A goldfish color, she called it. Fat fall pumpkins, I'd thought.

Madonna knocked on the shop's window. She wore a tight black dress that said without words *I don't give a damn.* And nobody would, except about her voluptuousness. "You'll steal the show from Trina in that," I said. She waved me away like she would a no-see-um gnat.

"Can you give me an updo?" She plopped in the black barber chair and took off her earrings. I loved the shop, with black and white tiles from the twenties when gambling and ice cream were big business. The room spread long and wide, so I displayed work by local artists on the walls. A hidden stereo for entertainment while I turned people's hair into living sculpture.

"Updo. Seems to be going around," I muttered. "Sure. I'll even put this red velvet ribbon around it." I pulled a thick ribbon from another event out of the drawer and held it up. She nodded, and I began brushing her full dark hair.

"You know the cab driver?" Madonna said.

"Cab driver? Yeah, Isabelle?" I said. Isabelle had a lucrative business, waiting for calls from tourists who'd flown onto the airstrip. She looked like the wicked witch of the west, only uglier, her flesh more grooved and dehydrated than smoked oysters. She was agelessly old. She always had a good story she'd tell while she smoked cigarettes in her taxi. She never let rich folks from the airstrip get away without paying her a juicy tip. "Yeah, crafty Isabelle," I said. "I'm going to put some mousse in your hair to make it stay, so don't freak out, okay?" I said. Madonna nodded and continued.

"So Isabelle came in to the Hook Wreck Wednesday late afternoon. Had a beer. Nobody else in the bar, so I guess she felt safe talking. She told me nobody was home on Monday. You know, at the Lutzes'."

"What do you mean, nobody was home?" She looked at me like I was stupid. The body had been found at home about that time, supposedly. "Okay, then, how would Isabelle know who was home if she was taxiing folks with airplanes around the islands?" I said. I swooped Madonna's thick shiny curls up and banded them. Then I began a French braid. "I mean, what would she be doing out at Live Oak Island? That woman can tell the biggest tales—"

"Rue, she was serious," said Madonna. "She was driving some rock star dude—you know how they borrow these rich people's houses for long weekends and stuff?"

"Yeah, go on," I said, second band in my teeth as I wrapped the braid.

"Well, Isabelle took the rock star to the house, that tacky pink house with dark pink shutters next to the Lutzes'?" She glanced in the mirror. I nodded. "The key to the pink house wasn't where it was supposed to be, so Isabelle went to the Lutzes' to see if Trina had a key to his house. Trina's Jeep was sitting in the garage under the house, and how can you mistake a red Jeep? No one was home, so, you know, around here?" she shrugged, "everybody knows everybody, and nobody locks up?"

"Ha," I shrugged. "Till now."

"Anyway, she went up to the house and knocked. When nobody came to the door, she walked in and found a key in the kitchen on the key holder by the door. She'd 'Hello'd,' you know? When nobody answered, she walked into the next room, Trina's study. She went to get a pencil and paper to leave a note, and nobody was there."

"Do you want to leave the braid hanging, or should I twirl it around? What time of day was that?" I said. Madonna's hair felt silky, malleable.

"Up, up," she said, using her fingers to create a swirl. "It was like, you know, after six and before seven in the evening."

"How do you know?"

"The sun had nearly set, the moon was rising. Isabelle swore to it."

"Where does she think . . . everybody was?" I pinned her hair into place and pulled the ribbon from the drawer.

"I know where Fletch was," Madonna said. Fletch Lutz, Trina's husband. She used her finger to point northwest. "Right there in the Hook Wreck. I was working, so don't ask me a bunch of suspicious questions, detective. He had gotten a meal at the Pelican and brought it in to eat at the lounge. I remember 'cause I was hungry about that time and he offered me some. He was already plastered. So I ate most of his fried grouper and soft shell crab."

"You're knock-out pretty." I stepped back. "But where was Trina, then?"

"Ain't that the question?" Madonna stood up and peered in the mirror.

Shrugged. "Like I said, her Jeep was there." She stood up, whirled around, her eyebrows raised and said, "*That's* the question." She left me a ten-dollar tip.

THE GRAVEYARD was settled on a mound of large water oaks. The mound overlooked one of the coves. Graves dated back to the eighteenth century, some wrapped with wrought iron fences. Others were tiny, former slaves' graves. Sadly, St. Annes had sent most of the black people off the island and into bigger towns to find work.

In the 1940s when the broom factory went out of business, it was the last straw for black folks still living on the island. I wondered if descendants knew where their ancestors lay. I'd want to spend eternity on this hill overlooking the cove. This mound where ospreys screeched and oyster boats purred in the distance, and moss strands swayed like resigned angels in the wind.

This morning, people parked and walked slowly in the chill. We north Floridians do not thrive in what we call winter. When the temperature hits the forties, we slow down, curl up like lizards and snakes. Everyone was peering into a graying sky, hoping for a warm front to ride in. Usually, the opposite happened. Like at this moment. A gust of wind flew through. Women held their skirts down while men put their hands to their Sunday best fedoras.

Fletch Lutz looked like he'd gotten hit by a semi. He stood with arms folded in front of him. He stared into space, shocked. His face held a gray tint. He'd slicked his thick salt and pepper hair back and wore a bolo with his dark suit. I suddenly appreciated Taylor's ban-country-music shirt. I searched the crowd for Tay.

Trina's casket was closed, heaps of yellow daisies and white roses atop it.

Laura drove up, so I wandered over. She wore brilliant blue earrings to match the jacket. "Fancy meeting you here," she said.

"I'm kind of looking for Taylor," I said. "Want to walk?" She nodded. We wandered around the oak-covered graveyard, leaves fallen and crisp. "Lots of people have been dropping lately," I said. "From cancer. Before you got here, I counted five graves of known cancer deaths over the past year. All kinds—lung, skin, ovarian, prostate, you name it."

"Cheerful as usual, Rue," she said. "Actually, I think it's in the water." Laura paused. "I'm trying to get a news story on the topic."

"Everybody knows the water's awful," I said. "It's brackish. That's not news. Anybody who doesn't have a filter system is brain-dead."

"Sensitive, are we?" she said chuckling. She pulled her coat close to her and shivered.

"Forget it," I said. "So what'd you find out?"

She looked around. "Nothing," she said. "As in, nothing out of the ordinary. Everything looks clean as a Dutchman's kitchen. Only they didn't do an autopsy."

"I thought you had to do an autopsy when it's a suicide," I said. She shook her head no.

"Only if a family member or someone requests it," she said. "You know, you're the only person I know of who's seen the body besides Cooter—if he indeed did. Cooter and the funeral director. And the walls of the morgue, if the morgue has eyes." She pointed towards the crowd forming a circle now. "So be careful Rue. For now, keep this between you, me, and Jackson."

"And Madonna," I reminded her. Then I briefed her on what Madonna had told me about the key and car in Trina's driveway.

"Right, of course," she nodded, thinking. "So this may mean the time of death was different, or Isabelle was off. This is getting weirder."

A cool dry rush of wind came up by the cove on the other side of the graveyard, and we both shivered in the chill. Laura pointed towards the water.

Taylor sat on a gravestone closer to the cove, his back to the crowd. He had balled up fists and was staring at the ground. I sat down and put my arm around him. Big tears splashed down onto his pants. He leaned into me and sobbed quietly for a minute. I didn't dare say anything. I patted him on the back and held him with both my arms. Suddenly, he sat up and wiped his eyes. I took his arm, which he shook off.

"It's okay. I'm okay. Let's get over there. I don't want to miss it." He stood, snuffled, and walked towards the crowd.

Tiffany appeared sick to her stomach and wan, standing next to Mac, who looked sharp with his white linen jacket and tanned skin. He smiled halfway when I waved.

Randy stood alone, a crease between his eyebrows. Cargos, as always, a button-down flannel shirt. A light khaki jacket. At least he had not worn a bolo. Taylor walked back to stand with Randy, who put a hand on my son's thin shoulder. They were nearly the same height, which shocked me. Apparently, someone had let Mary out of rehab or jail or wherever. She blinked, like she was trying to focus, and leaned on Cooter. As always, he stood in uniform, his legs straddled. He nodded at me solemnly while I stole a look around for Laura. She was craning her neck from the back of the crowd. I went and stood by her.

Madonna showed up late and made a scene getting out of the car in her tight black dress and short stole. She swaggered to the front of the crowd. Men's eyes followed her. She winked at Laura and me.

It was a suicide funeral, and the minister mused about Trina the way funeral functionaries talk about death and suicide. God's hands now, peace finally hers, in another place. The funeral parlor guy with the thick glasses had driven up. The casket was lowered into the ground, and Fletch still stood there, looking grim. Mary staggered over and put her arm around him and let him hold her up.

"She was a good woman," Mary slurred. "I don't understand why she did it." Fletch picked up her arm and took it off his.

Then the crowd started to disperse. No one spoke. In a small community, where you feel responsible for the whole, many of us wondered secretly if somehow we might have prevented this. I walked with Taylor to the car. He'd hiked over from school, so I was giving him a ride uptown to meet his girlfriend. I turned back around to see the funeral home guy embrace Fletch stiffly. The funeral home guy caught my eye and stepped out of the hug to stare me down. I ducked into my car and shuddered in the chill.

OKAY, OKAY, I said to Grandma Happy's voice in my head. Home in my downtown apartment alone, I picked up the tea, tonic as she had called it, and tucked it into the beauty supply bag. "I was probably supposed to take this to the funeral," I said aloud. I grabbed the big straw bag of hair supplies and headed down to the Island Hotel, now a historic bed and breakfast. The wind was picking up, and the air was growing colder. The midafternoon sun didn't peer out over the clouds. Back in the day, the locals hung out in the Island Hotel bar and the bikers banged on the piano in the lobby, some real musicians.

Then a true outsider woman came to town, bought the place, turned it into a linen-tablecloth and fine-china kind of hotel and restaurant. For a while, she was unpopular. Finally, everyone got used to it as the hotel began to attract a tony crowd. This meant money would be pumped into small businesses in town.

The original structure was still intact, built as a hardware store before 1850. During the Civil War, the building was transformed into a whorehouse. You could still tell, too. Upstairs, comfortable seats had been built into the hallway walls as a waiting or entertaining area. The hotel had a lot of business in those days, people said. Grandma Happy said the story was that Union soldiers had taken over Lighthouse Island, which you could see from our apartment. Several hundred soldiers occupied the place, guarding captured Indians to turn them into soldiers for the Union army.

The bride coming today from Tampa wealth had no idea about all this, of course. She was busy freaking out in the warmth of the hotel. "Ohmygod, where's the other flower girl, Mother?" she said as I headed up the steps to the parlor. I walked past her and on to the bridesmaids' room.

"Hair stylist," I announced. "Who's first?" I spent two hours putting hot comb curls into straight hair, struggling to make ponytails out of short hair, tying ribbons into curls. No one even complained. When I was done, I left quietly so as not to have to redo any hair. I missed the wedding altogether. Laura walked three blocks from her office and grabbed me to head back down to the dock street. We'd hang with Madonna at the Hook Wreck, since the work day had come to a close. The bars usually sat dark and empty in late afternoon, only to pick up again in the evening.

"Why would anybody get married on a Friday?" Madonna grumbled when we walked in. We found her washing the last of the glasses from the night before and restocking shelves. She wanted to go to the reception but couldn't get a substitute bartender. We stood on the other side of the bar, elbows on the table, brushing our hands together to get warm. The sun had appeared, and the slant light glimmered coppery on the Gulf.

"Did you see how drunk Mary was already at the funeral?" I said. "Her head was nodding. I shouldn't—I've been there myself, but—"

"So much for detox," Laura said, settling onto a barstool.

"Why don't y'all have a Heineken, on that note," Madonna said cheerily. She plopped down two bottles before us.

"Well, maybe you can get one of the old timers to come around behind the bar to work. That way, you can sneak off to the reception later," I offered Madonna. She opened herself a beer, illegal up in cities, but down on the islands, people looked the other way.

"Yeah," Madonna said. "I hear they've got decent music for a change. Some reggae band." She took a swig. "I saw on TV that oil from the spill killed more than eight thousand birds. Lemme see if I can remember some of them—pelicans, terns, gulls, plovers, oystercatchers . . . " she said in her twang, counting on her fingers, holding up her hand to show a full hand. "Wonder what it's killing underwater that we can't see."

"I just read a university press release that at some point all that sunk oil won't get eaten by the microbes," Laura said. "That this will cause already low oxygen in the water to go lower. Bottom of the food chain has no oxygen."

"Not good," I said. We all took a sip of beer and stared out at the Gulf. The surface, now gray as a chalkboard, always made me think of skin, waves of tree bark, this living and huge organism. We all sat glum.

"Oh, boy, I say let's forget the spill today. Get ready for the limbo," Madonna said, dancing around behind the bar. She took a swig of beer. "Come on, you two—a toast to the limbo." We toasted and murmured about how dance cures a lot of earthly ills.

"You know, all those graves we walked by this morning?" Laura said, turning to me.

"Yeah?" Which ones, I wondered. The clumps of old family plots, the fresher graves, the tiny tombstones that marked the African-American community?

"The new ones, in the past decade, the people who all died of cancer?" Laura said. I nodded.

Laura went on. "One thing in common. They all owned property out on the county road. A lot in that Magnolia Gardens area. I looked it up, compared county records to the newspaper obits. I'm just trying to see what's going on, if it's coincidence, or if it's human made."

"Hey, nothing like making Rue's day, Laura," Madonna said. "It's not like her dad and grandmother aren't just up the river from there."

"But what could it be?" I said, watching the gray Gulf churn as the sun floated behind clouds. It seemed cleaner up there than down at St. Annes where all the motor oil and trash and human waste swirled.

"Maybe a coincidence," Laura shrugged. I wasn't reassured.

"For now, I'm just saying today has to get better," I said. We all three clinked our bottles and cheered to that and to the limbo again.

CHAPTER 8

GOLD RIBBONS TRAILED over the blue carpeted floor of the Cove's conference center room. Pumpkin satin dresses swished to reggae. We all were jumping along in a line dance. The party mood and Mac's turning the thermostat to a higher temp was warming us. It half convinced us that snow weather wasn't headed our way, and that we hadn't just attended a funeral. Locals turned out after the ritual wedding party dances and speeches and cake cutting were done. The dark had descended, but the party was ardent with the desire to forget trouble and to dance.

When Laura had moved to the islands, she'd wondered what the word "locals" meant. I'd shrugged and said, "I guess anybody who's endured the place for longer than the rest of us can remember."

The word locals meant more. Locals fought to keep this way of life alive, or fought to stay alive in this place. They'd watched as wealthier folks had come with big boats and pushed the real estate market to the levels unreachable to locals and their children.

Due to the difficult nature of the fishing industry, it was understandable that the locals had a word for folks who'd moved in—outsiders. But locals were slowly learning how to get what they needed from the wealth of the outsiders.

The locals gave the outsiders something, too. A way of being. Locals knew how to party, how to relax urban rules. High school boys danced with old ladies, people actually stomped and danced loose-hipped on the floor. The outsiders appreciated this live-and-let-live on the island. This meant the two groups generally intermingled with no thought of consequence. Live for today.

The bride and groom had sneaked off to change their clothes to escape for their honeymoon. The wedding guests had changed clothes and knew they'd be staying at the Cove Condos for the night. They had more champagne, punch, and food. I watched locals sneak in cheap bottles of vodka under jackets and spike the punch. Then I noticed the nearly full moon, crisp and white, rising in the velour black sky.

Fletch, the grieving widower, arrived in his funeral clothes, bolo and all, and danced with some of the wedding party. Cooter would stop in once in a while, strut around like Barney Fife, and then disappear to swagger on Main Street. The weather had cleared. The opaque Gulf reflected the moon in silver ribbons. Beyond, on Spangle Island, only a shadow of craggy trees—pines, water oaks, palms—shapes that exposed the island.

Dad had come to town for the festivities. He loped up and put his arm on my shoulder, nodded out towards the glistening Gulf, the night birds diving and rising again. The haunted island beyond. "This is why we moved here," he said. He was always apologizing for raising me in a Cracker island town by touting its uncultivated beauty. He couldn't help that my mother had died, leaving him at the helm to raise me. I'm sure he'd felt like the last sailor aboard ship to do the job of captain.

"I'm so glad to be back," I said. I'd moved a lot—to Gainesville for one degree, to North Carolina for a master's, scholarships to Ireland, England, and Spain. Then to Jacksonville with the kids after I married. My husband Walter, when he was around, began to ridicule me as soon as Tay was born. It started with my family. My father, a Cracker bureaucrat; Grandma Happy, a crackpot. Then it was me. Flaky, eccentric, selfish, a gypsy. I was trying to forget. But I got the message—my choices about having kids were peripheral to his life. He had no interest in being a dad.

When I was pregnant with Daisy, I had a recurring nightmare that I was trapped in a burning house. I couldn't move my arms or legs to get the kids or budge to get myself out. Two months after Daisy was born, Walter had wanted me to get back to work. He started calling Tay, who was six at the time, a loser. My father had just had a heart attack and a double bypass. I left with the kids. In the middle of the night, so he couldn't bully me into staying. I had come right home. Dad had welcomed me like it was the most natural thing in the world.

Now, I wrapped my arm around my tall father's waist. We were about the same height now, but I always thought of him as taller. "I love it here," I said to him. "I'm glad my kids are growing up in St. Annes."

He smiled, read my thoughts and took a sip of Diet Coke. "I don't think we're gonna see oil. I have a feeling other things are sneaking into the water anyway. But we'll just keep rolling, like always." He squeezed my shoulder. I wondered what he meant, but I let it go for now in the momentary bliss.

It hadn't been easy. The child support payments had slowed to a halt, and they didn't cover squat anyway. Then a second mortgage on the Panther Pit property. I moved to town to start the business. Local friends supported me, but they didn't have much. Fishermen usually don't. Neither do most small businesses. But I kept finding ways to keep afloat, like weddings, conventions, specials during tourist season. My nightmare now was the possibility that I'd lose my business ten years after losing the idea that a husband would contribute to the raising of his kids.

"Fletch doesn't look like he's just buried his wife, does he?" Dad said.

Fletch held Mary close as a slow song played. She tilted her head back and laughed.

"This town is full of drama," I said. "Always has been."

"That's why I like the pit," Dad said, glancing at his watch. "Almost nine, my bedtime. Your grandma wanted me to remind you to take your tonic."

"Oh, lord, yes, the tonic," I said, rolling my eyes. "Tell her I drank it, okay?" He gave me a quick wink and headed out the door.

The bride and groom fled from the downpour of sunflower seeds that the crowd threw, and the reception settled into a late party. The band cranked up, and the locals hit the punch. Most remaining wedding guests danced in a big knot of jumping around.

I scanned the room. Tiffany shook hands with Randy. Soon, they had their heads together in deep conversation. Mac Duncan was sidling up to Tiffany, too. They started talking furiously, and Randy began to use his hands to explain something. Suddenly someone was tugging on my arm. Taylor and Daisy had shown up. I'd paid Tay to babysit his sister on a Friday night. A real sacrifice for Taylor. So I had agreed that they could walk down Main Street to the reception. I'd take Daisy after the reception was over, so Tay could do his teen thing at eleven.

"Come on," Daisy said, pulling my arm, wanting to dance. I put down my drink and danced. Gumby and Tinkerbell. People made room for my daughter. She didn't know how good she was, but she took up the space naturally, spinning and swooping and tapping. Thank you, Trina, for the lessons, I thought. My eyes suddenly felt too full. I blinked back the teary pressure behind them.

Tay noticed and pulled me out of the center. "Mom, you okay?" he said. I nodded.

"It just hit me," I said. "How much Trina did for you. That's all." I shrugged and stared at the floor.

He put his arm around me and sighed. "Don't cry here, okay?" I nodded. No scenes from Mom. A cardinal rule of teens.

"I don't like dramas, anyway," I said. At least not those I was in. "Go on and take the night off. I'm fine." He asked if I was sure. He thought he needed to assume the masculine role in our household. He looked world weary, and impatient. "Go on," I insisted. "I'm fine. Have fun." He skulked off, then thought better of it, tickling his sister in the sides as he left. The wedding party finally departed. But the locals stayed. Mac had asked the band to play on.

Up walked Mac.

"You look like you just stepped off the plantation," I said.

He leaned over and kissed me on the cheek, unruffled. Weird, he had always treated me as if I was a sister, a daughter, and a lover, all at the same time.

"Where's that haircut you promised me?" he said.

"You want it now?" I said. He nodded. He was one of those vain clients who had to get his hair cut every two-and-a-half weeks.

"Now's as good a time as ever," he said. "I'll give you a hundred bucks to cut it right now." The locals were dancing, stumbling around. I had cut hair in many situations. One night at a late martini party on Live Oak Key for a bunch of bankers, I cut hair. The brother of the bank president had always worn long hair, and we convinced him to cut it all off. He did. The next day, he freaked out. But he never grew his hair long again. Once, I'd shaved the head of a friend who was losing her hair during chemo right there in the hospital. People sometimes gathered around when I cut hair in those situations. I looked at Mac, shrugged, said, "Let me finish this drink," and then nodded. I owed him for this gig.

I walked to the opposite side of the room and grabbed my bag. A sauced Mary was bending Randy's ear. I checked my watch. Already ten, and Daisy was dancing with her school friends in a circle. "It's just so sad," Mary was saying. "I can't imagine why she'd have done something like that." She was wandering that path towards more sodden.

"Hi, LaRue," Randy said, so I stopped. He'd changed out of his funeral shirt and wore cargoes and guayabera shirt. He wore everything well, being lanky and broad-shouldered.

Mary went on. "I heard you talking to Cooter about Afghanistan," she said to Randy. "Don't ever talk to him about that stuff," she said. "He gets so mad. He blames it on Clinton."

"What?" Randy said, exhaling in exasperated disbelief.

"Why?" I said.

"Oh, you know," she said, shifting unsteadily. "Bush." She stared at nothing in front of her. "He doesn't like Bush either."

"Which one?" I asked. "Former governor of Florida or his bro the former prez?"

"Both. Governor. He says even Bush let the lefties put all these rules on us about the wetlands and regulations out the wazoo. Can't anybody do business anymore. And now we have that, that . . . black for a president. That Muslim." Her face had turned blotchy red, shouting the way people drinking do when they don't know how loud they've become. "Cooter says people have been building houses out there by the St. Annes River since time began. Then here comes the government, telling us what to do. And saying they won't pay us but ten percent of what we'd have made after this oil spill. Some say they did it on purpose." Randy sighed, looked at the ceiling, nodded at me, and then walked off.

"I wanted to thank you," I said, calling after him. He stopped, turned, his jaw clenched. I didn't get this guy anymore. "You've been so good to Tay. This is a hard time for him."

"He's a great kid," Randy smiled, glancing at me, and then back at Mary. "I enjoy his company." End of conversation, unless I said something. I turned away from Mary and took a few steps toward Randy.

"I'm about to cut Mac Duncan's hair, but I was wondering. You walked away fast from that conversation."

"I don't have to listen to all that about the wetlands, our fragile situation here, contaminants that are going into the water, especially now. Redneck conspiracy theories." He shook his head. He took a sip of his drink.

"Well, besides Mary, how're you doing?" I said.

"What do you care?" he said. Whoa. Hostility city, I thought. That was exactly what he'd said to me the night I told him I was moving to Gainesville to attend college. He'd had another year of high school. I'd told him I needed to get out of St. Annes and see the world, use the small minority scholarship I'd been offered. I had told him then I still loved him. "No you don't. I'll be stuck here, and you'll be off partying, finding another boyfriend. What do you care?" he'd said as we swung in the kiddy swings looking at the blinking stars above the tiny county beach next to the Cove. Just beyond this hotel.

That night, I'd wondered if he was bitter about his holy roller father. His dad couldn't accept a son who didn't have Pentecostal beliefs. His father would never understand Randy's passion for the natural world, his need for science.

But this wasn't my problem now. I had two kids, two mortgages, and times were damn hard. He had money, a home, nobody who needed him. "What do I care?" I said. "Good question." I pointed a finger at him, and stomped off to get my stylist bag. After a minute, I saw that he was bewildered at my behavior. I felt a little smug, and then bored with myself over it, so I wandered over to Mary, who stood by the piano. Alone, she stared at the wall across the room.

"These are the best rolls and coffee I've ever tasted," I lied. "Come on." She followed me to the coffee table. Mac stood across the room sitting in a chair, waiting. He caught my eye, raised an eyebrow and beckoned, pointing to the chair. I nodded, waved, then poured Mary and myself a cup of coffee from the urn, and asked her if she took cream and sugar. Neither. I handed her a roll, which might soak up some alcohol. She watched with slow eyes. I took a bite of roll and a sip of coffee. "Really good." I glanced over at Mac. I gave him the hang-on-a-second sign.

Mary took a bite of roll. "Ummmm, delicious. You know, I haven't eaten all day."

"Well, here's to us," I said, clinking my mug gently against hers. She took a swig as I did. I remember my college roommate doing this for me one night when I was hog-faced drunk, as she called it. We'd been playing pool in a Gainesville bar called Hogsbreath. I remembered following her every movement, and being glad I'd eaten the biscuits later.

Now, I poured Mac a cup of coffee from the urn and set it on the table. I put my bag on my shoulder and walked over to Mac.

"Where do you want to sit?" I said. He pointed to the corner I'd just left by Randy and Mary. We moved back over to the corner. I fetched his cup of coffee from the table. He loved java and could drink it any time. I draped the salon cape around his neck and snapped it shut. As I started trimming his white hair, I glanced up to see Mary watching us. Was she having a fling with Mac, too? Three men would be tough to handle. She'd been ballroom-style dancing with Fletch half an hour ago.

"Nice reception, huh?" Mac said. The party began to thin out. About twenty-five people still milled around, some dancing, some nibbling desserts, some sitting or standing, talking, helping themselves to the spiked punch and the dregs in the bottoms of the wine bottles.

"Especially now that the wedding party's gone," I said. De Lions of Ja, the reggae band with a hip hop flare, were playing their last set.

"Your daughter is a natural out there," Mac said. Daisy danced alone now, twirling and choreographing her own world.

"My daughter didn't get that dance grace from me." I said. Laura had begun a conversation with Madonna, who'd just waltzed in. Then they began dancing. Mac took a slurp of coffee. I asked him for a sip. It tasted bitter. "Mac Duncan, how do you drink coffee so bitter? Black coffee is awful." He showed off by taking a big drain. The only thing close to me was the tonic, so I took it out of the bag and began drinking it. Delicious—sweet and sour together.

"I'm sure needing this, even if it is bitter," he said holding the coffee. "And you're right—it must be old and burnt." I noticed Mary was still watching us glumly as she chewed bread from across the room. Mac's mane already had the coiffure of a woman, so this cut was easy. A trim to the back and sides, some gel to flatten the long bangs in front. I felt slightly dizzy. I hadn't been drinking, just coffee and then just one big swallow of tea. Folks on the dance floor were laughing and shaking their heads at the "whatever, man" way we islanders have, cutting hair at odd hours in strange places.

"Want some of this," I asked, holding out the tonic that could easily substitute for such bitter coffee. "Grandma Happy's concoction."

"No way," he said, draining his cup. I drained the entire bottle of tonic down. Well, here's to the day of opposites, Grandma, I thought. I finished up Mac's hair with a little wax to keep it in place in the winter wind. Cooter had walked in again, and stared at his wife. Randy headed out, and glanced at me and waved as he left. I shook some talcum powder on the barber brush and flicked prickly hairs off Mac's neck.

"You need to come in tomorrow and get this neck shaved," I said. He nodded. "But not too early, hear?" I added. He got up to head across the room. I wiped the hair bristles out of the chair and made a note to use the hotel vacuum later. I gathered the cutting supplies while the reggae band played "No Woman, No Cry." The dance floor moved in my peripheral vision like an old mirror's reflection, slightly wavery. Maybe I'd sit down rather than dance, feeling this dizzy.

That's when I heard Daisy scream. I whirled around. Daisy was backing away from a heap on the floor, a human heap. In Mac's clothes. No, it *was* Mac. Huddled on the floor, wheezing. He was coughing, almost convulsing.

The band stopped, one member at a time, and people quit dancing, moving towards Mac on the floor. Daisy ran towards me, grabbing my legs. Mac was writhing on the blue-carpeted floor. He lay holding his throat, his face red. And why was I dizzy?

I patted Daisy who was saying, "Mama, what's wrong, what's wrong with Mister Mac?" People were gathering around Mac, watching. A buzzing shout rose up from the crowd into the ceiling.

"Move back, move back," Cooter said, pushing away the group who'd crowded around.

"What's going on?" I said to Cooter. He was already on his police radio, calling the county sheriff's office.

"You!" Mary pointed at me. I pushed Daisy behind me. She looked blurry moving towards me. "I saw you—you gave him that coffee! You poisoned him! You tried to give it to me, too. But I wouldn't drink it!" She had drunk it, but I hadn't the time to argue. The crowd of people looked from Mary to me. My face flushed, embarrassed. I shook my head no.

"He keeled over just after you cut his hair and gave him that coffee," she said. "You tried to kill Mac Duncan!"

I wheeled around and squatted, holding my daughter's arms, looking at her square on and said, "Don't listen to this."

"I'm not," she said, scratching her nose. "I don't like Miss Mary. She's weird."

Laura walked over, taking Daisy by the hand and said, "Come on, Daisy, let's go outside." She glanced at me, nodded, and led Daisy out the door.

Daisy looked at me, questioning. "It's fine, honey. I'll be out there soon. Let me just get this straightened out." I smiled, but saw in my mind Trina's cut throat and felt the cold of her skin. I shivered when Daisy turned to walk outside with Laura.

CHAPTER 9

AT FIRST I THOUGHT Mary was joking or just over-drunk. But she stared at me, coffee cup still in her one hand, pointing a finger with the other. Worse, usually composed Mac was moaning louder. The county sheriff had received a call over at Fish Camp Diner on the St. Annes upriver about a biker's fight. He hadn't shown up yet, as the drive was half an hour away. Folks murmured and turned their heads away. Somebody got on the phone. Someone else got a wet paper towel for Mac's head. Someone else got water, which he refused. Someone else asked if he'd indeed drunk coffee, or could it be the cake? Punch? I felt dizzy. I sat on the piano stool.

What would these people tell the cops, and would cops believe a hair stylist or a cop's wife? I started sweating, thinking about the jail up in Wellborn. Metal bars and bad mattresses, and the smell of dank fear and sweat and piss.

"Rue," Madonna said, beside me suddenly. "Let's go outside. I think you may be in shock." I followed her, admiring that the French braid was still holding after a funeral. We walked outside and down into the park where Randy and I had swung so many years ago. The streetlight shone on the jungle gym. The waves rumbled to shore, and wind thrashed the palms nearby.

I sat on the seesaw and grounded it, my back to the party. Madonna had followed me, and said, "Yeah, you just stay that way. Face the Gulf, and don't worry about what's going on back in the reception hall. You don't want to get back into the middle of things right now."

I nodded. I was remembering the last significant hurricane in 2004, Dennis. We'd watched the water leap up over the concrete and ooze into the street, one block from the apartment. We were trapped then. Now I thought of a filthy jail, other scared lonely losers turning over on the squeaky mattresses during the night. The noise of an ambulance and voices and a sheriff car's blinking light filtered into my consciousness. But I sat, hanging back in readiness, thinking of how black nights could get on a forgotten island in the Gulf.

I could hear Laura laughing. I grabbed at Madonna's arm, as I felt dizzy again. Daisy had climbed the only tree in the courtyard of The Cove hotel, one of the only cedars left. In the 1800s, the factory had wiped them all out, stripping them into pieces for pencils. The wind was whipping the palm and cedar- needled branches, causing a whirling sound. Laura and Randy sat at the picnic table under the tree.

I could hear my daughter talking. Everyone had pulled their jackets tightly around them. I suddenly felt jealous. Hell, what for? I thought. Laura's forty-two, childless, lonely, she and Randy both living on the same island. I was the same age, but had two half-grown kids. What man would be remotely interested in me? *Besides, LaRue Panther,* I thought to myself, *you're on your way to jail.*

"You look pale," Laura said, patting my arm. "I called Jackson. He'll be here soon. It won't hurt to have a former detective present anyway. He'll be looking in on this case."

"LaRue, you didn't do it, so you don't have to worry," Madonna said, reading my thoughts. Wisps of her hair were coming loose in the wind.

"Who's Jackson?" Randy asked.

"The Florida DLE investigator friend of mine," Laura said. "From Tallahassee. Remember. I told you about him."

Just then, Daisy hollered, "Help!" Randy turned around and grabbed her down from the branch before she slipped and fell.

"What do you think you are?" he said. "The monkey from another planet who can climb trees?" Daisy laughed and hugged Randy's neck, and he put her down.

She slung her arm around my neck. "I'm cold, Mama," she said, teeth chattering.

"Daisy, what do you say you spend the night with me?" Laura said. "We'll have French toast in the morning."

"And maybe I'll take you for a boat ride, you and your brother," Randy said.

"Oh goodie, oh cool," Daisy said, forgetting the cold, jumping and dancing in a circle. "Can I, Mama, can I?" I wasn't used to people taking this much care of the kids. I looked out at the bubbling, seething sea just a block away. Who's in charge anyway? I'd always known I wasn't. Put the boat on the water, so to speak, and let it float.

"Of course, honey," I told Daisy. I looked around at these friends. "Thanks, you guys. She needs her jacket."

"I'll stay here," Madonna said, sensing she should handle details. "Daisy doesn't need to be around all this. Laura can drop by and get Daisy some warm clothes and take her on to her house, okay?"

"You'll know Jackson when you see him," Laura said. "Classy guy. Sweet face. Tall-tall. He disguises cuteness with glasses. Call if you need me." I couldn't speak, so I hugged Daisy.

"Randy?" I finally said. "Will you check on Taylor? Make sure he's got a jacket?" He nodded.

I added, "He's probably out around town somewhere, he's probably—"

"I probably know where he is better than you do," he said. "I was a seventeen-year-old guy once, remember? I'll find him and let him sleep on the porch in a sleeping bag at my place, if weather permits. Almost like camping out on the beach."

"Tell him—"

"I'll tell him just what I need to tell him," he said. "Not much." He smiled, and I thanked him, and they were on their way.

"I don't know that I trust that guy," Madonna said. "He wants to get in your britches. Not only that, but he's so angry and off to himself. I'm not sure he'd help you out, either."

"Madonna!" I said. "No way he thinks of me that way." She shrugged.

Mac lay on a stretcher and was being hoisted into the ambulance. Tiffany crawled in after him. She'd insisted, Laura had said. The hospital helicopter ambulance stationed downtown had arrived one minute after Cooter called. Luckily, Tallahassee Regional had a poison unit and good emergency techs. They'd have results of blood and urine tests within an hour after Mac arrived.

"I need to face the music," I said, standing, with Madonna beside me. Inside, three county sheriff's department deputies crawled the place. Each wore plastic gloves. One took samples of all food and beverage as Madonna and I sat in chairs near the hair cutting by the bathroom. A few people also sat, partiers witness to the scene, and now looking tattered at the edges.

"Come, let's sit in the comfy chairs," Madonna said, dragging several from the supply room where they'd been put away for the reception.

The second deputy was dusting with black powder, everything, bowls, Mac's coffee cup, Mary's, mine. Madonna checked her watch. Almost midnight. She had to leave to finish up at the bar. We sat sideways, backwards, front, swapped chairs, and still I felt dizzy.

The third deputy grabbed my purse and went through it. They took my fingerprints as Madonna and I sat in the chairs. The band dismantled and glanced suspiciously at those of us left waiting to be questioned.

Madonna finally said she had to get back to the bar, but she'd check back when she got off after 2 a.m. The deputies took names of the fifteen or so people still standing or sitting around looking sad, or a little guilty. Others appeared self-satisfied and nosey, glancing at me and away. Mary looked dejected. All I could wonder was, had someone set me up?

JACKSON WOODARD WHISKED IN through the door about fifteen minutes later. Cooter introduced us to him as if announcing the arrival of the president of the United States. This Jackson had three inches on me. Guys smaller than I was always felt intimidated by my six-foot self. He commanded authority in his bones. A self-assured quiet. A steadiness. His red hair would be curly if he'd let it grow. He had an Irish complexion, freckled. Laura was right. He tried to cover his sweet face with glasses. He wore a light cashmere jacket and shirt that I knew were vintage. I had no idea state investigators could dress with such cool.

"She's the one who poisoned Mac," Mary said, pointing at me, her head wobbly. Jackson's eyes swept the room.

"Nobody leave. You're all witnesses, and I need to hear from each of you. I'll be as quick as possible. I'll ask questions in there," he said, pointing down the hall to Mac's lobby office.

I checked out Mary, now passed out in a chair across from me. I was ready to throw cold water on her and send her away, I was so angry with her. They fingerprinted her next.

Quickly, one by one, the partiers were shuttled to the makeshift interrogation room. I was sure most people had seen nothing, which spelled trouble for me. My business would be toast if this Jackson fellow couldn't find anyone to hang this on. And if I were the suspect, word would get around. Who would visit a hair stylist who was the leading suspect in a poisoning case? I used sharp implements in my business—razors, scissors, clippers, too. Hell, the name of my business, Cutting Loose, could imply anything. I thought of Trina in the coffin. They'd be blaming me for that next. Except that nobody knew but me. I hoped. Finally, the interviewing came down to Mary and me, and Cooter came in the door when he saw that she was next.

He shook Mary awake and took her off to questioning. I paced the room, waiting my turn. Outside the big window facing the Gulf, the slice of moon had risen high. Its reflection zigzagged on the turbulent water, casting an eerie silver light onto Sprangle Island. A sudden flock of big birds flew up from the cemetery side of the abandoned island. Their winged shadows tackled one another like a chaos of dark, and then they all spread black into the partly occluded silver moon.

CHAPTER 10

"MS. PANTHER?" Jackson Woodard said to me. I stood near the hall-way to the office where he was holding questionings. The sheriff deputies had left. Apparently, they respected him and let him do the questioning. I whirled around and flattened against the wall. He smiled easily, suggesting a sense of humor. My back felt rigid against the wall. "Come with me," he added.

In Mac's back office, he sat in a comfortable chair next to the sofa where I perched. I felt skittish as a fish eyeing a hook. He offered his hand. "Jackson Woodard," he said. "The sheriff on duty is busy elsewhere, and I'm an FDLE investigator helping out. I need to ask you a few questions about what hap-pened tonight." I nodded. "You're . . . LaRue Panther?"

"Ms. LaRue Panther," I said. That was stupid. This usually didn't matter to me.

"Ms.," he said, raising one eyebrow. "Do you go by any other names?" he asked.

"That's my given name. My dad's name. I didn't take my husband's name when I got married, and I kept it when I got a divorce," I said. He took down my husband's name and the kids' full names, too. My mouth felt as if it had acquired a fish hook, dry and drooly together.

"You're from here, St. Annes?" he asked, interested. I nodded. He offered, "A great place. I have a friend here—"

"I know," I said. "Laura told me." He nodded, blinking, his eyes flickering with a little vulnerability. I had known of our connection before he did. He sat back.

"So you cut hair for a living?" he asked. I nodded. "And you—it's not un-usual for you to cut someone's hair at a wedding reception at—" he looked at his notes— "ten-oh-nine p.m. on a Friday night?"

"No. Not in a little town like this one," I said. I also felt I needed to explain why I had come back to the island, and why I wasn't a professor somewhere. I started to tell him about cutting the biker babe's hair at 3 a.m. last Arts Fes-tival weekend so she wouldn't beat up another biker chick, but he wouldn't understand. "I've cut hair at all hours, all places, all days. It's my business, and I make a bit of extra money when I can. Two kids to support. Alone." I sounded defensive.

"And do you normally take coffee to your customers?" he asked.

"I don't know—no—I mean, yes, and Mac is a friend. I was trying to help him out," I said.

"And Mary Lutz, you were just trying to 'help her out' by encouraging her to drink coffee and eat bread?" he asked.

"Well, yes, in fact. She's—she was—she'd had too much to drink, and she told me she hadn't eaten all day, so I was trying to get her to eat and maybe sober up. I didn't poison her." I spit a little drool when I said it, panicky.

"We'll get to that," he said, putting a hand up to stop me. I sighed and sank back in the chair.

"Did you see Mac—Mr. Duncan—eating anything unusual?" he asked.

"No."

"Do you know who made the coffee?" he asked.

"I think the condo staff," I said.

"But you served a cup of coffee to Mr. Duncan just before he went into a state in which he could not breathe?" he asked.

"I think you're leading the witness," I said.

He chuckled. "You've been watching too many episodes of *Law and Order*," he said. "I'm just asking questions."

"Yes, I served him coffee from those big aluminum coffee urns. I had a sip of it myself, by the way," I said. He looked interested.

"You drank from the coffee?" he said. I nodded.

"Yes. I commented that it was horribly bitter, too. I thought it was because it was black, and I don't drink coffee black." Hey, I felt dizzy, too, I wanted to say. Still do. But that would involve also talking about Grandma's tea, which I simply did not want to discuss. He gave me a curious look.

"What did he say?" Jackson asked.

"He said he needed the coffee, but that it tasted bitter," I said. "I started drinking—" Don't say your Indian grandmother gave you a tonic, I thought.

"Yes," he asked, looking up from his notes.

I took a deep breath and let it go. "I started drinking some tea I'd brought from home instead," I said.

"Tea. What kind of container was it in?" he asked.

"A thermos," I said.

"In your things, your stylist bag, if that's what you call it?" he asked. I nodded. Grandma and her teas. I'd kept the black bag by my side, hidden, but he'd spied it.

"What happened after you finished cutting Mr. Duncan's hair?" he asked.

"He got up and crossed the room. I started to pack my gear, and then I heard my daughter Daisy start screaming, and then there was Mac, writhing on the floor."

"Okay," he said, scooting his chair up towards the desk a little, "this is important," he said. "Did you remember seeing anyone else around you while you cut Mr. Duncan's hair?"

"Sure," I shrugged. "A lot of people."

"Anybody come to mind?"

I thought. "No," I said slowly. I couldn't think of anyone who'd try to kill Mac.

"Was Mr. Duncan arguing with anyone, talking with anyone before the incident?"

"I don't know—everybody. He's kind of, he makes the rounds. But no arguing. He talked with Cooter Lutz, the cop, and Mary Lutz, his wife, and Randy Dilburn, the lawyer. Nothing weird. My friend Laura, who you know, and Madonna who's coming back tonight, who you can meet." The photo behind Mac's office desk featured a boat with some guys standing around after a fishing trip. Mac and Fletch were in the black and white shot. "Oh, Fletch Lutz, Cooter's brother—half-brother, whose wife just died. Nick the jeweler and his girlfriend."

He was taking notes of all the names. "If you could give me any contact information on Mr. Dilburn, I'd appreciate it," he added. I told him how to get to Randy's house by the airstrip on the beach.

"Do you know anyone who was upset with Mr. Duncan?" he said.

"No. Everybody seems to like him," I said. "He kind of skims over the top of things, you know?"

I wondered if he did know, but he nodded.

"Well," I went on. "Actually, I don't think Trina Lutz liked Mac. Trina was Fletch's wife, who just died. But she didn't like her husband, either, I don't think. Come to think about it, I'm not sure who she liked. Kept to herself." I shocked myself saying that. He did know about Trina's suspicious death from Laura, but nothing more.

"The woman who was just buried today," he said, sitting taller and with interest.

"Right," I said. "Trina didn't much like Mary Lutz, either, or her husband," I said. "But you could say I'm trying to frame Mary, right? Because she witnessed me giving the coffee to Mac?"

"I'm not making any conclusions about anything right now, LaR—er . . . Ms. Panther. Is that a Seminole name?" he asked.

"Yes, it is. My dad is half. Makes me a quarter," I said. "But we don't kill white people. I mean, that is, I am a white person, basically." He laughed.

"I was just curious about the name," he said. "Okay, back to the questioning. Did she—Trina Lutz—tell you what she didn't like about the Lutz woman, or the other Lutz man?"

"First off, there are lots of Lutz men. Big family, eleven kids, six Lutz men.

I can't remember. I don't think anything specific. She would say disparaging things, you know? That Cooter didn't have the brains God gave him. She seemed to dislike but feel sorry for Mary. Talked about how Mary was always pickled. But felt Mary had led a hard life." I shrugged my right shoulder. "You know, hair stylists hear the gossip from clients."

He nodded, scribbling. Then he gave one of those penetrating looks. His eyes were the clear green of the pond on Daddy's place. I had one of those ridiculous sexual attraction waves. He got up, put on plastic gloves, picked up a Styrofoam coffee cup and walked around to my side of the table near the sofa. He smelled of pine deodorant. He squatted next to me to show me the inside of the cup. He tilted the cup slightly towards me. Now I smelled guy soap, but something exotic like frankincense.

"Don't touch it," he said. "Just look." Inside the bottom was a white filmy powder about half an inch high. "Do you know what that is?" he asked.

I shook my head no. His red hair was fine and short and wavy. He had begun to bald in front. I could fix that hair.

"I'm very sorry, but you're the leading suspect in the case for now," he said. "You'll be on release unless other evidence appears—"

"What!?" I said, pushing up and away, standing beside the chair. "What is it?" I pointed to the cup. He stood now.

"Percodan," he said. "Whoever wanted to do Duncan in really wanted him dead, and knew him well. He showed signs of an allergic reaction to the stuff. Do you have any experience with Percodan?"

"I—I—I think I took Percocet once. I had a kind of reaction to it. You know, a rashy thing," I answered, stumbling with my words. "Will he be okay?" I asked, rubbing my arms. Jackson moved back behind the desk, a wrinkle in his brow.

"Don't know yet. I'm trying to figure out why you didn't have any reaction to the coffee. I'm going to need to see what's in your thermos." My heart sank. I couldn't show hesitation though.

"Okay," I said.

He took the thermos. "We're taking your stylist's bag to the lab. Until we find out more, you're the leading suspect. It could make the news."

"You can't!" I said simply and grabbed the bag back, gave him the thermos. I plopped down hard in the chair. "I have two kids to support. No one will come to my shop if they think I killed someone!"

"It's the law, La . . . Ms. Panther," he said a little stonily. A change flickered over him. "I'll be in touch tomorrow," he said. "I think we were supposed to meet on this other matter anyway, if I'm not mistaken?" I looked into his eyes. I couldn't see anything.

Madonna was waiting for me as the door opened. She waved and looked at me questioningly.

"Right. Eleven tomorrow morning," I muttered to Jackson. "At the hotel? Breakfast? I'll try not to poison anything." It was a reckless thing to say, but he fought a smile.

"May I walk you ladies home?" he said. I wondered. Were we in danger? No, he probably had the hots for Madonna.

"That would be nice," I said. Damn, I had Southern manners down pat. I wanted to tell him where to go and what to do with his notes. Instead I was saying 'that would be nice.' "If you don't mind, could we take the long way around the dock to drop Madonna off at her car near work? I'm just—I'm so wound up now, I think a walk—"

"Of course," he said, opening the door for us both. "I'd enjoy that."

ON THE WAY HOME, Jackson, Madonna and I didn't talk much. The night wind blew cold and squally, so we huddled in our jackets and hurried along the dock street. The fog moved thick in the cove, and the clanking of metal sounded as a pulley banged up against the boom on a pleasure sailboat. The streetlights had fluttering haloes. Waves crashed and smashed against the sea wall, their bubbles leaping up into the air. A tabby cat skittered across the road. Jackson pulled each of us gently to the left side of the road when a car came up behind us and passed. A man and a woman from the wedding party, drunk, heads out the window, singing, *I would die for you, I would kill for you, I would steal for you, I'd do time for you.*

"That is a stupid and ugly song," Madonna said.

"I think it was their first dance song at the reception," I said.

Madonna bid us goodnight, key in the lock of her door as she looked at me like "Will you be okay?"

I nodded vaguely, and we said goodnight. On the bridge over the Marina Cove that connected the dock street on the Gulf to the corner of Riverside and Port St. Leon Street where I lived, Jackson lifted his nose and sniffed the ocean.

A white cat crossed in front of us. "Smell of ocean. Lots of cats in this town," Jackson said.

"Don't be surprised to see a raccoon's face peering at you from somebody's kitchen," I said. "They feast on the fiddler crabs and find their way into our old Cracker houses."

"Raccoons? In town?" Jackson said.

"Skunks, too. Out at my family property, the alligators eat the raccoons." I loved to shock people with this.

"You get more interesting by the minute," he said, as we walked to the stairway that took me to the apartment. "What's this family property you're talking about?" he asked.

"Oh, the rock pit and the spring," I told him. "Where my grandmother and dad live." I explained our magical spring, created from roadwork. Now we approached the stairs to my apartment.

"Stroke of luck," he said.

"I could use some of that right now." I felt nervous. "Well, thanks," I said, folding my arms. "See you in the morning."

He pointed to the top of the stairs where a yellow bulb lit the landing. "What's that?" A potted palm with a tag hanging from it sat at the top of the wooden steps. "I don't know," I said, surprised. Lately, I'd been trying to decorate the shop with a variety of palms. We walked up the stairwell to check it out.

"Don't touch it," Jackson said.

I leaned over to read the tag aloud. "Don't worry about Mac," the note said. "He deserves it." Typed on a typewriter from maybe the 1980s. No signature.

"May I?" Jackson said. He took out a handkerchief and held the card. He flipped it over. "May I take this as evidence?"

"Yeah," I waved as if to brush it away. I leaned against the wall. Since he'd been so protective and scrutinizing, I was trusting him. "Will you check out the inside for me?" I handed him the keys. He disappeared inside while I sat on the stoop. He came back out and assured me no one had tried to trespass. I got up and went to the doorway.

"I just want this day to be over," I said, sighing deeply. I turned and thanked him again. He smiled and showed his dimples, turned, the back of his jacket trim on his tall body. I shut and locked the door, glancing at the clock. It was nearly 3 a.m. Palms along the street clattered in the wind against the dining area screen. The quilt folded at the end of the bed was a welcome sight. It was the uncanny wind that whirled and reminded me a snow might roll in. The wind's whirring kept me awake for only a few minutes before my consciousness let go.

CHAPTER 11

I BOLTED UP IN BED, the digital clock radio flashing electric blue numbers. The day had begun without me. I stumbled to the kitchen to get coffee on, then scribbled out a list of people who might come to the shop for haircuts. If I were detained or called, shut down, I could at least eke out a living for rent, mortgage, and food now, and go under the table later if necessary. I jotted down thirty clients' names.

I watched the news as I made up the list. I couldn't stop following the spill's story in the mornings when the kids slept—and it seemed odd they weren't here this morning. The network ran a summary of what was happening: In April the explosion of the BP well had occurred, and it took until July for authorities to cap the gushing oil. That meant that the Gulf was covered under "a sheen of filth" that covered an area the size of Scotland. Then the drama of BP's money setting off cannons to scare the birds from the oil impact. By August, the Panama City Gulf beaches opened for business, but by September every storm brought more oil to shore. Now, we had holes in the food chain.

Fishermen out of work but working for BP now began to complain of their eyes burning. Those subcontractors who used dispersant to dissolve the oil began vomiting brown phlegm, had headaches, dizziness. Experts from the Exxon Valdez spill came down to help and noticed exactly the same symptoms in the two oil spills—high blood pressure, diarrhea, cancer, chronic fatigue— in five hundred workers.

As winter slowed the hurricane and storm weather down, things finally began to settle. And hell, it was Christmastime. People wanted to forget, and the news networks did as well.

At 9:30 I finished the list and picked up the phone to call Laura. The line seemed dead.

"Hello?" I said.

Someone cleared her throat. "LaRue?" came Mary's timid voice over the wire.

I felt like hanging up. "Yes?" I said.

"I'm sorry," she said, "I don't even remember—I barely remember last night. When I got up, Cooter told me what I'd done, accusing you and all. I—I don't know what to say."

"It's okay, Mary," I said, swallowing a long slug of coffee. "I can see how you'd have thought I did it. But I didn't. I did not. Mac is my—he helps me out business-wise. He's been good to me."

"I know. I don't know what came over me," she said. "I'm just real sorry."

"Well, I'm being watched," I said. Might as well let her know what she'd dumped on me. "And I have no way to make a living if I end up in jail. So I'd better get going."

"LaRue, I'm just real sorry—"

"It's okay. Have you heard how Mac is?" I asked.

"No. I think he's at the hospital. You could call his room." She added, "You know Mac's real special to me." I wondered again if she were having a fling with him, too.

"Right," I said.

"LaRue?" she said. If she apologized again, I was going to hang up. "Did you ever stop to think maybe from a different angle? Like maybe somebody's trying to put you out of business?"

I hadn't, but now I did. And thanks for your efforts in that, Mary, I wanted to say.

"Well, you've certainly given me some food for thought," I said. Clichés. I used clichés when I didn't really want to talk to people. "I need to go, Mary. But thanks for the call. And please do keep me informed." I hung up before she could say anything else.

I rang up Laura and told her about my grueling interrogation with Jackson. "So I'm a leading suspect now. Can I count on you as a witness for me?" I said.

"Of course, LaRue. And that's dismal. Daisy's just getting up. She's going to have that French toast I promised, and then I'll drop her off at Randy's. Okay by you? I'm supposed to have breakfast with you and Jackson, you know. Doesn't look like snow, but how would we know? Never snows here."

I decided the plan for the kids was okay, as long as Randy didn't mind. "See you at eleven."

Then I called Randy. "Taylor's sleeping like a cat," he said. "You know how cats sleep ninety percent of the time. Seems teenagers do the same."

"Yeah, he's storing up energy to find ways to point out my hypocrisies and faulty logic," I joked.

"He's a good kid, LaRue."

I asked him if he minded taking Daisy on the boat ride, as snow looked like it had traveled north.

"Of course not. I told you that last night. I like kids." Well. He liked kids.

"Thanks, Randy. I should be home by mid-afternoon. Make sure Daisy gets sunscreen." He promised, adding that it seemed odd to be worried about snow and sun damage at the same time. "The new weather," he said, and we hung up.

I called Tallahassee Memorial Hospital and was connected to Mac's room right away. Tiffany answered.

"Oh, hi, LaRue," she said.

"How is Mac?" I said.

"Oh, he's fine. They pumped his stomach. That stuff is really dangerous if you're allergic, but he was lucky. The poison ward here is one of the best in the country. He doesn't blame you, LaRue."

"Oh. Well," I said. "Can he talk?"

"No. They want him to rest. But maybe tonight if you wanted to come over. Or tomorrow." I'd known him longer than Tiffany had. This annoyed me, so I stayed silent. "LaRue?" she said. "Who'd want to kill Mac?"

"I don't know. Sure wish I did. I have no motive whatsoever. He sends me business. If you get any ideas about his enemies, will you let me know?"

I told her what had happened with Mary, and that I might have no business now, as the leading suspect in the murder. She didn't say anything except hmmm, then was quiet.

"Maybe Mary did it," she said.

"Why do you say that?"

"Oh, I don't know," she said, hesitant. "She was so quick to accuse you?"

"Well, she was drunk. Beyond drunk. I'm not sure what she's capable of."

"Well, I think she has a thing for Mac," she whispered. "The jealous type, you know?"

Oh, boy, I thought, maybe Mary is a true polygamist. "Well, I don't know about that. But I do know I could be sent to jail, damn it." I didn't say I'd never planned to be sole income earner for an extended family. I needed to pay December rent, a mortgage, buy groceries for kids. I didn't express just how dirty and tough things had been for me the past few years. Right now with the spill, everybody had that story. Still, I wasn't sure I wanted her to know. "Please tell Mac I'm sorry this happened. And I'll come visit tomorrow."

"I will," she said, sounding like she was thinking about anything but that. Bored. Preoccupied. If she'd been anything like I'd been at her age, her head was set on what she'd be doing tonight for fun. And how sad my boring, rotten life must be.

I hung up and headed out the door. The wind blew slowly, almost thoughtfully, in some nearby tall pines in a vacant lot. I spotted a pleasure boat out on the horizon as I made my way to the Island Hotel for breakfast. But what I really wanted was to get in that boat and float away.

LUCKILY, CARS OUTSIDE THE HOTEL had tags from Ontario and from nearby Florida counties to the north and west of us. Signs of Europeans abounded, too, as a rental Volvo, a VW, a Beamer, and a Mercedes outlined the perimeter of the place.

We were an eccentric mix, locals and implants, who had lived on the island awhile. We gossiped, but we cared. If someone had lost a job, people clustered to take them food for their pantries. When someone died, we gathered and prepared food. When someone was having an affair, somehow, most knew it. When someone had left someone, we often knew that, too. I was only hoping the same would happen to me, that people wouldn't speculate about my wanting to kill Mac or Trina.

Gray clouds were rolling in thick and low, but no snow. I picked a table out on the glassed-in sun porch, sat in the most hidden spot and waited, huddled in a winter jacket.

Jackson entered the room looking rested. "Morning," he said.

"Morning. Have a seat," I said with awkwardness.

He opened his napkin and placed it in his lap. "Well, the lab results are back," he said. "It was Percodan, and Mac is extremely allergic. The effects should have gotten to you, too, if you took a sip of his coffee." He asked the waitress for coffee and asked if I wanted some. I nodded. He went on. "This matches not only your story, but also Mary's and Mac's."

I shrugged. "I only had a small sip." Laura came in and gave Jackson a tap on the head and me a shoulder hug. She sat down, and we all took off our coats.

"Small sip of what?" Laura said. "I hate winter." Jackson ordered her coffee and briefed her on the lab findings.

"I did feel dizzy," I said.

"Yes, but you're allergic to Percodan, too, yet you didn't show any slight reactions, like a rash, nausea." I shrugged. I had a sneaking suspicion that Grandma Happy's tea may have helped.

"Yikes!" Laura said. "By the way, Jackson, you'll have to tell me if anything is off the record."

"Like I don't know that," he said. "I worked for the *Times*, too, remember?"

Then he turned to me and said, "What's odd is—" He turned back to Laura. "Off the record for now." Then he turned back to me. "Your—tea. What was it? Could it have been an antidote for the poison?"

I gulped.

Laura looked at me strangely. Then at Jackson.

"Surely you don't think LaRue—" Laura said.

"No, of course not. That's off the record, too. But I have to take everything into account." He turned to me. "But where did you get that tea? This is rather coincidental. The tea has Naloxone in it, which is the antidote for Oxycodone—

or Percodan. Though it does make you feel dizzy."

"Shit," I said. I put my head in my hands.

"What is it, Rue?" Laura said.

"It was one of Grandma Happy's concoctions," I said. "I didn't tell you, Jackson, because it was so—goofy."

"Who's this—Grandma Happy?" Jackson said.

Laura let out a short laugh and said, "LaRue's eccentric grandmother. She's Seminole, Native American, but she says that's white people's name for Indian. She's always coming up with some folk herbal tea for LaRue. She thinks LaRue needs her help."

"My grandmother didn't do it," I said. "She's ninety-four. She couldn't have, and please don't bother her. My dad had a bypass a few years ago, and I don't want him worrying about me." The two of them watched me sit up erect.

The waitress brought coffee, and we got quiet, cupping chilly hands around mugs for a few minutes. I breathed deeply to fight anxiety. I could feel the slow watery pulse of our lives here. Breakfast-goers spoke softly, the tinkle of glass and slow steps of waiters enveloped us. I noted that the waitress was a Colton, a distant relative of the Lutzes. She handed us each a menu, went through the litany of specials and walked back inside. Jackson looked over the menu. Laura gave him suggestions on brunch. He had a frown crease on his forehead.

"LaRue, your dad will worry about you a lot less if I can keep you from being the lone, leading suspect," Jackson said. "I'll need to talk with your grandmother if she made the tea."

I sighed. "She's sort of intuitive. And sometimes she's just short of weird. I don't know which Happy you'll get."

"It'll be interesting, at any rate," he said.

"By the way, the waitress is a Colton," I said quietly. "She's a cousin of the Lutzes and she will spread rumors like warm butter spreads on toast. Please be careful."

The rest of the time we enjoyed our meal. Jackson ate eggs Benedict with local shrimp. Laura watched us both as she ate an omelet. Her matchmaking skills were being put to the test, and she wanted to see how they were working. I pushed eggs around on my plate.

"Well, are you going to ask me questions or not?" I finally said. "About Trina Lutz?" We all glanced around. We were alone under a sun porch on a cloudy day.

"Sure," he said. "I can do that." He wiped his mouth, put down the cloth napkin and pulled out a small notepad and a pen. He said, "Laura tells me you saw something that the paper didn't report about Trina Lutz's suicide?"

"I didn't tell him anything yet," Laura offered. "I thought maybe you'd want to do the telling. I didn't want to get anything wrong." We waited as the waitress warmed up the coffee and left the check, which Jackson picked up.

As he put his credit card in the check holder, I told him exactly what I'd seen. And that unfortunately, I'd left that top button unbuttoned while the funeral home fellow had stood there. That I was finishing Trina's hair, and the funeral home director wouldn't go away. How even though the funeral was closed casket, Trina wanted to go below with good hair. Jackson jotted a few notes, losing all facial expression. I hoped that didn't convey character but a part of the job.

"What's the name of this funeral home fellow?"

I should have found out, I thought. I'm not so good at this. "I don't know. Edwards and Parsons Funeral Home. Up on State Road Sixty-seven up in Wellborn." He scribbled some notes.

"Can you describe this guy for me?" Jackson asked.

"Bad hair," I said. Jackson looked up, waiting. "You know—slicked back and black. Straight," I said. "Thick glasses, square and black. He looks like somebody, I just can't place exactly who."

"Well, do me a favor and try to place how you know him over the next few days, will you?" Jackson put away his notepad. Then a question came over his face. "Is he connected in any way to anyone who was at the reception last night?" Jackson said.

I shrugged. "Oh, for godsakes, I thought that might be *your* job," I said in an uncharacteristic burst of frustration, my hands fluttering. "He could be related to anybody. That's how it is around here, you know. A few big families, all scattered throughout the county. Everybody's cousins with everybody when you go back generations." I realized I was shouting. "Okay, I'll try to find out," I said, dropping my arms.

He held out a hand. "Take it easy, okay?" I took a deep sigh and glanced at Laura.

"Why don't you relax this afternoon," she said. "I'll go check on the kids at Randy's." I thought a minute. Maybe things were happening between her and Randy.

"Well, I really want to see the kids."

"They're fine, LaRue. They're better, really, not having your worrying. You're keyed up. Why don't you get some rest and then go see them tonight at Randy's. Or maybe at my place," she said, pulling a last sip off her coffee. "I'm going to run. Call if you need anything. See you, Jackson. Thanks for picking up the check."

After she left, we got quiet, sipping coffee, watching as the fast-moving clouds flew across the sky, darker. Then the sun broke out.

"Uh. I have to ask you this," Jackson said. "Did you put poison in Mac Duncan's coffee to make him sick or to kill him?"

I looked at him square on. "No. I most certainly did not. It would only hurt my business to try to hurt Mac. He's done a lot to bring customers to me. Don't shut my business down. And don't let out the news that I'm prime suspect just yet."

"Please tell me you knew nothing about what was in that tea your grandmother gave you."

"No. I. did. not. I tried to turn the tea down when she handed it to me, but then I took it anyway. She's stubborn. She said I was going to have a day of opposites and I needed it." I felt funny confessing about Grandma Happy.

"A day of opposites?" he asked.

"A funeral and a wedding," I said.

The Colton waitress came by again and took the bill holder. We waited until she left.

"How did she know?" he asked.

"My dad told her. And no, my dad did not poison Mac," I said.

"When I took the tea out, it was to drown out the bitter flavor of that coffee. That's all. The tea tasted sweet and sour. Very nice. Delicious, actually. I drank it all." I picked up my glass of water, the sides now covered with condensation. I put it back down. "Are you helping me, or are you trying to put me in jail?"

He ignored the question. "That could explain why you had no real reaction to the Percodan," he said. "Would you like to go somewhere more—less—you know, somewhere you'll be comfortable talking?" he said, looking around.

I kept trying to remember that Laura asked him to help me, even though he was the law, sort of. A state investigator not officially on the case, whatever that meant.

I sighed. "Sure," I said. The waitress brought back the receipt for him to sign. We were silent until she left. Then we stood and walked out to his car where the sun was shining.

"Where do you suggest we go?" Jackson said, putting his hands in his pockets, fishing for keys.

"My dad's boat." His eyes opened wide. "Don't get excited," I said, following him to his navy blue Toyota. "I'm not coming on to you. It's a rowboat out on the pond at Panther Pit. I think you'll like it. And if you must, you can question Happy and Dad. But you have to be gentle."

"And if I'm not, you'll all feed me to the pet alligator with an appetite for skunks?" he said, opening his door and using his unlock button to open the door on my side.

"That's right," I said, opening the passenger side door, grinning despite myself at the quick wit he seemed to have. Alligators and skunks, a combination to fear.

"Hey there," said a melodic voice on the street as we sat down in the car. She pulled four syllables out of two. Madonna. Wearing a cashmere midriff top and low-slung jeans. Jackson got an eyeful, then turned to peer at me.

"How you doing?" she said, cocking her head and giving him an appraisal. Then she looked at me and grinned sideways like I'd just caught the big swordfish.

I squinted in the bright sun. "I'm the prime suspect in the poisoning." I gave Jackson a dirty look. "He's making it official."

"Damn," she said. "That sucks." She looked at Jackson. "Well, I just wanted to tell you something about—well, something I heard. About Trina. Or the night Trina died." She glanced around and stepped closer to lean in close to the passenger side window.

"Go on," I said. She looked at him, then at me, and I nodded.

"Well, you know old OV?"

"OV Justus? Garbage man?" I asked.

"The very," she said. "You know how he lives at the canal between the main key and Way Key? Well, he was tooling around in his little oyster boat, he'd been working on it, and he took it out for a little spin before sundown the night of the suicide. He says he swears he saw Trina on Fletch's boat. You know the big yacht-looking thing?" She began to swing her arms and hips together. "I don't know what they're called, but it's big and white?"

I nodded. "Inboard-outboard? Bigger than most?"

She leaned in, nodding. "Right when she was supposedly at home killing herself."

"Yeah?" I said. "OV told you this when?"

"Last night when I went back to close up the bar. After the reception went kabloonk."

"Can you get me his name, address, and phone number?" Jackson said.

I looked at Madonna, and she shrugged. "Confidential information. I'll have to ask him if it's okay." Jackson shook his head, an amused smile across his face.

"I can question him anyway, but if you insist, you may ask him first."

"Jackson, you got to understand people around here," I said. "We all talk. We kind of trust each other. Kind of. And most folks don't trust the law. At all. Fishermen and islanders are not into authority. Some of these folks think they're freakin' cowboys." He nodded and then shook his head.

"Ms. . . . Madonna?" Jackson said. "Could you get the license number on that boat?" She nodded.

"Thanks, Madonna. I sure appreciate you. Every piece of information helps," I said as Jackson started the car.

"Let's go check out that boat tonight," she said under her breath so Jackson couldn't hear. I nodded and waved.

"I'll call you," I said.

CHAPTER 12

THE SUN WAS PLAYING shadow tag with our part of the world as Jackson and I drove through town. Over the first bridge, then the second of four. The weather would hold, no snow would fall. We headed away from the main island.

"Kiss-Me-Quick." Jackson read the sign at the next island. "Now there's an original."

I launched into how the old railroad ran parallel to the current road. "And when the train came through, it slowed way down and the locals would jump on, head towards the mainland. You'd be with your sweetheart, and when you hear the train, you'd say—"

"Kiss me, quick!" He raised his eyebrows and opened his mouth clownishly. I pulled away from him, and he smiled. He had dimples and sprinkles of freckles.

"Where are you from anyway?" I said.

"My parents came from New York," he said. "I grew up in Tallahassee."

"The capital. I went to grad school there. A political kid? Your dad was—something, a right-wing lobbyist, one of those guys who wanted BP to drill, baby, drill in the Gulf?"

"No. I mean, I'm probably more liberal than anybody in the department, if that's what you're asking," he said. "But to tell you the truth, LaRue, I just do what I think is right. That's the only reason I left the *Times*. I felt I might better serve the underserved. Folks who get into trouble with the law and have no money to get a good lawyer." God, he was killing me. We crossed the next two bridges.

"Where were the guys like you, the lawyers with ethics, when I was going through the divorce?" I pointed to the road, which split just ahead. "You want to turn right up there at the fork."

"I'm not the bad guy, LaRue. How far from here?" he said.

"About six miles." We passed big fat Phil, who had a box on a bike with a sign that said "Phil's Knife Sharpener." A Dixie flag hung in front of his box-bike.

"Hmm, nobody's killed him yet," Jackson said. "Dixie flags and knives somehow beg the question." I had to laugh.

I hugged my legs as we rode through the low land of sabal palms mixed with sand oaks and tall pines. We passed trailers, the bikers' property, old man Vickers', and the Coltons'. The folks I'd grown up around. An old statue of a lion sat in front of the Colton entrance. Someone had painted the lion with a Mexican cape over a Santa suit to bring in the season.

"Quite a bit of this land is for sale," he said. "Or just sold."

I shrugged. "Most of the old timers are dying out. Families are trying to sell these rural properties off after they die. Trouble is, most of it would never pass the wetlands codes today. Couldn't build on it."

"Who's buying it, do you know?" he asked.

"Hmm, not sure. Fletch Lutz has invested in some of it," I said. "Trina's husband. And Mac told me yesterday he was closing a deal out this way."

"Fletch—Trina Lutz's husband?" I affirmed that. "Anybody else?"

"I don't really know," I said. "Look, why don't you let me off the hook? You don't need to declare a leading suspect, and you know I didn't kill or poison anyone. I've got kids to support, and a lot of people won't come see a leading murder suspect to get their hair cut."

"Would you relax?" he said. "It's okay. You won't be under investigation for long, probably."

We passed the Church of God in Holy Heaven set up in a trailer. A billboard out front stated, "It takes a lot of faith to be an Atheist."

"Probably?" I let out a disgusted *pffft*. "Let me help out. I'll help you investigate."

He took his eyes off the road and studied me. Then laughed a little.

"It's not funny," I said.

"Okay. Okay, then. If I hadn't noticed your haircuts, I probably wouldn't agree to do this, you know. I have a weakness for good taste." He combed my long body with his eyes.

I felt myself go red. I stared at the swamps on either side of the road. Lowcountry. Yellow winter grasses against blue sky.

He continued. "So, how many nurseries have businesses between here and Wellborn?"

"I'm not sure—one or two." A sky wader, a blue heron stood like a nun, guarding her space up ahead on the road, working the shallows.

"And in Wellborn?" he said.

"I don't know—maybe four, six nurseries at the most, if you count Walmart."

"Find out where that palm came from," Jackson suggested. On slow wings, a hawk was patrolling its possibilities.

"That's not fair," I said. "I could end up—"

"And find out, too, who's buying up this property. That should be easy enough. Have Laura check the sales records in the County Courthouse." This was trivial stuff. The hawk soared, slid down almost to ground level, radar eye to its prey that we couldn't see.

"Can you think of anybody who didn't like Trina?" he said. The swamps blurred as we sped on.

"Everybody liked and respected Trina. She was all over the oil spill thing. When BP came to the community meeting and Tallahassee came down with TV cameras, she stood up and raised hell in that meeting about how the fishermen who'd gone to work for BP had no health benefits. And how BP had made workers sign a waiver not to request liability coverage in case the workers had chemical or psychological damage while working for them." We were passing the lower part of the river area, evidenced by the flocks of egrets flying overhead.

"That could cause a lot of trouble," Jackson said. "That could get any number of people upset."

"The video caused a stir. Fishermen began to stand up and say, 'I don't know what I'm going to do, I'm having trouble breathing,' or 'I have chemical burns I don't know how to treat,' or 'I don't know how I'm going to pay the rent this month without an income if I'm sick.' " He was nodding.

"She sounds like someone who didn't fit the standard female role down here," Jackson said. "But Laura's not exactly a prototype either."

"What the hell ever," I said. "It got BP to our community and setting up a clinic for anyone who needed chemical testing or counseling." I wondered if he thought I was a St. Annes prototype. Like Mary, for example, eccentric, crazy. Meeting my family would put the nail in that coffin.

"Who did Trina do accounts for?" he asked. I didn't know. "And how about Mac?" he said. "Who doesn't like him? Customers? Bad business deals? Anyone at the capitol?" I shook my head no. We passed the Stewards' place where the pinto and palomino stood out front warming their sleek bodies. I loved the swamps, home. The sun had begun to relax my tense muscles.

"Okay, I'll check Mac's history," Jackson said. "You seem to know most residents around here. Why don't you listen out for anything unusual. Find out who does business with whom around here, underground or above."

"Yeah. Everybody," I said sulky. "Lawmakers in Tallahassee, in the whole greedy state. And builders, big business, all those people."

"Fletch Lutz. What kind of business does Mac have? Or Fletch, for example?"

"I don't know. They buy and sell boats and real estate. The two have a small enterprise downtown. They take turns being captain and boating folks out on a pontoon. They charge too much, let tourists walk on an abandoned island where the pelicans and ospreys, turtles and frogs, poisonous and non-poisonous snakes are trying to survive."

"Interesting," he said. "Have you taken that boat ride?"

"Of course not," I said with scorn. "Locals can borrow a boat any time to go out on any island of their choice." He didn't let scorn ruffle him.

"Is this the place?" He slowed at the Panther Pit sign with the two stone horses at the gate.

"Sorry," I said, a general Southern 'I'm sorry' that's supposed to cover everything: Sorry I'm bitching at you, sorry for bad directions, sorry for slavery, sorry sorry, sorry. The British are sorry, too, I noticed while there on scholarship as an undergrad. If you bump into an English person, they say 'Sorry.' I went into a slight panic as we slowed to turn into the family property.

"Sorry, yeah, turn in right here, and realize it's nothing fancy. Sorry. And please don't tell Dad I'm the leading suspect. And don't tell him—anything. He's got heart trouble."

Jackson shook his head, a one-sided smile on his face. The man knew a high-strung Southern woman when he heard one. That alone earned him a few points.

We turned in and drove straight to the pine cabin, to the right of the entrance. He stopped the car and looked around the twenty acres including the water, which sat in the middle of the property, two acres of spring-fed pond. All around pines, cedars, and scrub oaks grew. A meadow sat between Dad's and Grandma's places. Across the pond, the woods stretched for miles into pine forest. The water held a clarity that made the colors aqua and bright green. Lime rock made water look dazzling.

"Wow. This is the prettiest place on the west coast of Florida," Jackson said. Oh, boy, wait till you see Grandma's trailer, I thought. I did cherish the property, or I wouldn't be working so hard to pay the mortgage. We climbed out of the car, and Dad met us at the screen door. Jackson stuck out his hand immediately and introduced himself to Dad, who slowly opened the squeaky screen door and stared at Jackson's feet. "Nice boots," he said. I'd forgotten Dad's affection for boots and hadn't noticed Jackson's shoes. Since Dad had grown up on the reservation herding cows, where boots counted, he liked Jackson straight up, no matter what I thought of the guy. Dad offered us soup and grilled cheese for lunch.

"That's okay, Dad, we just ate," I said. We shuffled onto the big porch that looked out on the pond. It shaded us not just with roof, but also with Virginia creeper vines climbing up and down every screen. The leaves now had turned red and yellow, and we could watch them falling off the trees as the wind gusted through. As a kid, I had slept on the porch in late fall after all the fierce no-see-um bugs, who could squeeze through screen holes and bite, had died off for the season. I could listen for hours to the whippoorwills across the pond. I'd dream to the frog songs and an occasional alligator growl. These sounds were a comfort.

The porch furniture included old metal patio sitters and four green wooden rockers. We gravitated towards the rockers, pulling the wool blankets on the backs of the chairs over our shoulders. Dad leaned down and turned on the electric heater by our feet. The weather had grown too severe for porch sleeping this year. Dad made three cups of tea, and we settled in to talk.

"You were at the wedding reception last night, right Mr. Panther?" Jackson asked. Dad nodded, looking confused. "I just need to ask you a few questions. I assume you don't know that Mac Duncan was poisoned there, do you?"

"No. Didn't know." Daddy looked my direction.

I shrugged.

"How about that. Did he live?" Dad was still looking at me for cues about what to say.

With that, I couldn't take sitting around and listening. "I'll go untie the boat and get the oars," I said to Jackson. "It's okay, Daddy. He's safe."

Fifteen minutes later, the boat rope sat wound in my lap as the boat floated in the water. Jackson hadn't showed up, and I'd grown tired of squinting at the sun flashing diamonds off water. I decided to warn Grandma Happy that Jackson would pay her a visit next and why. I threw the rope back over the dock post and wandered to her trailer.

"There you are," she said, standing with her billowy and multicolored Seminole skirt and the necklaces piled high on her neck. Striking woman. This always surprised me about her. TV was blaring. "Come in. Too cold out there." Once we were settled in her sagging sofa, Grandma said, "Did it work?"

"Did what work?" I was irritated with her, but it wasn't as if she could know about what was poisonous and what the antidote for that poison was.

"The tea. Protect you?"

"Well, yes and no, Grandma."

"Huh?" she said, so I turned down the TV. I proceeded to tell the whole story of how Mac was poisoned by a cup of coffee I gave him, and that now I was the prime suspect in the crime. And that an investigator at Dad's would talk to her next. And that the detective knew the tea Grandma had given me was the antidote.

She gave a high-pitched belly laugh. She was tough. She had taken everything that came her way and had survived anyway.

"So the tea saved you." She grinned, and the gaps where her teeth used to be showed. Then she laughed again. "The fancy policeman's gonna try to take an old Indian lady to jail?" She chuckled again and shook her head. "I told you it was a day of opposites. You didn't believe me. You don't listen to your Granny." She shook her head and then sat still. "You need to step in that man's shoes."

"What man's shoes?" I said.

"Policeman's shoes. You have the know-how. He's a match."

"A match?"

"A pair. Not opposites, a match. You do it together."

"Do what?" I said, frowning.

"You know the answer to that, not me."

"I'm trying, Grandma," I said. "I'm trying to get him to find the person who poisoned Mac, but you're not really helping. So this investigator. He's coming over here, but don't tell him too much, okay?"

She leaned over into me. "Indians been fooling white men for centuries. Don't you worry about me." She stood with a couple of ouches and ooches. She walked slowly over to the pot boiling on the stove. "Want some tea?"

"No, Grandma! And don't offer him one of your remedies. He'll think you're a witch or something."

Grandma turned around pointing with the wooden spoon in her hand and said, "He thinks that, that's his problem. I'm gonna make you some kava. Or maybe a new recipe, chamomile and lavender. Passionflower. You need to relax." So she made herbal tea and offered ginger cookies while we watched "Sponge Bob Square Pants." The cartoon entertained Grandma to no end. I caught her up on the kids, avoiding anything that might make her want to create a new tea.

Finally, Jackson and Daddy came pounding on the door. Jackson acted a little reverential towards Grandma, bowing and saying what an honor to meet an Indian, which she used to her advantage, bossing him around. She pointed to the lumpy sofa.

"Sit over there next to your partner," she said, pointing in my direction. I moaned. Jackson did as he was told. Grandma went on. "Maybe I should be an investigator. I know things." Jackson gave me a half smile.

"Mrs. Panther?" he said. "I assume?" He looked at me and said, "Matrilineal culture, right? Children take the mother's name, so hers is Panther?" I nodded, surprised he knew.

"That's me," she said, sitting in the rocker. "What do you want to know?"

Dad sat in the easy chair, winked at me, and then latched onto Sponge Bob's dilemma of the day.

Jackson launched into what had happened the night before. All but the accusations against me. "And I have a few questions I need to ask you, Mrs. Panther, because the tea LaRue says you gave her kept her from getting sick."

"That Mary is crazy. She lives with them two brothers," Grandma said out of the blue. "Bad brothers. That one man named after a turtle," she said, "Cooter. A turtle name. Indians don't like white people taking Indian names. They's better names than Cooter, anyway. Panther or water or tiger names." Jackson looked at me. Jackson had not mentioned Mary's name. I shrugged.

Jackson cleared his throat. "Did you know anything about Mac Duncan's being poisoned, Mrs. Panther?" he asked.

"No. It was a day of opposites. I made the tea the Little People told me to make for my grandchild, LaRue. She needs a lot of strength, raising those two kids alone. Working. By herself. I do what I can."

"Little people?" Jackson said. I groaned, louder this time.

"The Little People." She walked to the window and pointed outside. "They likes the pine trees best. Sometimes they is mischievous, sometimes they helps."

"Do you see them?" Jackson said.

"Oh, sometimes. But mostly I hears them. Something bad in the water out here. They telling me. Killing everybody here. People needs to honor the water. Thank it for being there for us. It's more gold than gold."

I stood up, embarrassed. "I'll see you when you're done with your anthropological study, Jackson," I said. "I'll be at the boat, waiting."

"Damn," I said when I got to the dock where Daddy had followed me. I didn't usually curse in front of my father. "Grandma's on one of her tears, this time about honoring water and the Little People and—"

"Honey, she's who she is," he said. "And that man, he's okay. He's honest, I think. Hard to find these days." We walked to the boat.

"I know you're a suspect," he said. "And I know you didn't want me worrying. But I need to know things like this. I can find work if you're concerned about the payments. I'd work at the Seven-Eleven," he said. Then he contradicted himself. "Just wish I could work." He'd retired from the gunpowder plant five years ago. His doctor up in Tallahassee was emphatic. The stress was getting to his heart.

"No, you don't need to work," I said. "I just hope they find out who poisoned Mac soon. Need to get to the bottom of things." The mid-afternoon was warming us on the rickety wooden dock. A bass blooped on the surface of the water. An osprey swooped in, over and back across the pond, eyeing the water for fish. I sat down and said, "Whatever she's saying to Jackson, I just have to hope he'll accept Grandma as she is."

"That's my girl." Dad put his hands in his pockets, turned, and walked back to his place. I stretched out on the dock. What was our town coming to, that someone would try to kill the guy who invited them to a party and then frame some innocent person there. Eventually, I just tried to think about nothing.

When Jackson came out to the dock, his footsteps vibrated down the walkway. He held one Miami Dolphins baseball cap and one that said Just Fishin'. He was grinning. "You've got the coolest family." He walked the dock to stand next to where I lay and handed me a hat. "And your grandma wants us to wear these."

"Don't patronize me," I said. "My ex told me how bizarre Grandma was, so just don't." I sat up, put on the hat and glared.

"I'm not patronizing you. Your family's feisty. They're doing what most of us wish we had the wisdom and acceptance to do. No pretentions. It's refreshing." He shook his head and put his hat on. I sighed.

"They don't have any money," I said. Still, I was grateful a city guy appreciated this simplicity. We stepped into the small rowboat. I sat in front, holding a paddle, and he in back with the other paddle. We weren't rowing anywhere, this was just a cruise around the pond.

We let the boat glide us to the center of the pond, the boat's movement lifting us from so much gravity. Gliding like birds in air. I leaned over and scooped up the cold water and splashed my face. Neither of us moved much for a long time. Bass swam near the surface, swam away. The smallest breezes passed through the pines.

"I haven't relaxed like this in forever," he said.

"Well, you have a secure job and aren't a suspect in a crime."

"Would you lighten up?" he said.

"Have you ever been the lead suspect in a crime of poisoning? Or seen a dead woman's real cause of death when everybody in control is lying about it?" I was muttering in complaint, but the smell of mud and earth, the fresh scent of pine and rainwater, the mineral hint of lime-rock pond did lift me.

"No, I've not. But I've seen plenty."

"Like what?"

"My mother," he said. "She had a terrible drinking problem after my dad died. She lived a few blocks from me in Tallahassee. She'd set the house alarm, then forget, and walk out and back in, setting off the alarm. The cops were forever coming to rescue her from herself," he said. "Eventually, they threatened to Baker Act her. I had to put her in a home. She died of a heart attack the day after she was admitted."

"I'm sorry. That sounds—really hard," I said, turning to glance at him. He stared into the water.

Then he looked over at the woods. "It was. Is that where the alligator lives?" He pointed toward the piney woods.

"The alligator mama and her babies."

"Whew," he said. "I've had to track down some dangerous people in dangerous places, but never an alligator mother." He half-smiled and adjusted his hat. "Once I was investigating this heist in Miami for the *Herald*—that's the paper where I started my career. Suddenly, I'm on Atlantic Avenue at the end of South Beach back in the day, when Miami was called the murder capital of the country. Before they cleaned up Miami Beach. Remember that time?"

"Oh, yeah. Blood and guts capital, we fondly named it," I said.

"And I'm walking," he said. He was gesturing now, and the boat began to sway back and forth. "And suddenly there's this car, a black limo, speeding down the street my way. From every window of the limo a machine gun is sticking out." The boat was swaying wildly now. "It sounded like small bombs going off, one after another, the gunfire. Somehow I had the sense to lie down just as the limo was passing me, so I didn't get hit."

"Wow." I held onto the side of the boat. He hadn't noticed the swaying boat, so caught up in his story. "Scary. Did anybody die?"

"Five people," he said, grim and sitting still, resting the paddle on his legs now. The boat slowed its sway. "All innocent. Just—" he shrugged and swallowed, "going about their day. Two kids." He sighed. The osprey floated high over the pond, coasting, surveying for food. Something in the day shifted. We'd passed mid-afternoon.

"Sorry," I said. I supposed journalists and investigators lived in a war zone of sorts. We went quiet. A breeze came up and turned into wind. The clouds moved in like a heavy smoke, so we paddled back to the dock and tied up. Grandma was sleeping when I walked over, so we told Dad goodbye.

We drove down the county road, where on either side we passed the salt grasses, tolerant of tidal flooding and salinity. The home and food of so many wild animals. The swamp thistle was in bloom, bold purple with wicked thorns. They didn't like being touched, and they let human skin know it by biting back with those thorns.

Nature can level anyone, in good and bad ways. I had a new respect for Jackson because he seemed to know this. I hoped nature had the power Grandma believed it did. She said it would always come back, even stronger sometimes, from human ways. I wondered where we fit into that picture on the Gulf.

Jackson reached over and pinched my elbow slightly. "Relax," he said, his eyes amused. I shrugged and looked away. My stomach flipped. What was I to do with this feeling I had falling over me? His decisions would be killing my business. And I still liked him.

My mind wandered. I was figuring already when I'd call people about their haircuts. Maybe I could get Madonna to let me sub for her some nights at the bar. And maybe Mac would let me clean his condos. If he didn't think I had tried to poison him. And who left that plant on my stoop?

Jackson Woodard parked and walked me upstairs to the door again. He gave me a long gaze. He seemed to be struggling with something.

"I'll be up with you this week," he finally said. He put his hands in his pockets and took the stairs back down two at a time.

CHAPTER 13

I SLEPT THE REST OF THE DAY. The kids spilled into the apartment, exhausted and hungry as the sun fell slowly towards the horizon. I pulled myself up from the bed and found Daisy and Tay preparing their own version of pasta: loads of olive oil and garlic. No meat, no vegetables. At least they were preparing their own meal, and were bounteous full of their trip to the islands.

"Mama, we saw a big snake!" Daisy said, tipping the bottle of olive oil. My eyes darted to Taylor.

"On Seahorse Key," Tay explained, taking the olive oil and putting it on the shelf.

"Yeah, and it was a monster!" Daisy said. "Six feet long and about as big around as Mr. Randy's thigh." She grabbed her stool to peer into the pot of pasta boiling.

"Rattlesnake," Taylor said, illustrating with his hands, about three times the thickness of a ripe watermelon, "and it was huge. But—"

"But it didn't get us," Daisy said. "Mr. Randy, he threw stuff at the snake, and it slithered to the middle of the island where there's a swamp."

"Good grief," I said, opening the refrigerator.

"Don't worry, Mama," Daisy said, scooting off the stool to hug my waist. "We were safe."

"Yeah, it was really cool, Mom," Taylor said as Daisy returned to the stool. "All these pelicans were roosting in the trees. I thought of a New York tenement house." He grinned. "They're all yakking at each other. Living on top of each other in the mangroves, and side by side, sitting on their nests. Daisy, pay attention or you'll get burned!" He pushed her down from the stool and took the pot off the burner.

"Yeah, and they're really funny," Daisy said. "They fight."

I laughed. "Maybe all families do."

After we sat down to eat the kids' pasta dish in the living room, I let the kids know the bad news: I was under suspicion until further notice and for bizarre reasons. And that my business would lose customers. They both looked confused and glum.

"But you didn't poison him, did you, Mama?" Daisy said, sucking spaghetti into her mouth.

"Of course not, you idiot," Taylor said, looking at the ceiling. He was tired.

"Tay," I said. "She is not an idiot."

"But Mom, you know she knows you didn't do it. Why do you think she asks, except to get attention." He picked up the remote and turned on the TV to ABC's news, which showed the oil as it had gushed into the Gulf for all those many weeks, and the months after.

"Honey, you used to ask questions like that. It wasn't so long ago either," I said.

He sat back with a huff.

"You didn't do it, did you, Mama?" Daisy said softly.

"Of course not, honey," I said, continuing with a conversation about living with less. I launched into no allowance, no extras like videos, snacks, and Taylor would have to find some kind of work to pay his car insurance.

"Great," Tay said, turning up the volume of the TV. "Dishwashing at one of the scum-bag restaurants on the dock." I ignored his remark. I didn't add that he probably wouldn't even find work at a scum-bag anything right now. Tourists had abandoned our stretch of water and sand.

"Tay?" I said. "I need you to babysit tonight." It was Saturday night, so he argued.

"You can have Stephie over if you want," I said. The girlfriend whom I'd never allowed over without me around.

"Yeah, cool!" Daisy said. Taylor blew out his breath in disgust. I asked Daisy to get ice cream. When she had trotted out of hearing range, I turned a full look to Taylor.

"Tay," I said. "I really need you—I have something I need to do—trust me on this."

He looked at me hard and curious, then folded his arms over his chest and said, "Okay."

I CALLED MAC'S HOSPITAL ROOM at 5:30 p.m. Tiffany answered and told me Fletch would be visiting tonight, and that tomorrow would look better for Mac. Good, I thought. No one could find us snooping. I told nurse Tiffany to please tell Mac I'd see him tomorrow. Then I called Madonna and invited her to hang out around eight.

I drove over to Piney Point. This was crazy, I knew, but I had to find out more about Trina. She'd never invited me into her home. The kids had visited, but not me. She and Fletch never entertained that I knew of either.

Piney Point burst with natural life and therefore became attractive as the choice spot for new construction on the islands these past years. Oaks and pine trees kept the island cool in summer. Deep, old growth woods. Luckily, the pencil mogul who'd ravaged St. Annes had only lumbered cedars and left the other trees untouched. Piney Point sat right on the Gulf, too, just north and east of the island where Randy and Laura lived. I parked at the old professor's house, vacant now, and walked to the water's edge to Trina's house. The sun had just sunk out of view.

I approached the house, walking past it first. It perched on stilts like all newer houses on the Gulf these days. Under the house, Fletch's truck was missing. But Trina's red Jeep sat in the weather, covered in a small coat of leaves, untouched for days. The house was built of cypress, expensive wood that resisted all manner of insects and water rot. I saw that Trina had grown sunflowers out back near the Gulf. And a fountain she'd made using lime rock burbled among the ferns in the shade. A suicidal woman wouldn't have designed a landscape this thoughtful, I decided. I walked towards the fountain, closer to the house.

Fletch, I hoped, had taken his truck to the bar where he hung out all the time. Tiffany might think he was going to the hospital, but that man never made an unnecessary trip off the islands. A statue of an angel praying stood a foot deep in water. Was it one of those by Liza Jane Gardner, who signed the bottoms of her work? Nosey me, I picked it up to look. Signed, of course. Trina liked the best, and could afford it, being an accountant. What I saw then made my throat constrict. A key lay in the spot where the statue's bottom had sat. I looked around. Nothing, nobody around. I picked up the key. It was labeled with a rusty tag that said, "Back door." I brushed away the dirt, thrust the key into my jeans pocket and walked back to the water's edge.

I STOPPED AND BOUGHT a pint container of mullet dip at Kiss-Me-Quick and headed back across the bridge from the Fish House. I would figure out how to get into Trina's house later. The day grew dark. I parked my car in the usual spot behind the grocery store and ran in to grab some crackers. Hell, go on and shop, I thought. The cupboard's damn bare. I grabbed a cart, found vegetables and cheese, and wandered down to the back of the store. In the butcher area, Jim Smiley, the owner, was packaging meat. Usually he took weekends off during the colder months. He had good if thinning hair and a thick mustache.

"Sorry to hear you got accused of something you didn't do," Jim said, leaning on the counter. He had the freshest meat in the county.

"Oh, boy," I said. "Small towns. You lift a finger, and everybody knows. Business will be bad for me. Got some chicken breast meat? About a pound?"

"Hey, murder or attempted murder ain't good for my business, either," he said. "Suicide here, murder attempt there, and any tourists left who'll come down will take their dollars to the east coast where the oil's *not* done spilled." He wrapped the poultry and marked the meat with black crayon, handing it over. The summer had been rough. The media blitz had scared tourists away.

"I can barely stay open. Got too much inventory. Not a good thing in a grocery store." He shook his head.

"Sorry, Jim. Everybody's saying the same thing. They won't know what they're missing if they go east," I joked. The east or Atlantic coast was far more popular, but we still had nature on the Gulf coast. And no high rises.

"Look," he leaned up on the meat case. "I could use a trim." He pointed to his head and then his mustache. "If you want to book me this coming week. Everybody needs to know we can trust you with a pair of scissors." He winked, picked up his butcher knife, and began to sharpen it.

"Thanks, Jim." I pulled out my day calendar. "When's convenient?"

He shrugged. "Tomorrow, say before eleven? It gets busy, you know, after church."

"That'd be fine," I said, cheered. I figured Madonna and I wouldn't be sneaking around until really late tonight, but I could be ready to give a haircut in the morning. "Just walk over. I'll be in the shop." I waved and headed down the aisle. Then I walked back, looked him straight in the eyes and said, "Jim. I didn't do it."

"Rue, everybody who knows you knows that. Everybody but the evidence gets that."

"Will you spread the word that I will cut hair? And I'll clean houses — whatever." He nodded.

I turned around and pushed the cart back up the aisle. "Don't worry," I said. "We'll be okay." He nodded.

Sometimes there were benefits to living in a small town. I piled my purchases on the conveyor belt. The cashier looked glum and very pregnant. A youngster who'd gone to school with Tay before she got pregnant and dropped out. Tay was one of twelve in the senior class. The other twenty who'd begun with him when we moved back in his eighth grade had either quit to become fishermen or had gotten pregnant or married. This island inertia had Tay both frustrated and confused. I had felt grateful to Trina for showing Tay the many ways a computer could work for a kid. And I appreciated Randy for taking Tay out. Nothing got in Daisy's way. At least not yet, I thought, carrying the two bags of groceries out the store's old squawky double doors. Once in the car, I checked the grocery receipt. Jim hadn't charged me a cent for the chicken.

Cars slowly cruised the highway, turning at the only corner in town with a traffic signal onto Main Street, where I lived, and headed to bars and restaurants. I left the car at the grocery store because it was in the same short block where our apartment was. I hefted the two bags down the block towards the apartment. Folks were steadily parading their Saturday-night way into town from everywhere else on the highway. Back when I'd first moved into the upstairs house on the corner, I'd be up all night hearing the cars and trucks. Now I slept right through most of it.

When I walked inside, Madonna was sitting on the sofa with a cup of coffee. Laura sat in the E-Z-Boy with a glass of white wine. Both kids were asleep on the floor. "Well, that's different," I said when I walked in. "The party came to me, and the kids are asleep."

"You should start locking the doors, Rue," Laura said.

"Oh, I see you decided to illustrate the dangers for me by making yourselves at home." I went to the coffee pot and poured a cup. I unloaded groceries and put the mullet dip on the coffee table with the crackers. Madonna carried Daisy to her bedroom and shook Tay awake enough to send him to his room. Maybe Tay's girlfriend wouldn't even be in the house if I was lucky.

"Hey, how about coloring my hair, LaRue?" Laura said, walking into the kitchen.

"Sure. I'll give you a deal." I dug into the mullet dip. "Delicious. But it would be so much better with a glass of red wine."

"Nope. No red wine for the boat investigators, and no inexpensive hair deals. Full price. I know what this color thing costs in Tallahassee. I'm paying Tallahassee prices." She drained her glass. I wanted to hug her, but instead gulped more coffee.

Madonna was perusing the newspaper and began to frown. "Laura, this funeral notice you wrote says the beloved Trina Lutz died of suicide. She shot herself in the heart at home."

"Madonna, I'm going with the lie for now," Laura said, pouring herself another glass of white and dipping a cracker into mullet dip.

Madonna went on. "Says she grew up in Atlanta and went to school at Duke. Business College. Brainy. Or her parents had money. Who could pay Duke tuition?" She scooped up some mullet dip on a cracker. "How'd she end up with creepy old Fletch?"

"Oh, the women I see with some men," Laura said, shaking her head. "Slim pickings out there." I walked downstairs and got the new color and scissors, put a chair in the middle of the living room, newspaper underneath.

"Her parents died when she was young, the article says. Hey, she was valedictorian of her senior class," Madonna added. I pulled a cape around Laura and mixed the color chemicals. Madonna went on, looking at the newspaper, musing. "Laura, you got a lot of quotes to show people were surprised. Dang, everybody was surprised. I think it was that damn Fletch who killed her. After her money. Truth be told, I'd have grabbed the gun and turned it on him. Or knife, or whatever the weapon was."

None of us said anything. I squeezed the frosting cap over Laura's head and pulled strips of hair through. Madonna read about the reception poisoning. "You don't sound very guilty, LaRue, thanks to Laura's writing," Madonna said.

"Well, I'm not guilty," I said, mixing up the bleach and applying it to Laura's hair. Then I showed Laura the two colors and the catalyst.

"You do it—I trust you," Laura said.

Madonna folded up the paper and turned on TV. Controversy about what dispersants really did or might do in deep waters. "Shit," Madonna said. "Where's Andy Griffith when you need him?"

There was a knock at the door. "I'm doing Laura's hair for free," I whispered. I could be in real trouble if I was found doing hair under the table by someone who wanted me shut down. Madonna answered the door. AJ Lutz, neat, trim owner of the Fish House, brother of Cooter and Fletch Lutz. How one mother could turn out such a variety of men, I couldn't figure. He took off his fishing hat and nodded. He was a more attractive, older version of Cooter, and better looking than Fletch. A more relaxed and earnest Lutz. He still had hair, salt and pepper, styled old school rockabilly. We all said "Hey" and invited him in. He had gentlemanly ways, hat in hand, nodding his head, calling us all Miss Laura, Miss Madonna, Miss LaRue, like the old-timers did.

"Think I could get a haircut?" he said. You could hear the wind chuffling laughter through palms. It was that quiet.

"Uh—AJ, I'd love to but I'm not working tonight. I'm doing this for Laura—I owe her one." A lie. "Actually, you might not want to get your hair cut by me." I figured he'd heard the poisoning news.

"All the more reason to be taking it under the table," he said. So he knew I'd need business, and he didn't care what others thought. "Making a little extra in case you got to get you a lawyer." Another silence. "Listen," he drawled. "I done plenty of under the table in my day. Times when weather's bad, the fish ain't biting, my fishermen's out on drunks. Right now, we're all working for BP, working for the devil hisself over Louisiana way and west Florida, and that's the only reason we're afloat." He cleared his throat in the silence. "I know you ain't done it."

Madonna stood up with the crackers and dip and offered snacks to him. "You're a sweet soul, AJ. Have some crackers. Miss Polly's dip's got extra spice in it." He shook his head no, but I took Madonna's words as a cue.

"Okay," I said. "That'd be great, AJ, but you please have to keep this to yourself." AJ nodded his cool head. "Is there a good time for you? And where do you want to meet?" I asked. We decided on Monday morning at the Fish House when it was closed, after I got the kids off to school. He nodded his goodbyes.

"You're not out of business yet," Laura said after his footsteps faded down the stairs and into the street.

"Unless somebody squeals about my black market haircuts," I joked. "Then it could be trouble."

We watched the news. A fisherman was trolling the waters of Barataria Bay in his johnboat, flashing on globs of oil on dying grass in Louisiana. The fisherman was saying, *It's eerie, quiet. It's all gonna die. You don't hear the birds. You don't hear the shrimp pop in the water, that li'l splash. You don't hear the redfish rolling on a pod of minnows up on the edge of the marsh. This is my way of life. This— it's pulling everything outta my heart.* None of us said anything. We ate mullet dip and drank coffee. Madonna talked about a bird, an oriole she picked up on the road and took to the refuge for injured birds. No one could figure out why the pale bird seemed so disoriented and couldn't fly, but everyone seemed to know the spill's poison had gotten to the yellow bird.

The poisonous smell had gotten to us all on the island. We saw no goo, but everyone in town had felt nauseous from the smell of oil. I'd called my respiratory therapy nurse friend in Tallahassee, and I asked her if hypochondria was getting the best of me when the petrol smell rolled in off the water and gave me a headache. She said to get inside and not come out until it passed.

"Sure it's multi-billion dollars BP will pay us, but we won't see a dime of it for two or three years," Laura said as I rinsed her hair. We all talked about how businesses would go under completely before any benefit to people on the Gulf would occur. I shortened the length of Laura's hair, blew it dry, and showed her the new look in the mirror.

"God, I look young," Laura said.

Madonna said, "I'd think you were those ladies in 'Sex and the City,' only you're not getting laid enough." Very funny, hahaha, Laura said.

Madonna and I had to prepare to go out to the boat. Laura agreed to stay over in case the kids woke up. She'd sleep in my bed. I'd come back and sleep on the sofa, and Madonna would head home.

Another knock on the door. We all looked at each other. 9:23 p.m. by the kitchen clock. "Who is it?" I said.

"Just Tiffany," she said. She walked in, her youthful glowing skin, her pale exterior and eyebrows going up and down in nervous energy. She did have beautifully shaped brows and doe eyes. She looked from one of us to the next. We all shifted in our seats and muttered hello. "What's up?" she said.

"Oh, we're fixing to call it a night," Madonna said, casual. "We should be asking you. What's up? How's Mac?"

She came in and sat down. "Doing pretty fine," she said. "They'll let him go tomorrow, so you don't need to go to Tallahassee. Or call." She looked pale, her eyes not lighting on anything.

"That's good news," I said. "We'll go see him at home, then." She eyed me suspiciously. "I didn't poison him, Tiffany," I added.

"I didn't think so," she said. "I just wonder who did." She stared at the floor. We all stared at her.

"So, if you have any evidence—do you know anybody who doesn't like Mac?" I asked.

"Trina," she said. "Trina didn't like him." She looked at me. "Trina and Mac got into a big argument about a month before she killed herself. I'm not sure why."

"How do you know?" I said, trying not to sound like I was fishing.

"I heard them. In the real estate office. It wasn't like a shouting match—well, it kind of was, but—" she shrugged. "They didn't sound ferocious. Not like Fletch and Trina. Just like they had a disagreement."

"Trina couldn't have tried to poison him," I said, gentle as I could. "She was already dead."

"I know. But you asked."

"Well, thanks for letting me know," I said.

"You say Fletch and Trina argued?" Laura ventured.

"All the time," she said. "Trina would call the real estate office looking for him. When he was there by chance, they'd get into it. 'Fuck you this and fuck you that.' I never saw them together. Just thought they had a not-so-good marriage." She shrugged.

"Have you stayed at the hospital all this time?" I asked.

She nodded. "I thought he was going to die," she said. "And he really doesn't have anybody, you know?" As if you do, I thought. I couldn't see Mac nursemaiding Tiffany.

Madonna yawned. "Well, I think we should all get to bed, don't you, girls? Tiffany, you've gone beyond the call of duty. I hope you get some rest." Madonna and Laura started to gather their things, as if they were leaving. Tiffany turned and left after I gave her a box of chamomile tea to help her sleep.

"She's doing him, sure as the world," Madonna said as soon as the door was shut after her. We all stifled conspiratorial laughter.

"But why?" Laura said.

"Classic professor-student, rich businessman-underling thing," Madonna said.

"Total waste of time," Laura said. "That's what it's all about—pedophilia." We all snorted back our hilarity like preteen girls telling dirty jokes during a church sermon.

Then we got to work. Laura retrieved plastic bags from the drawer and instructed us to put anything that looked like evidence into them. "Get going," she said, pushing us out the door. "Before you two start drinking and get sloppy." She tripped over the new plant, and all three of us burst out laughing.

"Hey, do you guys recognize what nursery this plant came from?" I asked.

They looked at me like I was crazy. I told them about the note the night of the poisoning.

"Logan's, maybe, on Sixty-seven just the other side of Wellborn," Laura said.

"Wal-Mart," Madonna said, up in Wellborn.

Laura stripped the key code sticker off and said, "Take this with you and see." She put it in a plastic bag, and I shoved it into my pocket. "Sometimes they can run it down. Now go on, you Nancy Drews." Suddenly, I felt a similar dread to the fisherman on television who measured his life by the grass, shrimp, mullet, and the birds. *It's all gonna die,* he said. I tried to push his words away.

CHAPTER 14

THE NIGHT SKY was a black satin gown with white gemstones scattered throughout. A crisp winter night. For half an hour we'd sat in the shadows of the marina between Main and Dock Streets that surrounded the cove on three sides. Huddled and shivering, walking five steps forward, five back to keep warm. We were about to trespass, and we didn't know why.

Saturday night traffic came in pulses. People drove in for dinner or the bars. St. Annes party culture assisted people in the night-off rituals we were used to—the shouting of drinkers, the wailing of the jukebox, the clank of beer bottles thrown in the garbage by bartenders or waiters. So every time we thought we might walk over to Mac's boat, people left a bar on Dock or Main. We made a run back to the apartment to change into dark jackets over navy T-shirts and long jeans.

"We'd never get our badges if we tried out for Boy Scouts," Madonna said, gloomily. Suddenly, a lull. I fingered the tiny flashlight in the pocket of my jacket.

"Okay. Now," I said. We took off our shoes, leaving only our dark socks on. No footprints, no shoe prints.

"Here, put these on," I said, handing her hairdresser's gloves. This protected stylists' hands from dyeing chemicals. We each stuffed several plastic bags in jeans pockets.

"Why are you whispering?" Madonna asked as we crossed the street by the hardware and fish bait store, heading for the moored boats.

"I don't know," I whispered.

"Well, stop. It's so obvious."

We stepped onto the starboard side of the twenty-four-foot boat. It swayed, and we both walked straight to the stern, farther from the dock and the streetlight.

"Look for—" I said in a low voice.

"Anything," Madonna said. We slid on the gloves.

We silently scoured every inch of the port side of the boat with our flashlights. I examined the floor while she explored the flanks. A well-cleaned boat smelling of a bleach-and-water scrub. Madonna tapped me on the shoulder and thumbed down towards the cabin. We took steep steps into the cabin.

On either side of the center aisle lay two slim beds. The carpet and beds were dark blue. Beyond that, the inner cabin. "You take starboard, I'll take port," Madonna said.

I checked the padded cushions. Under the mattresses were boarded seats that opened to storage. An old fishing net, some nice deep-sea fishing poles, a hammer and screwdriver. A Swiss Army knife. I dropped that into a bag, moving towards the inner cabin.

On the wall, photos with ends curling from ocean humidity were tacked up on the paneling, ends curling from humidity and time. One photo of a younger Fletch and Trina standing beside a small boat. They beamed, and between them stood a boy about five years old.

Another photo of Fletch and some guys holding up a goliath grouper. I smoothed the brittle, curling photo and placed both snapshots into the bag. Madonna was brushing her gloved hands along the other side. Her white glove against the dark boat looked like sea anemones swimming.

Another photo struck me. Trina as a young woman, with maybe a baby brother. This child, the same kid that stood between Fletch and Trina, only older now? No, they didn't look the same. The boy was about four, and Trina looked about eighteen or twenty. The kid was familiar. I stashed the photo in the bag and headed for the inner cabin.

"Check it out," Madonna said from the other cabin. She had removed the padding off the other bed and was curled inside, under the bottom of the bed that served as a sofa during the day. She held her flashlight on a big splotch beside her under the boarded bed. A blob of rusty red ran from above and had stained the storage wall.

"Here," I said, opening the Swiss Army knife. "Get a bag and hold it right below this. I'll scrape."

"Hang on," she said. She squirmed inside the box to get more comfortable. "Okay, go." I scraped the red that now crumbled off the knife and fell into the bag. The cove's waves slapped the sides of the boat. "Good going," I said.

"Well, it might be paint or fish blood, so don't get your hopes up," she said.

"Jackson said he never excluded anything," I said. "Let's check the inner cabin."

"You go ahead," Madonna said. "I'm going to look at these pictures on the starboard side." She flashed her light on the strange mosaic of pictures and squinted. I entered the inner cabin. A musty smell. Benches were built into the front, but not much else except storage shelves on either side.

Suddenly, the boat dipped sideways, and then began to sway back and forth. The slapping of the waves against the boat got louder, quicker, like the wake of another boat. Then I heard a footstep above. Ducking through the door, I reached up and lightly touched Madonna's elbow and pulled her down.

"Shh," I said. I pointed up. Her eyes got huge as she turned towards me, then winced, blinded by my light. She tiptoed towards me, and we shut the inner cabin doors behind us without a sound. Footsteps clomped above, all around the boat. Heart thumping, I turned on the flashlight again and picked up a shoe iron and handed it to Madonna. She found a hammer on her side of the shelving and handed the shoe iron back to me. I clicked off the light.

I could hear our shallow breathing. The sound of footsteps coming down the ladder. A flashlight clicked on, and I could see the silhouette of legs, someone scanning and then rummaging the room. A thin male, maybe? One shadow of an arm reached up where the photos were, then came back down. The person turned and walked back upside. We stood still, quiet, sweating. The waves against the boat slapping. Two minutes later, we felt the boat dip to starboard when the person stepped off and back onto the dock. We stayed completely still and quiet for about five minutes.

"Mary, Joseph, and the baby Jesus," Madonna finally whispered, letting out a deep sigh.

"Let's give it a minute more," I said. We waited five minutes and then slowly replaced the heavy implements. One of the photos was missing. Whoever it was had taken it. Neither of us spoke. Before now, neither of us thought of ourselves as women who would crack someone's skull open. After another five minutes, Madonna poked her head out and looked. We slowly made our way upside, breathing clean air.

We crouched on the floor so as not to be seen, listening to people bar hopping, laughing, singing, occasionally yelling in bursts. We waited another five minutes. I had to pee. We stepped off the boat, found our legs, peeled off the gloves, stuffing them into our pockets. My hands were shaking. Without saying anything, we put on our shoes where we'd left them by the marina door just across the cove. Madonna led the way one block to my apartment away from the cove. Once inside, we bolted the door.

"What in freaking hell? . . . " Madonna said, staring at me.

"What happened?" Laura said, going to the refrigerator and getting two beers for us.

"Who was that?" I said. We each plopped down on opposite sofas, popped open the two beers, and nearly sucked both all down.

"Thanks." I put the bottle on the table, then stood, too freaked out to talk, and checked on my sleeping kids. Still slumbering hard, thank the gods of sacked-out babies. I lightly touched the heads of my soft-haired children. Daisy in her old white canopy bed, Tay in his upper bunk, the collection of bones, arrowheads, and rocks on his bureau.

When I returned, Madonna and Laura were already talking in low murmurs. Laura kept shaking her head and staring at the floor. She finally said, "I can't believe how close you two came to getting caught. Remind me not to let you two do that again." I nodded, turning on CNN.

We forgot ourselves in the new bad news, as I lay across a sofa, watching. Scientists were concerned about holes in the food chain in the Gulf. The mainstream news had finally decided to report that the people BP had hired to spread dispersant in Louisiana and Mississippi, mainly out-of-work fishermen, had burning eyes. Subcontractors who took boats out to spread the dispersant were vomiting brown phlegm, had headaches, dizziness.

And there was no compensation. I wondered when the poison would wander over to us, but it didn't matter. The Gulf coast people were our Gulf coast people. It looked like we were screwed. My mind followed the terns, the oysters and shrimp. Dolphins. And then I went below the surface, to sleep.

I WOKE UP in the living room as the phone rang. Daisy thundered down the hallway to answer it. The sun had made its way above the horizon and well into the sky. I'd left the TV on, and CNN was telling us the world's spanking new bad news. The heavy storms might follow up with snow. Tropical storm-like weather was headed to the Gulf. It would surely send more trouble into Louisiana, which could handle it least of all. This storm might drive the poisonous goo to the northwest coast of Florida.

Madonna had crashed hard on the other sofa. She hadn't heard the phone ring, even the second time.

"Hello?" Daisy said sweetly into the phone. "Oh," she said with disappointment. "Mama, it's for you. Some man. Mama, why is Laura in your bed? I'm hungry." I took the phone, sat up and pointed to the kitchen. Mother sign language for 'You know where the food is.'

"Hello?" I said, groggy, clearing my throat and turning off the TV.

"So island people sleep in. I'd always suspected it." It was Jackson.

"What's up, Investigator? It's so damn early on a Sunday. What could you want?"

"It's nine-thirty a.m.," he said. "I could want any number of things." Was he teasing? Passing time? I staggered to the kitchen to make coffee. Daisy was pulling waffles from the freezer.

"Yeah, pretty damn early," I muttered. "I was working until late last night cutting hair."

"Opening the shop at night?" Daisy went to the living room and turned on TV cartoons. Madonna groaned, stretched, got up, and staggered to Daisy's room to sleep. I put the coffee on.

"I didn't—I cut friends' hair. That's all." Not even a white lie. "It was Laura's hair—she's your friend. You want to arrest us both? I can see it now in the headlines: Famous investigator arrests single mother and friend for cutting hair in apartment."

"I know what you think. Cops and investigators are stupid, don't do their job, so I'll just help them out and help myself out, too. Can't trust cops anyway, right?" he said.

"It's an old island tradition not to trust authority," I said. "Sometimes we get up late, too. You should know that." I walked onto my slanting wooden balcony porch, a risky endeavor. The wood was old and rotting just like every other porch on Main. The balconies stayed there for looks only nowadays. Still, the sun beat down and warmed things up, and the water was calm as gray satin, the light glittering off its smoothness. The sun was a huge orange pill in the sky.

"Okay, well." There was a silence on the line, and I checked, squinting into the window to the kitchen, to see if coffee was filling the pot.

"It's gorgeous out here this morning," I said to soften the conversation. "Water's calm, seagulls and pelicans flying across the Gulf."

"Oh, yeah?" he said. "Just foggy, muggy, and chilly here in the city. So much cement will be the downfall of us all."

"Yeah, why do we keep covering up Earth, I wonder. Anyway, I'm going to take some wildflowers and maybe some cookies to Mac," I said. "He gets home from the hospital today."

"How about asking him who he thinks might have done it," Jackson said. "He probably trusts you more than cops." I agreed. He went on. "Something else," he said. "Mary Lutz was committed to a mental health unit of Tallahassee Memorial last spring. Have any idea why?"

"Hmmm . . . she's crazy?" I said. "Seriously, I didn't know that. I thought she left to visit family up in Georgia." The silence again ensued, and I said, "Well, I haven't found out much of anything. I'll go check on the plant thing. And grill poor Mac, too."

"Ask him if Trina kept his books," he said. "And I'll tell you what." He paused. "Let me take your underemployed, single-mom self to dinner tonight and we can compare notes."

My stomach tightened. I wasn't paying enough attention to what he was saying. What I was realizing at the wrong time was that I'd faced being a possible murderer until last night, holding a heavy metal tool. I also understood that I would have been willing to crush someone's skull in to save the kids or myself or friends. I finally understood the murderer, whoever it might have been, and how that person might want to crush me.

"Hello? LaRue?" he said, noticing the silence between us.

"In Tallahassee?" I said, dreading a trip into that traffic and the complicated life of malls, suburbs, school districts, and cement.

"Such disdain!" he said. "No. St. Annes. The Pelican."

"The Pelican sucks," I said. "Everything's boiled in bad oil. The only thing they have is view."

"Well, what's your preference?" he said.

"The hotel," I said. "Pricey, pricey."

"You mothers are a picky lot," he said. "Okay, sounds fine. Say six, before the sun sets?"

"Now you're talking like an islander. Okay, meet you—we could meet at the dock on Dock Street if you want to watch the sun set, and walk over to the hotel."

"Sounds good," he said. I could order pizza for the kids. Maybe Daisy was old enough to stay alone for a bit. If she got scared, she could walk down Main Street to the hotel. If not, I'd ask Tiffany to sit. I resented just a little that he didn't have to think of any of this. "What about your kids?" he said.

"Covered," I said. But my stomach still hurt. "Okay, see you for some visual drama at the dock at six," I said and hung up.

Back inside, I hugged Daisy and said, "Let's bake some cookies for Mr. Duncan!"

"And some for us, too?" she said, putting the TV remote down. So we stirred up a double batch of chocolate chip oatmeal cookies and slid the first pans into the oven. Meanwhile, Laura had gotten up from my bed and grabbed a cup of coffee. The apartment began to fill with the scent of baking butter, sugar, and chocolate. The house warmed and Madonna stirred, rose for coffee, and then Tay was up hunting orange juice. One of Daisy's friends knocked on the door, and the two girls dove into her bedroom and shut the door. That left me with the cookies. Everyone else was sitting around the table with morning drinks and toast.

"So how are you feeling about last night?" Laura asked.

I walked behind Tay and gave Laura the shush sign, not wanting him to know too much.

"Well, we nearly got busted," Madonna said.

Too late to keep it from Taylor now. In fact, these women were helping me raise my kids. I certainly didn't know how to do it alone. So I took my cue from them and went on. "Someone we don't know came onto the boat while we were searching the cabin, so we hid," I said.

"What boat?" Taylor said, turning quickly to frown at me.

"Laura, you explain it," I said. "You know, why we got on the boat." So Laura explained.

"Murder?" Taylor sat upright and stared at me.

I plopped down and told him about Trina's throat, the fact that she'd had no gunshot wound, and the funeral home experience. Tay stared into the table, his mouth open, his eyes sparkling, wide.

"Someone—somebody *killed* her?" he said with wonder. He looked around the table at each of us. Laura and Madonna gave him the whole scenario and why we'd gone on the boat—that the garbage man had told Madonna where Trina was last spotted—on the boat. Meanwhile, the timer dinged, and I slid the first sheet of cookies out of the oven to cool and shoved the next one in.

Taylor was looking at me in a different way. "So you went on the boat looking for stuff that might show she got killed?" He looked excited, his big dark eyes full of possibility and adventure.

"I don't recommend doing this yourself, Taylor, sneaking around," Madonna said. "Though we did find some stuff." She pulled out the baggie of scraped red rust. I walked back to the bathroom where I'd gone to change clothes, got the photos I found on the boat and laid them on the table. Madonna added a photo to the bunch.

"This is evidence?" Laura said.

I shrugged. "Could be." I handed her the photo of Trina, Fletch, and the little boy. "Tell me this doesn't look like a happy little family. Maybe thirty years ago."

"Trina was quite the cute young woman," Laura said. "They do look happy."

"I saw that picture," Taylor said. "In their house. Except bigger. In a frame. And some others of the same kid in the living room."

"Did she ever say who he was?" Madonna asked.

"No, but I always thought it was their kid. I had the idea he had died, and she didn't like to talk about stuff like that."

"Fletch wasn't ugly, either," Madonna said. "Maybe that's why he thinks he's such a lady's man now. Forgot he got old, not just old but lech-old."

"Check this one out," I said. "Who's this with Fletch? One of his brothers? They kind of look alike, but he seems too young to be a brother."

"Let me see," Laura said. She studied it awhile. "That face—seems like I've seen it recently, but I can't place it."

"I thought the same," I said, bringing a plate of cookies to the table.

"And how about this shot," Madonna said, grabbing a cookie. Mac stood tallest, in the middle of a group of six men. He held up a huge cobia that one or all of them had reeled in. "The Boarders," was scribbled underneath in pen.

"Ooo, there's old man Fielding," Laura pointed. "The late senator himself. And . . ." She squinted. "I know I've seen that one," she said, pointing to a smaller, heavy man, handsome middle-aged face and dark eyes. She shook her head as she munched a cookie. "Some meeting. Maybe county commission? And there's Fletch. Can't determine these others."

"So who are 'The Boarders?'" Taylor displayed quote signs like Austin Powers.

"Good question," I said. "And now for maybe the best, maybe lamest evidence. Madonna?"

She pulled out the baggie and dropped it on the table. It looked empty.

"That's pretty lame, you guys," Taylor said, thrusting a whole cookie in his mouth and grabbing another.

I picked up the baggie. "Dark rusty stuff. Maybe blood."

"Oh, man, you are really digging." Laura shook her head.

"I told her that," Madonna said.

"Come on, you all," I said. "Give it a chance."

"What I want to know is how Fletch can get it on down there with his lard ass on those skinny beds," Madonna said. "That's the real mystery." Everybody laughed, including Taylor. If I'd said it, he'd have said, *Mom, how gross.*

"What's so funny, Mama?" Daisy said, running down the hall, friend in tow. "Do I smell cookies?" They all grabbed a cookie. Daisy tried to peer at the photos.

"We're just laughing about Mr. Lutz sleeping on those skinny mattresses in a boat we rode in once," I said. "That's all."

"Oh," she said, studying each of us with suspicion. Tay smirked as he sauntered off to his room.

"I'll talk to you about it later, honey, okay?" I whispered. She nodded and gave her friend a pointed look and sigh.

"Well, I've got to get going," Laura said. "Did Jackson tell you—hey, what do you think of him?"

"I don't know," I said, low, staring at the table. Daisy walked over to eavesdrop. "I just don't—it's been years since I've . . . dated. I don't know what I'm supposed to do anymore."

"It's like riding a bike," Madonna said. "You never forget. It's time you got yourself some, Rue."

"Madonna, shh!" I thumbed at Daisy and her friend. Madonna shrugged, winking at Daisy who was watching all our faces.

"He's a good guy," Laura said. "He doesn't . . . expect things."

"Anyway, you were asking me if he told me something?" I said, skirting the issue.

"Yeah, did he tell you he turned me onto a big story on the river?" she said. "Looks like they've got some nasty runoff pouring into the river."

"Gasoline? The oil spill was about sweet crude, not gasoline," I said.

"Yeah, like that's news," Madonna said. "Which river?"

"Oh, this is news. St. Annes, but they think it's running straight into the Magnolia Springs. They've got—well, they've got more than we ever knew about. I can't say now, but I'll tell you when I get more facts. It's not sexy like oil or gas. It's septic tank seepage running along the aquifer."

"Oh, they always leave you hanging when it comes to the shit," I said, feigning heartbreak. "Still. Wait." I thought again. "Another water pollution story? It's a surprise we have any water to drink at all. The Magnolia? Our gem? The spring that feeds all the fresh water?"

"Rue, you're ranting. You need to watch less oil spill news. I gotta go, too," Madonna said, gathering her things to leave. "Got to get some rest." Tonight she would work steady weekend drunks and the folks depressed about Monday. And the guys working the spill. "None of my customers tip enough, but at least I've got customers." She shook her head. The Rusty Rim waiters, she'd said, had just lost weekly hours.

Daisy and I scraped the last of the cookies off the sheets and onto waxed paper. We had a chocolate chip oatmeal cookie infestation. I was going to see Mac in a while, and I'd be giving the grocer a hair and mustache trim. Later, I'd go to the nurseries to check out the plants.

I was working with a guy who liked me. Dread rolled over me.

CHAPTER 15

DAISY HAD GALLIVANTED OFF to play with her friend up the street, and Taylor was on the phone, explaining to his girlfriend why he slept through Saturday night. This meant he'd get in the van and zoom off soon, too. He'd surprisingly offered to babysit Daisy so that I could go out. The weather sat stubborn in the low fifties, but the sun always has its way with the islands. Now sun's fullness shone in the Main Street windows. I was placing the cooled cookies in several containers when a knock came at the door.

"Is it already that close to ten?" I said. It was Jim, the grocer.

"Yep. Morning is my best time," Jim said, "and it's gone before I know it."

I told him where to sit and covered him up with a silver cape. "Don't worry, I won't offer you any coffee."

He laughed. "Wouldn't mind some, really." So I poured him a cup. I offered him cookies, too, which he took. He wanted a hair and mustache trim, and I got to work clipping. When you touch people, they'll talk to you. It's a funny thing about us humans. Jim and I traded teenage horror stories since he was raising a son a year older than Tay. "Finally, he's started coming around again," Jim said of his boy. "For a while there, we thought he was gonna drop out of school like the rest of them around here. But he decided to stick it out. Now he's on his way to junior college."

"I know you're relieved," I said. I had expressed worry that Tay wouldn't finish out of sheer boredom. "We look for the good signs, don't we, Jim? Have to."

"I see you've got a picture of Fletch and Trina with little Curtis," Jim said, pointing to the table. I had forgotten to remove the photo from the table. I'd put the rest of the evidence in a big Ziploc to show Jackson later.

"Curtis—oh, yeah, the picture. Yeah, Taylor brought this home from the Lutzes' house once," I lied. "I was thinking about getting it redone for Tay to remember Trina by." Who was this Curtis he was talking about?

"That was a tragedy," he said.

"I didn't know Curtis," I said.

"You were a young'un then," he said. "Curtis was only a child himself," Jim said. "Fell off the boat when he was out with Fletch and Preston. Drowned before Fletch could even get to him. Out on the Magnolia River up by the bluff. Trina never forgave him, I don't think. How can a mother go on after a child has died?" He shook his head. "And Fletch, that ole Fletch got the message out that he didn't like nobody talking about it."

"Oh," I said. I wanted to sit down. Poor Trina. So she *had* been a mother. A teen mother. My kids served as her grandkid substitute. Indeed, how does a mother live her life after her child dies, I wondered. Or live with a husband she feels had responsibility in the child's death? How do they go on together? And who the hell was Preston? Why hadn't I known about the child? Fletch had really put a cap on any talk, that was certain. "Jim, do you think Trina was—depressed?" I said.

He turned his head and looked at me. "'Tween you and me?" I nodded. "I think there was hanky panky going on there."

"Hanky panky? You mean she was having an affair? What makes you say that?" I said.

"No, not that kind," Jim said, waving his hand. "Take it from me." He looked at me pointedly. "Trina was honest as a summer day is long, and Fletch is just as dishonest." Then he shut his mouth. I trimmed his mustache, trying not to tickle, and not to cut anything besides hair. "You know some of them Coltons got hired by BP," he said after a bit. "Said they won't let the fellas wear respirators when they're working with them chemicals. Said they'll sack 'em if they wear any protection."

"That's horrible," I said. "Those big companies don't care a thing about the Gulf's farmers. We can't fish, so we have to go get poisoned cleaning up their mess." I stepped back and looked at his hair. "There," I said. "All done." He stood and went for his wallet.

"LaRue, between you and me, those books them guys kept of their businesses?" he said, shaking his head. "They were screwy. Trina came to me complaining, since I run a clean business. She kept the books for all of us around here, you know. And she told me she was scared." He shook his head and pulled out a hundred-dollar bill. "All kinds of funny money around here, swapping it up here and yonder, and she couldn't keep hide nor hair of it. Knew it would be her hide if anybody got caught." He handed me the bill.

"Oh, I don't have change—" I said, putting my hands in my back pockets.

"I don't want change," he said. "I may have to count on you for the same sometime." He threw the bill on the table. "So just don't forget me."

"Jim?" I said. "I can't take this—"

"Rue," he said, sternly.

"Well," I said, sighing and dropping my shoulders. "Okay. I won't forget it. But there's something I wanna ask. Did Fletch and Trina fight much? The books? Or—" I trailed off, then pointed to the photo. "Or Curtis?"

"I don't know about that," Jim said, pointing to the photo. "But the funny money? All the time," he said. "Trina, she tried to get people to come clean, but they ignored her." He shook his head. "Well, you take care, now, hear?

And don't be a stranger. Hope you get your reputation back soon!" He smiled, waved and was gone.

THE FIRST NURSERY on the county road took almost twenty minutes to reach. I'd almost gotten to Wellborn. All kinds of showy pinks, purples, and oranges sat out front at Logan's Nursery, a new building made of light wood. I wondered how a business kept from folding in a recession. I entered the fenced area and began to saunter, searching for the palms. They stood toward the back of the main room. Sure enough, palm trees that looked like the one that landed on my front stoop. Only in different-sized pots.

I asked a sales clerk if he could check the bar code for fitting their inventory or cash register. He sized me up, shrugged, and ran it through. "Yep," he said. "Purchased here October first." Whoever delivered the plant to me had bought it five weeks earlier. The premeditated precision made the skin on my back crawl.

I asked if he could trace who'd purchased the fern, and he shook his head no. I thanked him and checked out some hibiscus I wanted to plant at Panther Pit, a coral color. By the time I made it back to the island, the sun had passed towards mid-afternoon.

An hour later, I was standing at Mac's door, knocking. Mary answered, wearing a scanty white nightshirt thing, surprising me. I knew she saw my expression, and she said, "Oh, um, I'm just helping Mac out until he can be up on his feet. Come in." I followed her to the kitchen.

"Want a beer?" She grabbed one for herself and popped the top. I stared at the hallway that led to Mac's room. I'd just stolen onto a boat he owned. I'd supposedly poisoned him several days ago. I'd just found out he kept iffy books. Of course I wanted a beer. But I figured I'd better not.

"No, thanks," I said. "But some tea or water would be great. Whatever you've got." I leaned on the marble bar of his modern gleaming kitchen. Black and white carpet, red leather furniture in the living room. Very Asian, teak and sleek. The windows with their angular shapes stretched across the Gulf side of the high-ceiling living room.

"He's getting damn frustrating," Mary said, pouring a glass of water. She handed the tumbler to me, plunking a piece of ice in it as an afterthought. "Wants to get back to work. Says he needs to see this guy, got to get a loan from that bank, and call somebody about the other project. And he's been watching those football games." She took a deep glug of beer. "He gets as mad as that Spurrier guy used to get when the Gators did something wrong. You know how that coach used to throw his hat on the ground like a spoiled brat?" I nodded. "Last night, you'd have thought Mac was the coach the way he threw pillows at the TV." She shook her head. "I thought he was gonna cry when that team—whoever it was—started losing the whatever game today." She took another long drink and sighed.

"Maybe that's his way of getting frustration out," I said. "He's really a dedicated worker. He loves work. Lives work. You know. When do you think he'll be back at it?"

"Tomorrow, probably. The doctor said not until next week, but if the man can walk, the man will work," she said. "Thank the Lord." She finished her beer, crushed the can and hesitated. She looked at the tin of cookies I'd brought. "How nice of you."

"Think I can see him?" I said.

"Sure. Wait here." She opened the fridge, popped another beer, and headed up the stairs. I sneaked into his study, scanning. Papers from a Tallahassee law firm, stationery with the heading ECOL, a legal document that looked like a property description. Somewhere out the county road. I stole back into the kitchen. Mary descended holding her beer can.

"You can go up in a minute," she said. She turned around in that skimpy pj's thing. She was married to Cooter, probably out on patrol. If not, he was drinking at the Hook Wreck, or sleeping off a hangover. Mary had some presence the men liked, like Tiffany. They were always swarming around her. Now Mary seemed to be hovering around Mac.

"Mary, you know I didn't put that poison in Mac's coffee, right?" I asked.

"Of course, LaRue," she said, not looking me in the eye.

"Do you know who did?" I asked.

"Nope," she said, staring into her beer can, frowning. "Sure don't." Tight lips.

"Come on, surely you have an idea of who hates him, you know, who's jealous, or greedy, or vengeful," I said. "You're around him a lot."

"Dang," she said. "Greedy, vengeful, jealous? You make it sound like a Greek tragedy." I was often surprised by Mary. She sounded like a drunk humanities major. And she'd been committed to a mental ward, now on her way to drunk. She was hanging out with a guy twice her age, married to a cop without the brains God gave him. Talk about your Greek tragedies.

"Help me out, Mary. I didn't poison him. I need to get back to business, and the only way to do that is to find out who—"

"I don't know," she said, her words flying. Her neck grew red. "I really don't. Go on up and see him. Take him the cookies. I have a headache." She put her arm to her forehead and took a sip of beer. I headed up the steps.

The bedroom sprawled huge, white, navy, and austere. The furniture, scant and nautical. A skylight was set in the ceiling over the king-size bed. The headboard brought to mind a ship's wheel. "Well, there she is," Mac said, "the evil witch with the poisoned apple."

He sat with newspapers, coffee cups, and dishes expanding in disarray around him. The sailor in his shining pajamas. Mac did have beautiful hair, and the tan, media-star handsome against his white hair. But his eyes looked puffy.

"Here, sit on the bed," he said, then saw my face. "Or grab that chair and pull it up." He pointed at a white wicker chair in the corner. "What'd you bring me?"

I handed him the tin, and as he opened it, his eyes gleamed. He pulled a cookie out and held it up. "Now, some folks would tell me not to touch what you brought me." He took a bite. "Umm mmm. But I'd say to them, 'Don't you fret over Mac Duncan. He and LaRue Panther, they're tight.' " He winked, and smiled. We'd helped each other in business, referred people to each other, been active in the local chamber of commerce together. But I'd never been in his home, next to his bed with cookies, or talking around murder attempts versus trust.

"Daisy and I baked these for you this morning," I said. "Laura and Madonna said they're thinking about you and send you their best." They'd done no such thing. My eyes roamed the room. "Nice bedroom."

"So folks still thinking you did this to me?" he said. I didn't know how to answer.

He sat up, fluffed his pillows, working a fierce, menacing look onto his face. Raised his eyebrows and gave a steely look meant for some unknown enemy. "Don't you worry about all this, LaRue." He went on. "I'm sorry you've been implicated. I know it's a hardship, and if you'd like, I'll try to get you more work."

"Thanks, Mac. I really appreciate it," I said. I rose and looked at my watch. "I've got a dinner meeting here in a little while, so I'd better get moving."

"I've been telling people," he said with a short laugh. "What the hell does that girl have to gain by killing me? Nothing. If I die, a few other people would stand to gain, but not her." He laughed hard, in a gallows-humored way. It echoed through the big house.

CHAPTER 16

VIEWING A GORGEOUS ST. ANNES SUNSET proved to be a bust. Jackson and I met at the end of the pier, where low gray clouds hovered. A storm blew up and cracked open the heavens, part of the hurricane that had luckily wimped out. He knew Lighthouse Key lay across the Gulf to the right from the dock. That Sprangle Island was settled across from the cove and the Gulf. But he studied farther left, caught a glimpse of the silver conical-shaped buildings at the tip of land twenty miles away. He wondered what it was.

"Crystal Power Plant," I said, "the nuclear power plant."

He nodded, raised his eyebrows and said, "Aha."

The wind had begun to blow rain, and the sun dove beneath the horizon, so we'd walked hurriedly down the street towards the hotel for dinner. The jukebox at the L&M Bar one block over and beyond offered Waylon Jennings and Hank Williams. The hotel restaurant offered a muffled and wavery Bach. I'd rather have Lucinda Williams or the Decemberists piped through the rooms, but Bach made for a nice change from the usual St. Annes fare.

We pushed through the double screen doors. The parrot in the lobby squawked a hokie "Hello, Mate!" and we began to warm to mauve tablecloths covering antique tables. Waiters were clinking silverware and glasses as they set a semi-formal table. A denial of poverty, I figured.

Jackson pulled out the chair for me. When I looked at him quizzically, he shrugged his shoulders. I felt silly but went with the pretend we're-both-young-single-on-a-date routine.

After the waiter handed us menus and took our drink orders, I suggested Jackson ask about the fresh catch. "The fishermen come to the back door every day and sell what they've just caught," I said. "It's usually better than anything else. Fresh." Jackson nodded, searching the menu like it held the answers to the universe. "'Course everything's good here, you know."

"I want one of everything," he said, patting his flat belly. I wondered if he worked out. Next to his six-three frame, I wasn't quite so tall. I still made a note not to wear heels around him, though I rarely did anyway. At six feet who needs any help? I glanced from my hands to his, measuring them in comparison. His palms were larger, but my fingers might be as long as his. I put my gawky hands in my lap. Still, something about his barrel chest, his muscular strength, comforted me.

"So who cuts your hair?" I asked.

"What's left of it?" he joked. He was balding near the forehead.

"Men are too sensitive about baldness," I said. "We women care what's inside, not how many hairs you have on your head."

"I don't think you were a man in your former lifetime," he said. "When *you* start losing *your* hair and don't mind it, give me a call."

"Fair enough. You didn't answer the question," I said. "Who cuts your hair?"

"Someone in Tallahassee," he said. "But there's a rumor about this talented woman on a nearby island who does a great haircut. She's been accused of poisoning a local businessman, but I don't believe them. I'll be at the shop soon to prove them wrong."

"Yeah, okay," I said. "Rumor has it some merciless investigator wants to use her as bait to bring out the murderer. A letter-of-the-law guy who doesn't understand her need to pay rent, car loan, and a property mortgage." I couldn't help myself. "Come on, Jackson. You know I didn't try to kill him. Get me off the hook."

"Huh," he said. "Mad at me already." He half-smiled and studied the menu. "You know I can't do that," he went on. "If I did, I'd be wondering how to pay *my* rent and car payment. I'm an investigator, LaRue, I can't just arbitrarily—"

"Enough," I said. "Let's order." I didn't want the waiter hearing the conversation and spreading more rumors.

"So, you're savoring the moment," he said with a dry smile. "Actually, I think you're a woman who shields herself with rough humor."

"Okay, yeah, it's a shield. And laughing gets me through the day. It keeps me from weeping, too. Except that I can't think of anything funny about, say, the oil spill."

"Fair enough. I'm sure you'll find a way, if there is one."

After we ordered the grouper and redfish specials, I got down to business.

"Okay, I found these photos on the boat," I said. I showed him the photos and told him what AJ had said about Trina and Fletch's drowned son Curtis.

Next, I pointed to the photo of "the Boarders," with Senator Fielding, Mac, Fletch, a county commissioner, and two others I didn't recognize. Jackson picked the photo up and squinted.

"That's Bob Sturkey," Jackson said with interest. "CEO of the power plant. Totally believes nukes are the energy of the future. He's like a religious fanatic about it. Now that oil has a dirty name, he's salivating. I don't know who the other guy is."

"All I have to say is, 'the sun.' Do you know that on the east coast, down by fancy-schmancy Boca Raton, the people didn't want windmills in the water? Said they were *unsightly.* Now they're all freaking out every time a tiny tar ball rolls up." He listened, making me nervous, the way he watched. I was fiddling with my water glass, running my fingers down the designs of the cut glass. "They run the damn tar balls to the lab to see if it's our Gulf oil spill blighting their Atlantic beaches. Define unsightly, I say."

"Whoa, I can see the spill isn't funny to you yet. You're still in the lecturing phase," Jackson said. I liked that he could push back.

"Okay, never mind," I said waving my hand. I pulled out the next photo. "Then there's this one," I said. "I don't know who this is." The photo of Trina as a teenager, a child standing next to her. "Do you recognize this person? I found these on the boat."

"I haven't got a clue," he said. "How would this be evidence?"

I shrugged, feeling both silly and impatient that he wouldn't consider anything as possible evidence. I went on. "I also found out that Trina didn't like Mac."

"What's your source?" Jackson asked. The waitress brought us crab-filled mushrooms.

"Tiffany," I said. "Tiffany works in the real estate office, remember her?"

"Youngish woman? Kind of washed out and lost-looking?" I nodded. At least he had deeper observational skills than most. "She spent some time in the hospital with Mac, yes?"

"The very one. And Jim, the grocer, told me that Trina confided in him about how messed up Fletch and Mac's books were. Others, too, around town, cheating on taxes. She kept trying to get folks to get straight on their numbers, but they wouldn't. Tiffany said Trina and Mac had a big row in the real estate office once."

"Row? Since when did you turn British?"

"I studied in London. I pick stuff up. Sometimes I don't even know what I'll say next."

"Okay, let's back up a minute," Jackson said. "You say you went on this boat *when*?"

"Midnight last night," I said, my fingers tracing the glass again. Our drinks came, and Jackson picked up his scotch on the rocks.

"With his permission, no doubt," he said dryly, sipping.

"Of course not," I said. "The garbage man said—"

"Okay," Jackson, said putting down his drink and listing off my sources with his fingers. "You've heard from the garbage man, the grocer, the real estate clerk . . . and now you're telling me you trespassed on the boat of the man you're accused of trying to poison and stole his personal photos?" he said. "And this, I'm guessing," he said, sipping again on the scotch, "is what you want me to submit as evidence to a judge? 'Your honor, the garbage man said

. . .' " He shrugged.

"Let me finish," I said, impatient. "Are you being condescending? Garbage men know more about people's troubles than anybody, wouldn't you think?" I heard my own condescension. Still, I rather enjoyed this heady banter. I picked up my glass of beer and played at the foam.

"Sorry," Jackson said, sitting back, taking another sip of scotch. "Go on."

"Okay, same back. We Southerners are sorry for everything, aren't we?" I smiled for the first time that night, I realized. "The garbage man lives on the canal just past the school. The mouth of the canal opens up at the Gulf near Way Key." I drew an invisible map on the tablecloth with a fork. "And he has an oyster boat. So, he was off work, you know, they start early, get off early, garbage men, and he took his boat on a cruise that afternoon. The afternoon Trina allegedly shot herself.

"He told Madonna that he saw Trina on a boat—Mac's boat. Right around six p.m." I was tapping my fork hard on the table. "OV, the garbage man, said she was sitting up in the *front* of the *boat*. OV said Trina waved at him and smiled, and he waved back. At the exact time she was supposedly shooting herself at home."

"Relax, LaRue," Jackson said. I was leaning forward into his face. He leaned back. "Let's have a nice meal and enjoy each other, okay? We're helping each other out."

"Oh, really?" I said. "I wouldn't count on the St. Annes PD to keep a goldfish alive in a self-feeding bowl. And that goes for the Sheriff's Department and the State Patrol too, for that matter. Or in Tallahassee or Gainesville or Orlando, or anywhere."

"Well," he said, nibbling on a crab-filled mushroom, "Now we're all clear on where we stand. This crab is delicious. Just enough spice."

I picked up a mushroom, waving it around on the fork. "Seriously, Jackson, this thing happened on Monday, and now it's what, Sunday?" Jackson watched the mushroom in my hand as I gestured. "What've you found out? At least I've gotten somewhere."

"Look, it's the gloaming," Jackson said, pointing out the front window at the purplish-black sky.

"Twilight," I said, sighing, letting him change the subject again. We peered out the window, locating Orion, then Canis Major, chasing after the great Greek hunter. We were quiet, enjoying our appetizer and drinks for a few minutes.

Out of the blue, Jackson put both hands flat to the table and cleared his throat. "Okay, did you look for any implements, you know, murder weapons? On the boat?"

"We found a Swiss Army knife," I said. "I took it."

"*You what?*" he said.

I shrugged. "We had slipped on hair dressers' gloves. We found something red and hoped it would—we saw red streaked across a spot under and behind the cushions of the bed, in the crevices? We scraped it into a bag."

"Okay," he said. "That could be evidence. Can you give it to me so I can have it analyzed?" I nodded. "What else did you find?"

"The photos," I said, leaning into him. "Somebody got on the boat while we were there."

"Oh, another thief?" he said. "What did he do? Or she?"

I told Jackson how we'd hid below, and that the person was looking for something in the cabin, and grabbed a photo. "Interesting," he murmured. "Describe this person. And it would help to know what lay in the compartments under the beds. And I won't even lecture you on how dangerous that moment was." He stopped and stared at the ceiling. Then he looked at me. "I'm not suggesting you get back on that boat." He looked at me sharply. "Yet in a crime scene, you look at every single detail."

"Okay," I said, waving him away, changing the subject. "So I found out a little about the plant I got that night." I told him about Logan's Nursery. "Don't know by whom, though. What have you found out, Mr. Investigator?" I said.

"Have you heard of a company called ECOL?" he asked. I told him I'd seen the letterhead at Mac's. "It stands for Ecological Corporation of Oceanic Living," he went on. "Sounds like an environmental organization by the acronym, wouldn't you agree?" I nodded, and he went on. "They're buying up property out the county road near your dad's place."

"Who are they?" I said.

"I don't know yet," he said.

"Oh, great," I said. "But you'll find out?" He said he'd get on it right away. Our salads arrived, and we ate. I explained that the heart of palm salad, invented by the original owner of the hotel in the fifties, involved killing a whole palm for the fruit in the salad. No longer, I told him. Pineapple replaced the palm.

"Interesting how appalling such waste seemed to us in the late twentieth century," he said.

"And then seemed to be forgotten in the early years of the twenty-first. Nothing like the threat of—ooooo, terrorism—to take you off the destruction of the natural world," I said.

"And now with the big pile of junk oil we're dealing with in what was the most naturally preserved body of water in the country—"

"Momentary renewed interest in the environment."

"So. I made a call to Miami where your Mac Duncan is from," Jackson said. "Graduated from the University of Miami's architecture school. Went to work for a large firm there. He's not the most well-regarded architect in the world. Guy I talked to said there's more, but I need to talk to the one who investigated the case. But he's left and moved to Oaxaca."

"Oaxaca!" I said. "Mexico? Why?"

"Why not? Easier to cover up crime there than in Miami," he said. "Leave the country with your big bag of money and an economy that's cheaper. Nobody can touch you."

"That's it?" I said. "That's all you have?"

"I have to talk to the investigator," he said. "Notes on a case don't mean anything unless you get the story from the person who took the case. I've got a call in to him. You know how Mexico is, though. They'll get the message to him when they get the message to him."

"Nothing else?"

"About Mary's mental health case. She and her husband have tried to keep it under wraps, the diagnosis. She's a manic-depressive alcoholic, who's also been arrested for assault and battery," he said. I raised my eyebrows in a question. "On Cooter," he said.

"Oh, my god, don't tell me Cooter can't—"

"She was fighting with him about something, some hysterical pregnancy she had. She blamed him, and then came at him with a knife. Poor bastard had fifteen stitches in his right leg. He lied and said it was cop work."

Oh, my god, I thought. But poor bastard? Maybe dumb bastard. "Look," I said. "He's the poor bastard who lied on the police report about Trina's death. So did she go to jail? What's a hysterical pregnancy, anyway?"

He shook his head. "No jail time. Cooter got her off, and Mac Duncan had her admitted to the TMH's Mental Health Facility. A hysterical pregnancy happens when a woman thinks she's pregnant, but she's not. She shows symptoms, but she's not biologically pregnant."

"Weird," I said. "Poor Mary." Then we both glanced at each other and away, towards the Gulf. A glassy gulf. I wondered how it would look in six months.

"Poor Mary," we said in unison, chuckling. "Fifteen stitches, huh?" I said. Why did Mac get involved, I wondered. Our fish was laid before us, and we ate in silence. Jackson offered me a bite of his grouper, which I took. My kids' father never shared food.

"When I was at Mac's today, I kind of snooped around in his office," I said. "Only saw the ECOL stationery."

He washed down his fish with water. "You kind of 'snooped around in his office'?" he said. "I asked you to check out two things. You don't need to snoop around in offices or steal onto boats." He looked at me pleadingly. "For god sakes, you're already the primary suspect in the poisoning case, don't give anybody ammunition."

"Ha!" I said, grinning. "Look, I'm going through some of Trina's things, too." I wanted him to lecture me again. I guessed I was flirting. I'd forgotten what flirtation felt like. I liked his concern. I felt the trust thing oozing through me. I hated it, I loved it.

"For god sakes. It would be different if you'd found a bloody knife or something that was evidence, LaRue. You've got nothing—"

"It's fine for you to call Miami and find out a few little things, but I need to move this investigation forward."

"Whoa, there," he said, chuckling. "I thought maybe you at least wanted a good meal out of this? A social event? No? All business and chewing me out?"

I took in a deep breath and let it go. I started twirling the front of my straight black hair, a habit I'd nearly broken. "Thanks for dinner," I murmured. I leaned a little closer. Then away. "I'm going to the bathroom. I'll be right back," I said. I headed across the dining room, through the lobby, and into the old bar with the Neptune mural. Then to the back of the room, which sagged downhill, and into the bathroom. I splashed my face with water. Turned upside down, shook my hair out, stood up, and stared at the mirror. I looked like a madwoman with hair askew. Why was I acting so intense? Who was this guy? Or was it me? My wanting not to trust him? I brushed my hair smooth.

My ex had been a fantastic liar. Told me to leave with the kids, that he wanted the house if I'd chosen to leave the marriage, I thought as I put on lipstick. Then he had never made another payment on the house again and lived in the house for a year. Meanwhile, I had struggled with a new business and paid rent downtown for an apartment. I hadn't known about his non-payments until a year later when I received a copy of the foreclosure papers in the mail.

I wiped the lipstick with a paper towel, remembering how my husband had run off and left me horrible credit and a tax debt, too. He'd lied about his income and then had gotten audited. And since we had been married, I had to pay. I wasn't thrilled with the law. It had never benefited most women in general. Law was one thing, justice another altogether. I decided I looked dead, so reapplied the lipstick I'd put on before leaving home.

And people ask me about child support. Ha. I had been lucky to pay off the taxes and the charge card bills he left me in order to clear up my credit report. Trust? It was something stupid people did. I put a layer of plum over the pink lipstick and headed back out to the dining room. There just weren't any men in their late thirties or forties who weren't attached, divorced, rigid, or weird. Laura and I had complained endlessly about the no-guys-to-meet-or-date factor, especially on St. Annes. The reason we joked so much about Randy. I made a note to ask Laura why a dude Jackson's age was single.

BACK IN THE DINING ROOM, there she sat, in my chair next to Jackson— Daisy. Panic struck me—what could have gone so wrong that she'd walked four Main Street blocks to the restaurant? And sat with a stranger? She and Jackson were talking. She was eating from a new plate. Grapes. She ate one, then put one on Jackson's plate, which he then ate. Suddenly she burst out in gales of laughter. Jackson was wiggling something black in her face. I walked over. A big black plastic cockroach. She was screaming with laughter and near-ly dumping herself out of the chair.

"What are you doing here?" I said to Daisy with some alarm. "And where did you get this?" I said to Jackson, pointing to the cockroach. They both sat up straight and got quiet.

"I just walked down, Mama," she said. "I got lonely, and . . ." She shrugged.

"She's fine, LaRue," Jackson said. "The cockroach is something I have to entertain kids when there are stressful situations. I keep it in the pocket—" He shrugged, looked a little embarrassed. "We ordered some grapes, and we're having a feast. Right, Daisy?" He brightened, looking at her for help.

"Mama, he's got a gun," Daisy said. "He showed it to me. Sometimes he has to use it."

"Well, what I said was—" Jackson tried to explain, but I interrupted by pointing to Daisy to sit in another chair. She ignored me.

"Is everything okay?" I said.

"Fine, Mama," she said. "It's boring in the apartment."

"She's fine, LaRue," he said.

"You know you can call me," I said. "Why did you leave? Someone could have—. Scoot over," I said. Then I waved an *Oh, forget it* hand and sat on the other side of Jackson.

"I think it's safe to say she just decided to take a walk in the neighbor-hood," Jackson said, then saw my face. He turned to Daisy. "You know you need to follow your mom's instructions about leaving the house. If she wants you to call before you leave, you need to do so." He looked at me. I touched his hand under the table. I didn't know why. Maybe I was too afraid, too alone. I didn't really know what I was doing, frankly. He continued, steady. "And she should know where you are all the time."

"Okay," she said. "Can I have a glass of chocolate milk?"

"Of course," Jackson said, holding his hand up for the waiter. "Should we all have dessert then? Daisy, how would you like some ice cream?" He ordered ice cream for her, but he and I were full.

"Mama, Mr. Jackson is cool," Daisy said when her ice cream arrived.

"Right," I said. "He's the one who—"

"Who's trying to help your mother find out who we need to put in jail around here," Jackson said.

"Will you use your gun?" she said. "I think you should. It's so cool." I groaned.

Suddenly, Mary was standing by the empty chair at our table, holding a beer with one hand and patting Daisy on the head with the other. It creeped me out, but I asked if she wanted to sit down.

"Maybe for a minute," she slurred. She was two-and-a-half sheets to the wind. "Daisy, you're growing up so, Baby." She sat in the only empty seat, put her elbow on the table, her head resting on her hand, staring at Daisy eating ice cream.

"I know," Daisy said. A lack of confidence was nothing I'd have to worry about with this child. Then Mary sat up, as if remembering the adults at the table.

"How y'all doing tonight?" she said, but she stared at Jackson. "You're the detective," she said. "You find out who did it?"

"Still working on it," Jackson said, glancing at me. "State investigator," he corrected. "It's not my case, exactly . . ."

"Well, I sure don't know," Mary said, pulling off her beer. She stared at nothing, eyes wide, looking in the distance. She turned her head to me. "Did you see that wreath?" She didn't look directly at me.

"Which wreath, Mary?" I asked.

"Well, not exactly a wreath, but this . . ." She waved her hands around in the air. "thing. Of flowers. One with the big-ass silver cross," she said. "Sorry, Daisy, that was bad of me to potty mouth." She turned her drunken attention back to me. "At Trina's grave." She reminded me of myself early on after the divorce when I'd go out with friends. I'd just wanted to leave planet Earth for a while.

I glanced at Jackson and rolled my eyes in a who-knows way. "Silver cross?" I said.

"Yeah, big styrofoam job with mums all spray-painted silver. Gaudy as shit," she said. "Oops, sorry, Daisy."

"No. I missed that," I said. "I was thinking about doing wedding hair, I have to admit."

Mary leaned forward into the table and whispered. "They say this black woman sent it." No black people lived on St. Annes, unfortunately. The black population had left and never come back when the fiber factory folded. It spoke to Madonna's inner strength and charm that she could mix it up as a brown person on our island. Jackson and I exchanged looks.

"Who was it?" I asked. She shrugged, turning her half-focus back onto Daisy, patting her hair.

"Always wanted a pretty little girl," she said. She finished off her beer, then got up from the table and walked out the door.

"Well then," I said.

"Mama, Mary's drunk again," Daisy said. "I remember the time you got so drunk you forgot where I was."

Jackson chuckled. I said, "Okay, that's enough."

"Follow up on it," Jackson said, raising an eyebrow at me. I understood what he meant. Check out the cross, the name, whatever the connection might be. I felt like it would be a waste of good time but would check the graveyard on my way to breaking into Trina's house. Something he didn't need to know about. I nodded.

Jackson asked for the check, paid for the meal, and we all walked down dark and cold Main Street to the apartment. Daisy insisted on skipping between us and holding our hands. The crescent moon floated in a hazy sky. The wind was blowing hard, and I decided with chattering teeth to invite Jackson in for a hot cocoa.

WHEN DAISY finally fell into sleep on the sofa, we watched Tallahassee's evening news. Three guys with Spanish last names had been arrested for animal cruelty after being found running around in a back yard covered with blood, a slaughtered goat nearby. The newscaster connected it with the Cuban Santeria. Jackson shook his head and put down his mug.

"This is more about insanity than Santeria," Jackson said. "I know these guys. Tomorrow somebody will find a murder victim in a seedy apartment. They were celebrating the death of the other gang's member, mark my words." He slumped down in his chair and let out a huge sigh. "All these kids killing other kids. It's insane. I'll be busy next week. TV makes it look like a Hispanic thing when it's an economic thing." Of course my mind wandered straight to my son of the same age.

"I wonder where Taylor is," I said. "He should be home in a while."

"If I were you, I'd be keeping close tabs on that kid," Jackson said. "Just being careful."

"Oh, Mr. How-to-raise-children, how many children do you have?" I said. He gave a half-smile. He seemed to get a kick out of my faux toughness.

"Just mentioning it," he said. "I don't mean to offend you. And by the way, I respect your ability with this case, in some ways." He drained his cup of chocolate. "It seems like people have an easier time talking to you than they would me. Even if you do get rough with me, you're not that way with your townies. And folks seem to talk to your friend Madonna. And Laura digs until she finds the information she needs. I'm just saying, use what you do well without getting a B&E charge, hear?" I wouldn't look at him. He leaned in towards me. "I've made you mad now. Can I make it up to you?"

He had ruffled my feathers about my son. I wasn't used to men telling me what to do anymore. "No, I don't think so," I said.

"We need to follow up—the Mexico thing, blood analysis, the funeral wreath. How about we get up next week?"

"Nope," I said.

"Can I cook your family dinner?" he tried.

I hesitated, thinking about how full my life was. How nice he was. I didn't trust it. "I need to get this monkey of a crime off my back. That's my first concern."

"Okay, we'll solve this monkey of a crime, then," he said.

"Well, you make it sound like you need some deep research or something, like a dissertation, for god sakes," I said, talking fast now. "I don't have a fellowship to feed me for five years, Jackson. I am the sole provider for five people, okay? I need to get cleared of this stupid crime I clearly did not commit. You need to find out things. Like who the hell is the coroner who let it slip by him that the death was by a cut throat and not a shot in the heart? And how do we really think it was suicide? I mean, she didn't leave a note."

"Notes don't mean anything," he said. "And this guy was a doctor, some yokel county doctor who's hard to find. He's been out of town and not returning calls. I will be stepping into a dangerous game. And you'll be at high risk."

"Find him," I pleaded. "And see if you can dig up anything about these guys in the photos, the Boarders or whoever."

"I'll see what I can do," he said.

"Well, thanks for dinner," I said. "And for entertaining Daisy."

"She's a pistol, so to speak," he said. I nodded. He went on. "Say, find out more about Mary. And Tiffany. Something's going on there. Why are two young women, one married, hanging around men so much older? Follow the money, they say. And you're welcome. Let's do it again soon."

Suddenly, I felt heavy as a whale. I nodded, yawning. We stood up, and I saw him to the door. He turned around. "Look, you be careful," he said. Before I could protest, he said, "If someone tried to kill Mac with poison and put it on you, they'll try to kill again. Be very careful. Don't worry, just be vigilant. We'll have this cleared up very soon."

"Stay cool and drive safely," I said. "Thanks, again. Good night."

I FELL ASLEEP dreaming that a maniac from a foreign country who spoke a language we couldn't understand had kidnapped Laura and me. We were held captive in a tent, and our captor had a piece of art that the other side wanted. I began to realize that I was in fact wearing the art they wanted—a dress. A purple silky dress with black hieroglyphic figures in some ancient language no one understood anymore. Laura kept trying to phone Jackson, but she couldn't get through. The maniac was saying, "Huh, hah huh, haha huh huh." We couldn't comprehend his words.

That's when I woke up in my bed and heard those very sounds in the living room. I got up and tiptoed out to the front. There stood Taylor, performing karate moves with a fierce frown on his face.

"Huh, hah huh, haha huh huh," he said.

"Taylor, what are you doing?" I said.

"GoKu," he said, not looking at me, not pausing from making hand and leg strikes. "From *Dragonball Z*." He'd told me before *Dragonball Z* was a male soap opera in Japanese animation. The main character practiced a variety of martial arts on the screen.

"Why are you doing this?" I said. "It's like two a.m. I'm trying to sleep."

"You never know what'll happen at school tomorrow," he said, knifing the air with his hands.

"What are you talking about?" I said.

"A night is only a grain of salt in the ocean of time, Mom," he said, twirling around and giving the air another kick.

"Honey, please get to bed," I said. What was going on with him, anyway? "Come on, I'm tired. Let's get to bed."

"Okay," he said, loosening his body and straightening up. "But Mom, don't ever sneak up on me like that again. Huh Huh!" He chopped at a mystery foe.

CHAPTER 17

THE NEXT MORNING after the kids had left for school, and still nobody was visiting the shop, AJ Lutz called to see if I'd cut his hair on a house call. AJ, Fletch and Cooter's older, smarter brother, wanted me to walk to the Fish House. He'd avoided saying anything about Mac's poisoning; this was Southern for *I want to help you out.* I carried the supplies bag for the short, scenic stroll that led past the grocery store and car parts place, then past two Victorian houses where the back cove sat. I could smell the salt sea tang. The air was slightly warm, gentle. I was suddenly suffused with happiness, transient though it often was. I'd left my hoodie at home, and the long-sleeved T-shirt and black jeans were enough. No cars headed towards town, typical for a Monday. Laughing gulls called overhead, in case I might toss them some fish heads, like fishermen sometimes did.

I rather liked that they were trying to communicate, even if for food. Right now, the Gulf birds west of us needed room, sympathy and food. BP was currently setting off cannons to scare the shore birds from the shores of Louisiana where they'd be covered in oil if they landed looking for food. Not to mention being poisoned.

Pelicans and seagulls perched on old dock pilings out in the hushed cove. I passed a few herons and egrets that stood in the oyster beds picking meat out of the shells. In some ways, this place had not changed much since Europeans had discovered the continent. In others, we had managed to compromise all of life here.

The heavy bait scent hit when I knocked on the front door of the Fish House. AJ had haircuts about three times a year. He didn't fuss over his appearance, but he had the manners of a nineteenth-century English gentleman. He didn't schmooze around the bars every day, and he worked hard for a living. The closed sign hung in the door window. Through the shop glass, I could see inside. Cases sat empty. Normally, they displayed the raw oysters, shrimp, stone crab claws, red fish, and the catch of the day. People had stopped buying seafood. AJ came to the door and took off his baseball cap. He opened the door and bowed slightly, squinting at the sun.

"Miss LaRue," he said, nodding, beckoning me in. "Nice morning, ain't it?"

"How're you, AJ?" I said. I automatically circled him, inspecting his hair, picking and fluffing the crown. "Looking healthy," I said. His hair, though fine-stranded, was dense and chocolate. He stood still while I felt the back of his hair. I suggested we find a chair.

"Out yonder," he beckoned. He shuffled behind the counter and guided me to the rear, where two weighing machines hung. He pulled up a chair and sat by the dock at the inlet where the fishermen brought boats to weigh and sell their catch. The late morning sun beamed on us.

"Just do the usual," he said, as I fastened my barber's cloak around his neck. He must trust me, I figured, as I pulled out the hair-thinning shears. Here I was with sharp implements where no one could see us. And AJ didn't even have a mirror to look as I did the cutting. "Thanks for the business, AJ," I said as I began to thin his hair.

"I wouldn't leave you stranded," he said. "You and me, we go way back. I know you didn't poison no Mac Duncan. Bunch of foolishness."

"Does it worry you that there's somebody out there who's, you know, trying to poison people?" I said.

"Nah," he said, waving his hand. "I've seen some stuff. Once in a while there's somebody dies. You know that, LaRue. Some of them around here, they got some enemies." He chuckled. "Fletch and Cooter's my brothers, but I'll tell you what, they both got their hands full."

"Yeah?" I said, shaving the back of his neck first, opposite the way I was taught. But it cleaned things up so you could see the landscape.

"Cooter, now he's got the most problems, seems to me," he said. "It's one thing to have your wife kill herself like Trina done on Fletch. Sad. Real sad. But—" He shrugged. "Cooter, he's got a wife wants to kill *him!*"

"Mary?" I said.

"You didn't hear about that?" he asked, turning around to look at me. I shook my head no. "Mary, she ended up in the nut ward up in Gainesville 'cause she took a knife to old Cooter."

"A knife?" I asked, putting the shears away and pulling out the scissors. I felt like Old Testament Delilah. I wanted to hear Cooter's brother's version of the story. "Why a knife—I mean, why did she try to kill him?"

"Some fight over this baby thing," he said. "She's always wanted a child, and they can't get one. Seems he can't. She claimed she was pregnant, though."

"She tried to kill him 'cause he can't get her pregnant, but she was pregnant?" I said.

"Well you know she's a drunk, LaRue. Like half the people on this island. Me, I love to have a drink, get loose, go over to the Rusty Rim and sometimes even to the Hook Wreck and dance, but not every damn day." I mentally counted, realized I'd been drinking every day lately. What the hell, holiday season, I thought.

"Yeah, we've seen them come and go, haven't we, AJ? I'm seeing what you mean. Remember when they had to cart ole Axman off in a straight jacket?"

I laughed, remembering watching Axman get hauled off during P.E. class. I leaned into AJ's left side, working at the plot of hair on top of his head, trimming. "Ole Axman hasn't changed a bit! He still thinks everybody's out to get him. Madonna tells me when somebody says something he doesn't like, he threatens to go get his ax and take 'em out. The man wouldn't hurt a mosquito in winter, but he can sure talk. So did Cooter call the mental ward on Mary?"

"Nah. That was Mac," he said. "I sure don't know how he got involved. I think there's hanky panky going on there, but every time I try to talk to Cooter about it, he don't listen. He ain't the smartest brother I got." I took out the trimmers to clean up around his ears.

"AJ, do you think Trina killed herself?" I said.

"What?" he said, then rubbed a few hairs off his nose. "You think somebody killed her?"

"Oh, I don't know. Just wondering."

"I don't know. She and Fletch, they had a history their own selves. Fought all the time. She didn't like his business dealings. She used to come over here and say, 'AJ, you're the only honest one in that family.' She did my books and all, you know." He shrugged. "You never know about someone though. She kept to herself a lot. Didn't ever seem to belong here anyway. Came here young and seemed a little desperate. Latched onto Fletch right away." This didn't sound like the Trina I had known. "I don't think Fletch would kill his wife."

It struck me as strange for a brother to say "I *don't think* Fletch would kill his wife." I'd finished the cut and started shaving his neck. "What about Mac? Do you think that poisoning was accidental or what?"

I took off the purple-sheened blue cape, shook some talc onto a soft boar brush, and swept off his neck. "He's got some enemies."

"Like who?" I said.

He shrugged. "I just heard about it in the Rusty Rim. He done some damage down in Miami or some funny name place in Mexico, something Wah-cah-cah? I heard those people's still chasing after him. Heard he owes them some money."

"What do you know about that?" I said.

"You're asking a lot of questions," he said.

I shrugged, moving to the right side of his head. "Sorry. Curiosity, I guess, AJ. You know how it is around here. We've never had any weird suicides or poisonings around here. We always thought it was a safe little island. Hell, I just started locking the doors last week."

"Girl, you got a bad memory. Remember Dorman, died out near the Panther Pit? Over drugs, they say. Looked like hit and run."

"I was off at school then," I said. "I'd forgotten about all that."

"You know five people have died over the past few years, and all of them lived out on the county road?" he said. He cocked his head and looked at me. Not as if he knew anything, just contemplating it.

"Cancer," I said. "Mainly."

"Not old Dorman," he said. "That cat got run over."

"Well, they're so weird anyway, a bunch of recluses, and all those guys had long hair, never ever bathed. Oh, that hair bothered me. So stringy, and looked like it'd never been touched by shampoo." I felt bad as soon as I said it. They were human, and no one deserves to be run over by a car that I know.

But he laughed and I combed out his hair, stepped back, and gave him a thumbs-up. AJ raised his eyebrows, more concerned about the county road intrigue than his appearance, it seemed. "Yeah, they's something else, all right. But, you know, his daddy got run over the year before him, remember?" he said. "Near the same place, walking home down the county road. Now the land's for sale." I thought down the list. One neighbor died, supposedly of drowning in the swamp, drunk. Another died of lung cancer in the hospital. Another of a strange rare cancer. My head was spinning.

"What's the connection?" I said.

He shrugged. "Hell if I know." He smiled. "Probably ain't one." He handed me a fifty.

"I can't take that," I said, packing up the stylist bag. "You're a working man, and who knows when anybody will buy Florida seafood again."

"And you're a working woman, ain't you? Accused of a crime? Kids to feed? You'd do it for me, wouldn't you? Besides, I got my papers I'm filling out to send to BP. They ain't gonna like how much I'm losing this year," he said, holding his hand up to say *Don't give it back*. If he'd been accused, like I was, of poisoning someone, I'd pay him every chance I could under the table to help him out. I'd pay him twice what it cost, too. This was also a matter of pride. He wanted to help. So I shook his hand, and put my left hand over our handshake.

"Yes, I'd do it for you, AJ. Thanks. You take care, okay?"

"LaRue?" AJ said. I turned around.

"Watch out around here, okay? Don't be asking too many questions." I stood stock-still and resisted another question. I nodded and waved as I headed out the front door. He locked it behind me.

"HOOK WRECK," Madonna said. She sounded slightly bored as she answered the phone. Early afternoon's sun burned on the water's surface, blazing into everything on the island. But her boredom was faked, as she was now playing her part.

I swung the car up into the graveyard where moss dripped from the trees, and magnolias down near the water buffered the wind and sun. I put the Saturn in park as I worked my plan out with Madonna on the cell. Laura's kayak was tied to the top of my car. "Hey, girl," I said. "He there?" I'd asked her to lure Fletch into the bar a couple of hours before school let out so I could snoop in his house.

"Yep. We open at noon, and don't close for another fourteen hours after that," she said. This meant Fletch sat at the bar close enough to hear the conversation.

"Okay, I'm only going to need about an hour and a half, two hours. Just keep him there long enough for me to check the house," I said, fingering the key I had stolen, now in my jeans pocket. "Slow dance with him if you have to."

"Sure, come on by. But I don't dance with no strangers," she said.

"You will be richly rewarded," I said in an Eastern European accent to represent gypsies or fairy tales or something hokey in cartoons. Acting goofy was a way to stave off the fear.

"Okay. I'm sure," she said. "Talk to you soon."

I drove the car over to Trina's grave. At the front of the granite stone stood a three-foot-tall cross of Styrofoam with silver mums attached. Unlike Mary, I loved the arrangement. It seemed to celebrate life. Resilience. The card attached to the Styrofoam, though slightly frayed in the island weather, said "In memory of Trina E. from Eunice M." Who the hell was Eunice M.? I copied the message verbatim onto a corner of an old bank receipt.

The envelope said Busy Bee Florist and featured a picture of a bright-eyed bee. The address was up in Wellborn. I jotted that down on the receipt. Who was Trina E., I wondered? Was that her maiden name? How would this person know something like that? I drove out of the serene graveyard, down past Gulf Drive, and headed beyond the old fort. Nine different peoples had warred over its spot over four or five centuries. Several of those were Indians, as Grandma loved to remind me. Billy Bowlegs for one, a hero of hers. I parked under a three-hundred-year-old oak forty feet wide near the old yellow house. Once owned by a retired professor, now dead, the house was vacant.

Luckily, there was a scruffy beach where I could launch. I untied the kayak stacked on life preservers, threw the ropes and preservers in the trunk and locked the car. I pushed the kayak, shishing through sand, to the brackish waters where the Gulf met the river. The cold water shocked my flip-flopped feet, but the down jacket and wool scarf helped. The water sloshed rough, but once in the boat, earth's gravity lifted. I caught the incoming tide, but the wind came from the other direction. Not an easy run, and yellow was a conspicuous kayak color for someone wanting to sneak into a house. Yet no one was around.

The water lapped in more lazily along the river, and mullet jumped in the water nearby. A dolphin rolled up for air about a house lot away. Approaching Trina's house, I could smell the rich scent of decaying leaves. A bundle of pied-billed grebes peeped and rolled backwards into the water. The shade dappled the ground of Trina's yard. She had picked this spot to build her house years ago. On the Gulf, the river, and the woods. A careful accountant's planning. I knew more than ever that the plot against her had been real. Someone this in love with the world would not commit suicide.

A heavy silence lay over the yard and house. The elegant windows of the cedar home on stilts looked like empty eyes. Trina's car sat in the driveway under the house. Fletch's truck was gone, of course. I'd waited for the high tide when a boater could easily climb up the dock and enter from the water. A cormorant flew off a post of the dark dock. I flung the flip-flops into the bushes, put on a pair of hair-dyeing gloves, then headed through the back yard.

Trina and Fletch hadn't put in security yet. Until now, our community had hung on to the idea that we were safe. Fishing gear leaned against the house. An ice chest, several poles. I tried the back porch door with the key. The door squawked open. I could hear a clock ticking as I ducked in. The white carpet in the living room felt thick as sea foam. I tiptoed through the living room and stopped cold when I saw the photograph of the boy—the boy in the picture on the boat. The kid who stood with Trina when she couldn't have been more than about eighteen. Who was he? I almost recognized him. She held his hand, and she looked a little lost, as teenagers often do. Confident and lost together. Exactly how I'd describe Taylor.

I walked into the kitchen. Spic and span except for a pile of dirty dishes in the sink, probably left by Fletch over the past two weeks. It looked like an accountant's kitchen. The pots hung by size from the ceiling. A sampler that said, "God Bless Our Home." Another sign said, "God grant me the Courage to change the things I can, the Patience to accept the things I cannot, and the Wisdom to know the difference." Not the inspirational message of someone who'd off themselves. But both truisms seemed ironic now.

I stole into her office. Not a sign of blood anywhere. White carpet, no blood stains. A ledger sat open and a pencil lay in the crease of the book. A shiver went through me. Her CD's lay stacked in a CD rack, alphabetized by artist. One CD sat in the computer as though waiting to be played. I pushed the mouse. Nothing. The computer wasn't on, of course. I turned on the computer and the screen. There on the screen was another photo of that child, the second child, the mystery child from the photo we took from the boat. This was not their son who had drowned. This was someone else. Who?

I began to open drawers. In the top drawer was a sealed envelope addressed in Trina's hand to ECOL, the company Jackson had mentioned to me that was buying up land. I shoved it into my jeans pocket. I looked for other things in the drawers, but began to feel a strangeness in the house, a presence. I felt my good luck was coming to an end. I heard a faint thud.

Then the front door sucked quietly open and closed like a whisper. I heard someone walking down the front steps. I jumped behind the desk and waited. Nothing. Not a sound. Then I heard a car start up next door. I ran to the front window. A turquoise Ford. Had someone been following me? My stomach turned over. Still, I memorized the numbers on the license plate, Magnolia County tag. I wrote them down, then walked back to the desk and shuffled the papers around on Trina's typing stand. At the very back of the stack sat a calendar. I opened to November 6, the day Trina died.

She'd listed an appointment with the dentist at 1 p.m. in Wellborn, and the word "Cove" at 3 p.m. Suicidal people don't go to the dentist before they do the drastic deed, I guessed as I stole out the back door, returning the key to the fountain statue. Who else had a key? What did they want?

As I walked across the yard, I noticed the tide had risen, a more chilling wind blew, and the water was getting choppy. The sky had grown overcast with gray clouds behind a few silvery cumulus in front, typical north Florida winter weather. Cove, what could Trina have meant by "Cove?" I ran back to my flip-flops in the piney backyard, rumbled down the dock, and climbed into the kayak. The water had risen a whole step up toward the dock. I untied and paddled quickly away towards the old professor's house as if I were a stealthy Indian.

CHAPTER 18

THAT NIGHT, I lay on our green sofa, reading a story in the *Chronicler* by Laura in a rare moment of quiet—Daisy had walked with Taylor down to the city dock. She wanted to look at the shape of the moon for her school project on planets. I'd argued that I should go, but they acted like I was crazy.

I was now on the verge of worrying about them, so I texted Taylor. He texted back, "Relax. Back in a few."

Laura's news story had sucked me in. She'd showed discretion by avoiding news of Trina Lutz's death or Mac's poisoning. As far as anyone knew officially, Trina's death was a non-issue, and the cops were on the case of the poisoning.

Even though Laura would call this a fluff piece, she loved them, because she could sneak in stories about folks in the area who'd never normally get publicity. This story covered Norma Redding, who had built her own facility to care for sick and injured wildlife. Norma'd given up her IBM job to come out to the sticks of the county to save wild animals.

Norma had told Laura that a plethora of birds got injured with fishing line, which they'd thought was live bait. The line would get wrapped around wings, which caused injury and death. She pointed out that the area just an hour west of St. Annes had been overfished before the oil catastrophe. This led to more birds diving for fish hooks. Laura had quoted Mac as saying this was a tragedy for our birds, and we needed to come up with bird-friendly lures. Mac, I discovered reading the paper, headed the Save the Wildlife Club in St. Annes.

That's when the phone rang. I answered it with an I'm-tired-who's-this? voice.

"Hey, LaRue, how're the kids?" It was Jackson. I sat up, remembering Laura had called Rocky to get a security light put over the storefront window.

"Oh, hey. Can we skip the chitchat? What did you find out about the coroner who signed the death certificate? Or local doctor, let's guess, filling in for the coroner." I'd push him first.

"Very strange," he said. "And sloppy. Unprofessional."

"Welcome to the Undiscovered Coast of Florida," I said, standing up, walking to the porch to peer out and look for my kids. "The Redneck Riviera, the Panhandle, where nothing gets done right today that can get done wrong tomorrow. Or say, maybe they took lessons from oil companies."

He ignored my rant. "Both the coroner and the assistant coroner were on an overnight deep-sea fishing trip when the body came in on Monday evening. This according to the office secretary. Not that she knows. She wasn't in. The body arrived during the night. The coroner's office did call in a local doctor. I didn't realize earlier because the secretary hadn't told me then that the doctor was also along on the trip."

"Wait. What?" I couldn't see my kids and was considering bundling up to search for them. "You're saying the coroner, the coroner's assistant, and the doctor were all on the same deep-sea fishing trip?"

"Right—the pro, his stand-in, and the stand-in's stand-in. Supposedly the doctor's assistant assigned another doctor to look in and sign off on the body. This according to the secretary," he said, taking a breath.

"Who *wasn't* on the friggin' fishing trip?" I said, sighing, walking back to my warm bed. If the kids didn't show up in ten minutes, I would go after them, crazy or not.

"She gave me the name, but I can't find this person anywhere. Nobody seems to know who this is. The doctor said he'd authorized the assistant to sign off on routine business. He thought normal procedure had been followed. Seems someone just showed up out of the blue and signed."

"What? What's the name?" I said.

"He signed the form with the Gainesville backup of the backup doctor's name. An Indian name. Dr. Singh," he said. "The secretary at the coroner's office said no one else was there, that Singh had the key, and they don't know anything else. I'd swear this signature looks kind of girlish."

"Girlish," I said, sneering.

"Well, you'll say I'm stereotyping, but it looks, well, rounded letters, extra neat writing, you know."

"Can you bring it to me to look at?" I asked. "I just want to see it."

"Okay," he said. I relaxed. He was working on this case after all. I'd thought he would say he couldn't get back to the island, too busy, blah blah blah. "Amazing how these small counties can be so laissez-faire. Had a friend in central Florida who found a woman who'd been dead a week with six dogs in her house. No one knew, and a neighbor went and found her. The cops didn't even show up for a couple of days after that. And the body sat in the funeral home for three weeks waiting for someone to claim—"

"Okay, that's creepy. I don't want to think about shit like that," I said, breathless. "Anyway, I found another picture of that kid who was in the photo on the boat," I said.

"All right, Scrapbook Queen, what'd you find?"

"Don't make fun of me," I said, pulling the covers up to my chin. I'd text Tay again when I got off the phone with Jackson. "You forget that relationships are why people kill."

"Are you implying that you'll kill me?' he joked.

"No. I'm saying you don't understand that what people say, who's in their pictures, what gossips tell you, that that's as important as blood on knives."

"Huh," he said, neutral. "Tell that to a court of law. So where'd you find the new photo?"

"On Trina's computer screen," I said. "So it must be someone important." A long silence followed.

"Don't tell me you're breaking and entering *her* house now," he said, exasperated. God, he was by the book. This man just wouldn't break a rule. And I was even more exasperated and didn't want to tell him why.

"Just once," I said. "And hey, I need you to track down a license plate for me, will you?"

"So you can go break and enter there, too?" he said. "LaRue, you can't just go ransacking people's—"

"I'm not ransacking anything," I said, feeling hot, throwing the covers off. "Do you know that Trina also had a dentist appointment at one p.m. on the day of her death?" The line went silent. "And she had written down the word 'Cove' at three o'clock? At about four, she was on a boat, Mac's boat. After that sometime, she died." I didn't let him speak. I went on, stomping through the house, putting on water for tea. Hell, I'd go find the kids. "There was someone in the house while I was there, Jackson, and it wasn't Fletch. Madonna lured Fletch to the bar so that I could get in and look. I need you to get the tag number because whoever it was sneaked out the front door."

"LaRue, this is not the Keystone Cops," Jackson said with some forced patience. "You could get *killed* if there's a murderer out there who's trying to keep things quiet. I want you to stay away from that house." I could tell he was getting agitated. I reminded myself I had good reason not to tell him about the hair and shoe polish warning. I also made a note to ask Madonna to check the license plate instead.

"I know it's not Keystone—hey, don't get condescending with me, *buddy*," I said. "Just because you live in a big city and have a professional job doesn't mean squat. I'm out here with two kids who need to eat, and you're in Tallahassee sitting on your thumbs for all I know." I could see the spit flying out of my mouth. I was glad he couldn't.

I remembered the letter addressed to ECOL. How could I have forgotten it? I'd put it in my underwear drawer. I'd look at it later. I wasn't about to tell him about this yet either. The line was silent for a good several seconds.

"*Buddy,* huh?" he said. "Sitting on my thumbs, huh?" He snickered. "You're a feisty one. Okay, you've convinced me there's a lot more going on than meets the eye, LaRue. But a screensaver with a boy's picture on it doesn't—" he broke off, fearing I'd blow up again. "I need hard facts. Evidence. I have to stay on my work at the state. I'm worried about your safety, too."

My snooping around in houses probably did seem less important than his keeping a job. "I'm sorry you have to deal with grim things. And this might seem like trivia to you, Jackson," I said, my voice starting to shake, "but my kids' friend and mine had her neck slashed and died for no damn reason. That's serious. To me, that's grim as well."

"Okay," he said. "Don't cry on me, I can't stand that. Give me the license plate number. I'll chase it down for you. Sorry. A lot's going on around here right now. Just let me tell you what else I found out for you between interviews with gang members," he said.

"I'm listening," I said, snuffling. "But first the license plate." I gave him the number.

"I found out our little Tiffany spent the last two years of high school in PACE, a school for wayward girls," he said. "And Sturkey's the Chairman of ECOL and the Chair of the County Commission in Madison County, right next to you."

"Sheesh," I said. "Sturkey's a crook in cahoots with our Sheriff's Department for our county and the big realtors. What'd *Tiffany* do?"

"She stopped talking to anyone, went from sulky teen to not talking—and started doing tricks for drugs."

"Dang," I said. "Doing *tricks?* Who ever knows about another person?" All the humanity who came to St. Annes, running and running from life, from concrete, from the law. Thinking somehow this place was a haven. Thinking Saint Anne could save them, was the end of the universe. People ran until they got to the edge of land, and all that was left was water. When the water didn't baptize them, they tended to crash and burn. Or leave. But not Tiffany. It looked as though she was learning the architecture and real estate business. I could almost feel for her, that desperation.

"Jackson?" I said. "There was no blood on the carpet in Trina's study. No stains, nothing. And the carpet is white."

"Yeah," he said. "Despite your law breaking ways, I'm convinced she didn't die in her house."

"Thanks," I said. *Finally,* I thought. *An admission.*

"Oh, I called the garbage man, OV," he said. "He wouldn't talk. He hung up on me."

"That's not really surprising, Jackson. He doesn't know you," I said. "You'd have to get Laura or me to take you over there, someone from here."

He agreed. It was late, so I hung up and collapsed in the bed to rest my eyes before I went to check on the kids.

I HEARD THE SHOUTING downstairs in the street. *Now what*, I thought. The last time anybody'd made a scene downtown was when that raccoon tried to get a bag of groceries from old Winnie Destin, the oldest, loudest woman on the island late last summer. Finally, Tay had gone down and shooed the raccoon off.

I stepped out onto the balcony that overlooked Main Street. Taylor was standing straddled in the street like a dueling cowboy, and Daisy hid behind him. He was shouting at a boy who looked about twelve, one of the oystermen's sons, Ronnie Hastings. Taylor had him by nearly a foot in height.

"What did you say?" Taylor said, his fists balled. "Say it again. Say it again, and I'll knock your head off!"

"I didn't say nothin'," the Hastings boy said.

"Say it again!" Taylor crouched now, his hands now open and stiff the way I'd seen them when he was doing the karate stuff. "I'll show you what a Japanese kung fu fighter does for a living."

"I ain't said nothin'."

"Don't you ever say *nothin* like that again, you hear me?" Taylor said. "You will not have a voice to tell it again, 'cause I will knock your throat out. Nobody picks on my sister. I know what you said."

I waited, praying *please Tay, give it up, please give it up*. Finally the boy's face changed, drooped, and out of his mouth came, "I ain't goin' near her." He turned and walked away. Taylor was frozen in his karate stance, looking a lot like his dad, thin and strong, far too angry and lost together. His dad didn't have violent tendencies, but he'd habitually hung out in St. Annes bars when we'd visited from Jacksonville and one night ended up getting beat up by a boatload of loggers. Cracked three of his ribs. Daisy was clinging to Tay's T-shirt. Slowly, as the boy backed away, Tay straightened.

"Let's go, Daisy," Taylor said. I heard them climbing the steps. I was making myself a brandy when they walked in. They entered looking winded and guilty. Their eyes both were wide, and they plopped down on opposite sides of the living room, each on a sofa, breathing heavily.

"So what was that all about?" I said, sitting in the rocker at the end of the living room sofas, between them. They looked at each other.

"Nothing, Mom," Taylor said, making a fist and pounding it into his other fist.

"Nothing, Mom," Daisy said. Sometimes they had a deeper alliance with each other that drove me nuts, but wasn't that what a mother wanted? For her kids to share a loyalty for the rest of their lives?

"Didn't sound like 'nothing' to me," I said. "Sounded like maybe you were threatening someone smaller and younger than yourself."

"Mom, you don't know everything," Taylor said, smoldering. He kicked the coffee table, which I ignored.

"Yeah, Mom," Daisy said.

Suddenly, Taylor stood, his fists balled, and he said, "Stay away from him, Daisy. I mean it." She cowered.

"Taylor!" I said. His breath came in and out, rasping. He never shouted like this at his sister.

"I will," Daisy said in a small voice. He stomped back to his bedroom and slammed the door. I sat on the sofa with Daisy and she held onto me tight. I sang to her, *Just another manic Monday.*

AFTER THE KIDS had left for school the next morning, I walked over to City Hall to put an index card on the bulletin board advertising myself as a hair stylist. Sometimes rich tourists might want a cut and dye during big fishing weekends. And some folks might come for a week's vacation and decide it's time for changes, and why not start with a new hairstyle?

Then I got in the truck and headed for Wellborn to look for Busy Bee Florist. In Wellborn, I found the shop in the most dead of three strip malls across from the big Wal-Mart. The store spread out across what had housed a Pic N Save. As I pushed the door open, I was welcomed by the rich scent of fresh plants, that cool damp feel of greenhouses. Orange tiger lilies, yellow mums, and white daisies sat loosely in shiny buckets decorated with cheesy dolphins and rainbows. Primroses in vases. Tropicals and semi-tropicals decorated with orange and red ribbons for Thanksgiving and turkeys with bows. At the back, two women worked. One, short and excessively blonde, was laying out her victim roses, pulling leaves, cutting stems, then rolling the flowers in colored cellophane. The other, a medium-sized woman with a trim brown-shaded pageboy, was twisting off flower heads and sticking them on a wreath in the shape of a heart. It reminded me of the big silver cross near Trina's grave. I caught the eye of the brown-haired woman, who came out, wiping her hands on her apron.

"Hey," I said. "I'm from St. Annes. I'm helping out a lawyer who represents Trina Lutz's estate, and I wonder whether you can help us. On November tenth, she was kindly sent a wreath, a silver mum cross, by a Eunice M? Fletch Lutz has lost the address and we would like to thank her."

"I don't think we did any flowers on November tenth by that name," she said.

"Would you do me a favor?" I said, "and just check your records to be sure?"

"Name was Parsons," said the small blonde woman from the back.

"What?" the brown-haired woman said, looking one-upped.

"The name is Parsons. I remember 'cause she was black. And she wanted that color, silver. Put Eunice M on the card, but paid with a check that said Parsons. Little old lady," she said, wiping her hands and coming out front. The brown-haired woman had some frizz, and she could be a gorgeous auburn. She went to the back, glancing curiously around at me. She brought the small card file to the front and pulled one under P. "Yep. Eunice M. Parsons. Signed the card as Eunice M. thirteen-eighty Southwest Fourth Street, Wellborn. You need the zip?"

"No, thank you," I said. "You've been a huge help. Do you ever go to St. Annes?"

"I love St. Annes," she said. "You're lucky to live there. My boyfriend and I love to fish there. He's got a little bass boat, so we don't go out far, but we like to ride along the Magnolia River below the lower bridge. Guess we'd better get down there before the oil creeps in. We been meaning to. God's country."

I handed her a Cutting Loose card. "I do hair if you ever come in. I'm on the corner of Main Street at the highway. I'll give you a good price on a first-time color. My color's a bargain, too." I have a fault of not liking to see good people with botched hair color. She thanked me, and I waved goodbye. I felt sure the women would wonder why a hair stylist was enquiring for an attorney.

I was in the back streets of town, the old Wellborn, Black Wellborn. A white clapboard church stood on the corner of Second Avenue. I turned and cruised down a narrow street shaded with old oaks and Spanish moss. On one side stood a long graveyard and baseball field. On the other, shotgun houses—one-way-in and one-way-out houses—painted bright colors like purple and yellow and green. This old neighborhood even had a sidewalk, uncommon for this part of Florida. Gardens out back. I passed Eunice M.'s house. The mailbox said Eunice Parsons. I pulled off to the other side of the road, walked across the street and up the front walkway. No one answered the door. The next-door neighbor opened her door and looked out.

"You looking for Eunice?" she asked.

"Yes, I am," I said. "Is she around?"

"She's off visiting her daughter over in St. Joe for the holiday," she said, eyeing me up and down. Thanksgiving was tiptoeing in. It would be upon us in two days. Vacation was not on my brain.

"Oh, well, I'm just a friend of Trina Lutz's down in St. Annes, somebody who was an old friend of hers. Passed away a couple of weeks ago," I said.

"Oh, yeah, that lady who killed herself?" she said.

"Yes," I said. I hadn't hesitated. "Sad, wasn't it?"

"Uh huh," she said, giving me the up and down again.

"Well, I'm LaRue Panther," I said. "I'm from St. Annes. I knew Trina was friends with Eunice. I'll come back another time. I just wanted to catch up with her is all." I tried to smile. I waved as I headed back to the truck.

"She should be home Thursday evening," the neighbor offered. "She can't stay away from that garden for long. Baby lettuce and these impatiens need real good care in the winter weather."

"I'll try back then, hear?" I said. On the way home, I stopped to see Daddy and Grandma Happy. They were both sitting in Daddy's living room. Daddy was reading a magazine, and Grandma was looking at an herb catalogue. I invited them to a turkey dinner. I dreaded the invitation, because Grandma always had a lecture about how Americans didn't have good holidays. No fancy dancing, she said. No Green Corn Dance.

"I ain't thankful for nothing white people did," Grandma Happy said, plopping down her magazine when I mentioned our getting together to be grateful for having each other in the cold season.

"Now, Ma," Daddy said, winking at me, "you love your grandchildren, don't you? They're white, too."

"No, they ain't. Long as I'm alive, they's Indian." She loved to go on about how Indians could have blue eyes on the reservation. Unfortunately, my kids weren't culturally Native American, but saying that would only pour kerosene on the fire.

"Grandma, Thanksgiving will taste great," I said. "I'm doing a beer can turkey, too, that you taught me to make, on the grill." Actually, the recipe called for chicken, but I thought I'd try it with turkey. What it amounted to was putting a half-drunk beer can filled back up with secret sauce into the center of the turkey, standing the bird on its rump in a pan, and letting it cook over a fire so that the steam tenderized the meat. She just stared at me, so I said, "And if you'd make some squash, the kids would get to see how Indians on the rez really eat."

"Humph," she said.

"We'll be able to watch the pre-season games," I said.

"Seminoles playing?" she said. She meant the Florida State University team nicknamed Seminoles, not the tribe. The Seminole and Miccosukee Indians on south Florida reservations were huge fans of the Seminole football team.

"Okay, then," she said, grinning. "I like that football."

CHAPTER 19

TWO DAYS LATER, it was a Thanksgiving holiday morning. I put Randy on the beer can turkey outside at the grill around eleven. The deal was that I'd cut his hair in return. Which was no small order. He had a vain streak and usually had about five ideas for his hair very specifically laid out in his mind, most of which wouldn't work. Still, it guaranteed I wouldn't be blamed for a bad turkey. I'd manage upstairs while he cooked on the ground-floor patio.

As usual, a November winter day in St. Annes meant low gray clouds, little sun, and maybe a heavy rain, a day of humidity like a sauna bath. "Yeah, the sunshine state," I mumbled as I stared out the front window. Daisy and Taylor were in charge of setting up a buffet table for the food. Everyone would have to do cafeteria style and sit where they found a place in my house.

Laura arrived with a blueberry pie and whipping cream. "What can I do to help?" she asked. I told her "Nothing," as I took the pie. She went to the sink and began washing the used dishes. Madonna breezed in a little later with potato salad and her boyfriend Mickey, who'd been on the road in a truck for a month. "We pounded way too many beers last night," Madonna said. "Celebrating our reunion."

"Come on in," I said. "I heard turkey and a Guinness is the antidote for a hangover."

Daddy and Grandma Happy showed up at noon. Daddy had some of his sweet corn and heirloom tomatoes he'd canned from the summer, and Grandma brought the squash dish. The soon-to-be-licensed-in-something-at-community-college Tiffany meandered in to see what we were up to. She asked for a haircut, which I promised to give her later in the day to get rid of her. I didn't trust her to spend a meal with my family.

"Where's the TV?" Grandma Happy said once she'd put down her casserole dish.

"Over here where it always is, Grandma," Taylor said, pointing to the sofa nearest the screen.

"How about making me some coffee, Taylor," Grandma said. "Just some Folgers in the can for me. Don't give me none of that goddamn seven-dollar-a-cup Starbucks. Don't like the taste. Just boil up some water and throw in the coffee. Best way to have coffee, you ask me."

"Mom," Taylor came in the kitchen saying, "what's she want me to do?" I explained that you just boil water, throw in the coffee grounds, let them boil for a couple of minutes, let them settle for a few minutes, then pour the coffee into a mug. "Yuk," he said, shaking his head.

"Oh, you know she loves you best," I said. "That's why she wants you to wait on her."

"Taylor?" Grandma called from the living room. "Where's the Seminoles on this thing?"

Meanwhile Daddy wanted to know where the grilling was going on, so I asked Madonna's boyfriend to accompany him to the courtyard downstairs.

"The Seminoles aren't playing yet, Grandma," Taylor said.

"What'd he say?" Grandma said. Laura went to the living room and turned on the pregame show. Laura, quiet as usual, watched amused. Grandma seemed blissful watching the sports announcers anticipate who'd win, while in the background the cheerleaders waved their pompoms around fiercely.

Madonna got herself a beer from the fridge, held it up, and said, "You're right, Rue. This *is* the best cure for a hangover." She settled down on the sofa next to Grandma, and they watched the starting lineup get introduced.

"Your grandmother—she enjoys watching near blood sport, kids bashing their heads together for entertainment," Laura said as she set the table with forks and napkins with care. "It's because of the name Seminole."

"The only place where her home nation has any national attention," I said, shrugging. "I admit it, I can scream for the Noles myself. Something in us loves this crap."

Of course Grandma didn't hear a bit of this, nodding her head to what was within her range of hearing, the pre-game bands playing. Taylor took Grandma her coffee while Daisy played solitaire at the dining table.

I clumped downstairs to see how the beer turkey experiment was going.

"The worst haircut I've ever seen is on that old Fletch Lutz," said Daddy. "That has to be the ugliest—why would anybody want a cut that makes them look like they been wrestling with a razor?"

"I seen a fellow over in Seattle had a jar head cut like that, only he'd colored it like a rainbow," Madonna's boyfriend Mickey said. Mickey was a homeboy out-of-work fisherman who was now working on the BP trucks in Mississippi.

"Hey, is that the guy who holds up the John three-sixteen sign at all the Seahawks games?" Randy said. They hadn't even noticed that I'd entered their conversation. The women were talking about football and beer, and the men were talking haircuts.

"Sounds like a hairdo I'd enjoy creating," I said. "Did you know if you stretched out a head of hair over time, what we grow in a lifetime would extend from Chicago to New York? So how's the cooking going, guys?"

"Should be ready in about thirty minutes, I'd say," said Randy.

"That's if it don't explode before that," Mickey said.

"Oh, no," Daddy said. "Never seen it do that. Seen it blow up fat as a puffer fish, but not go boom, kablooey."

Randy gave me a smile. I stood enjoying the smoky smell and felt a hand on my neck, gentle, natural, and surprising as a dragonfly landing on your arm. It was Randy. I hadn't expected that. My stomach flipped violently. I wasn't ready to feel things like this, but I liked it. I froze, not knowing what to do. The talk shifted to the weather. I stood quietly, Randy's warm hand on my neck. Dad either hadn't noticed or pretended not to. As Randy began talking about the hurricane that hit when we were in high school, he started describing everyone leaving town at the same time. The line of cars, headed north on the highway, something never seen in St. Annes, aimed towards higher ground north. Randy moved his hand away from my neck to demonstrate how far out the long line of cars extended. It felt a little like relief. I headed back in. "Half an hour, then," I said.

THE APARTMENT FILLED with the scent of blueberries bubbling and nutty squash toasting, the fire smell of grilled turkey. Randy had carved the bird. The beer turkey had turned out okay. The game had hit halftime, so we consumed. At first everyone sat quietly and ate and raved about the food. Then Laura began talking about the story she was on.

"I didn't realize how close Magnolia Gardens was," Laura said, "to the Magnolia River. It's only quarter of a mile as a crow flies through those woods."

"And five minutes to walk through that dense woods. I used to hunt there in the fall," Dad said.

"Did you know about the septic problems?" Laura said.

"Yep. Only three feet at most down to the aquifer," Dad said. "And no paved roads. During Katrina, homeowners couldn't get out. It's so close to sea level. That, and the roads were under water. But it was the only place a lot of folks around here could afford to buy a house."

"Well, it's incredibly dirty for the river, too," Laura said. "Nutrients just flood in there."

"What's she saying?" Grandma Happy said.

"Septic tanks are dangerous," Taylor shouted for her to hear. "When they fill up, there's no earth for them to perk through to clean up the water. Learned about it in science class last year."

"It'll kill you," Grandma Happy said. "Any fool knows that."

"It's expensive to get new septic systems, too," Laura said. "Like ten thousand a pop. And the pollution you can't see. It runs underground."

"And it's the hydrilla that's the indicator," Randy added. "Eventually, the nutrient level could kill the whole of animal and plant life in the springs and river." Everybody looked at him. He shrugged. "I've been studying it."

"White men making money, killing theyselves," Grandma Happy said. "Old story. Turn up that TV, Taylor, the game's back on." Taylor shook his head and rolled his eyes at me. Then he raised the TV volume and pulled up a rocker for Grandma right in front of the TV so she could watch.

"So folks in that huge neighborhood just repair their old septic tanks, or get their brother-in-law to. Then the tank keeps leaking nitrates into the aquifer," Laura said. "It's not regulated."

"You should see these catfish we found while I was working for BP, you know, on Dauphine Island out there off Louisiana," Mickey piped up. "Catfish with burns on their heads and bodies. Big ole holes in their heads. It's weird. And nobody knows if it's the oil or the dispersants or what causing it. Downright freaky-looking."

Everybody got quiet again, grim looks on their faces. The media had been speculating that it could be a decade before the Gulf came back.

"What used to worry me at the gunpowder plant," Dad said, "was how close we were to the St. Annes."

"Exactly," Laura said, "those rivers are sitting only a few miles from the plant and from our sewage. This was never meant to happen." She shook her head.

"What do you mean?" I said.

"Safety-wise, Magnolia Gardens should never have been built without a sewage system down this way. And then there's Tallahassee's runoff and sewage and the fertilizers they were using on the spray field farm," she explained. "I'm trying to get a story out of all this, but it's not easy. Information is so tough to pull out of officials."

"Stay on this, Laura," Randy said, suddenly banging his fist on the table. He jutted his neck out. "It's important." We had all weathered a very bad storm with this unstoppable petrol heaving up out of the bottom of the deep ocean. But we were spent by it.

"Since when are you a political activist, Randy?" I joked.

"Since it affects me," he said. "Directly." A tangible pall hovered over us all. Then Randy got up and went to the buffet. "This squash casserole is the best thing I ever tasted."

"Old Indian recipe," Grandma Happy piped up. Daisy, Taylor, and Daddy got up to heap more food on their plates and began commenting on how good this and that was. It was as if we all needed to lighten up.

"Mama, are we going to die?" Daisy said loudly.

"Not for a long time if you got any Indian genes," Grandma Happy said. Everybody chuckled, and Daisy skipped to the living room to ask her grandmother how she made her skirt with so many layers of triangles. The party reignited.

We stuffed ourselves with blueberry pie and real whipped cream, as if it were our last dessert on earth. "I'll give free haircuts to anyone who will help out with the cleanup," I announced.

"Don't be ridiculous, LaRue. We'll all pay regular prices for haircuts," Madonna said. So I cut hair all afternoon and into the evening. Not only Randy, but Dad, Mickey. A few locals stopped by to say hello when they saw Dad's truck, Randy's car, and Mickey's Jeep, and they sat down for cuts, too. I ended up with cash enough for the mortgages for another month, since everyone paid so well. This Thanksgiving, we took what luck we could get.

As usual, it rained Thanksgiving night. We needed it, so no one complained.

I WAS ASLEEP, or in that near asleep state where you're finally gone and you don't even know you're gone and then something jolts you awake. The letter. I'd totally forgotten about the letter from Trina to ECOL. The contents sat safely in my underwear drawer. The clock beside my bed said 12:53 a.m. The world was hushed. The wind had calmed down, the bars mellowed. I could even hear the Gulf's waves in the distance. Daisy was asleep, and I'd allowed Taylor to stay out until two with Stephie.

I turned on the bedside light, got up, and found the letter. The rain had brought in a cold front that felt like a possible freeze. I shivered and slid under the covers to read.

The envelope felt rich and linenlike in my hands. It was taped shut, so Trina had probably not made a decision about not sending it right away. The business letter was typed and signed on paper with a logo that said, "Trina Lutz, Accountant."

The date in the center of the page was October 18th. The letter said:

To the Partners of Ecological Corporation of Living Well:

I am currently collecting and separating the receipts, expenses and resource data back up results for the year in order to begin reporting the tax files for the coming year.

As you know, this past summer I submitted to you a letter detailing that I had discovered that the entire data results for the environmental study pertaining to Cases C-522387 and V-384021 properties had gone missing. They were replaced, but with numbers that are false.

As a professional accountant, I must warn you that if these files do not have the correct data, it is my ethical duty to go to the proper authorities to report this incorrect material.

Sincerely

Ms. Trina Lutz

Lutz Accounting

cc: Preston Edwards

It was all in code, numbers and letters that meant nothing to me. I reached for the cell phone to text Jackson, so he'd see it in the morning. Instead, there was a message from the school principal, left Wednesday before the close of the day. "Now what?" I thought. I hadn't checked the cell for twenty-four hours.

I'd have to call Jackson in the morning. Jackson had done cop duty all weekend, or I'd have invited him to the Thanksgiving dinner. This reminded me of Randy's hand on my neck. The shadows on my bedroom wall made huge hands waving like claws. It was only the palm outside moving in the night wind.

CHAPTER 20

FRIDAY, I threw on jeans and added a nice sweater for Southern politeness, left Taylor with Daisy, and drove up to Wellborn. I couldn't call the principal at school to see what was up, probably with Taylor. School was closed down for the holidays.

The sky was a gray blanket without sun. I wended through the narrow streets of the black section of town, coming from the island side this time, and parked on the corner of the block where Mrs. Parsons' house sat. The walk proved pleasant on the tree-lined street. Folks sat by the windows staring out, wondering what this stranger had in mind to do in their neighborhood.

When I got to Mrs. Parsons' gate, I stood and watched her for a minute. She must have been about seventy-five or so, and she wore a cornflower-blue housedress and a wide-brimmed hat with a blue ribbon. She was stooped with her back to me on her knees digging in the garden. She had dug holes and was placing marigolds into the ground, then covering them with dirt. She then doused them with water. I hoped she didn't mind that I opened the gate and walked up the path. She sat back on her heels and turned around looking at me that way older people do—no fear, no resentment, not even much curiosity.

"Sturdy bug repellants," she said, pointing to the marigolds with her trowel. "They give you color even though summer's gone. I'll have to cover them once the next frost comes, crazy weather. They're all fragile that way."

"Yes, they are," I said. "Your whole yard is beautiful. I live on St. Annes Island where it's sometimes hard to work a garden or grow flowers. Except for a few places. But I'm a block from the water."

"I like having a variety. I change it up all the time, too," she said. Then she gave me the once over. "You know, lily-of-the-Nile will do right fine in the sun. Maybe hibiscus." She was pointing with her trowel. "Nice purple color, the lilies. An orange hibiscus mixed in would be nice. I love flowers. And you know lantana grows like a weed in the sun. You'll get a passel of butterflies if you have lantana around. And lilies, they're easy anywhere. Not just at funerals."

"Well, thanks," I said. "I'll try to remember all that when I start working on the family place. Don't seem to have much time right now."

"Chrysanthemums," she said, wiping her brow. "Easy to grow." She held up her hand. "Help me up, will you, baby?" I took her hand and put my other hand on her other elbow.

"Did you donate those to the florist shop for the arrangement you sent

Trina Lutz?" I asked. I winced at my bad segue.

"Oh, heavens no. I let the florist do all that. Did you see that, then? I liked it. Silver. A color she liked all her life. Poor thing," she said, shaking her head, brushing off her dress.

Then she looked up at me with eyes slightly narrowed, showing interest.

"So you knew Mrs. Lutz," she said. "You her secretary or something?"

"No, ma'am, not secretary," I said. "I was a friend of hers. My kids haven't really had a grandmother. My mom died when I was born. So Trina kind of took it upon herself to spoil mine rotten," I said, smiling. "It's funny she never talked about you."

"Oh, no, I wasn't her nursemaid, baby. I was the woman who raised up her *boy*," she said, slowly walking up the stairs. "Can I get you a glass of water?"

"No—I mean, yes, ma'am, that would be nice," I said. Old-time women, black or white, liked to be ma'amed. It showed decent manners. And I didn't want her to disappear into the house without discovering more.

"Come on up here," she said, pointing to the rocking chairs on the porch. She had a high wooden porch painted gray and three rocking chairs with fading green and black paint. "I'll fetch us some water. I am nearly dying of thirst." She came back outside and sat.

"So you raised up that child who later drowned?" I said. "That must have been hard for Trina." I pulled my jacket snug as she set water down on a TV tray between us.

"Oh, no. Not that one," she said, then took a long drink of water. "The older one. I reared that white boy right here in this house. Only saw Trina on the weekends. It's a shame what that father talked her into. Having someone else raise up that child as if it wasn't hers." She took a long drink of water and held onto the glass.

"Oh, the older one," I said, as if I knew. "I didn't know him. What was his name again?"

"Preston," she said. "Preston Edwards. She gave him her family name. Kind of cold out here." We were both huddled in our rockers, shivering. "I'm gonna make us tea. You sit tight."

She went back inside, which gave me time to rock and think and rub my arms and legs warmer. Where had I seen that name Preston Edwards? It was the cc: on Trina's letter to ECOL. Preston Edwards. Would this guy have killed his mother? For money? To hide something?

"Put you a teaspoon of sugar," she said, handing me a cup.

"Thank you, ma'am. Would you like me to turn on this space heater and put it right on you? I'm not so cold myself," I lied. I didn't want her to go inside, so before she had a chance to say anything, I angled the heater at her and clicked it on.

"Thank you, dear," she said, sitting back, sipping now on her tea.

"Nice heater. Those big metal ones do the trick." I took a sip of tea, putting the cup under my chin, steam rising and warming my neck.

"Got it on sale," she said. "Up in Tallahassee. Only twenty-five dollars. I think it was on sale when we were having that heat wave back in May before the oil spill. People aren't thinking about heaters and heat waves at the same time," she said, chuckling. She stared out at the ball field across from her house. She turned with wide serious eyes now. "So how's things down St. Annes way, what with the spill and all?"

I told her how tough times were down on the water. Fishermen out of work. "Fish seem okay, but folks don't trust the water. The fishermen who have work are over in Mississippi and Louisiana helping with the cleanup."

"Nasty stuff," she said. "Don't know why they build stuff if they don't know how it's gonna do, if it's gonna blow up or something." She shook her head.

"So, Miss Parsons, why did you raise him up, Preston?" I said. "I am not just nosey. I really—it's important for me to know."

"Important, is it?" she said, looking across the street again, but beyond to the graveyard. "Don't know why it should be. All the past now. She's dead now, poor lady." She looked down at her garden. "Yeah, I reckon I taught Preston pretty good. He runs a whole funeral business now. He comes around and sees me every Saturday."

The one at the funeral home, the director who covered up the means of death? The way he was behaving, so casual? I leaned in to her without thinking. It couldn't be him, I thought.

"Yes, ma'am," I said. "I'm sure you're proud of him. Do you think of him as your own?"

"Sure do," she said. "And he calls me Mama. Now his real mama's gone, I'm all he got. She paid me good the first five years of her boy's life." She looked at me. "Paid me to take care of him. Well, I loved that boy so much, I said, 'Don't be paying me no more for this child, you hear? This is the Lord's blessing on me.' But she insisted. Wanted him to have the best. And we did. We had a good life together."

"You say he runs a funeral parlor?" I said.

"Yeah, the one that buried Trina," she said. "Edwards & Parsons Funeral Home. He named it that after his two mamas."

Suddenly pieces were fitting together: the photo of a young Trina with a boy I recognized, the fellow at the funeral home who hovered over me with the slicked back hair who must have known I'd seen Trina's stitched-up neck.

"And what about his daddy?" I said.

"He still don't claim nothing of his daddy," she said, looking at me like I'd better not talk about it. "Greedy old man."

"Can you tell me about how you came to raise Trina's son—Preston?" I asked.

"Oh, she was so young, Trina. Sixteen. Too young to know what to do with a child. That man had brought her down here with him, and then left her to her own resources when she got in the family way. Said she couldn't prove it was his, he couldn't have no babies, said he was sterile, and claimed maybe she was doing some hanky-panky," Mrs. Parsons said. "Can you imagine a man saying such a thing? He's become a politician now."

"I met her pregnant five months and just about to turn sixteen in the health clinic where I worked then," she said. "I was Mrs. Moser then. Mr. Moser, he run off, and I took back my own name then."

"I'm sorry," I said. "I did the same thing when I left my ex-husband. It was one way to forget."

"That's right," she said. "Don't want no ghosts hanging round."

"So you met her at a clinic?" I asked.

"Yeah, and we got to know one another. That man was paying for her apartment and claiming he wasn't no father. I want you to know, how can somebody's words be louder than they actions?"

"I hear you," I said. "And you agreed to raise the boy?"

"Well, yeah. I offered," she said. "I didn't have nobody. Daughter was gone off to Thomasville where she got herself a job nursing. Good money in that. And I felt for Trina, you know? Just a child. She came from up Atlanta way, and she didn't treat black people like they was less. I respected that she wasn't ignorant like so many white people was back then. No offense, baby," she said.

"None taken," I said. "I respect your being so open yourself, to bring a white child to your neighborhood."

"Trina treated me like a friend. I figured half the boy's genes wasn't bad. So I said I'd raise up the boy if she'd help me out. People around here talk-ed. Oh, lord, they talked. But we did all right. After while, nobody talked no more, 'cause that boy grew up good." A door slammed and a middle-aged man walked down the sidewalk and waved and nodded at Mrs. Parsons.

"Do you know about the younger boy, Mr. Lutz's natural son?" I asked.

"Child that died?" she said, sipping her tea, narrowing her eyes at some-thing across the road. "They say he drowned. They say it was an accident." I decided to leave it at that. She was running out of steam and things to say.

"Did Preston resent that his real mother wasn't raising him?" I said.

She looked at me. "That boy know right from wrong. He know you got to get inside somebody else's skin to know how they feels. He's probably too much that way. Too nice, you ask me. He hasn't ever asked nothing of that man. His own daddy. Nothing."

"What man's that?" I said.

"The man that's his daddy," she said. She gave me a look again that warned me not to go there.

"Right," I said. "Well, there's a letter Trina wanted her boy Preston to get a copy of that she didn't have time to send. I need to get it to him. In person."

"You not looking for trouble?" she said, leaning in towards me. Her brown eyes had a milky ring around them. Kind eyes, but protective.

"No, ma'am," I said. "In fact, can I trust you about what I'm about to tell you?" I knew I could. I sat back in the rocker. "I think Trina Lutz was murdered." Mrs. Parsons sat back in her rocker.

"Lord have mercy," she said. "So that's why he been acting so strange," she said. "Preston, he always kept things close. You reckon he thinks the same?" She looked at me again in the eyes. "Don't you let my boy get in any danger. You hear me?"

"No, ma'am," I said. If he was in trouble, he'd gotten himself into it, I decided. "So I can find him at the funeral parlor?" I'd finished my tea and set it on the tiny side table between us.

"Reckon so," she said. I stood up, and shook her hand.

"I'll be praying for you, baby," she said. "You a tall one, ain't you?"

"Yes, ma'am. Got it from my tall Indian daddy's side, I guess. Thank you, Mrs. Parsons. I'll need it."

THE FUNERAL PARLOR looked the same as always. Like it wasn't what it was: a place to make dead people look alive and sleeping. I fiddled with the envelope, not knowing what to say to Preston Edwards. Maybe surprising him with the letter would catch him off guard.

A secretary in an outer office with wide open doors smiled at me, got up, and ushered me to a sofa before asking me what she could do for me.

"I need to see Preston Edwards," I said, shoulders high, head high.

"May I tell him who's calling?" she said, not paying much attention.

"LaRue Panther. I have something Trina Lutz wanted to give him," I said. Nothing on her face showed she knew anything. She disappeared.

He appeared before me, stone-faced, that Elvis haircut, the aristocratic nose, the smooth skin, the nerdy glasses. "Mrs. Panther?" he said.

"LaRue," I said. "Ms. Panther."

"LaRue, then," he said, holding his hand out with some stiffness. "We've met here before, but I don't know that we've been properly introduced. Preston Edwards." A very white name to have been reared by a black woman in a rural Southern town. But that was stereotyping, which only keeps us from the truth. We shook, and he invited me back to his office.

The office had carpeting and licenses framed on the wall. A photo of Mrs. Parsons sat on a bookshelf. I looked for a photo of Trina and didn't see one. He offered me a chair across from his desk and sat down himself. His hair was lovely, black and thick. If only he didn't slick it back like Elvis. I could put gorgeous layers into hair that thick. He had broad shoulders and stood about six feet tall.

"You have something for me?" he asked, folding his hands on the desk.

"Yes," I said. "Your *mother* left this in her drawer." He glanced at me nervously as I handed him the letter. He opened it slowly as if to fend off the bad news that was coming. He read silently. Then he refolded the letter and put it back in the envelope.

"This is ancient history," he said. "Why would you show it to me?"

"What do you mean, ancient history?" I said. "Who owns ECOL?"

"I don't know, and I don't really care," he said. A chill went through me. He handed the letter back to me.

"Mr. Edwards, you know as well as I do that there's something fishy about what happened to your birth mother," I said.

"Ms. Panther," he said, standing up. "I think it's time for you to leave." He opened the door for me without a word, and waited for me to head out. I left without turning around.

IN THE CAR, my back to the funeral home, I was too freaked out to think about what had just happened. What had I stepped into? He'd acted icy. As frigid as my Norwegian neighbor in grad school, the old lady next door who always said nothing except to talk bitterly about others, even her own children. Steely blue eyes you. Just thinking of her gave me the shivers.

I picked up the cell as I headed back to the islands and called the principal at school, expecting to leave a message. But she answered.

"Ms. Glick?" I said, unbelieving. "LaRue Panther. I can't believe you're in—I mean, I'm not even sure why I called this late, but—"

"Oh, I'm here. Lots of work to do. I'm afraid I'm a bit of a workaholic," she said. "Are you calling about Taylor?" My stomach went thud.

"I'm returning your call. Is there something going on with Taylor?" I said.

"Well, yes. Yes, there is. Do you think you can come over here to the school Monday morning? That way, we'll all feel refreshed, and we can have a good face-to-face conversation," she said.

"Okay, sure," I said, sounding like a bouncy soccer mom. "What time is good?"

"How's eleven?" she asked, but by her pushy tone, I knew the answer I needed to give.

"Oh, that's fine," I said.

"I'll meet you at the office, then." She sounded confident and disconnected while I had seemed needy and worried.

Great, I said to the air as I clicked the phone off.

WHEN I ROLLED into town, a few tourists had made their way down and were wandering on Dock Street. The water looked choppy, but the day had cleared, not a cloud anywhere. Still, it was cold, and I wanted a big glass of water.

I cruised down Dock Street. Most places were closed except for the restaurants. I headed straight for Mac's real estate office. I parked at the side of the building and noticed the light slanting onto the small wooden porch that led to the red front door. The sun can prove relentless in a Florida island summer, but even for a minute or so in winter, it's healing. I stood outside and basked, looking at land and homes posted for sale in the window.

Tiffany sat in the office with her shoulders slumped. Her hair needed a cut. Had she never heard of texturizing shampoos? Her hair sat so limp on her scalp. I walked inside. "Hey, there," I said, smiling.

"Hey," she said, lips pursed, glancing up. She was pale.

"Tiffany, are you feeling okay?" I said.

She was finishing up a letter on the computer. She punched save and said, "Sure. I'm just tired."

"Are you getting enough sleep?" I said. "And enough to eat?" My mother voice wouldn't turn off. "You know, you need a certain number of fruits and vegetables every day to stay healthy."

"I'm fine," she said, standing up, and then sitting back down heavily. She sighed and hit the print button. She started clearing off her desk.

"Well, then, maybe you'll tell me what you know about ECOL," I said.

She froze in the middle of opening a drawer.

"I have a letter that Trina had meant to send before she died," I said.

She said, "Well, um . . ." and then she shut the drawer.

"I didn't know you knew about ECOL," I said. "So you do."

"Not really," she said, lifting one shoulder and dropping it. "I've done one letter for them."

"Does it state who's in the corporation and what they're about?"

She pushed away from her desk. "I'm sorry," she said. "I'm really sorry, and I'm not feeling so good." She put her elbow on her desk and rested her head in her hand.

"What are you sorry about?" I said.

"I don't feel so hot. I'm a little queasy and tired," she said.

"Go home," I said. "Get a nap. I'll watch the office for you. I can't do anything, but I can sure tell folks about St. Annes. I'm not likely to poison anybody here."

She laughed despite herself. "Are you sure?" she said standing up, holding her stomach.

"Of course," I said. "Now go!"

"But what if Mac comes by?" she said.

"I'll tell him I'm watching the office," I said. "Look, go on. It'll be fine. Mac's in Tallahassee, though, isn't he?" I opened the door for her.

"No, Mac's in his Cove office," she said.

"Shoo," I said. "Go rest."

BEING ALONE in the office felt oddly relaxing and unsettling at the same time. I took a deep breath and then I got to work, first locking the front door. I opened the letter Trina had cc'd to her son and looked closely at the numbers. Then I started rummaging through files. Letters to clients about home sales. Home sales all over, the main business in St. Annes. Finally I saw the commercial real estate file drawer. I opened it, and started looking. Mostly boring crap about sales in Tallahassee, Tampa, and Miami. I slowed down in the Miami batch.

When I found a file with a lawsuit attached, I took it out and set it down on the desk. I sat down with the thick file stamped MISTRIAL on the front. I started reading through its pages. Inside, the case read "The State of Florida vs. Martin MacKenzie Duncan." Lots of trial stuff—depositions, interviews, and court reportage. I slipped the file into my big purse and zipped it shut. Then I went back to the filing cabinet.

The next file drawer down, I discovered the pattern of the numbers. The middle four numbers represented the year a folder was created; the letters in front represented the main names involved; and the last four or five letters or numbers represented the location by road. Maybe I was running down a deadend alley, I thought. Then I found it. ECOL: HPK2000SR347. A handful of beige folders sat within the larger green ECOL file. And someone was knocking on the door. I shut the drawer and straightened up, sticking a smile on my face.

A couple, Canadians. "Kinda warm, eh?" the man said.

"Yeah, I guess. I mean, no. Not if you're from Florida," I said. I'd make a rotten real estate salesperson.

"We thought Florida was the sunshine state," the woman offered. "But we didn't know it meant hot in winter." She began taking off her sweater. I had to admit, the humidity was uncomfortable, and the day was warm.

"Yep, that's us, the hellshine state," I said, peering out the window. "Usually this time of year it's chilly to us all the time. Stays dark long, too." Their faces fell.

"We were looking at the sign out there, the one for the condo behind the KOA?" the man said. "Could we take a look at it?"

"I'm just substituting today," I said. "I don't even know where the keys are. Do you think you could come back tomorrow?" Boy, I'd be fired as a lousy salesperson by the Florida Tourism Board. In fact, I realized right then: I didn't want anybody else coming to Florida. We were full and overflowing with people, problems, and legislators who didn't give a damn.

"I can't help with real estate, but I can recommend several restaurants in the area." Their faces grew long.

"Good seafood, you say?" the woman asked. I sent them on their way with directions to the Cove, Mac's place, the best hotel for a nice overnight condo stay and food, and a promise that someone would be available tomorrow. I locked the door and went back to the ECOL folder.

The main owners included Senator Fielding, Mac, Fletch, County Commissioner Eli Sturkey, Patrick Monahan, a name I didn't know, and Carl Vickery, head of the Magnolia State Bank. Not Preston Edwards.

I pulled out a file called PENDING. In it was a map of all the property between the fork in the road that led out to Dad's place up to Leon County between the Magnolia and St. Annes Rivers. It showed about twenty square miles worth of property, thousands of acres of swamps and small islands, including the federal preserve. Certain parts were yellowed with a highlighter, none in the preserve. Some blocks of property, and some individual properties—mostly on the opposite side of the highway from Dad and closer to the river area—were shaded yellow.

The yellow highlighted areas included the property that the long-haired loners owned, the ones who'd died in hit-and-run accidents last year, the Holy Rollers' property, and Mrs. Colton, who'd died six months ago of lung cancer. A huge block was yellowed out over by Magnolia Gardens.

Then I ran across a file that was sealed in plastic. PERSONAL was written in red on the outside. I lifted it out and muttered, "*My* personal business." I put it, too, in my big purse.

I glanced at the clock. Nearly five. I headed over to the Cove real estate office, condos and restaurant.

THE FRONT OFFICE of the Cove Restaurant and Condo Rental rivaled going into a *real* real estate office in a real town. The glass, the neon lights, the corkboard on a stand that told all the activities available, offering a free tour of the area if the attendees agreed to listen to the spiel to buy a condo. A small bribe for whoever was willing to take it. I took little comfort in the fact that I'd sent the nice Canadians here.

I ducked past the cork board and got to the front desk, an obstacle, a bar you couldn't go past unless you were *somebody*. Loreen McBride, who lived on Seventh Avenue, was tending the front, so I waved and headed into the back area.

"Do you have an appointment?" Loreen said. She was eighteen, and probably just doing her job.

"No," I said. "But I have business with Mac." I wound around, then headed to the very back where his private office was. The door stood open, so I waltzed in.

"Hi, Mac," I said as I entered. "Hope you don't mind my walking in like this."

"LaRue." He frowned, sitting at his desk. "You're not supposed to barge in here. I'm expecting a phone call. If you'll wait out front, I'll see you as soon as I can." He shifted in his seat.

"Oh, thanks, Mac," I said. I didn't look at him, but stared around at his office for the second time in a month. He had a collection of stuffed fish. All over the room. My body was swinging its tall nervous self, noticing one wall, the next, the next. "Tell me, Mac," I said, "do you have a deep hidden desire to be a deep sea fishing expert?"

He smiled, looking a bit like an aging movie star. Handsome, slick, white-haired. "You've turned into an analyst? If you'll just sit in the lobby, I'll be with you in a few minutes." Instead, I sat down on his white sofa, a piece of furniture I could only dream of owning. I was such a slob though. Maybe not.

"I don't want to buy a condo," I said.

He chuckled. "No, you wouldn't," he said, shaking his head. "You've got the prime real estate out off the highway with twenty acres and that two-acre spring-fed pond."

"Did you like the cookies?" I said. "Your hair's still looking good."

"So you're here to talk about hair?" he said, cocking his head at me. "Because I'm expecting an important call."

"I need to talk to you about business. Yours, mine. Both. If that's okay. I won't be long."

He grinned. Smile creases deep. Teeth a bit yellow-brown with age. "I don't know about hair styles, LaRue," he said.

"That's okay," I said, scanning the room. Another photo of the six guys. Mac was holding up a mammoth sailfish he'd apparently caught in the Atlantic. A shot of Mac and Tiffany, arms around each other. A man nearly dad's age dating someone my son's age.

"Mac," I said, a serious look in my eyes. "You know I didn't poison you. I didn't put that stuff in the coffee. But the cops have made me prime suspect until they know what's going on. It sounds simple enough, but it's not." I said that I knew about his Miami mistrial.

He wheeled his chair over to the sofa and leaned in to me, his hands clasped. "So if the hair thing doesn't work out, you're considering detective work?" He laughed aloud at his joke. "You know those reporters lie," he said. "They're trying to make a buck. Sensationalism is the name of the game. Guilty until proven innocent. And you won't find anything from the mistrial." He smiled again. "And I saw you going through the files at the real estate office," he said. "As I was walking by. Those are confidential." He looked like a father chastising his child for spilling milk on the floor.

"Did Preston Edwards ever threaten you?" I blurted out. "Because he kicked me out of his office this morning when I asked him about Trina and about some of your real estate dealings."

He turned his head to one side and looked back at me without blinking. Like I was a slow kid. "It's hard to lose a business interest, a friend. I was shocked myself. Saddened." So he thought Preston Edwards considered Trina a business interest.

"I'm sure." I cleared my throat. "How about Trina?"

"Who?" he said.

"Trina Lutz," I said, shocked. "Trina, who just died several weeks ago. Whose funeral you attended last week? Who also questioned you about your accounting, your books." I didn't know for sure this was true. And then I took a breath. "Who had an appointment to talk to you here at the Cove the day she died."

He shook his head and frowned. "LaRue, you've gotten things confused. A lot of things confused." He stood, put his hands in his pocket, the second time today I'd had a man signal me in exactly that same way that the interview was over. "Do you think Trina Lutz knew to put what was poison to me in my coffee? I don't think she could have crashed the wedding party and done that if she were dead, now could she? And my real estate files are confidential. Not your business. Now, why don't you go experiment with hair dyes or . . . new styles and let the police do their work?"

I stood and followed him to the doorway. "Why is there nothing in the files about Preston?" I said. My hands shook. He shrugged. "Why can't you tell me if or even why she was here the day she died? I mean, if you told her she was losing her job or something, wouldn't the cops want to know?"

He stopped at the entranceway of the door exactly the way Preston had. He said, "LaRue, Trina killed herself. That's what the cops have discovered. If they want to know something else, they can come and ask me. I need for you to go. I have a call coming in."

"But what about that property your company ECOL is buying? What is ECOL exactly, anyway? And . . ."

He held his hand out and said, "See you later, LaRue."

CHAPTER 21

SATURDAY NIGHT WAS A BUST, despite the fact that the city of St. Annes had put up red, white, and blue lights on the lampposts. We islanders preferred Christmas green and red, but the city officials seemed to think it cutting edge to go another way. Daisy was off spending the night with her friend Kevi. Taylor and I had argued over his new tattoo, which fortunately was henna and temporary. A picture of Uncle Sam hung by a rope at the neck was featured on my son's left bicep. "Kill Kapitalism" was the slogan underneath the unfortunate Sam.

"What will Daisy think?" I said as I sat down across from him at the dining table.

"She needs to know that material wealth is the scourge of the earth, Mom," he insisted. He had been scarfing down a bowl of cereal.

"Can't you just let her have a little magic in her life before—"

"It's not magic, Mom. It's chicanery." He'd slammed the door on his way out.

Just when I had decided to sulk and watch *African Queen* on my own, the cell rang. Jackson.

"How's it going out there in the land time forgot?" he said with a chipper tone. How could he feel so happy?

"Well, the patriotic lights are strung up on Main Street to get us stirred up for Christmas shopping. The locals are hollering as they wander from bar to bar up the street because they're reminded they can't participate in the spending spree," I said. "My kids are out, my Saturday night girlfriend get-together is a bust, and I'm feeling a whole host of self pities. How about you?"

"I'm tired up here," he said. "There's this new gang war going on. Black on black crime. Kinda depressing. I'm trying to find a hole in the middle of it before it explodes."

"Oh, wow," I said, fairly depressed myself. "How about finding some holes down here in the island murders, which time and a certain state investigator seems to have forgotten?"

"Hey, you're not even playing rough right now. There are those who say that investigators are just glorified secretaries with clipboards."

"Never heard that one. But I notice you don't even carry a clipboard."

"So you're still in a gleeful mood, I gather. Why don't you come up to Tallahassee, and you, your girlfriends get some culture? The New Seventy-Sixers are playing at the Mockingbird next week. I know you love that band."

I did. The best string blend of folk twanged up with old-time-religious mournfulness, country and rock in the region. He had me, but I couldn't leave right now. "I can't. Too much going on. God, I love that band. Maybe another time?" I said weakly.

"All work and no play. Okay, I see I'm beginning to wear you down. Wonder what it'll take. Tickets to see the Avett Brothers, I'm thinking. Anyway, I did find out about the turquoise Ford license plate," he said. "It's registered in Trina Lutz's name."

"I've never seen that car before," I said. He'd actually checked on the tag. "Everybody knows everybody else's cars around here, even if they're in the garage."

"That's the curious thing," he said. "Wellborn address. Take it down. Ninety-eighty-two Seventeeth Avenue North."

"I'll check it out, Boss," I said. "By the way, Trina has a son who was raised by a black woman." I told him what I'd discovered. He encouraged my above-board sleuthing skills. "Well, you won't like this," I said, and told him about my pilfering through the real estate office and confronting Mac but not getting anything out of him.

"Be careful, LaRue," he said. "You don't have anything on anybody yet. I know that's hard, because you have to ask questions." I hated nothing more than being told what to do.

"Okay, sure. Thanks," I said, explaining that I had to take a nap, and I hung up.

I clicked the video on, only to have someone knocking on the door. There stood quiet, solid, reliable Laura. She held in her hand a present for Taylor. A DVD of some survivalist game.

"Great," I said, plopping down on the sofa.

"You seem tense," she said sitting down with care, as always. She wore a long green and pink paisley skirt with a hot pink turtleneck. Her big eyes were disguised by thick glasses. She had a creamy complexion. I hadn't been spending enough time with her lately.

"Have you seen the tattoo on Taylor's arm?" I said. I described it.

"Ooo, kinda . . . deathly," she said in a mock-shudder. "Sounds . . . like a teenager." She always comforted me with her droll humor.

"And that frickin'—excuse my French—Jackson keeps giving me advice about raising Tay, and about not getting in trouble with the law myself," I said, "and meanwhile he's the one—"

"Who's put you nearly into jail. I know, LaRue, you've said that. A lot." She sat down next to me, tucking her leg under her and putting the DVD on the coffee table. "I hate that too, but I admire him for his honesty, you know?"

She glanced outside. "He cares about you. More than you can say for most. At least the ones we seem to know the most about."

I groaned.

"I think you're really attracted to him despite yourself," Laura said, her kind eyes twinkling.

I sat up facing her. "But on Thanksgiving, Randy put his hand on my neck. I can't tell you what that did to me." We sat quiet for a minute. "And money," I said. "My constant companion, worry about money."

Laura shrugged, clicked off the silent TV. "Join the rest of us. Meanwhile, I've got an idea," she said. "As I recall, you're an ace pool player. Didn't you tell me your father taught you the game at the old Rains Restaurant?" Daddy had indeed taught me pool at Rains in the mornings. Rains had the best breakfast in town, the local fisherman gossip that Daddy loved to hear, and a pool table open all hours. So we'd go first thing in the morning for breakfast, we'd play pool, and then Daddy would drop me off at school down the road most days.

Trouble was, I had been good at pool. The guys had started to cut me out of the game. "I used to be good," I muttered.

"Come on," she said. "You and I both need to go out and just raise a little hell, forget all this and have some fun." She stood up and grabbed my hand and pulled. "C'mon! 'Tis the season. I stood with a longneck in one hand, a pool cue in the other. I hadn't been here since I was eighteen and had finally been banned from playing pool in St. Annes. I'd pissed half the men in town off. The other half cheered me on. I played with focus. Daddy had taught me that. Grandma Happy said it was the Indian genes. I don't know what, but it had turned out to be a curse and a blessing. Some men loved that I could beat anybody in pool, others purely hated me for it.

I held the cold beer in one hand, the cue in the other. All I knew was, it was the same trick as doing hair. It was all physics. A player looked at what needed to go where and made sure it went there by way of gravity, entropy, and the path of least resistance. It was all a mental measurement of weight, gravity, and chemical makeup of the objects at hand, static electricity, all that.

I took a swallow of beer. A small crowd had gathered. It started when I signed up for the game. I supposed enough years had gone by to keep people's memories from protesting my playing. The bartender, new enough in town not to know me, said nothing.

I was taking a ladylike sip off my longneck standing next to Laura, who kept poking me affectionately with her elbow, telling me to go on. Across the smoky room stood a greasy brown-haired biker dude with a tattoo of blood dripping from a knife.

A passel of bikers, who also lived out the county road, took their places behind Mojo, as they called him. The colony of bikers varied in population from three permanent to three hundred temporary residents on their hundred acres, depending on the time of year. Biker chicks perched on stools lining the bar. Randy was hovering, but I couldn't think about that. Fletch stood by the bar.

And so the game began. Mojo broke with a quick snap, scattering the nine balls. The three dropped into a corner pocket. He sank the eight with a combo off the one, then a straight shot into the side with a long shot at the four that luckily went a little wide.

I took another ladylike sip off the longneck, handed the beer to Laura, and stared at the oh-so-familiar felt of green.

The four sat an inch off the wall. I studied, leaned into the table, squinted and thought. And then I saw what Daddy always told me to see—that faint lighter green line down the table that told me what the path of least resistance was and exactly where to shoot that ball, and how hard, and at what angle. I leaned into the cue ball and hit it down the line. The four went in.

Around the table, I found the light green line from the cue to the six-ball. I'd have to cut it sharp to send it sideways without the cue ball running into the far corner pocket. I studied it, then hit ever so gently. The cue nicked the six, and the six went right, into the side pocket.

"This chick might be good," some biker woman said. Others were muttering. I began to feel a bit woozy.

"Here, have a little sustenance." Laura handed me the longneck. I looked around and saw Mary staring at me. She looked completely lost. She'd lost her lamb. I drank long and hard. What was the lamb Mary'd lost, I wondered.

I looked back down at the pool table and saw the light green line from the cue to the distant five. I sent the cue to the five, the five to the corner pocket. Somebody let out a yell, and the bikers groaned.

I took a deep breath. "They might throw me out," I murmured to Laura.

She said. "That was twenty years ago."

I leaned over and dropped the two into a side, the seven in with a bank shot. Then the eight down the length of the table. The nine, an easy shot, rolled into the corner pocket. End of game. Then the crowd was yapping like gulls on the beach.

Mojo came up and held out his hand. He shook, saying, "Good game, dude."

What made me happy was the $300 I made on that game, and even more so, the $500 I won on the next. After that, I played one more, lost, and they were satisfied that I'd lost $100 on the game. After that, I quit. I didn't want to push my luck.

AS I WAS COLLECTING my remaining booty, someone put an arm around my neck. I turned around. Randy. "Good game, Ace," he grinned. Laura winked and waved goodbye. She was headed home to work on the Magnolia Gardens piece before early deadline Monday morning.

Randy lifted his beer. "Can I get you another?"

"Sure," I shrugged. I'd already had two, my limit. I didn't know when to quit sometimes, especially out at a St. Annes bar. That was an Indian gene, too, Grandma Happy said. We could handle tobacco, but not alcohol. Whatever the reason, it's why I didn't go out much.

We sat in a booth, and he grinned. "I remember you when you were in ninth grade," he said. "I was only in seventh, but I had this excruciating crush on you."

"Me?" I said. "I was TooTall." My high school nickname, TooTall Panther.

He shrugged. "Not too tall for me."

We talked about the years between—marriage, divorce, coming home. How things were changing on the island now. Suddenly, he leaned in towards me across the table.

"I don't think it was suicide, LaRue." He said it quietly, looking around afterwards.

"Huh?" I said. I was getting too woozy. So was he.

"Trina's death," he said. Then he looked around and leaned back in and said, "I think she was murdered."

He wouldn't say why he thought this, try as I might to get it out of him. I got up to pee and pushed through a hoard of people to get to the door. Inside, there was only room for one person waiting and one in the john. I heard a familiar voice behind the door.

"I really was pregnant. I was. They can say I wasn't all they want to, but I was." Mary, I deduced from lowering my head to peer under the stall door and see the high-heel black velvet shoes she'd worn at the funeral. She must be talking to herself. She was drunk. I cleared my throat to let her know someone was waiting. "Sure, Cooter's sterile. But Fletch ain't." I looked in the mirror to see my own shocked face.

She barged out of the bathroom and stumbled to the sink. "Oh, hey LaRue," she said, zipping up her pants, not knowing, I felt sure, what she'd just revealed. "Good game."

"Thanks," I said. "I've got to pee." I ducked into the stall. The next person pushed open the bathroom door, and Mary said to her, "He made me have an abortion, the jerk."

"Sorry, hon," the stranger said as Mary left.

I stumbled out of the bathroom and wanted to leave. This was too much alcoholified stimulus. I had gotten too off-duty. I looked toward the booth to signal to Randy that I wanted to leave. But just then I saw Fletch leaning on the bar. I walked up to him and said hello. He nodded. The grieving widower, out the next weekend.

"What do you know about ECOL?" I said. Catching him off guard might work.

"What?" he said. He leaned away from me.

"Did you get Mary pregnant? And what do you intend to do with the property you're buying out adjacent to Magnolia Gardens?" The room wasn't standing quite still anymore.

He straightened up and smiled at me. "Saucy, ain't you? That pool game's got you all wound up. Come on, let's dance," he said. I was under the influence enough to let him slow dance with me to "I'm Having Daydreams about Night Things." Then he steered me right back over to Randy. "Sit here with your date, Miss LaRue."

I plopped down, and Randy looked at me quizzically. "Let's get out of here," I muttered.

A STRANGE AND FICKLE ATMOSPHERIC CURRENT was blowing into St. Annes. Something akin to a northeaster was blasting through as Randy and I walked past Main Street and onto Dock Street by Mrs. Fielding's house. Randy put an arm around me, and my heart began beating faster.

"Randy, tell me why you think it wasn't suicide?" I said, turning to look up at him.

"I don't know," he said, watching my mouth. He licked his lips. We stood in the shadows of Mrs. Fielding's backyard cedar tree, our feet planted in the parking lot of the boat cove.

"Yes, you do," I said.

"You're right," he said, "I do." And he lowered his head to kiss me.

But he never got the chance, because suddenly Mrs. Fielding's voice yelled out from inside. "Knock it off, you beer-drinking sex fiends," she said. This startled me back into reality.

"I'm totally confused and slightly drunk," I said.

So he walked me home. "Why're you so interested in how Trina died?" I said as we cut through the side street between the bait shop and the bank to get back to Main.

He shrugged. "Business. She was my accountant. She knew who was into dirty business here. She had the honesty to get to the bottom of it, maybe. I think she was killed." He set his jaw hard.

I pushed. "That's kind of—" I swallowed, "melodrama, don't you think?"

I said softly.

"Melodrama?" he snickered. "Come down to my house next week sometime. I'll take you out to show you something," he said. "Something that will make you—just come out."

We'd reached my house, and I sneezed.

"Uh oh," I said, heading up the stairs. "Better get warm before this weather gets me."

I walked inside to a dark house and threw my keys and purse down and sat on the sofa, letting out a big sigh. I put my feet on the table. "What a night," I said aloud.

Something felt strange. I wasn't alone. Fear bolted through me like lightning on water. I turned on the standing lamp beside me.

There in the center of the room stood someone dressed in all black, including a ski mask. I screamed. He took off his mask. Taylor stood grinning.

"What in God's name—" I said, realizing I'd climbed up on the sofa. I jumped to the ground.

"I'm getting good, aren't I?" he grinned.

"Mary, Joseph, and the baby—you just about scared me to death," I said, sitting down.

"That's the point," he said, strolling down the hallway.

CHAPTER 22

I SLEPT IN SUNDAY, and my head and belly spent the rest of the day reminding me why I didn't do the bar scene anymore. I considered driving up to the cowboy bar past Wellborn and over to Southside Tallahassee to play a few pool tournaments and make some cash. But the freezing weather turned to all-day rain.

The kids tiptoed around me for a change. Tay and Daisy promised to serve me lunch in bed and brought me tea and aspirin when I asked for it. For a split second, I pondered becoming a drunk full-time to get service like this. But I thought better of it when the lunch arrived. The toast was burnt, the eggs underdone, the coffee weak.

MONDAY, AND THE COLD FRONT was passing by, making the world more bearable. But the ocean beyond roiled and the horizon was a yellow gray.

An appointment with the school principal, a trip to Wellborn to hunt down a turquoise Ford, a pool tournament, and a hair appointment with an eccentric rich man—all looked as unpromising as being a sun bunny right now.

Taylor and Daisy got up early, expecting perhaps that ole Mom had retired for good. I found them in the kitchen noisily making smoothies.

"Taylor's taking me to school today," Daisy said with what came across as smugness. What I knew was that she'd bonded with him in a brief moment and was giving me the aloof treatment. In order to get on in the older world, she figured, she'd have to play the part of an I-don't-care teen. I looked at Taylor.

"I figured you could use the break," he shrugged.

"Thanks," I muttered.

As I made coffee for myself, I talked to Taylor about getting us all keys and locking up the place and leaving lights on when we left at night. "It's easier to hide in the dark. With lights, I'd have to camo myself better," he said.

"But I don't understand," I said as he poured the thick juice and yogurt drink into a glass, "why you think you have to learn how to do this in the first place. Sneaking up on people, hiding in the dark, making yourself invisible."

"Mom, why do you always try to stop me from what I need to do?" he said. He and Daisy gathered their things to leave, and I sipped coffee. "I mean, other people do this. That cop guy you like must have learned it. Randy taught me how to do it. It's not like it's a crime." Then they were out the door. I decided not to talk to him about the school meeting. Not all teenagers wanted to camouflage themselves and scare their mothers at night.

IT TOOK A CERTAIN KIND OF PERSON to live here, I thought, as I stepped out of the door of Cutting Loose with a CLOSED sign over the door. Half the locals were avoiding the woman who may have poisoned the richest guy on the island. Main Street Monday morning, a breeze coming in from the north on the Intracoastal Waterway. More boats were bobbing in the slips on the pier than usual. This meant the water was rough out in the Gulf. I just hoped there wasn't a tropical storm or a too-late hurricane brewing. What we all feared— that a hurricane could easily blow the oil straight into our part of Florida, completely destroying our lives with something simple as wind and water currents.

I pushed against the wind up the street towards one-story tiny City Hall. Hollywood could have breezed in and filmed a cowboy Western in what seemed a ghost town. Except for the twenty-first-century cars parked next to shops and businesses on the street, the tough weathered balconies looked like Old West saloons and parlors and hotels. Up the hill, away from City Hall, Main Street wound around oaks hundreds of years old, then past old tall Georgian-style houses whose widows' walks allow their occupants to gaze out across the Gulf.

People came and went from here, but generally, we got along. Had to. Eccentrics, artists, swamp folks all agreed on this. We gossiped, fished, took life as easy as we could, working and playing hard, drinking hard, and some of us churching hard. We locals generally understood that we were the cash poor, and the tourists were the cash we needed to drive our place. We wanted them to visit. Fat chance now. Times were tough.

This morning, the cafe was quieter than usual. I watched Madonna cross the street two blocks from City Hall and head my store's direction, towards the local cafe. She waved, nodded, and crossed the street. It was time for a gossip session, even though I had to get to the school by eleven.

Inside, it felt warm and sticky. Fishermen sat in the corner together. Booths lined the walls on the right, kitchen in the left back. Red and white gingham tablecloths covered each table, and plastic topped the cloths. Fake Wal-Mart flowers sat in the middle of each table. We made our way to our favorite booth, along the middle to the left side of the restaurant. I faced the door today.

"I don't trust Mac," I said after AJ's son poured us some bad industrial coffee. "This stuff will be the death of me," I predicted, looking deep into the black liquid.

"You'd better not say that too loud," Madonna said, scanning the menu. "You're theoretically the one who tried to knock Mac off with the exact same liquid, remember? I think I'll have strawberry shortcake for breakfast."

"How do you stay so . . . voluptuous with your appetite?" I said. "Your hair looks great, by the way."

She shrugged. "Luck? So what happened with Mac?"

I told her about my confrontation in Mac's condo office. About the letter to ECOL from Trina and the information that I'd dug up in Mac's real estate office. And how he'd politely sent me on my way.

"Be careful, Rue," Madonna said. "You don't just go confronting people around here. This is a tiny town."

"I could also be facing jail time. And Jackson is tied up with some weird Santeria case. They found about a hundred birds on the big lake up there slaughtered, one wing torn off each. Animal sacrifice and refugees. He can't help me right now."

Her eyes went to the doorway. "Well, look what the wind brought in." she said. I turned around. Randy Dilburn, scanning the room, hands in his pockets. He saw us, and nodded. Waved at a few fishermen and sat in a corner alone.

"Speaking of trust," Madonna said, then waited while AJ's son put the shortcake mounded with whipped cream in front of her. When the waiter left, she muttered, "I don't trust that guy. I know you all think he's hot or whatever, but . . ." She shook her head and spooned whipped cream into her mouth and licked her lips. "Something about him. Negative energy."

"You sound like a New Ager, Madonna," I said. "Minus the positivism."

"He doesn't talk to anybody. He lives in an isolated house on a lonely peninsula, and argues with Mary about politics—a true exercise in futility," she drawled futility out for six syllables in her Southern syrupy way. She pushed her plate over to offer me some shortcake.

"I had that 'dinner date,' if you want to call it that, with Jackson," I said, spooning whipped cream into my mouth. "I just can't date him right now. He's so sweet to Daisy. But he doesn't seem that thrilled about helping me with the case. And he doesn't want to get into a relationship with a leading suspect when he's working the case anyway. And I'm not ready for someone like him. I'm more attracted to Randy."

Madonna rolled her eyes. "I heard Randy's pretty hung up on his dead wife," she said. "Gimme a break. That's been, what, five years? And he's got no sense of humor."

"Must be that Southern hardcore religious upbringing," I said.

She said she had something to tell me and leaned across the booth. "I was up in Wellborn picking up cleaning supplies for the bar and checked that address Jackson got on Trina's car. Guess who's name is on the mailbox?" I shrugged. "Parsons. The dude, the funeral home dude." I put my fork down and sat back. She beckoned me to lean in. "I went past the funeral home on the way back to the islands, and that turquoise car sat in the back of the funeral home."

"Something is definitely up with that guy," I said. "I can't tell if he's hiding something or if he's just sinister. I need to go find out. What the hell would he have been looking for in Trina's house? And why would he sneak out?"

"You just be careful, LaRue," Madonna said, pointing her spoon at me.

After we ate, she got up with that body to die for and swished it in her cowboy boots and tight pants to the bathroom to primp. I didn't even see Randy walk up, but suddenly he was beside me.

I jumped, startled.

"Sorry, didn't mean to scare you," he said, a crease in his forehead. I told him it was okay. "Would you like to come out on the boat with me this weekend? I thought I'd run out to Seahorse Key, where I took your kids. They enjoyed it."

"They told me about the snake," I said. He didn't smile. "I was joking," I said. "Yeah, why not? The kids . . ."

"I meant, just us," he said, putting his hands in his pockets. I leaned my chin onto my hands so he couldn't see my ribs—it felt like my heart was beating so hard, he couldn't help but see.

"Okay," I said.

"Okay," he said, his face relaxing into an almost smile. "So why don't you come to the house Saturday, say around nine o'clock? We can get a pretty early start that way." I nodded. Madonna was back and had heard that last part. I didn't look at her.

"Sounds good," I said. He nodded at Madonna, then turned and walked out the door.

"Hmm," Madonna said. "He'd been watching. Waiting to pounce while I was away," she teased. "Why do you always go for these intense types?"

"I can relate," I said, glancing at the clock on the wall opposite us. "And as for intense, at eleven, I have to go talk with the school principal."

"Daisy in trouble?" she asked.

"No, you know it's Tay. He's behaving strangely lately. In school, too."

"For god sakes, he's a teenager. Don't tell me you didn't act strange as a teen," she said. Just then a big *Pow!* sounded outside in the street. Everyone in the cafe looked around at each other. The first thing we all thought about nowadays was terrorism, even on a little island like St. Annes. We all rushed to the door, creeping cautiously out to the street. Across the street, the whole block had darkened windows. People all along Main Street walked from businesses and looked around.

Out came Tay from the apartment. Why wasn't he in school?

"Oh, boy," I muttered to Madonna.

Tay headed towards me. "Mom," he shouted, his black headband on his long hair making him look like something out of the sixties. "I think the burglar alarm system I was putting in shorted out the street." Great, I thought. He doesn't even know he's shouting, making a scene for this little town to freak out on. My son, who should be in school and is looking like something from the Black Panthers, has shorted out one whole side of Main Street.

"Why aren't you in school?" I asked as I met him in the street, keeping my voice low, hoping he'd catch on to keeping his down. "And where's your sister?" People on both sides of the street were watching us. "What are you doing putting an alarm system in the house without talking to me about it?"

"'Cause I'm trying to fucking protect us!" he shouted. "But forget it. I won't." He stomped off. He turned back around shouting. "My sister's in school. I took her, 'cause we didn't know if you'd still be lying around in bed!"

"So much for not causing a scene," Madonna muttered behind me.

TAY SQUEALED HIS WHEELS as he left for school. The town maintenance guy, WH, began working on the electrical blowout. I'd have offered to help, but I had the school meeting to attend. I put on my jacket and walked to the one school in our little island town while I still had any dignity about me.

The morning fog spilled over the island, so thick you couldn't see five feet in front of you. The clouds made a sheet above. From Main to the school, people were having morning coffee, or were slumbering, or had already slipped out into their boats hours earlier. Soon, the fishermen would be eating eggs and grits at Rains down by the Fish House after bringing in their haul.

Despite my appointment, I enjoyed walking up the hill through the old neighborhood with stately wood houses from the 1800s painted white with green shutters. Then the sharp-roofed turn-of-the-century Victorians, into the modest Depression-era bungalows and World War II block houses. Then past the old black churches and honky-tonks now converted to cottages.

Up at Fifth and E Street, I saw Randy's Honda hybrid parked by a house that had once been an African-American church at the southeast corner next to the last cove off St. Annes. I didn't know who lived there, but morning was early to be out visiting. I glanced around, yet didn't see signs of him, just the car. The inside of a car told you something about a person's daily life. I slowed down and glanced inside the passenger side. A clean car, a pile of papers that looked like a deposition done on an Orlando defendant, and—I went numb.

An ECOL envelope stuffed with something like what I'd stolen from Mac's office. Randy wasn't a member, was he? He could be representing the group. I tried the car door. Unlocked, of course. No one locked anything in St. Annes until lately. I opened the door, reached in and whisked up the envelope and slid it into the waist of my jeans in one fell swoop. I walked on without looking back. I would drop it back into his car tomorrow. He'd never miss it.

Randy was handsome, well-off, and he could have dated any single woman on the island, aside from Madonna, that is. The Gulf breathed its huge-lunged tidal breath at the top of Sixth Street. I felt seasick. I was stealing from a guy I'd decided I might date. The early morning grew darker, thicker with clouds. Up ahead sat the school administration building, the color of gunpowder.

FESTIVE WHITE LIGHTS blinked over the double doors of the entrance to the only K-12 school within forty miles. I pushed open the heavy door. In the glass trophy case of the entryway, I saw some blue ribbons, crinkled, and dusty. They'd sat in that horrible case since the 1930s. I turned right after dodging the school seal tiled into the floor. Back when I'd attended the school, kids could get a paddling for walking on the supposed sacred seal. Years ago, I'd leapt over it often.

The lockers, putty-colored, displayed all manner of teen paraphernalia sticking out of slammed doors—shoe laces, pieces of rumpled paper, notes folded elaborately and stuck in the vents for the locker user to find. The waxy smell of cleaned cheap floor tiles shook up my school memories—often fun, and sometimes trouble.

I walked into the first office on the right. Marge, the school secretary, pointed down a small corridor that ended to the left. From the doorway, I could see the long oval table. There sat the principal, Ms. Glick, medium height, distinguished, a nice pageboy shaped by an expensive cut from a larger town. Her jewelry was large and metallic and tasteful. She had that expectant look of one hoping to get a job in a real town and not look back.

I hadn't expected the other one, the youngish guy, the coach who'd played minor league soccer. Tay couldn't stand him because he wanted all the boys in competitive sports. Tay preferred martial arts, competing with himself. I gave them both a weak smile and sat in the only available chair. The principal and coach smiled, nodded, said hello.

"I thought—" I got out.

"Ms. Panther?" Ms. Glick said. She knew my name. I hated officious behavior disguised as competency, especially in women bureaucrats, who seemed to have it down better than the men sometimes.

"LaRue," I said.

"LaRue, we've been concerned over some behavior in your son Taylor's classes lately," the principal said. I noticed she didn't offer her first name to me.

"And out of class," the coach said. His abruptness reminded me of New York where I'd done an internship in psychology after college. I'd felt trapped there. It wasn't so much the people, curt and in a hurry, but the fact that I could not see more than thirty degrees of sky when I looked overhead. In a maze I couldn't escape. Like now.

"And out of school," Ms. Glick said.

"After hours," said the coach, who Ms. Glick had politely introduced me to. He was tight as a barrel, a shiny, half-bald head.

"Taylor and Daisy were close to Trina Lutz, is that right?" Ms. Glick said.

"Yes, they were," I said. "Since the . . . the . . . the divorce, they haven't really had a grandmother to speak of. My mother—she died the day I was born." They nodded sympathetically. Or was it pity? I hated telling people this, especially people who considered themselves a class up from me, because I was a hair stylist now. I had as much education as either of them, but the unemployment rate for higher degrees in English had astounded us all. Suddenly, an ancient wave of longing came over me. What would my mother have said to me today? Would she have invited me to the cabin out on the pond, made tea, told me it would all be okay? Would she have put her sixty-eight-year-old veiny and thin-skinned and tough hand over mine? I couldn't know.

On top of that, I remembered early days of being called TooTall, and aching for a mother who might tell me—well, whatever mothers tell their anxious teen daughters.

Ms. Glick cleared her throat. "We think this sudden death may be affecting Taylor's behavior in and out of school. On top of that, we have the oil spill. And of course your being lately in the media."

"Yes, I've noticed it, too," I said, glumly. In my monkey mind, I sat Jackson down in my salon chair and shaved his head bald.

"You probably don't know, though, that Taylor's hanging out at the Under There at night," she said. They both looked down at the table.

"The Under There?" I said.

"Yes. It's what they call the place. Lilith Robinson's parents' low, empty garage, usually too wet in the summers." Anything low in our county was a disaster waiting to happen structurally. If you dug down at all, you'd reach water pretty quickly. Lilith was one of the hair-sheared kids who'd dropped out of college. The principal went on. "They're drinking, smoking pot, and—"

"LaRue, they're drinking cough syrup. This particular one gets them high if they drink enough of it," the coach said.

"Some of these kids—this group—are really at risk," Ms. Glick said. "The stuff can be addictive." How much cough syrup would it take? I wondered.

I sat back and sighed, folded my arms, stared at the wall across from me.

They were analyzing me, an adult with two mortgages, Grandma's, Daddy's, and of course the rent on my apartment downtown. Who did they think they were?

"Taylor is a good kid." The principal backstepped, trying to appease me. "He started off the year really well. He has this thirst to learn that some kids don't. He probably has a higher IQ than other kids in the school, and this makes it hard for him to connect. Most of them are trying to get pregnant or get someone pregnant, or *not* trying to get pregnant but getting pregnant anyway."

The coach finished for her. "And considering that fishing is what the boys assume they'll be fated to do forever, they just roll with it, if you will."

"Right," I said, when I wanted to say, Wrong. Not Taylor.

"Right," said the principal. "Even though he's better read and more worldly, he's exhibiting some odd behaviors. Not only is he neglecting his work, but he uses the time to . . . to plot defense and security measures. For what, I don't know. It's paranoid, slightly. Even though these are strange times." She shrugged.

"He's not doing his work in class?" I said.

"No. And he doesn't apologize for it. He says, 'I'm working on something far more important.' " The coach imitated Tay and exchanged looks with Ms. Glick. "He has a whole system of how to camouflage himself plotted out on paper."

"LaRue, I hate to do this, but I must. We found this on Taylor's person earlier in the week. He was showing it off to a friend in the Under There crowd, and I had to bring him to the office," said the principal. She pulled out Taylor's Swiss Army knife.

"Oh," I said. "Oh. He knows he's not supposed to bring that to school."

"The five of his teachers, who I'm representing, are suggesting he seek counseling," the coach announced.

"Counseling?" I said. "He went through counseling during the divorce. It helped him then, but he's pretty cynical about counselors now." Not now, I thought. Please, not now. He's a teenager. Do you remember that time in your life, people? God, what if they'd seen me just now, stealing things out of a guy's car when all I'm doing is trying to figure out who killed Trina Lutz. I cringed at authority sometimes. I also heard what was between the lines: Columbine. Mass teen murderers. Insane people carrying weapons. My son was no killer.

"We think you'd be making a mistake not to get him counseling," the principal said.

"Not yet," I blurted out. "I'm—I think it will pass. He's a sensitive—"

"It's the sensitive ones who need it," said the coach. His head of hair was hopeless.

"I'll think about it," I said. I took in a big breath and let it go. My nose felt clogged, stuffed up with years of dust and humanity.

Finally I said, "Is that all?" They looked at each other with knowing glances, and I stood up. They couldn't make me do this. "I appreciate all you're doing, all you've revealed to me. I will think this over and watch him carefully. I think I should monitor his nights more closely at any rate. I'll check back in a week, okay?"

They both shook my hand gravely, and I blew out of there. It felt too much like jail. The ECOL letter was stashed under the newspaper on the front seat. I should be more careful. Randy could come by and just snatch the thing right back.

CHAPTER 23

FLORIDIANS BEHAVE LIKE SCARED GOATS when the weather gets chilly. We bleat and fret and huddle together, saying "It's cold!" when someone from the Midwest would laugh and call it a warm fall day. The only time I spent time in a Northeastern city in winter, curse words spewed out of my mouth when I went outside. I was literally in pain from the cold. Not at all like a chilly December in north Florida. But I guess without all that cold winter weather, the Santa Claus, reindeer, sled-and-snow and down-the-chimney thing just gets surreal. Nobody really believes a guy in a red suit with white fur when it's 70 degrees outside.

So it was in the low 60s, and as I looked out the shop window, a light rain was misting in the air. I called Madonna, who couldn't believe anyone would wake her up at such an hour—during her after-breakfast nap so she could cope with staying up until two a.m. I told her about "the horrid school conference." She listened without a word.

"This is why I dropped out of school," she said finally. "School sucks, LaRue. I'm younger than you. Have you been to a public high school lately? Almost a third of kids don't even graduate, okay? Just read that in—I don't know—somewhere important, I'm sure. Tay's a good kid." She hung up, but I wondered. When it's your own kid, you worry. You know the principal doesn't know how your kid's doing, but do you, the parent?

The clouds covered the whole sky, a low, heavy ceiling, and promising change yet again. At least there was no big wind, no hurricane pushing the oil our way. I remembered talking to the owner of the Island Hotel a few days after the spill. Clyde fished and ran the restaurant. We'd sat outside on the swing at the front of the hotel in the heat of early May, commenting under our breath about how our eyes stung and there was a strange smell in the air. "If we get a hurricane, and the oil comes this way," he said. "Just burn it all down, the top of the water, the buildings along the Gulf, everything. Take it all down," he'd said. We'd nodded gravely in agreement. Everyone felt this way, but no one else had said this aloud. It was just that devastating to us all.

But some rain wouldn't be a bad thing. I swallowed a bagel and threw down a cup of coffee behind it. In the distance, I could hear the clanging of metal on the mast of a sailboat in the harbor.

For a change, a few customers began to arrive at the shop. In walked Fletch and his too-long crew cut. Behind him, a walk-in tourist in skimpy dress with starfish on it. Wasn't she freezing? Behind him, Isabelle the taxi driver.

I booked the tourist for forty-five minutes later. One hour sounded like too long a wait to a tourist, but forty-five minutes gave me time to really spend with the local ahead of her. Isabelle looked at Fletch out of the corner of her eye and asked if I could book her after the tourist. Friday had often proved hectic, an unpredictable day. I tried to make room for as many appointments as possible. After the flurry of walk-in booking activity, now the shop sat empty except for Fletch and me.

"Have a seat, Fletch," I said, patting the top of the chair. "Can I start on your sideburns? They're back in style, you know."

"Nope," he said, as always. I loathed giving him the crew cut. Asking me to do a crew cut was sort of like asking Picasso to paint your bedroom in white paint—not that I thought I was a Picasso, but that lack of creative generosity made me impatient. But a hair stylist gives the customer what the customer wants, within reason. That is, if we can't gingerly talk them out of something drastically bad.

"Just the usual," he said, as always.

"So how are you doing, then?" I asked. "I'm so sorry about Trina." We pretended our bar conversation after pool hadn't happened.

"She loved those kids of yours," he said, smoothing his hand over his head. His eyes suddenly took the color of steel. I'd seen Fletch smooth his hands over his head like that before.

"They're having a rough time, especially Taylor," I said. Fletch didn't seem to be. He looked rested as I pulled the cape over him.

"Yep. It's tough," he said. "So how's your pop?"

"Dad? Daddy? Dad's fine," I said. "Enjoying his garden." I thought I'd try to catch him off guard. "So what's this group called ECOL?"

"ECOL?" he said. The hand went up to his head, even though my scissors were in the hair on the side of his skull. "Don't believe I've heard of it."

"That's funny, because I saw an envelope with the stationery and your name on it when I was subbing for Tiffany in the office the other day, along with the Senator and some—"

"Oh, that," he said. "It's an economic, ecological growth package we're working on." This didn't fit his vocabulary. He'd never left the island, so didn't switch from country to college in a heartbeat. But he'd spouted this ECOL explanation out like it was rote. Like he'd programmed himself to sound semi-knowledgeable if asked. "We got a park and some low-density residential property development." He tripped over that phrase.

"On wetlands?" I said. I was trimming the back short.

"LaRue, we're developing with the agreement of the county and state regulations." He said the words as if he were talking to a naughty, stupid child.

"I get the impression that Trina didn't like it," I said. He sat up a little, then went still.

"Trina didn't approve of a lot of things, bless her heart. Why don't you stick to the haircuts and get out of the Nancy Drew business, honey. Trina was an unhappy woman. I'm afraid I knew that too well. I loved her dearly, of course." His hand went to his head again. "Wasn't nothing I could do to console her." He sat back in the chair with a set mouth, his jowls sagging. Steely eyes stared back from the mirror.

I realized I shouldn't have confronted him. I apologized. Fletch was one thing, but Mac came from city culture. You could confront Mac, and he wouldn't think much of it. Fletch? Well. Many older Southern men will never forgive a truly confrontational woman who makes them lose face. And he had clout in the community. He could make it hard for us—Dad, Grandma, Daisy, Taylor. So I apologized profusely.

"You're right, Fletch," I said. "I shouldn't bring up these things right now. I know it's hard for you." In my fantasies, I was giving him a Mohawk and dying it purple. In walked the tourist, and the talk between Fletch and me turned to weather.

I finished up Fletch, and he paid me well, and tipped well as usual. But a chill ran through me as he left. Call it intuition. He was cold as a Chicago winter. But I didn't have time to process it. I trimmed the tourist woman's straight blonde hair and used the iron to make a flat round curl, first teasing it a little to give her some volume. Voila, soft curls for the day—they matched the dress. I sprayed the heck out of it because of the weather. She felt perky and tipped well. If she liked the cut and style, she'd go tell others about my place.

In walked Isabelle. She already wore a pageboy and had healthy silvery hair. Yet her face looked a bit like cooled lava on a craggy mountain.

She sat down. I could tell she didn't need anything haircut-wise. She wanted to talk. "How about a shampoo and a bang trim?" I suggested.

"Sounds about right," she said. Her voice sounded as crackly as a radio talk station that doesn't quite come in. During the lavender shampoo, I gave her a good scalp massage. She began to talk.

"That damn Fletch," she said. "He is one home wrecker. Done been carrying on with his brother's wife for years. I mean *years* while Trina was at home working hard."

"Who, Isabelle, which brother?" I said. It sounded Old Testament, somehow, and important.

"Cooter, who else." She shook her head and shrugged her shoulders.

"Fletch?" I said, trying to sound neutral and unknowing.

"LaRue, they got this place up yonder at Cureall," she said. "Lotsa times,

I'm out on the road, you know, taking folks back to the airport up Tallahassee way?"

"Cureall?" I said. She nodded, went on. I pulled out the razor to texture her boxy bangs for softness.

"Well, they're one or the other of the two of them always turning off on the same little rut road back into the woods. You know the sign with the squirrel on it? Says 'Squirrel's Nest?' "

"Yeah, I've seen it," I said. "Doesn't it stink to high heavens over in Cureall?"

"Naw, you're thinking of in the town. I'm talking about up closer to Tallahassee from there in the woods. It don't stink. Anyhow, I seen 'em turning in there to do their hanky pank for years now."

"Years. How long?" I said.

"Oh, twenty, say," she said as hair drifted into her face and she spit it away. I'd talked her out of color about a year ago. Her silver hair was prettier than anything in a bottle.

"Twenty years?!" I said. "It's like a, a marriage! Are you sure it's been that long?"

"Well, I came here from Georgia twenty-two years ago, and started taxi driving a year later. Almost the whole time I been seeing 'em turning up into their little love nest, yes sir. I 'bout lost my accent now, my Georgia one," she said. Hardly, I thought. She went on. "'Cept he wouldn't leave Trina for nothing. Set in his ways, you know."

"Don't I know it," I said. "I can't even get him to grow sideburns."

"Mary despised Trina, you know," Isabelle said. "All she ever wanted was to get her hands on Fletch, and his money wouldn't hurt her none, neither, know what I mean? She felt Trina was taking all that from her, when it was really flipped the other way round."

"But Mary—Mary would have—okay, Mary would have been fourteen when they started seeing each other," I said, horrified. Younger than Taylor, only a few years older than Daisy.

"I'm telling you, that Fletch is a skunk. And I think Mary married Cooter to get close as she could to Fletch," Isabelle said.

"Ew," I said, realizing I sounded like Tay's friends. I clicked on the hair dryer, trying to sort through all this. "It makes sense that she's—well, kind of off. Guess that's why she's always acting drunk and crazy."

"Now don't go all soft, LaRue," she said. "You coulda done the same with what all you been through. She ain't got no morals is her problem. She's just a whore." I winced, but didn't want to get into the semantics of moral ambiguity or calling women sexist names. Hairdressers don't do that in a small town or they'd close down faster than mullet jumps when you aren't looking. "I think she wanted to kill Cooter when she went at him with the knife," Isabelle said.

Luckily, the phone in my pocket buzzed. Jackson. I told him I'd call him after I finished Isabelle's blow dry.

I decided to put on the Avett Brothers, music to cheer myself up. Isabelle and I sang "I and Love and You" together as I dried her hair. She didn't know the words or the band, but they sounded country and the words were simple enough that she caught on. *My hands they shake, my head, it spins. Ah, Brooklyn, Brooklyn, take me in. Are you aware the shape I'm in.*

She tipped big, and then left. I finally had earned Christmas money. I did a little jig.

"Did you call because I broke the law, Officer?" I deadpanned Jackson when I called him back.

"No, but I might have to fire you, Señora Panther," he said in a Mexican accent.

I had to laugh. "You're rotten. What a stereotype."

He put on the thick Hispanic accent again. "You have not been checking out this Mary and this Tiffany as I requested. But if you like, I can tell you about Señor Mac and the Mexico connection."

"Really?" I said, relieved. "I hope it's good. It's so far a rough day. And I do have some word on Mary. You first, though."

"Well, first things first. Are you doing okay?" he said. I told him about the horrid school conference.

"Kids are kids," he said. "Boys his age don't belong in school. At least not in the kind of schools most public education provides. Hey, he's coping. But I hope you'll pull him home weeknights, not that it's any of my bus—"

"Nope. Sure isn't," I said, and then softened. "But I will."

"Okay, then. Never tell a single mom how to raise her kids. Point taken. Next, Mexico," he said, the professional tone setting in. "Mac had a mistrial in a case of money laundering in Guatemala. Seems he was fired, and whatever it was got covered up. But there wasn't enough evidence to convict him of anything."

"And?" I said.

"That's all I could get for now," he said. I could hear phones ringing and people talking in the background.

I figured he was busy, so I started. "I'm wondering about—"

"Wait. Couple more things," he said. "The blood in the bag you gave me from the boat matches the blood on the knife. Most significant thing is, it's human blood. And the blood type matches Trina's blood type. Good work. It's something we can go on. But we need more if we want to exhume the body without using your testimony." Her blood had spilled on that boat. With a knife.

"Also, I'm going to send you a copy of the coroner's report on Trina's cause of death. Remember I told you the signature looked girly? See what you think. I'll fax it to Laura's office after we get off the phone. You should go directly over there when we hang up so that it doesn't get into any other hands."

I glanced across the street. Laura's office lights gleamed. "Got it. Thanks," I said. I meant it. He'd been good to me. I told him what Isabelle had said to me regarding Fletch and Mary's twenty-year relationship.

"Mary's—twenty years? She's how old?" he said.

"Fourteen. That is, she was fourteen when it started," I said. Silence on the line. I went on. "She's married to his brother, Cooter, you know."

"Well, that explains the abortion or false pregnancy, and the mental ward. Possibly the alcohol habit, although that's a chicken-and-egg question and a personality-type question, too. What kind of knife did she come at Cooter with?" he asked.

"How am I supposed—okay, can you find out?" I said with a sigh. "Can you track down her health records for the past decade or two?" I said.

"Sure, only, what, seven thousand days of possible medical problems, give or take? No problem," he said.

"I'm sorry, I just . . . I'll go get the fax. Anything you can do would be helpful," I said. He'd been more than just helpful. Someone in the background slammed a desk drawer and shouted at someone else. He'd told me before that at any law enforcement office, emotions could get high. "Jackson, thanks. I mean really. Thanks."

"Sure thing, LaRue," he said. He lowered his voice. "You're still not so sure about me, huh? You know this case is extra. But it's important to me." As an afterthought, he laughed and said, "Let's see what instrument of cruelty Mary is capable of using on poor ole Cooter."

I blurted out, "Want to go to the Full Moon party at the Cove? Next weekend?"

"Hmm. Sure. I happen to be off, and have a case or two in St. Annes that need looking at. The weather report says it's supposed to clear up soon."

"I hope so," I said, hung up, and crossed the street catty corner to Laura's office. What was I thinking, complicating my life any more?

I shook the rain mist from my hair and sweater before I walked into the newspaper office, a converted one-story wooden home on the corner. Laura had made it homey-professional with two beige sofas, a rectangular tile table between them, loads of fluffy pillows, and a fake bear rug underneath. The house smelled faintly of cedar wood. Laura wore her signature working clothes—a bright red long dress with arty earrings to match.

"How's it going?" Laura said, ushering me over to her desk in a corner of the living room. "Seems like forever since I saw you. It's funny how a few days can sometimes seem like a lifetime." She handed me the coroner's report that she hadn't looked at yet. I sat down across the organized desk from her. She had piles stacked all over her wide, deep desk. She probably knew what lay in each pile, too. Her eyes behind her big black glasses looked quizzical.

"Sheesh,'" I said. "Don't even ask." But I told her anyway. About Jackson's being busy, about Tay blowing half of Main Street out electrically. About the horrid school conference. About my asking Mac and then Fletch about ECOL. About Mary and Fletch's sordid, long-term tryst. About the Mexico thing. The blood types on knife and bunker on the boat matching and proving to be human blood.

With each bit of news, her eyes got bigger. She shook her head and her red earrings danced.

"I'm totally disgusted," she said. Like me, she focused on the child-porn aspect to Fletch first. "Mary at fourteen? And Fletch married? And Trina's second son died while Fletch was with the kid? Surely Trina knew about Mary. I'd have committed hari-kari, not—"

"Oh, my god," I said, standing up, staring at the coroner's report.

"*Now what?*" she said, staring up at me.

"I can't be absolutely sure, but I'd swear this was Tiffany's signature. Pretending to be . . ." I squinted, then threw down the report. "How original," I said waving my arms, voice dripping with sarcasm. "She—if it is she—she signed some Indian name to it."

"You mean she said Trina was Indian? Native American-Indian or India-Indian?" she said.

"India-Indian, of course. No, not Trina's name. The doctor's signature. How many Native Americans in Florida are doctors? Probably approximately one, though Granny thinks she's the medical authority of north Florida," I said. Kidding around about Indianness made people feel less uncomfortable about having to be politically correct. I'd seen real Indians do this with finesse. They had the best sense of humor in the world.

"How can you tell it's Tiffany's signature?" Laura said. "You have to be so careful about these things."

"I'm not certain, but the way she pulls out the ends of some words when she writes? I've seen her do it when she writes checks or in the office. She's left me notes at the house. And that classic way she makes her small "e's." I leaned across the desk to show Laura. "And the way she'll write an 'i,' dot it, then swipe the 'i' towards the next letter, like this. That's totally Tiffany." I leaned across the desk to show her the "i." Laura stared. Then she opened a drawer and pulled out the Tallahassee phone book.

"Spell that Indian name for me," she said, wryly. "I think I need to go to a Tallahassee doctor. I'm feeling pretty darn sick." She picked up the phone, frowning.

I was pacing in front of the desk now, thinking. OV, the garbage man. What had Madonna said that OV had told her? She said OV had been tooling around in his little oyster boat, he'd been working on it, and he took it out for a spin before sundown the night of the suicide. He says he swears he saw Trina on Fletch's boat. I reminded Laura of this as she dialed. As the phone rang, she thought through things.

"Okay, so that's hearsay, but let's assume it's true. Was she steering the boat? Who else did OV see on the boat? Where exactly were they? And at what time?" She held the phone to her shoulder as she numbered these things off on her fingers.

"Well, we can ask the source to ask the source," I said. "Where's Madonna right now?" I peered out the fogging window looking down the cowboy-Western street. I whirled around. "Hey—has Fletch tried to frame me and tried to kill Mac himself?" How close I'd stood to Fletch this morning cutting his hair!

"Possibly," Laura said in her flat calm way. "Let's conjecture, but don't assume anything. I'm getting a recording." She jotted down the number where the doctor could be reached. She scanned physicians in the yellow pages, looking for another way to get ahold of the guy. "And then there's Mary, who I can easily picture going at Trina with a knife. If Trina were out of the way, she'd have everything she ever wanted." She looked up at me. "We need to get Mary's alibi."

"Oh, Laura, I should never have mouthed off to Fletch," I moaned aloud, squeezing my face in my hands. Laura hung up the phone and scribbled notes. "He'll try to poison *me* next," I added, putting my head in my hands.

"Hold on. I'm thinking. . . . You know, Fletch may not know anything," she said, looking thoughtfully past me. She was so analytical that every time I got in a nervous snit, she calmly talked me out of it in a roundabout way. "Mac could have been poisoned by the Miami connection. How would we know?" She was making circles with her hands, the pen in her right hand now. "The wedding party came from out of town. Someone from Miami or Mexico or Honduras could easily have mixed in with the bunch of us—locals and wedding party." She shrugged and went on. "Who'd have known? Probably not, but in other words, it could be anyone. How about that funeral guy? He could have arranged the whole thing. Don't assume anything."

"God, I'm confused," I moaned. "And my kid's in trouble."

She looked at me placidly, got up from the desk, and beckoned me to go sit on the sofa with her. "Look," she said, sitting next to me. "My mom always told me to pretend—it was in reference to men, of course, but it still applies here—she said *pretend* you're not concerned. Act cool. For you, it means meditating on the idea that you're on a low dose of Valium."

I started to protest. She put her hand up. "I know, I know. But you sometimes just want to be subtle, blasé, and quiet as a cat. Let's have some graham crackers and brie. Best dessert lunch in the world. I'll make some tea. Let's just chill, as Daisy loves to say. Breathe, deep breaths." She disappeared into the kitchen area. She always had lunch on hand, having a big kitchen at work. She rarely stopped work to go home for lunch, and just ate what was in the kitchen. She kept it stocked. I could hear plates and metal and the pantry door squeak open. Breathing deeply did help. And domesticity was calming.

"It's a French picnic lunch," I said when she set a plate of cheese, crackers, and sliced apples on the tile table. The fragrance of apple suddenly filled the air. She sat down beside me. "My mother would be proud," I said, having no idea what my mother would really have thought.

In walked Madonna. "Just in time!" she said, grabbing a slice of apple and sitting across from us on the other sofa. "God, you look terrible," she said to me. Laura laundry-listed all the reasons I couldn't relax.

"Hot damn," Madonna said, cutting a big hunk of brie. "We kick *ass* as 007, don't we? Blood types match!" And though I didn't feel her sense of accomplishment, I smiled when she high-fived me. She held up a cracker with brie. "God, I love this stuff." She crammed a big cracker with a mammoth hunk of cheese into her mouth.

"I don't think the French would approve of your manners, Madonna," I said. Brie was squeezing out the sides of her mouth. Laura pointed at her and started chuckling. Then I was laughing. Then Madonna had to empty her mouth to laugh. Sure, it was stupid, but there we were, all laughing uncontrollably, tears running beside my big Seminole nose. Finally we stopped, gasping for breath.

We got quiet in that way deep friendships can. We ate and did not discuss murder or poisoning. We um'd and ohm'd occasionally, especially when Laura brought out a chocolate cheesecake. We each sat back and sighed afterwards. Madonna wiped her mouth with the back of her hand and then licked it. "Sex without sex," she said, then tilted her head and put a serious look on her face. "I have to say, Ruey, I hope you won't mind, but I went through Tay's junk at your apartment."

I looked at her with alarm. "It's a good thing we're friends," I said.

She shrugged defensively, and said, "I was worried. I went through his room. He's got *nothing*. Not even a pack of cigarettes. I found *one* girly magazine. It's my opinion that he's just hanging with the wild ones right now. But I did find this." She stood up and pulled out an envelope from her purse with a letter scrawled in Trina's hand. I looked at her. "Didn't read it," she said. "Just saw it. In Tay's undies drawer."

For a moment, I thought I was going to throw up. Too much was happening. "Well, okay," I said. "Now we're both thieves." I shoved the envelope in my purse. "I can't deal with this right now. I've got appointments this afternoon." I picked up the coroner's report and stood. "I gotta get back to work, you guys."

"Enjoyed lunch, especially the brie squishing out Madonna's cheeks," Laura said. We all laughed again.

"Maybe we can meet at the Hook Wreck tonight, before it gets busy?" I asked. We agreed.

"Maybe we can't figure out what from which, but I got a drink that'll go right to your elbows and knees," Madonna said. "So nobody better need to drive home tonight." Fair warning, I decided.

CHAPTER 24

THE NEXT PERSON to walk into Cutting Loose wanted cornrows. A college kid passing through, a backpack on her arm. Tedious job, but it paid well. And I had a tiny TV to listen to and glance at. Drilling experts revealed on the news that BP had valued speed over safety in the oil rig disaster, the news caster was saying. The screen flashed a picture of a raccoon looking into a camera, puzzled, as it walked through the sludge at the edge of a Louisiana marsh. "How to explain to a raccoon why this is happening, man," the college kid said.

Next a tourist came down wanting foil highlights. I decided to give the brunette woman some gold streaks. You tend to forget about the brunettes and the fun that can be had with their color. I used a 20-volume gold coverage on her. Thunder muttered outside. While the client was "cooking," I handed her some trash magazines and a cup of tea. I slipped out, walking the three blocks in the misting rain to the white post office building.

A rain started up and was spitting sideways, so the fishermen had come in early. A line had formed at the P.O. with people buying stamps and beginning to send Christmas gifts. I nodded and waved at a few locals and pushed the glass door into the postal box room, about the size of a living room. Rows of metal boxes lined three walls. The smell of gummy paper permeated the place. My box was situated in the corner. I had nothing much but bills and "buy our stuff" catalogs.

I pulled out the coroner's report from my pocket again as I stood at the box, my back to the door. Was anything else odd about it besides a signature that looked like Tiffany's? A heavy loud clap of thunder shook the place.

"A letter?" said Mac over my shoulder. I turned around, and he stood just behind me. Instinctively, I folded the report.

"Hmm, from a sweetheart?" he said. I shook my head no. "Why so secretive? Still playing Nancy Drew?" I glanced at the large window, the fourth wall of the room. It began to rain harder. I sighed. I hadn't brought an umbrella.

"Why? You see something familiar?" I said, stuffing the report into my pocket. He was at eye-level, a small advantage a tall woman sometimes has. I could smell his aftershave, a lemony cedar scent.

"No," he said, backing away a step. "I just thought that since you feel free to look through my real estate files, you wouldn't mind my seeing your lemon-scented love letters." He was smirking, looking with piercing blue eyes. I looked at him right back.

"Gotta get back to the shop," I said. "I'm in the middle of a foil highlights." I felt trapped in the stuffy room, but said, glancing at his umbrella, "If you wouldn't mind walking me down?" I didn't want him to think I was afraid.

"I wouldn't mind accompanying a pretty lady," he smiled, opening the glass door for me. Outside, we stood under the eaves. Rain was clattering on the sidewalk and street. It felt sharply chilly.

"Mac, you flatterer," I said. "I'm tall and intimidating as a French cathedral. And this nose could hook a twenty-pound grouper. Forget buttering me up. It's okay. We're cool." I straightened up as he opened his umbrella.

"You tall girls underestimate yourselves," he winked. "Well, I do want to tell you something, clear something up," he said, offering for me to walk under his umbrella.

"About your trial?" I said.

"That was years ago," he said, waving his hand casually. "It's best left in the past. At any rate, it was a mistrial. The company I was working for fired me. Unfortunately, almost took me down, because they were going down."

He glanced at me, and we crossed the street where the old decayed ice cream parlor one block from my shop sat empty. Its overhead porch offered shelter from the rain. Then we continued to walk down the covered sidewalk. "They had cooked the books. It's why I hired Trina Lutz. She was a straight shooter. We didn't agree on everything, but she was honest. I respected that in her. And in you." We were passing the only grassy lot on Main Street now, which fronted the sewage system and sometimes smelled like, well, like a sewer. I thought of the fishing widow who'd lived in the little house next door there for years before she died. Then my thoughts went back to Trina on a boat, dead before she had time to think.

"Do you think she was happily married?" I said as we hurried past the vacant lot next to my apartment building.

"I have a sense that they had their problems, like any couple. LaRue," he said, stopping to look me in the eye. "I believe she was an unhappy woman. Depressed. The world wasn't . . . perfect for her. And you know how emotional some women can be." Weary, I ignored the sexist remark.

"Affairs?" I suggested. "Someone else in love with Fletch who wanted Trina dead?" He looked at the sidewalk and guided me by the arm towards the salon.

"LaRue, we've all got to let her go. She died. She killed herself, and I deeply regret that. I wish she'd reached out more. Maybe—" He stopped in front of the salon and stared at the ground. "I know you're distraught about the possibility that you could be charged with attempting to kill me." His eyes softened. "I know you wouldn't. I know you feel frustrated. I'll be happy to loan you a couple of thousand dollars to get you through if a court appearance ties you up." In the three-second silence that meant *No,* a local fisherman hollered at the four-way stop at another fisherman about party plans. I turned and looked at Mac straight on.

"Someone tried to kill you," I said. "Aren't you worried they'll try again?" He shrugged. "Do you think Fletch would want to kill you?" He had been looking back at the ground, and for a moment his eyes flickered as he looked into mine. Then they went back to their steady gaze at the ground.

"I'm leaving it to the police. They'll figure it out." He shrugged. "Meanwhile, you and I need to move on. If there's one thing I've learned in life, it's that we all have to pick up and look forward, not back." He peered out over Main Street and up into the steely sky. "Figured you'd be too proud to take money from me." He smiled and opened the door for me.

"Hello, there," said the tourist woman with silver foil layered all over her head.

"Hello, Mrs. Banks," Mac said, nodding.

"You were right, I needed this! She's giving me a little gold blonde!" she said.

"I sure hope this clears up," I said. "The weather, I mean." So Mac was still referring people from the condos down to me. I smiled and waved as he turned to leave.

I had two more local appointments after Mrs. Banks. One was an Ootz who lived next to Dad and Grandma. I liked Matteo Ootz, an Italian-German mix whom we all grew up calling Matt. But he had a gorilla in a cage for a pet. He smelled of zoo.

The other, a church lady, would quote Bible verses and talk about the blood of the lamb. I had my serious reservations about church. I headed to the coffee pot in the shop.

According to Dad, my mom's French ancestors died for their faith. As Huguenots, their parents were tortured, imprisoned and had their throats slit for ministering to peasants, so the French Catholics killed her great-great-great etc. grandmother and grandfather. Didn't I owe it to them to practice my faith?

But my life came 350 years later, I rationalized. We needed a new faith, or a faith not unlike Grandma's to remind us of nature's power. I felt as weary as a dying civilization. I would need some of my special Ethiopian java to get me through the day, so mounded double my allotment of the ground beans.

IT WAS IMPERATIVE that I wash Matt's hair. I added some bergamot oil to his neck and just under my nose. It smelled the way Earl Grey tea tasted. The cut was simple: a Beatles bowl cut for a quiet, kind man who happened to have a gigantic gorilla for a pet. But he had such thick hair that fat and muffy fur grew over his ears. So I decided to do a triangle cutout. This would pull the weight from the area. I didn't want any of my clients walking around looking goofy.

"So how about Trina's suicide, Girl?" Matt said. We'd grown up together, had listened to bad eighties music together. And Cindy Lauper's "Girls Just Want to Have Fun." That's when he started calling me Girl.

"It wasn't suicide, Matt," I said, trimming the bottom of his hair first. He sat up and turned around slowly and looked at me.

"Know what? Somehow, I knew that," he said. "She wasn't the type. But who did her in?"

"Been trying to find out," I said, shrugging. "Turn around, unless you want me to trim your eyelashes. I think—okay, between us, okay?" He nodded and sat back in the chair. "I think Trina knew too much about *something*. Or somebody wanted her money. Or someone wanted to marry her husband." I began picking up the crown of his hair and cutting. He had perfect hair— shiny, straight but with body, dark like Italian men you see in fancy magazine ads. I ran my hand through it while cutting. "Gorgeous hair," I reminded him.

"Would you stop that?" he said. "It's making me think evil thoughts." I slapped him on the head like I would have when we were eight. "You call Fletch a husband?" he said. "Fletch hadn't lived with Trina for years. I did yard work for her. Some mornings, I'd go work before the sun was up. Fletch always drove in around six-thirty a.m."

"Know anything about where he might have been?" I said. He shook his head no.

"Know anything about ECOL, this group that seems to be buying up land out our way?" I asked. He turned around to look at me. "I can tell you what I've seen," he said, shifting a little in his seat. I was onto the bangs now. He was cute, after all, gorilla or not. "Dish," I said.

"I was down at the lower Magnolia basin last month, near the wildlife refuge, you know? And I put my canoe in and drifted out of the park and down to where the Colberts used to live. You know how Mr. Colbert died of leukemia, and his wife died of sadness about a month later? Not one of the Coltons, the Colberts."

"Right," I said. "Mr. Colbert looked just awful at the end. His lips, under his eyes—everything was kind of purple."

"Worst kind of cancer, cancer of the blood," he said. "Anyway, out one of those dirt roads the government put in there? All these big dump trucks came roaring through. Out in the middle of nowhere," he said. "Disappeared just as fast. Sort of across the river from Magnolia Gardens, you know, near that spot where you got married out on the river?"

"Don't remind me," I said. "What'd these trucks look like? Did you see any names on the machinery?" I asked.

"Looked like they'd been painted kinda camo," he said. "Dull and splotchy green and brown and beige. Mostly dump trucks painted over." I put the scissors down and combed through his hair.

"Like army trucks?" I said, disbelieving.

"Sorta," he said. "They're probably trying to build condos out there. Hey, the hair looks good. You're no good at keeping a husband, but you sure can cut hair." I slapped his head again.

"I have dirty words to describe people who mess with the wetlands," I said. "Swamps. And you know as well as I do, that's all there is out there. It's no place to build jack shit."

"They're changing this place, Girl," he said wistfully. "But you," he said, teasing, pointing at me, "You better worry about getting *your* derriere off the hook first," he said. "They find anything else out about Mac's poisoning?" He saw my face fall. "Don't worry, I'll vouch for you in court."

"Great," I muttered, brushing hair off his shoulders. "A guy who owns a gorilla near the swamps will verify that I'm sane and not a murderer." He handed me two twenties. "No," I said. I handed back one of them. "You don't have this to give me. You've got a big fat monkey to feed."

He kissed me on the cheek like a brother. I held my breath like a sister with a stinky brother, and he left. Later I found the other twenty sitting by the cash register.

IN WALKED MISS MURPHY, who wore her silver hair in a knot and sported a big mother-of-pearl cross around her neck. She had that old lady smell about her, of Kleenex and dust and White Shoulders perfume. She needed some honey color in her toilet-paper-white hair. But today, she wanted simply to talk about Trina and how we could possibly get a hurricane *and* oil pushing up to shore, according to the Weather Channel. Always in polyester black pants and a twin set, today she wore her jacket trimmed with fox fur, the type where the actual fox feet are imbedded in the fur. I guessed someday I'd understand why modern people wore dead animals' fur.

"I can't believe that Trina is gone," she said primly. She pulled off her jacket and handed it to me, then plopped into the chair by the basin. She clasped her little cloth purse in her lap. She never let me put the clutch on the desk where I worked. I washed her hair once a week, so I leaned her back in the black speckled basin and sprayed warm water over her pink scalp. Miss Murphy went on. "She was such a lady. She praised God. I just don't believe she did that."

She was referring to suicide. I wrapped the towel around her hair and we went to the cutting chair. I wouldn't cut much today, but I could sure create a better fifties look by flat pinning the hair, teasing it for a lift, using a thumbing technique for a simple elegant style.

Miss Murphy kept talking. "Though she had had a hard time of it all those years, grieving for that baby boy she lost. Imagine, having your husband lose a child that way. How would you ever forgive him?"

"I know what you mean, Miss Murphy," I said. What I was thinking was *What happened to your forgive-and-forget and turn-the-other-cheek stuff?* Also, what did she mean by 'lose a child that way?' I trimmed her hair at the bottom a little as she talked.

"Then the other boy, he ended up in Chiefland. I don't think she ever healed from all that. The Lord will heal your heart if you let him," she said, raising her eyebrows and pointing in the mirror before us.

"Yes, ma'am," I said, thinking maybe she was more superstitious than Grandma Happy. At least Grandma knew a broken heart sometimes couldn't be mended. I bit my tongue, smoothing styling gel into her hair, flat pinning it, and thumbing for a clean look.

"I'm glad she had that Randy Dilburn boy to sit with in church," she said. "They seemed close. They always shared a pew on Sundays."

"Randy Dilburn, the lawyer Randy Dilburn?" I asked, trying not to sound too interested.

Had Trina been robbing the cradle? She looked great for a woman of sixty, sure, but with Randy Dilburn, twenty years her junior? And why not? Older men with younger women was always on the big screen, *ad nauseum.*

"Yeah. I believe they attended some church and—what do you call those nature lovers—ecologicals? Yeah, ecological conferences together, too," she said.

"Really?" I said.

"Yeah. And they went on some African mission work, you probably already know." I knew about the mission work in Africa, vaguely, but I hadn't known it was Randy and Trina. She went on. "One time, they were gone six weeks helping a village in Kenya, I believe it was. Helping those poor people get some clean water." She was clutching her purse under the big cape I'd put on her. "See, water's scarce and they were building some way to catch and keep water for everybody. Some people don't even have clean water, did you know it?" she drawled.

I pictured Randy and Trina in a tent in the bush, getting it on, drinking Coca Cola and . . . I stopped myself. I respected anyone who put aside six weeks of their own pursuits to try to get people clean water.

"Randy's got some pretty hibiscus growing out in front of his yard," she said. "He's got quite the green thumb." I thought of having wanted some myself up at the nursery.

I put Miss Murphy under the dryer and started thinking about closing up shop. The water kept haunting me. I wondered how long we'd have clean water out in the swamps or in town or at the springs with the oil spill, the runoff pollution, and whatever else. How could anyone do that without some interference from the government? Unless no one knew. Since I didn't want Miss Murphy to get suspicious of my asking too many questions, I handed her a gossip magazine. She was such a gossip, she could run right to the wrong people about my enquiries. I walked outside to get a breath of sweet rainy air.

AFTER WORK, I sauntered across the bridge of the cove to hang out with Madonna and Laura. Now I was looking out the window at the gray Gulf of Mexico from the Hook Wreck. I thought about the Indians I came from, probably floating back and forth across from the Yucatan to these islands. The Gulf, a water vortex. A mere fissure in the earth between the two peninsulas. Those people, thousands of years ago, made their way over cross currents, white caps, and deep water.

"The uterine sea of our dreams haunted by the true dream," said Madonna, dreamily. She sat across from Laura and me as we all sipped drinks.

"Pretty esoteric for a high school dropout," Laura teased. "Who said it?"

"SJ Perse," Madonna said. "I was smart enough to quit school. What's your excuse?"

"Boarding school," Laura said. "I couldn't quit. At least, I didn't think I could."

"This drink is called White Cloud," Madonna said, eyeing me, talking to Laura. Madonna held up the whitish translucent drink she'd made and poured into martini glasses. "White crème de menthe and vodka."

"You were right—it goes directly to your elbows and knees," Laura said. "I hope nobody needs to drive anywhere tonight."

"Not me," we each said. We watched the white caps, the uterine sea of our dreams and sipped in silence.

"Was Jackson ever married?" I asked Laura.

"He's been in several committed relationships," Laura said, "but he tends to pick Super Professional women. You know, the ones who really marry their jobs."

"Hmm, maybe he wants that," I said. "It means he doesn't have to really commit."

"Oh, I don't think so," she said. "He's more conventional than you might think. They tend to leave him about the time he wants to get married. He just likes interesting, challenging women, I guess."

"Why would you introduce him to me?" I said. "I'm a homegirl hair stylist."

Laura and Madonna exchanged looks and rolled their eyes. "She's hopeless," Laura said. Madonna made us each another drink, and we toasted to finding the poisoner.

Finally, Madonna decided to get playful. She said, "So LaRue is going to get nekked with Randy Dilburn." We all snorted.

"Hardly," I said, reddening.

"Well, he is a babe," Laura said. "I wouldn't mind slipping between the sheets with the likes of him."

"You guys are ridiculous," I said. "I don't even know *how* to do this dating thing anymore. I don't think I ever did. Did any of you ever really go on a date? It was always more like, 'Wanna go to the Mounds Saturday? We'll hang out and party down!' "

"It's not about a date. It's about how to be with a guy. It's like a bicycle," Laura said.

"You never forget how. Or you never learn how, depending," I said.

"Or like eating a chocolate ice cream cone," Madonna said. "Come on, Panther. Give yourself over to pleasure once in a while. Bet he's great between the sheets. Ooo, he's got those pretty lips, and think of that tongue on a chocolate—"

"All right, you guys, knock it off!" I said.

"Tell me if he's got a fine ass, LaRue," Laura said.

"Laura!" I said.

"Oh, that's right," Madonna said. "Randy goes to church. He and LaRue don't do stuff like that. LaRue begat Daisy and Tay through . . . hmmm, what's it called? Immaculate Preconception."

We started laughing and hooting and slamming our hands on the table when the door to the outside creaked open. Then the sound of its closing echoed through the bar, and Fletch stood at the entrance. Madonna muttered to us. "Okay, girls, here I go with my pretend-you-like-him routine. He's a good tipper anyway." We all got up. Madonna slid behind the bar, Laura sat next to Fletch, and I headed out the door.

CHAPTER 25

THE NEXT MORNING, the Saturn puttered me out past Gulf Point and onto Wakulla Key to see Randy. I'd left Daisy and Taylor with Dad. The night before, I had left Laura and Madonna with Fletch, despite the fact that my knees and elbows did, in fact, wobble.

The grass by the school nearly vibrated green after the rain. Out on the peninsula, the Gulf effect kept the earth's surface slightly cooler than in the main residential part of the island.

The houses on the drive to Randy's sat low. Due to the dunes, higher land elevation, and the way these houses were situated by the channels, they tended to fend off the brunt of hurricanes. Pines, tall cabbage palms, a few spindly oaks. The airstrip ran parallel to the road, but private planes flew in only on weekends. The yards consisted of the stuff Grandma used for medicine and fragrances, like dollar weed, sea lavender, rosemary, and aloe yucca.

Randy lived in a small house about halfway down the peninsula. I pulled in behind his hybrid parked out by the road near his new hibiscus bushes. The boat was already launched in the canal.

The file that I took from his car was the same file I had seen at the real estate office. I had to return the ECOL file to Randy's car without his notice.

I got out of the car, threw the file into his, and went to the door and knocked. I had a slight headache. "No more White Clouds for you," I said aloud facing the door.

"Talking to the door?" Randy said behind me. I jumped. He snickered. "I was on the side deck and heard you drive up. Coffee? Inside." He smiled warmly, raising his cup. I nodded, worrying that he may have seen me put the file into his car, and followed him around to the deck that faced the Gulf, and then into the sliding glass doors. As flat as his house was, one story on an island, he had the million-dollar view of the water and beyond to the out islands. In the other direction, he had a huge glass window facing the strip where planes landed, mangroves beyond. And a view across the inlet back up towards the river near Magnolia Gardens.

"Great view," I said. "Views, that is."

"I see more than most," he said grimly from the kitchen. This is one intense guy, I thought. "Sugar, cream?"

"Don't need any more, thanks," I said, noticing he had only one chair in the living-dining room area. Maps of the islands were spread across the dining table almost like a heritage tablecloth.

"Waiting for the furniture truck, are we?" I said, plopping into the one chair.

"I like it clean," he said. But the house felt dusty, stuffy, and bacheloresque. He brought the coffee and stood near the dining table about four feet away.

"Thanks for your work with Tay," I said.

"He's smart and seems pretty grown up," Randy said. "I've enjoyed him. He appreciates the natural world. Doesn't want to see it destroyed."

"You . . . uh, it's hard raising kids," I said. "Being a single parent . . ." I drifted off. "Staying married is hard enough." One thing a person didn't do on a date was talk about past loves.

He picked up his binoculars and looked out to the Gulf. His broad shoulders, the lean torso and legs. I remembered this from high school days—all our make-out sessions when we'd sneak into his dad's church's fellowship hall.

"See anything interesting?" I asked from the one chair in the room.

"Too much sometimes," he sighed. I wondered if what they said about him was true—still in love with his wife.

"Miss Murphy just told me you and Trina Lutz sat in church together every Sunday," I said. He lowered his binoculars and looked at me blankly.

"She had a lot of loss in her life," he said, a wrinkle appearing between his eyes.

"You traveled together," I said, shifting in the chair.

"We worked together," he said. "Went to Africa—Ghana—got water for a village. The people there really appreciated just having clean water. We tried to help them find environmentally sound ways to vary their crops."

"You and Trina were friends or what?" I said.

"Does it make a difference?" he said, staring again into the binoculars.

"Guess not," I said. "Just wondering your thoughts on the suicide-murder argument." He didn't say anything. The chair wasn't very comfortable, so I wiggled out of it and slid onto the thick carpet.

"Look," I said, "my son was close to her. And now I've been accused of trying to poison Mac just after she died. My son's very upset about it all." He was still silent. "Do you know what she and Mac—what the relationship was?"

"Aren't the state detectives on this?" he said. "Aren't you dating some cop? Shouldn't you be asking *him* these questions?"

"I went to dinner with the cop, Randy," I said. Why should I have to defend myself? "I could go to jail. I'm just trying to get myself out of this. The local cops are totally corrupt, and the county? You know that. No, the guy I went to dinner with is helping with what he can. But he's busy with Florida's urban crime."

"You want information about Trina?" he said, walking toward the chair.

"Of course," I said, lying down on the thick carpet now, hands behind my head.

"She thought Fletch actually drowned her younger son," he blurted out. "It's why she gave the older boy up for adoption. Fletch is capable of extreme violence. He killed someone when he was young—about eighteen. But the county called it manslaughter. I don't think she—I think she blamed herself for not being a good mom. But I don't think she killed herself. I think she was shot."

A bolt of shock went through me. How specific he was, yet what he didn't know.

He stood up. "You have sunscreen?" he said, frowning. "You know how the sun gets in a boat on the water." He walked to a kitchen drawer and rummaged around until he pulled out a drugstore brand sunscreen with 50 SPF. He brought it over. "Let's go," he said, putting out a hand to help me up.

"Let me take a stop in the ladies' room, first, okay?" I said. He nodded and put the binoculars in the case. I dove into the bathroom. Maybe it wasn't a date. He seemed tense and unfriendly. I pulled ChapStick from my shirt pocket and realized the letter Madonna had snagged from Tay's pocket was still there. Some detective I was.

The letter said:

11/5

Dear Taylor,

I'd love to have you out to help me put in an herb garden! Thanks for the suggestion.

I can't do it this week. You know how you think some people don't understand your way of thinking that we have to preserve the natural world? How you don't know what to do sometimes? I am going through that. And I have to do something about it this week!

How about next weekend? I'll make your favorite, chili and carrot cake.

I have new camping gear for you, too.

Let me know Monday if you can garden next week!

Love,
Aunt Trina

My eyes welled. Tay hadn't managed to see Trina that week, I thought, leaning back against the wall. I flushed the toilet to make Randy think I'd used it. I sniffled a little. Trina was dead the day after she wrote the missive. The day after Tay got and read the note. He was still basically a kid. Had she been pulling him into her problems?

And Tay. He'd walked around for weeks with this knowledge and had told no one. No wonder he had been behaving in an edgy way, pulling away, hanging out with kids who were trying to escape.

I burst out of the bathroom after I crammed the note into my pocket. I raced to the boat to release some energy, some paranoia about my son's safety now, my own, Randy's weirdness.

We stepped down into the inboard/outboard, and Randy and I wordlessly untied the ropes from starboard and shoved off. He cranked the motor, and the water gurgled and left bubbles behind us, and we were off. The boat slipped through the sparkling gray water. The sun was rising slow and orange as late butterflies. A cloudless sky. I swore boating felt like a bird must feel during an effortless flight, almost weightless, with a dash of the exhilarating danger thrown in.

We cruised down the peninsula to the tip. The sand beach sat brilliant, almost too much white. I'd forgotten about this beach. Randy shocked me by continuing back towards the swamps, the opposite direction from the Gulf. He pulled the throttle, and we sped across the dark water towards the side of the old Indian mound. I'd not seen the mound from water since Grandma and I canoed down there decades ago. She had told me she knew panthers still lived around here. Randy stopped the boat and turned off the motor. Waves lapped gently along the sides of the boat.

"This is a bizarre way to get to the out islands," I kidded. "Do you see any unusual or dangerous animal life here?" I was thinking about the bears I'd heard from Matteo that lived around here.

Randy didn't say anything. He pulled out his binoculars and peered towards the mound. "Want to see unusual animal life?" he said. "We have to climb the mound, but this is what I brought you out here to see." We anchored and got our land legs, the waves bubbling around us, the waves hissing onshore. We climbed the steep mound full of shells and weeds and pottery shards until we reached a clearing, and then the top. We could see for what seemed like miles.

He handed me the binoculars and rolled up his sleeves and pointed as I looked through the binoculars. "See that tall palm? Look right past it and focus," he said.

Far into the swamps I saw movement. Large movement. Like dinosaurs. No—trucks. Slowly I began to hear faint grinding. Trucks were pulling up earth, dripping organic muck, and putting it on the shore. The camo machinery Matteo had mentioned. A couple sat on the top of a truck, the man with his arm around the woman. I zoomed in with the binoculars. Mary and Fletch. Sitting, watching from the top of his truck.

"So it's true," I said. No response. "How long has this—" I waved my arm around the swampy area with all the activity back upriver.

"The relationship or the machines?" he said. I let him tell me as he stood, thumbs on his hips. "Years. Let's say decades. How long have the machines been out there making a big mess? Couple of months, I'd say."

"What are they doing?" I said.

"I'm not sure. I got a file on the purchasers of the property—a group called ECOL. I've been suspicious of this group for a while. They keep it way below the radar, know what I mean?"

"But aren't they digging awfully close to Magnolia Gardens?" I said.

"Let's get down and head back to the boat," Randy said, helping me down the steep mound. "There was nothing in any media about the purchase. Laura can't seem to pull anything from them. She does have an appointment to see the power plant. Mac, Fletch, Bob Sturkey from the power plant, the widow Fielding are all on the paperwork. I can't find the file, though. I was sure I put it in the hybrid," he said.

"Oh, it'll probably turn up," I said, feeling queasy. We were back on flat land and sloshed into the salty, chilly Gulf and back into the boat.

"Just not sure what they're up to, but I know it's no good," he said, mysteriously. Then he changed his whole demeanor, smiling, reaching for his ice chest.

"I made you some special sandwiches," he said. "Grouper. I caught it myself, out too deep yesterday with this little boat. Figured I'd better go out before the fish had either eaten up the oil or were eaten up with oil. Well worth it." He pulled out sandwiches and a jug of water.

We sat and ate quietly. I tried not to think about lying on his chest, or what his whole body would feel like flat next to mine.

"Delicious," I said. "Thanks. Okay, you still haven't exactly told me anything I didn't know. I mean, I'd heard about this—both things. Seeing it is revolting, but . . ."

"What did you want to know?" He offered me half an orange, which I didn't take.

"Okay, what's ECOL about, exactly?" I said.

"Not sure," he said. "I think it has to do with this new development. This is a totally underground activity. They don't have permits to do this digging."

"What a surprise that is!" I said with sarcasm. "Where'd you get information about ECOL?"

"Trina gave me a file." He went on. "She was going to have me look into what they were doing. The machinery was rented from the military base, shipped in by water from an ex-military guy in the Panhandle. On paper, it looks like . . ." he shrugged, "it looks like they're legit, you know, just buying property and renting machinery to use at the power plant. They bring the machinery on a barge from the power plant, and unload up here where no one can see what's going on. It's been constant, though. They're working fast and furious, sunup to sundown."

"Okay, is Mary a part of ECOL?" I asked. "Mac and Fletch, I know, because of the real estate factor. But who else, I don't know. Sturkey has invested with them before. You know old Fielding was a crook. And how does this—what would Fletch and Mary be doing out here? Do you think they—do you think Trina knew and protested? And one of them . . ."

He eyed me knowingly. Then shrugged. "You'd be amazed what people will do," he said, starting up the boat to head back. "Safety or health or murder issues are not a problem for these people. Or it's a total disconnect. I honestly can't say what makes them behave the way they do. Greed. The unforgivable sin," he said grimly. Boy, was he ever raised Baptist.

BY THE TIME we returned the boat to the dock at Randy's house, the sun was at its apex and though windy, the day had warmed. I was dreaming of having a dark hot chocolate, or even a tea, but Randy offered neither. We sank into the quiet carpet of his living room floor, perpendicular to each other. It was good to be out of the wind, the sun, the cold, and the salt spray. We both relaxed for a few minutes in the quiet.

"Can I get something warm to drink?" I finally asked. His eyes had a faraway, almost absent look.

"One more thing. Got something else to show you," he said, rolling to his side. He patted his pocket for his car keys. Then he stood, focused on the sliding glass doors.

"Oh, my god, do we have to go?" I whined. "Okay, but—" I stood heavily, following his lead.

"I'll get you some hot chocolate at the Minit Mart. You cold?" he said, putting both his hands on my arms from behind, rubbing me warm.

About twenty minutes later, we arrived at the Magnolia Springs entrance with a stone and wooden toll booth. We paid the $4 entry fee and drove slowly into another world, one full of ancient cypress trees, red, orange, and brown now in the winter, with long strands of Spanish moss hanging from the limbs. In some ways, it felt like Middle Earth. The land lay below the road, and I'd sometimes seen it flood.

"This spring pumps out as much as one-fifty to six hundred thousand gallons of water per minute," Randy said as we parked and walked to the spring head. Only one lone couple was swimming. A small cluster of people waited for the boat ride we would take. It had been a few years since I'd visited the spring, and the familiar kabloosh of the one swimmer off the diving board returned me to childhood memories. Dad had brought carloads of us kids in the summer. School end-of-year picnics happened here. Great white egrets sat in the cypress across from us, and some moorhens screamed like monkeys from the near side of the river.

We walked onto the boat, and Randy intentionally sat us in the front. Far from the back-of-the-boat guide who gave talks as he steered over the river. "A few years ago, Trina and I were here with the Friends of the Magnolia, pulling hydrilla," he said as the boat took off and the motor drowned his voice from tourists' ears farther back. I knew hydrilla was a plant that signaled excess nitrates or pollution in a water body. Laura had covered the threatened status of the limpkin population in Florida. Their primary food source, apple snails, had vanished because of the hydrilla problem.

"You know, Magnolia Springs and its septic problems, I assume," Randy went on, paying the guide for our tickets.

"Well, sort of," I nodded. I pulled my jacket tight. Bright green eelgrass under the spring-fed river swayed as if in slow motion. A few bream swam past. Above water, the orange-leafed cypress trees made islands in the middle of the river. The Spanish moss draping them looked like ladies' stockings drying languid in the sun.

Randy turned to me, urgency in his eyes. "There were thirty-five thousand septic tanks pouring leakage into the watershed back then, including Magnolia Springs and up Leon County way. Because the underground lime rock passageways in north and north central Florida are so interconnected, the dirty water—all water—seeps through the surface and enters the system. Once it flows down here, the pressure is high. So the pressure from the water pushes that dirty water back up into the spring, right?" he said as the boat backed out of its parking spot and turned to head south down the river.

He continued, pointing to the water. "Hydrilla is like an uncontrollable monster. You couldn't stop it when the Friends were trying to get rid of it. The stuff grows an inch a day, the water was that dirty with nitrates. And it was as if the water was fertilized, there were so many nitrates."

I nodded. He pointed across the river, no longer looking at me. He was staring at the other side of the river from the boat. I felt like a kid he was teaching at.

"We eventually had to start mowing the spring."

"*Mowing* the spring?"

"We mowed the spring," he repeated. "It was that bad. The hydrilla had taken over and the boats couldn't even get through."

"To add to that, there's a *black* bacteria growing on the back side of the spring now," Randy said, pointing towards the side of the river where the new secret neighborhoods would be located. Even as we floated down the river, the swamplands were being dug, platted, and dug deeper for septic tanks.

I said nothing. I had no idea what all that meant.

"People get sick from it," he said. He nearly spit it out the way I heard his father could spit out a sermon. For a minute, I was repulsed by his anger, but he meant well. He seemed to carry the weight of the Gulf and the rivers on his shoulders.

I wanted to put a name to it to have it make sense. "What's the name of this bacteria?"

"*Lyngbya majuscule,* a cyanobacterium. Seems to be increasing in frequency in blooms across the planet these days. It seems to attack humans with acute skin lesions and respiratory and eye problems. Toxic. It affects the ecological health of marine reptiles, too." He sounded like a robot science teacher from the future.

"So." I didn't know what to ask next. "So who let that happen?" I asked. "It doesn't appear out of nowhere."

"It kind of does, because it's underground. You know we're linked by sinkholes, right?" I thought of the many places where I'd swung from ropes into the deep sinkholes that filled with the underground aquifer water east, west, every which way in the county.

"Yeah, okay, the big system below the surface, water running towards the Gulf."

"Everything gets in it if the ground doesn't perk it," he said. I wished he'd face me. His legs were still so hot, his shoulders broad, his face square and tan.

"So in the best of situations, the water, even say dirty water, gets filtered by the earth. Then the water you get when it hits aquifer is clear, clean. But when you only have a foot of soil before you hit the aquifer, the water doesn't clean up. It doesn't have enough earth to filter it well."

"Okay," I said, shifting in my seat. A couple of moorhens screamed their monkey scream, which echoed through the waterway. An alligator slid off a log to the water so that only its eyes floated on the surface. The tourists ran to the side of the boat and started oh'ing and ah'ing. "So, like Magnolia Gardens, right? How does that fit the septic problem?"

"Old septic tanks leak. Those folks don't have money to repair them. And so where do you think that nitrous-filled crap goes? One to three feet below? The aquifer."

"Ew, shit," I said.

"Exactly," he nodded. "Nothing wrong with it in nature, but in such concentrations, it's poisonous. Add to that the street waste—gas, oil, city soot that all washes off the roads and into water, holding ponds, what have you, and gets into the aquifer. Worldwide, this toxic combo is being linked to cancer."

"Yuk," I said, depressed, looking at the ancient cypress trees with Spanish moss, the great blue heron lifting off and flying to a higher branch, the female anhinga with her black and silver wings, her fluff of a brown neck like a stole this time of year.

"So why are they allowed to keep creating these places, people like ECOL?" I said.

"You know the county. They've been passing money hand to hand under the table for as long as the county has existed."

"Starting with the senator," I said. We all knew Fielding had planned the first set of condos on the Island against all kinds of protest, from crabbers to shop owners. But Mac came in from out of town and quickly got permitted and contracted and the first high rise on the island popped up.

And the problem was everywhere and involved all of us, I thought. Sure, it was big business, it was the county commission, the state legislature. Fresh water bodies all over Florida. But it was as simple and unsexy as poop and pee, too. Ours. All of ours. In our waters now.

"Men should all pee outside," I said suddenly. I sounded like Madonna, I knew, but it was true. In rural settings, where's the harm in that?

Randy laughed despite himself. "How about I pee over the side of the boat right now?" He leaned as if to do just that, saw my shocked expression and sat down, shaking his head and laughing still.

The wind was picking up across the river, making ripples on the water and pushing the boat back down the river towards the Gulf as the tour guide talked about Tarzan, and how the movies were sometimes filmed on this river.

I imagined how much warmer Randy's house would be. I conjured up the idea of hot chocolate with marshmallows on top as I pulled my jacket tighter. I thought of those graves of people who'd died of different kinds of cancer.

"It Never Rains in Southern California" went through my head. Randy and I had listened to that as teenagers. A soppy sentimental song. We'd driven around the graveyard drunk, singing at the top of our lungs. Then we'd made out on the old Mr. Field's grave until we'd heard an oyster boat across the bay and realized it was just before dawn and the fishermen were out. We'd stayed up all night, drinking, singing, and getting hot and bothered.

Now, the tour guide cranked the boat up. We headed back up to the springhead as the sun was setting, red and fiery and glorious as our young relationship had been. As we reached the car, we said nothing much, but held hands briefly, walking to the car in the chilly air.

RANDY ZIPPED UP HIS JACKET as we headed for his sliding glass door. We hadn't spoken since the pee conversation and his countenance was back to sobriety.

A few crazy mullet were jumping in the Gulf beyond Randy's deck. People were as mysterious as the fish that flew into the air for no apparent reason. What did we humans know about the animal world? We hadn't even learned where to pee and poop safely.

Randy held his hand out to pull me into the house, but I refused. For just a moment, I wanted to breathe in the briny scent of Gulf, to watch the mullet do their mystery dance in the air, navigating between water and air in a way we humans weren't designed to do. Randy's cheeks were flushed red, and I could smell the scent of his cologne. Something intangibly Eastern, like frankincense. It was as cedary and wise-man and biblical as he did not want to be. Our deep past was a comfort, but our nearer past so fractured, so fragile.

I began shivering and just wanted to warm up and welcomed heading into the warm but sparse house. Exhaustion pulled all the way to my bones, but in a good, relaxed way.

Randy heated up some water for herbal tea while I wandered around the house. No furniture in any room, a mattress on the floor of his bedroom, a laptop beside it, with papers all over the floor in piles. There was one other piece of furniture—a desk with fat law books where he did his freelance work.

In the second bedroom, he had carpeting and a bookcase. I lay down on the carpet and began to study his books, picking up one called *A Land So Strange* about the explorer Cabeza de Vaca from Spain. Shipwrecked in Mexico, he and the remaining sailors traveled through the Gulf region learning survival skills in the wild place. He passed right through what later became our town, but was then a fort. He went back to Spain changed, saying conquering others wasn't the answer.

Next thing I knew, Randy was shaking me awake by the shoulder, holding a glass of wine and an open bottle in front of me.

"I changed my mind," he said. "I let you sleep through tea, then decided to pull out a bottle of this. Hope you don't mind. I've got a stash of pinots from California." He headed to the kitchen to get his glass.

"I thought you'd never ask," I grinned when he returned. He sat cross-legged across from me. It felt good to know that Tay and Daisy were okay, freewheeling for a change. After a glass each, we were remembering when . . . school dances both of us sat as wallflowers.

"I'd have asked you, but you were so intimidating!" Randy said, his eyes going wide.

"I was terrified," I said. "No guy would ask me to dance, tall as I was. You chicken," I said, kicking him in the leg and laughing. We'd never have gotten this playful without the wine.

We remembered the time a brawl broke out at a pep rally just before a big basketball game between the future oystermen and the future crabbers. "Remember how ole Red Bird thought he could get into the middle of it and break it up?" I said.

"He was so old, they tossed him aside like a set of tongs," Randy laughed. His face had begun to relax and flush.

He lay across from me, and his face softened. He asked, "What year was it that the hurricane drove all but four residents off the island?" I shrugged. He went on. "Those old coots stuck it out while the hurricane flooded Main Street. I don't know whether to salute them or walk a mile around folks like that."

"Yeah, how about the year school closed down for a week when that tourist lady was found dead in the water face down," I said, looking for the bottle.

"You mean that woman who'd gotten so drunk she'd tried to walk the sea wall on the dock street and fell into the Intracoastal water?" Randy added.

"Crazy times," I said, pouring us both another glass.

Randy leaned in, toasting to those days.

We polished off the next glass, and so began the talk about how BP thought it could change CEOs and make us believe that everything would get back to normal. How the earth was out of balance.

I said, "The Native Americans—not just Granny, I read this somewhere—say that the earth has a crack in it, deep inside. Because we're taking so much from her and not giving back. Sounds corny, the "her" stuff, the crack in the middle, but who knows?"

"I don't think it's corny, LaRue," he said. "And I think you don't give enough credence to your grandmother, and you worry too much about Tay." His eyes showed sympathy and concern, even if his words felt a tad preachy. "Know what Tay says about you?" He emptied his glass, set it on the ledge of the bookshelf and leaned his back against the wall.

"Do I *want* to?" I said, staring into my empty wine glass, and setting it down next to his.

"He thinks you're a cool mom," he said. "He knows how hard you work for him and Daisy."

I looked at him. Warmth spread over me. My son did think I mattered. Randy's lips were tinted dark red from the wine. The day was waning, and outside a purple-blue resolve had taken over the sky. The sun had set, but twilight wasn't yet radiating its absolute purple blue. I crouched on my hands and leaned over and placed my lips on his. Peaches just picked off the tree in August, I thought. Or pumpkin pie in late fall. He pulled me towards him and then on top of him.

CHAPTER 26

I WOKE UP WITH A START at 3 a.m. half asleep, and rose in my nightgown to reach the bedroom chair, grabbing the blouse I'd taken off before I'd crashed into bed. The smell—it was haunting me. I had driven home before I got myself or Randy into a drowning-in-kisses problem. I had been exhausted. Boat riding wore me out—wind, sun, salt water, the push back of boat—they all take their toll. I took in a deep whiff of the shirt.

Oh, my god, I thought, *that* was it—the shirt smelled of that distinctive deodorant. Kind of sharp pine, but softened by something else. The scent of Randy. The same smell I caught on the boat the night Madonna and I had found the knife and blood. The tall, thin shadow of a man searching. I'd blocked it before now—Randy and the way he moved his arms, the way he stood on a boat. He was the one. But why? But a lot of people wore deodorant or cologne, and not enough fishermen, if you asked me. Still, I knew in my bones the man on Mac's boat had been Randy.

What had I done with the photos we took from the boat that night?

Instinctively I went to the kids' bedrooms first. Daisy's bed was full of stuffed animals, but otherwise empty, of course. She'd probably twisted her grandfather's arm to let her stay up late and watch bad TV. She had most likely drifted off only a couple of hours before, which meant a cranky Sunday for her. Taylor slept quietly in his bed, the moon milking his face sweet, light, and angelic, his long-jawed, Indian seriousness.

Then I scrounged around my bedside table and found the photos—Trina's son! Had Fletch murdered that child? We had clear evidence of a possible murder on the boat far more recently. But as Jackson would say, the court didn't know I'd gotten it through inadmissible evidence, and what did it prove anyway? Too bad Madonna and I had taken things off the boat without a warrant. Sleep had fled me, but I flung myself back into bed anyway.

And then there was Preston Edwards, the funeral parlor guy who had reason to kill. His mom had amassed a small fortune, probably, being a smart accountant. Maybe it had nothing to do with ECOL at all, or couples who couldn't be couples until certain spouses were out of the way. Or with Mexican mistrials. But what was Randy looking for on that boat?

I was glad I had taken Monday off. I had a trip to make to a funeral home in Wellborn to see a certain Preston Edwards. Early Monday morning, I'd catch the guy off guard.

"Mom," I heard. "Hey, Mom." I woke up Sunday morning to Taylor looking down at me frowning. Outside, it was full daylight. "We're supposed to have lunch at the pit, remember? It's eleven already."

I sprang up. Taylor began practicing tai chi in the living room. Daisy was already out at the pit expecting us any minute. Tay's slender body suddenly looked vulnerable. He'd always been short until ninth grade when he zoomed up, taller than most kids in school. Suddenly, he'd become extremely thin, tall, and fit.

"Tay," I said. "I'm so proud of you." He stopped mid-pose, and his face lit up.

"You are?" he said. The surprise in his voice stabbed at me.

"Of course," I said. "I know school is hard for you. I know the teachers confiscated your knife. And I know you're not doing your schoolwork."

"Mom, school is so fucking stupid," he said. "I'm so bored! You don't know how stupid kids act. Or how teachers make you just practice the same stuff over and over. I took my knife—I'm just trying to protect us. Weird stuff's happened, and I want to be prepared."

"I know," I said. "I understand." He came and plopped down beside me. I put an arm around him. Maybe I had a laissez-faire attitude with my kids, but who's their ally in this world if not mom? I understood in a very specific way why my son disobeyed the school rules.

"You've been in such a bad mood lately," he said.

"So have you," I said.

"Yeah," he said, sighing. He draped his arm awkwardly around me. We sat watching the sun strike like liquid metal off the Gulf.

IT WAS RAINING AGAIN. Tay and I were headed in my car out to the pit. This time the winter brought a misting. The temperatures were getting more warm and humid by the minute. Tay wore headphones, listening to his hip hop standards. He wanted me to hear it too on the radio. Oh, joy, I thought, turning the AC on low to chase out the damp. But I kept my mouth shut. Some hip hop, I was all about it, as Tay would say. And some needed incineration. But I would keep these strong opinions to myself.

The swamp brush along the sides of the state road had a burnished look, an abstract of browns and beiges to match the grayish white of sky.

"'Zat Great Happy?" Tay said, pulling his ear buds out. That's what he called his great-grandmother. He pointed in the distance along the side of the road. A lone and tiny swath of blurry but bright turquoise and pink moved along slowly.

"What the hell?" I said. There she was, Grandma Happy, carrying what appeared to be a big blue bucket in one hand and old Bank of America umbrella in the other, wearing her pink overshirt and her long turquoise skirt with black rickrack. The billowy skirt reminded me of the skirts of jellyfish floating. I pulled the car up beside her.

"Well, damnation," she said. "It's about time I got some help." Tay stepped out and picked up the bucket and heaved it sloshing into the front seat.

"Gosh, this is heavy," he said. Then he helped Grandma shut the umbrella. He situated her in the back seat.

"*Water?*" I said staring into the bucket. I knew better, but sometimes she needled me.

"Damn right, water," she said, breathing heavily. "Poison in the drinking water from the faucet. It ain't good. It's killing water."

"Grandma, where'd you get this water?" I said. Tay shut her back car door and rode shotgun.

She looked at me and tilted her head. "At a spring. At my special place." She looked away and frowned as if I'd asked her when her last bowel movement had taken place.

"But where?" I said. Tay sighed. She took a bit to catch her breath.

"Oh, I got a place," she said, vaguely. She would never tell me all the elements she put in her potions either.

"Why didn't you get Dad to take you?" I said. "You'll get sick walking out here like this."

"Let's go," Tay whispered.

Grandma replied, "Your father got enough to do. Got Daisy while you're off gallivanting with some man. She can't be drinking that poison water." Grandma pointed a slightly crooked finger out the window, south. "Them people down the road, they got the swamp water all turned upside down." How could she know about this?

"What people?" I said, pulling the car back onto the road. No one came or went on the rural road cut through the swamps.

"White people. Make a mess of everything. Can't trust a one of them," she said.

"Grandma, I'm white," I said.

"You ain't. Stop talking like a white person," she scolded. "You don't know what you're talking about, young damn know-it-all." She continued to slow her breath down. "It's time you learned to speak Seminole. And get your son learning it, too." Tay was smiling next to me, silent. She stared out the window at the sky. "Going to go to tornado winds in the next hour or so."

"Grandma, we've never had a tornado here," I argued. A small group of black skimmers sailed overhead with their akak, ak akak sounds.

"You watch, smart tart," she said. I watched the skimmers' colors, like distinguished gentlemen in tuxedos. Long red noses and long red stockings to match. A colony must live nearby on the river shallows or in an estuary in the river. Their habitats were endangered because of coastal development.

Taylor was absorbing everything Grandma said. So when we got to the pit, he offered to help her over to the trailer with her bucket of water. Grandma Happy told him she had a special concoction that he could use to make loud explosive noises.

"I'm not so sure that's a great idea," I called out behind them as they walked to her trailer. I stood at the small pond between the house and pond, watching them ignore me.

"You mind your business," Grandma said, not looking back. "This boy won't hurt nothing unless he has to." Tay turned around and waved, grinning, the water in the bucket sloshing.

"Nothing at school, Tay. Hear me?" I said. Just then Daisy raced outside and almost knocked me into the tiny pond between Dad's and Grandma's with her hug. Grandma and Taylor saw the moment as their opportunity to escape further scrutiny. Daisy was already saying her mantra of "There's nothing to eat in the house."

"Let's see what we can find for lunch," I said as we opened the screechy screen door and entered. I heard a mourning dove starting up outside.

Dad gave me a long hug and said, "I tried to stop your grandmother, but you know you can't stop her."

"I know, Dad," I said. "You doing okay?" The TV was on low.

"Good as I can," he said. "Better than the alternative. By the way, your friend Madonna called here. Something about a Tiffany?"

"Right," I said. "But first, what've you got to eat?" I went to the refrigerator and grabbed the butternut squash and spinach and turned on the oven. Then I pulled out some cheese and started a pot of water on the stove.

When lunch was just about ready, I heard some *pow* explosions next door.

"Dad, check on them, will you?" I said. He nodded and headed over to Grandma Happy's. A couple of minutes later, Taylor and Grandma followed Dad. All of them piled into the cabin talking about how windy it had gotten. Taylor washed up, and he and Daisy set the table. Grandma watched the Miami Dolphins heaping onto the New York Jets.

We were just sitting down to eat when Dad looked at the TV and whistled. "What do you know. Big tornado just off the west coast of Florida." Grandma chuckled and sat at the table, nibbling at her food.

"Is it headed this way?" I said.

"Naw, gonna hit just east of here near the Wassacoochee River." You could hear the sudden gusts that precede a big windstorm outdoors. As I looked out the window, pines bent deeply towards the pond water. "Ain't gonna say I told you," Grandma said. The kids ate fast and heartily and then ran outside, their arms lifted, twirling around, open to the sky. I demanded they come back inside, that they could get hit by branches and who knew what. Reluctantly, they trudged upstairs to watch a movie.

Happy returned to her football game. Dad settled, stretching out on the sofa to pretend to watch, but really to catch a nap. I tiptoed upstairs to my old bedroom, which hadn't changed much. The same late-seventies bedspread with red poppy curtains to match. I picked up the landline and called Madonna. I told her about the wind at the pit.

"Really?" she said. "I want to come out and play in it. It's nothing but gray over on the Gulf. Lots of sloshing water, and the birds have disappeared."

"I wouldn't want to be where you are on a Sunday this quiet with a tornado on the Gulf. This is when most of the restaurants start thinking about closing up for the day."

"Yeah, right," she said. "Speaking of days, Tiffany came in last night. We talked for a long time. She was in the juice last night. Told me she'd been in Juvie for a while. Wanna know why?"

"Juvie? Juvenile detention? I'm all ears," I said.

"Forging prescriptions for scheduled drugs," she said.

"How convenient," I said. "I knew she was shifty. I've had a weird sense about her. And after hearing that she did tricks, I'm so not surprised."

"She also told me she feels for Fletch." I could hear her opening and shutting the freezer at work. Someone had come in ordering drinks.

"Fletch? She hasn't got a clue, does she?" I said. "Hey, by the way, do you remember any pine scent, some exotic smell on the boat? That night we sneaked on? And someone came onto the boat?"

"God, LaRue," she said. "I was terrified. No. Why?"

"Never mind. Just a stray hunch," I said. I didn't want her to know I thought Randy was on the boat. I was afraid she'd discourage me from seeing him again.

"Hey, how was your big date?" she asked.

"The date was okay," I said carefully. "It . . . man, the boy can kiss."

She laughed. "Kiss where?" I knew the road she was headed onto. "On the study floor."

"Aw, Panther kisses and don't tell," she teased. "Anyway, what smells like pine, exotic pine?"

"I don't know. I was just wondering," I said. I couldn't face telling her my silly hunches. "Anything from OV?"

"I didn't see our witness, the garbage man OV, last night," she said. "Okay,

I'm thinking about closing up. There's no one here but one tourist couple who just came in to get ice."

I heard the door slam and the kids arguing in the room next to me, the room Taylor used. I could hear, "You're cheating." They must be playing Clue, I figured. Soon, they settled in and started murmuring. I quietly picked up the landline again and called Laura.

"How was your night?" she said, quietly.

"Oh, interesting. I don't think he's a candy man, maybe. You want it, but that one bite is plenty." I hadn't known I felt that way until I said it.

"One bite, huh?" she said. I heard in her voice the hope that I'd get more interested in Jackson.

"Or maybe a second bite. His lips are mighty peachy. So what's up with you?"

"Peachy, huh?" she said. "All I did was hang out with Madonna at the bar. But I did find out some interesting stuff there."

She told me she called the Indian doctor. "He's the third they call if nobody else is available to do a weekend coroner's report. He never got a call. I didn't tell him anything either. I asked as a reporter. He even checked the answering service to be sure. Nada. In fact, he never gets called much, because he's got a bad habit of always finding mistakes the Magnolia County coroner's office doesn't, he claims. When he brings it up, he says they just get quiet. He says he feels a strange hostility there. You know the don't-trust-an-outsider thing."

"Hmm." I said. "Sounds like I need to pay that funeral parlor guy a visit again. I think I let him chase me off too quickly."

"Be careful," she said. "Someone's calling me anonymously and telling me to mind my own business then hanging up. They just say 'mind your own business' and hang up. I've tried to trace it, but it comes from payphones. None here in St. Annes."

"Oh, god, yuk. We're being watched. Laura, get off the case. I don't want you or Madonna . . . You two just forget this case, okay?"

"Bullshit," Laura said. "You must take us for a couple of pussies." I had to laugh.

CHAPTER 27

I DROVE OUT IN THE FOG and dripping rain to Kiss-Me-Quick, an island in the St. Annes cluster of peopled islands. It was swollen with live oaks and moss dripping from the trees. Too bad it also held the most trailers per square inch of all the islands, and the highest percentage of broken-down cars, on or off blocks, in the southern U.S.

Mary and Cooter's mobile home rested on the back side of the tiny island by the cove, in a formerly-saturated-blue now faded-by-sun single-wide. Not particularly poetic. It reminded me of where I could end up living divorced with two kids.

I banged on the front door, and Mary opened it. She wore a faded pink bathrobe spotted with stains. Her hair looked worse than a pelican's roost. She held what looked like a vodka and V-8 juice. Not that I looked so much better in my faded U2 sweatshirt.

"Oh, hello, LaRue," she said, backing up, taking a sip. "Come on in. I was just having a little breakfast." She clinked the ice in her glass and led me to the table next to the kitchen. Sitting down at the small table, I saw no food. But the Smirnoff bottle sat on the linoleum countertop. She reached into the refrigerator and pulled out a wilted celery stalk and stabbed it into the glass. "Healthy," she said, holding up the glass. "Want one?" I shook my head no. She shrugged and sat down hard. A bottle of anti-anxiety medication stood next to her salt and pepper shakers, a ceramic pig couple dressed in fishing attire.

"Mary, I know you've been seeing Fletch for years," I said. She sat up and opened her mouth to speak, but I went on. "It's not my business. I understand how marriages aren't always so fulfilling," I said, rolling my eyes. "Believe me, I'm no one to judge that. I'm wondering what you know about Fletch and ECOL?"

"ECOL?" she said. She stared blankly at the fishing pig couple on the table. She wasn't bluffing. Sometimes our hometown girls often never imagined they might have to pay attention, learn things, go anywhere. I'd watched my own generation over time not giving directions to tourists, simply because they didn't even know or care to know what was up the road or down the street.

"I know you and Fletch are working out on the east side of the Magnolia River on some kind of project," I said. She sat up straighter. Her face hardened.

"It's just a landfill thing," she said.

"Landfill?" I said, leaning back in. Her deliberate ignorance infuriated me.

"You know, just putting some extra garbage—just getting rid of some—

clearing some stuff."

"What stuff?" I said. "What I'm getting at is that I know Mac is in on the land purchase, too. Somebody tried to kill Mac. Someone's conveniently trying to pin the poisoning on me. And I could go to jail."

"There are worst places," she said, staring at the ceramic fishing pigs.

"I'm serious, Mary. Did somebody try to kill Mac because of ECOL? I'm afraid someone is going to try to kill him again. And I don't want to go to jail."

"I don't know, LaRue," Mary said. She pulled out a cigarette and lit it with a plastic lighter.

"Trina was murdered," I said. Mary looked at me and went pale.

"What makes you think that?" she said, looking out the window, then at a fingernail, nervously at me, then chewing on the nail. She downed the rest of her drink.

"Look, Mary," I said. "You can talk or not talk. But I think you know more than you're saying."

"All I know is that the landfill development is a big secret. Trina knew about it, and something about it upset her. She threatened Fletch and I think maybe Mac, and she warned them that she'd let it out that they were—that something was going on. Some pollution thing." She threw up her hands in disgust. "You know how those Magnolia Gardens people just keep complaining about their roads and all that. Trina said this new thing would affect them. This new development. And—" She got up and plinked more ice into the glass, pouring half the tumbler with vodka. I sat in the chair at the table not daring to take my eyes off her.

"Where were you the weekend Fletch and Mac were deep-sea fishing, the weekend that Trina was murdered?" I pushed.

She turned around, her face red, swollen, angry.

"You're ruining everything, you and your hippie son and that spoiled rotten daughter. You had a good thing with that man, and then he left you 'cause you're TooTall Panther. He found himself a young thing. A pretty blonde chick." She could see that she was hitting where it hurt. I sat stunned. I couldn't begin to ask her what kind of knife she used to stab her husband with. She pointed at me. "You look here," she said, "I finally got what I need, and now you're trying to ruin it all." She was shouting and spitting as she spoke. "You just don't want anybody else to be happy, 'cause you ain't happy." She pointed at me and then at the floor, the way drunk people sometimes do, just staring at something only they see. She continued. I thought about how the guys at the pep rally had pummeled each other that day. I clenched my fists and stood up. She stood by the refrigerator, glass in one hand, waving the other.

"Trina was an unhappy bitch too. And tried to make everybody feel guilty about everything. All she wanted was like all liberals want, to get our taxes raised so some people who complain all the time could get roads in and their water fixed. The world's not perfect, you know. I'm not taking this shit anymore. Out!" She pointed her finger to the door.

Now I was mad enough to slap some sense into her. She opened the door and pointed again. "Get out," she screamed as I stomped out like a giant, fe fi fo fum. Mary ranted on. "Just get out. Stop nosing around in business that ain't yours, you hear me?"

I WAS DRIVING TOO FAST back towards town. But I figured when I got mad, I should use the adrenaline. I pulled up at the real estate office and bolted to the door. It was locked. I stood, breathing hard, fuming. I stormed down our Main Street of dusty old buildings towards Tiffany's apartment across the street from mine, taking two stairs at a time. I banged on the door. Nothing. Banged again, harder, faster, longer. Feet stumbled to the door.

"Oh, hi, LaRue," Tiffany blinked. "What's wrong?" Her living room looked as empty as a small warehouse, had one easy chair with a TV stacked on cinderblocks. The dining room contained a circular table with one washed-out orange vinyl chair and one metal chair. She stood in her sexy little pajamas, blue velvet tank top and belly-showing bottoms.

I pulled out the now worn and crinkled fax of the coroner's report. I pointed at the signature.

"That's your handwriting," I said. "Why?"

She frowned and looked defensive. "Why what?"

"Why did you risk your record to go back to forging a doctor's name? And this isn't prescriptions. This is *lying* about someone's *death*." She was backing up, then stopped.

"Mac told me I wouldn't get in trouble. Mac said—" She took another step back, away from me.

"Mac put you up to this."

"He said it wasn't a big deal, LaRue," she said, shrugging. "He said I was just doing the doctor on call a favor." As she said it, she turned her head aside, backed away another step, and I took one towards her. She stepped back again, and said, "I didn't have anything to do with Trina. I don't know what you mean about lying." Tiffany was lying. Lying and shrugging her shoulders, her arms hanging, palms facing me. I had that maternal radar for lying young people. I'd done it myself in my youth.

"So you know she was murdered."

"No, I just know you came in here and said she was," she said, her brow wrinkling. She stepped back again and looked to the doorway.

"And it didn't occur to you that maybe there was a connection between his asking you, someone who's not authorized to sign a death certificate, to sign it? That it was illegal? That he might be covering something up? He asked you to put your neck on the line for him." I was shouting. I was furious at women who'd risked their own sense of self, women like the woman I had been with my ex.

"I don't know," she said. "He's my boss. I did what he asked. I'm just trying to do my job!" Now she was yelling.

"You've trusted the wrong people, Tiffany," I said, lowering the fax. "Do you know who poisoned Mac?" I said.

She shook her head, still not looking at me. "I don't understand why you're asking me any of this." She sounded smug all of a sudden.

"Do you know about ECOL?"

"It's a group of people who purchase property for disposal purposes," she said. "What's the big deal?" She tucked her leg under her and plopped into her chair.

"The big deal is they're willing to kill people, Tiffany," I said. I paced as she sat.

"I don't believe it," she said, folding her arms. "Mac is the nicest man I've ever met. He's done a lot to help me out. You, too. You should be grateful."

"Right," I said. "Right." I left and slammed the door behind me. The whole building shook. How had it withstood all those hurricanes, I wondered.

"LOOK, COULD YOU JUST STAY OUT OF IT for a couple of days? I think we're headed somewhere."

"Jackson, ever the cautious cop," I growled into the cell phone. I was driving towards Wellborn, now passing the turnoff to the mound road, wooded wetlands where Indians used to throw their garbage. Only with no oil products like plastic bags. Now I cut through the expanse of wetland, the bayous most people never see. The tin-roof shacks and the beat-up mobile homes along the way. A bald eagle soared way overhead. It was noon and gorgeous, and I was dangerously hungry.

"LaRue," Jackson sounded impatient. He slowed down his speech. "Now that I've got the match for blood, I think I can subpoena for an autopsy. In a court of law, we need evidence. You do have Tiffany's signature, yes. And what the garbage collector thinks he saw? What you think you saw through binoculars?" Jackson said.

"I didn't think I saw, I saw!" I shouted into the cell phone.

What was Randy really up to, and what had he been up to with Trina? Why was Mary in such denial? What was making my son so angry he'd explode things and obsess about karate chops and try to scare even me in the dark? And Tiffany—she'd bought into the whole men-with-money-can-save-you idea.

"Why would anyone want to destroy this?" I said, my voice starting to shake. "Why would they want to upturn the cabbage palms, the old Indian mounds?" I said, distraught. "They're going to destroy everything that was beautiful about this place."

"LaRue—"

"None of this answers who's trying to kill Mac," I said. "It's not going to be easy to get me off the hook, Jackson."

"Wow, who woke up next to the bear?" he said.

"Whatever, Jackson," I said.

"LaRue, I'm trying to keep you from getting into deeper water. You're messing with people who will hide a cause of death at the very least. Murder probably. If someone's trying to kill Mac, they will try again. Maybe again when others are around so that the killer will be hidden in a crowd of people. And they wouldn't think twice about killing you, too, or trying to peg you again. You're mad as a nest of wasps, and this isn't the time to use your analytical skills."

"Shut up," I said, as I hit the steering wheel. I rolled down the windows.

He didn't. "And don't think I don't know about the phone calls someone's making to Laura, and next it will be Madonna. You don't want your friends in danger, do you? Lay low, I'm telling you."

I said nothing. I was more determined than ever to not lay low.

"Hey, I'm looking forward to seeing you this weekend, right?" Jackson said hopefully. I was passing the pit now, regretting so many things. Ever marrying, not knowing a good guy from a bad one. Jackson was a great guy. That fell on me like a pile of lime rock. He was putting up with my saying "Shut up."

"What EVER!" I sounded like Taylor. I didn't want to. "After this talk with Trina's son, I will stop. I promise."

I turned off the cell and threw it into the passenger's seat.

Up ahead I saw again the bright tiny turquoise vision of Grandma Happy on the side of the road. She was stooped over picking something. Thistle milk, she had said, was good for your skin. Maybe she was collecting a winter skin potion. Even though they'd pierce you in a second with their prickly thorns, the flower looked like a burst of purple prism.

I couldn't not pull over.

"Grandma, what are you doing?" I asked, breathing fast.

She turned around slowly, her turquoise and orange beads as always layered waterfall-like down her slender neck. A thin tidy bun on her head, mostly salt with some pepper. Gleaming in the sunlight. Even though I was mad and disappointed and afraid, I had to admit, she was a beautiful old lady.

"You in trouble," she said, pointing a bony finger at me through the passenger side window.

"Oh, no, not that again, Grandma," I said. "What are you doing out here on the road? I don't want you to get run over."

"You ain't got the sense I reared you with," she said stepping slowly towards the car. "You think I'm gonna walk out into the road? Goddang it—"

"Can I give you a ride back?" I said, not wanting to hear her disappointment in me. She was holding a bag of something.

She looked around. "No. I got things to do. Just picked this. Good for a stomach ache. Tastes like lemonade, good for a cold, too. Used to just grow in the Everglades, but it's warming up here. I found a patch in a sunny spot. You be careful or there's gonna be more killing." A chill went down to my toes. She opened the car door to climb in.

"Grandma, I'm just going out to Wellborn to talk to someone. I'll be back this afternoon," I said.

She pointed her bony, arthritic finger at me again. "Call Taylor on that moving phone. Tell him to come out this afternoon. I got some things for him." I knew not to contradict her.

"Okay. You sure you don't want a ride back? What are you growing this winter, anyway?"

"Something." She said it firmly and then opened the car door and sat slowly down. This calmed me somehow. "You stop at my place," she commanded. "You need to drink some chamomile and kava tea before you go to town. Mixed in with a little passionflower. Calm you down. I see you're mad at yourself and everybody else. Won't do no good that way." I was turning the car around too fast, and she hung onto the door. "Slow this killing machine down," she said. I did.

"Grandma, I don't want to calm down or to slow down," I said. "You know I don't get upset, but now I'm very upset. They're destroying the river just up from the Indian Mound. They're somehow putting poison in the water. I have to figure this out. I need this anger to drive me to—"

She grinned and chuckled. "That's the Indian," she said. "You got the panther warrior in you now." She beamed. "Stop this car." I pulled off. She grinned back at me, all five of her teeth showing. "Using that fire to make bread. You don't need no tea. You got the fire under control now. You finally listening. I been telling you that water's poison." She opened the car door and began to get out with her mystery bag and purple thistle.

I hated it when she was right. "Grandma, please get back in the car," I said.

"You turn around and run fast up there to that Wellborn. You know your ancestors used to go there in the harvest season to live and grow crops. They knew better'n to be on that water in a hurricane. They'd come back down to the coast in the winter."

I had heard this story a bajillion times.

"They was smarter'n you think," she said. "They didn't drill no holes a mile down the water, neither, messing up the whole world, not asking the ocean permission." She handed me a Swiss Army knife. "For luck. Now go. Tell that boy to come see me today. Soon as school's out." She slammed the door and twirled her fingers to say, Turn around and go. I did as I was told.

I WAS HEADED TOWARDS STONEY BLUFF by the river, where divers had found Indian artifacts, proving that a huge civilization used to live there. Pipes, pottery, bones, arrowheads, the stuff of whole nations, buried. A history about 15,000 years old. This made the Bible of my youth seem infantile at about 5,000 years old. Maybe Grandma *could* smell the wind and know what animals were passing through. Maybe she *did* know what potions worked.

"OV had interesting information," Madonna said. I was thinking so hard I didn't answer. She'd called me on the cell. I passed into the bluff's higher ground with oaks and grass, hardwoods just past bayou country, then past fresh pretty water on the St. Annes River where you could easily launch a boat.

If I trusted the garbage man, why not trust Grandma Happy? I wondered. She had predicted the tornado. I fingered the knife, then opened and closed it and put it in my jeans pocket.

"LaRue, you there?" Madonna said.

"Okay, yeah," I said. "I was just putting a knife in my pocket. What did our garbage man see?"

"He said some guy with slicked back black hair rode on the boat with her. He was driving, actually. OV said he recognized the driver as some guy in Wellborn," Madonna said. "He thinks he's the guy who buried Trina."

"Madonna, I think that's who I'm going to see right now," I answered. "Remember the guy in the photos we stole? That's him. He's Trina's son." A bobcat blazed across the road ahead of me.

"Shit, girl," she said. "Don't go." Suddenly I was elated, having seen a bobcat.

"I have to. He can't do anything to me at his office," I said.

"Ha. As if, girl. Someone killed Trina on her own boat." I imagined her hands tied, the knife across her throat.

"I have an Army knife if I need it," I said. "Blessed by Grandma Happy." I took the knife out again and flipped it in and out.

"You be careful. Call me when you get out," she said.

CHAPTER 28

I PULLED INTO THE FUNERAL HOME PARKING LOT and breezed past the receptionist area. The receptionist protested with some one-syllable sounds, jumped up, and followed me straight into Preston Edwards' wood-paneled office. Someone needed to tell Preston to grow about an inch of sideburns, let the back grow in a tad, and blow the length out for a surfer boy/streetwise look rather than old man slick-back style from the fifties. I pulled out the fax of the copied coroner's report and opened it up to face him. He came around the desk and told the receptionist, "Thank you, I'll handle this." He shut the door of the office on her face. He turned towards me with a stiff neck.

"Please, have a seat, Ms. Panther," he said, extending his hand, formal and rigid. He beckoned me to sit in a chair across from his desk. The surface of the desk had only a carved penholder and a marble paperweight, which held no paper under it. The only paper on the desk was a calendar. He returned to his side of the desk and sat with a sigh. I paced in front of his desk rather than sitting.

"You know about this," I said stabbing my finger into the now tattered copy of the coroner's report. "That's your mother," I said pointing to Trina's name. "You knew about this. And you covered it up. Or you killed her." He winced. I stepped back away from his desk, hands on hips. I fingered the knife in my front jeans pocket.

"Will you please stop shouting," he said, looking coldly at me. He sat down himself heavily in his chair behind the desk. "This office has ears," he said. Suddenly, he looked weary, his face long, and he looked at me with pleading eyes that nearly made me stop.

"What the hell is going on here?" I said. "Did you try to kill Mac Duncan? I know who raised you, and I know why, too. So don't start any bullshit with me, mister."

"Ms. Panther," he said quiet as an accountant. "If you will lower your voice, I will try to communicate with you. Please." He pointed to the door. "The office has ears. And please," he gestured to the chair in front of his desk where I stood, "sit."

I sat down, scooted the chair close and leaned towards him across the desk. "Okay, talk," I said. "First, why did you let this go?" I pointed to the crinkly coroner's report.

"They would have killed me, too," he said. "Yes, it was Mother." He took a breath that shuddered in. He blew it out. "You think I don't know how bad this is?" He looked at me, his eyes blinking. Were his eyes watering? A photo of a St. Annes bayou, with palms leaning in towards each other, hung behind the desk. I stuck my hand in my pocket and felt the position of the knife.

"So?" I said.

"The group of them. The whole bunch. My dad would just as easily kill me as look at me. Like he did my brother." He looked me dead in the eyes. I remembered what Isabelle had said, that some thought Fletch had pushed the boy in. Others, that the boy had fallen in and Fletch decided not to save him.

"What did your mom know that made 'the whole bunch' kill her?" I asked.

"She knew about the construction, the secret construction close to the river," he said. "She knew they were planning to build on wetlands that would send effluent into the already polluted river. And that the effluent can cause cancers of all sorts."

"What construction?" I said. "At Magnolia Gardens?"

"ECOL," he said. "Across the river. They're pushing through a development that they're not calling a development on the Magnolia River across the way from Magnolia Gardens."

I knew this, but hearing it verified by him angered me. I stood up. My fists were balls. I started pacing.

"Please, LaRue," he said, going informal. "The receptionist is Fletch's second cousin. I just found out last week. I don't dare fire her right now." He motioned for me to sit down, and he leaned over the desk. I sat. He put his head in his hands and spoke softly.

"They had me drive the boat—at gunpoint—up the back of the Magnolia, near St. Annes in a small cove," he said, his voice quivering. "I tried to knock the gun out of this big thug's—dude's—hand, and they knocked me out and the rest I don't know. . . . Except—" He stopped, and drew his lips in. He glanced at me, then shut his eyes and put his head in his hands again. "When I woke up, I was here—in there," he pointed to the door, "where you were later when you were doing her hair." I nodded. He cleared his throat and steeled himself. "I woke up on the floor next to Mom's coffin. Fletch, my father, was sitting next to me, waiting for me to wake up, a gun in his hand. He threatened me. Said I would be next if I opened my mouth."

"So it was Fletch?" I said.

He shook his head no and shrugged, bouncing a look at me and away as if he were talking to the floor. "I can't say for sure. Fletch was there, but there was some big lug ex-military guy with a silencer and a—"

"Then why did they kill her with a fishing knife?" I said. "The blood on the knife on the boat—it was human blood. I know, I found the knife on that boat days after."

"To pin me, I expect, in case it ever came out," he said. "It would look like an inside job, not a professional thing. I do get her inheritance, another reason he might want me dead."

A reason for this funeral director to want her dead, too. I took in a deep breath and let it go. "How do I know you're not lying?" I said.

"You don't," he said, looking at me. "I just hope you can see it in my eyes. Because they *will* come after me if this gets out." A long silence lingered between us. He leaned back in his chair, pale. He seemed so alone suddenly. "I just hope you know what you're doing. But you check for yourself," he said, whispering. "Go out to the place where they're digging. See if they're not building roads and signs and surveying lots and putting in old-time septics. They work at night. And on weekends."

"That's my place, my home. People are dying left and right," I said, my voice shaking with anger. "Who said they could— I will— How can they get away with this?"

An oil spill was beyond my control. Hurricanes and floods, droughts. But not this. This was home. A family spring, the sinkholes for swimming, the rivers we all fished in and swam in, the place we all worked our butts off to keep.

"It's their secret," he said. "And Mom found out. She was ready to go to the Feds about it, and they shut her up." He was looking at the floor.

"How do you know?" I stood up again. "I— I— I'm sorry. She was my kids' friend." I took in a breath and let it go. "I'm sorry you lost your mom. Your first mom." I sat down again. The room was quiet, and I heard the AC click on. "How do you know this?" I said. "I'm trying to find out. I've been pegged with trying to kill Mac Duncan, and I could take the rap for something I have no clue about. I just stepped into the middle of it without knowing. I have two kids, and I need not to be in jail, okay?"

"I'm in the same boat, so to speak," he said grimly. He stood up and wrung his hands, walked to the door, tried it to make certain it was locked. "It's the ECOL group," he said, turning around. "Since Fletch works with Sturkey at the nuclear power plant, and Mac has money and real estate, they're working together. Someone is paying Fletch to do the work of getting the machines out there. Paying people off to keep quiet." He came back to face me. We both sat down in the two chairs in front of his desk.

I looked at Preston next to me, as I was beginning to think of him. His mother dead. No brother. Is this what murderers did to innocents? Snatch away their loved ones and leave them with only silence?

"Why would anyone do these things?" I said. "Kill a stepson, kill the water, the animals in it, kill his own son?"

He shook his head slowly. "You'd have to ask him. I have a feeling he's—" He put his finger to his head to indicate that Fletch was crazy. "He doesn't care about anything. He's borderline psychopathic if you ask me."

"Okay, if Mac's in on it—and you think he is?" I said.

He nodded, gave a one-shouldered shrug. "Can't be sure, but wouldn't he have some notion, all that work going on?"

"Of course he does—he had Tiffany forge the signature," I reasoned, slowly. I was in way over my head. Why can't I just cut, color, and style hair and be done with it?

"How do you know the receptionist is . . . spying?" I said.

He winced. "They told me as much. Said they were watching me. When Mother called to tell me she wanted to show me what they were doing, they knew. They could only know from hearing the phone conversation here. I remember—when I swung open the door to go—Mother had sounded urgent on the phone—the receptionist was just hanging up the phone herself. I'd thought she was listening in on occasion, but I didn't know. After that, it was all over." He looked at the floor. "When Mother and I met to take the boat out, we had left the main docking area, you know, by the Cove?" I nodded. "Well, Fletch drove up in his speed boat with Mac and another guy, began talking to Mom."

He stopped, swallowed his shaking voice, and went on. "And they anchored the speed boat, came aboard, and the big guy with Fletch took over the driving. We were far enough out on the waterway that no one from shore could see us, you know. They drove us at gunpoint up to the Magnolia River."

His whole demeanor had changed. His eyes showed terror and a haunted vacancy.

"Okay," I said. "I'll go to the back side of the Indian mound upriver to see if you're telling the truth. I'm taking protection with me, so if there's anything . . ."

He stood, staring at me. "Be careful," he said. "If I were you, I'd take guns." He looked at me meaningfully. "And back up." I nodded and turned for the door, not looking back as I braced myself for passing the snitch.

I breezed past the receptionist, beaming. I recognized her. She was a Colton, the one out in the swamps who'd nailed a sign on the highway that said, "Kill Obama." I gave her a wave and said, "Have a great day!"

"TAY, GRANDMA WANTS YOU TO DRIVE OUT THERE," I said, headed back to St. Annes and on my cell phone. "She has something for you." My kids at home, four blocks away from a possible murderer.

"Cool!" he said. "Just what I've been waiting for! Got my knife back today."

"Honey, you leave that knife at home," I said. "I mean—don't take it to school again." I felt like a hypocrite.

"Mom, I know," he said. "I know, I know, I know."

"How's your sister doing?"

"She's hungry," he said.

"Please fix her something to eat, okay? For me? I'm on the road from Wellborn."

"Whoa!" he said. "The fire truck just went by." I could hear it from the phone. That was rare.

"Well, you stay put or go out to Grandma Happy's. You've got your sister. Just stay put for now, please? I'll be home soon. Probably a restaurant fire. See you soon."

OSPREYS AND EVEN EAGLES soared over the swamp grass, which looked like wheat, spotted with small clearings where water lay, reflecting the brilliant blue sky. Taylor's van headed the opposite direction on the road, towards me. Towards the pit. I slowed and held my hand out the window. We stopped on the county road, side by side, facing opposite directions, as no one was coming either way but the two of us—mom and son.

"Don't worry, Mom," he said. "Madonna is with Daisy. I'm going to spend the night out here, okay?" I frowned, hesitated. "Come on, Mom," he said. "I'm hanging out with Grandma. What kind of trouble could that be?"

"What kind of question is that?" I said. "Okay, then. See you tomorrow." I reached my arm out of the car across the middle of the highway and he reached his out of the van. We clasped and I squeezed his hand.

"You worry too much, Mom," he said. We drove off. I called Laura. I figured I'd tell Laura to give Madonna a call, catching them both up on the day's events.

"Laura Knight," she said, out of breath.

"It's me," I said. "Have I got news."

"So do I," she said grimly. "Just found out Mary's probably dead."

"What?" I said. "Did you say, 'Mary's probably dead'?"

"I need to go, LaRue. Don't know anything yet, but I want to get to their trailer before Cooter does. Heard it on the police radio. You know, they can't confirm the death, but that's what the police said to the ambulance. A neighbor found her on the floor. Dead, the neighbor said. No visible signs of a murder attempt. Just comatose. Then—"

"Oh, my god," I said. "I was just there a few hours ago. Oh, shit. Laura—"

She spoke calmly, quietly. "Meet me there, at their trailer, on your way back to town. You didn't do it. Be there. We need to talk to whoever we can to get the real story before whoever starts trying to cover it up. Jackson will be there, too."

Jackson walked over to greet me when I arrived at Mary's trailer. He wore plastic gloves and held a couple of small opaque bags.

"How did you get here so fast?" I said. A Leon County ambulance had pulled out just as I turned in.

"I'm an investigator," he reminded me, pointing to the sporty navy Nissan he was driving. I jumped out of the car, adrenalized. He must have seen that I was freaking out. He shrugged. "Seriously, I heard it on the radio and came down to collect evidence before it could get botched up. She's not dead, just nearly dead. The neighbor found her and thought she was dead. I have another detective with me." He tossed his head towards the trailer. His hair looked softly red, golden, beautifully curling without any stylist help from me.

"Oh, god," I said, looking at the yellow tape he had stretched across the open door. The other detective ducked under the tape and headed down the trailer's shaky stairs. I was shocked. Suddenly, I realized that Jackson, despite all he had to do, had made the effort to haul ass down and bring another cop along. And that, in fact, he'd always been listening, paying attention to the police radio after the poison incident in my little county.

"What'd you find?" I said, leaning on the car, fiddling nervously with the knife in my front pocket. He shrugged.

"She was poisoned," he said. "Rather not talk about it right now," he said, glancing at Fletch in his truck, who was just squealing to a halt. "Stay cool, LaRue," he said out of the side of his mouth.

Jackson raised his hand to welcome Laura, who pulled up behind Fletch. Jackson leaned in close. Why was I feeling like kissing him at a time like this? I actually wanted to push him down on the ground and cover him. "I don't want you to get rattled, okay? Keep a very low profile." His eyes pleaded.

"Okay," I nodded. "In fact, maybe I should go."

"LaRue?" he said. "Do." He waved his arms for emphasis. "Go home. Please, do as I ask." He lowered his voice. "First, speak to Fletch. Tell him you're sorry to hear the news. Then get in the car and have Madonna keep you and the kids company. I'll come by after that. Don't open the door for anyone besides us."

"Tay's visiting Grandma," I said. He must have heard the distress in my voice.

"He's probably better off out there," he said. "I'll be by soon. I'll alert your father, but no one else. Okay?" I nodded, smiling a weak half-smile.

WHEN I WALKED into the house, Madonna was looking through cookbooks, seeing what dessert my daughter might want. "How about strawberry short-cake?" Madonna said to Daisy as I opened the door.

"Jesus, Mary, and the baby Jesus. This is freaking me out, all this killing," Madonna said when I appeared in the door.

"What killing, Mama?" Daisy said, running from behind Madonna to cling to my waist.

"Oh, Mary's sick," I said. "She went off to the hospital in Tallahassee. Madonna's just talking." I was trying to keep the shake out of my voice and hands.

Now, I kissed her face and sat her down with a glass of milk that Madonna handed me. "Mac and cheese will be ready in about two minutes."

CHAPTER 29

LATER THAT EVENING, when Jackson arrived, I wanted only to cling to him, someone, and stay there, to forget everything. Instead, I handed him a bowl of mac and cheese. I was feeling impatient, wanting Daisy to be asleep.

And faking that everything was okay. Waiting for Jackson, tall, lean and calm, to finish eating his mac and cheese with Daisy. I listened to his middle-range voice as he read her a story on the sofa, and then I watched as he tucked her in. And I waited for her to drift off to sleep. But finally the time did come, and I filled him in on my conversation with Preston at the funeral home. He didn't say anything. He said his first concern was for my safety.

"Want a beer?" I said. Madonna had left for the Hook Wreck to take over for her sub.

"I have to drive back to Tallahassee," Jackson said. He was wearing a jacket, but he'd ditched the tie back at the scene. His curly hair was ruffled on one side, which made him endearing.

"Well, I'm gonna have one," I said, pulling out a Molson.

"Actually, maybe I should stay here," he said, glancing quizzically at me as he sat on the sofa, then looked out the window. "I'm not . . . coming on to you. I mean, for your safety. You stirred up a hornet's nest, and the insects are coming back to bite."

"Shit," I said, sitting back down on the sofa next to him. I pulled on the beer, handing it to him to share. "Okay." I walked back to the refrigerator to get him a beer.

"Never had a woman say that to me when I offered to stay," he said. "So okay, force me to have a beer, then. By the way, the other detective took the lab samples and will get some answers by tomorrow, I hope."

"What did you find?" I said, sitting a little too close for just friends. Handing him the fresh beer, I took mine back. "How is Mary?" I tipped the beer up. It felt good going down.

"Mary's comatose. She OD'd on the same stuff Mac was poisoned by— Percodan." He shrugged. "And booze. And other tranquilizers." I stood up in alarm and faced him. "But we have some hair that doesn't belong to you in the trailer, too, found near her body. You know, DNA testing doesn't have all the answers. It's just one way. And you're a suspect." He pointed the beer neck at me as he said it.

I clicked my bottle with his, and, hand on hip, said, "A toast. I didn't poison Mary." I took another sip and sat back on the sofa. "I didn't poison Mary,"

I said again. "But she was worked up when she found out I knew so much. And when she found out I knew Trina had been killed. And then I asked her what her alibi was."

"So they'll be after you next," he said, looking at me seriously. "Right now, Fletch is beside himself. He's a zombie. He's at ICU with her now. He doesn't know she's probably not going to live through the night."

"God, poor woman," I said. "So she didn't do herself in?"

He shrugged. "No evidence. Why would she choose to die that way instead of taking an overdose of pills with the booze? Someone is desperate now, it seems."

We both finished off our beers in silence, listening to the bar noise coming faintly down the street. He looked at me and said, "Let's turn in. First thing tomorrow, I'm going to take you out to the pit and show you how to shoot a thirty-eight."

"Some kind of *gun?*" I said. He turned to me with eyes like the Gulf on a rainy day, deep, cloudy, brown-green. He put his hands on my shoulders as we faced each other on the sofa.

"You have to do this," he said. "You don't know who might be after you." Here was this guy who wasn't exactly being paid a lot to do any of it. He had the sweetest face I'd seen on a cop. I'd tried so hard to not like him. I'd tried to lust after Randy instead. Jackson was actually hotter in his way. He was classy, unassuming, smart without the baggage. And tall.

"I'm not sure that's legal," I said, teasing. "Aren't you an on-duty cop? And you're going to teach a murder suspect how to use a gun?" I leaned in and kissed him. I kissed him hard. He was surprised and pulled away.

"I can't do this," Jackson said, his eyes almost pleading. "I'm on this case. We can't—"

I leaned in and said, "Shut up." His eyes reminded me of the Magnolia River as I remembered it in childhood. That depth and clarity. He was looking back, diluting the angry fire in me. He took my face in his hands and kissed me on the forehead. Suddenly, his freckles, his slight baldness in the front of his scalp, his innocent face had all the sex appeal in the world. He pulled me closer. This was not peaches, but down comforter. Maybe a little bit of .38 pistol, too. He picked me up and took me to the bedroom, tucked me into bed and disappeared. I did not come to until Jackson's phone rang.

"We were wrong about the poison," Laura said on Jackson's phone. I'd been sacked out for a few hours. It was the darkest time of night. Jackson appeared in the bedroom and had the phone on speaker. "It was a Dilaudid and Percodan overdose. Dilaudid is a Schedule Two narcotic. She couldn't have gotten a Schedule Two without the doctor's signature. And it hadn't been prescribed for her. I checked. In whatever way the narcotic entered her system, she's comatose." Jackson was sitting up, putting on his sweater automatically.

"Are you at the hospital?" Jackson asked. Laura said yes. "Don't leave alone," he commanded. I was reaching for my sweatshirt, glancing down the hall at Daisy's room. The hallway nightlight, a kitschy Virgin Mary, glowed red and blue. Quiet, luckily. Daisy tended to sleep like a bear in winter.

"I won't. An old friend from the *Sun* is here with me," Laura said. "He's offered to let me stay at his place tonight. I gave him this story, so he gave me a place to stay."

"Laura," Jackson said, grabbing my hand as I stood up, squeezing it. "Someone's calling you with threats. You may have someone tailing you."

"Not a chance," Laura said. "I'm not that important. But one thing—about ECOL." We both waited. "This ECOL group formed five years ago and immediately started buying up wetlands around the river. At about that time, the county commission worked up a report that's been under lock and key by local government officials since, covering up the sewage problem along the rivers and in the aquifer."

"So they've been *burying* information about the problems in the wetlands?" I said.

"Yep. All the information about what nitrates can do, not to mention the bacteria on the other side of the river that can make you so sick. Australia has the same bacteria in some of its waters, and they're doing a more thorough job of investigating the results. Plants die, people get cancer. Scientists have been conjecturing for years now that infection causes cancer, especially this kind." It explained the leukemia, lung cancer, lymphoma, birth defects—the list of health problems contracted by people out my dad's way. Grandma may be right again, I thought.

"Where'd you get the supporting documents?" Jackson said.

"I subpoenaed them," Laura said, "and drove over and picked them up at the commission office when the big shots were on vacation—Christmastime is perfect for that."

"What exactly did you find?" I said.

"First study was four years ago. Back up the Tallahassee waste water area, before they repaired their city sewage to keep it from free-flowing down our way," Laura said. I knew that water ran straight down towards the Indian mound, all through the area where the Colberts, the Vickers, and the Coltons had lived. My family had only been lucky because we lived on a spring, which pumped water from its own source. Then again, the source was the same, it was all interconnected. But now Grandma was saying our water was bad. My kids, my dad, we'd all been drinking well water.

"Why—don't they give a shit about people's lives?" I said.

"LaRue, this guy at the power plant down the way, this Sturkey guy?" Laura said. "He used federal money to order the machines to do the development work. Sturkey isn't going to let anything get in his way—certainly not the truth. I've seen others like him in action. I've seen him at commission meetings, at his workplace. It's a religion to him, making money in whatever way necessary. He considers it progress, growth in the county."

Jackson gave the phone to me. I paced, listening. "These kind of fanatics will ignore all the research that says the effluent causes infections and possibly auto-immune deficiencies, cancers, brain damage. The coal people who want to stick a plant up the road in Perry are the same way. I don't even need to mention BP, do I?" I looked out the window at the Gulf, shimmying purplish under the nearly full moon.

Laura went on. "Same old problems—run-off and waste in the water. Same denial. Sturkey and ECOL, they're all willing to do anything to keep the negativity covered up. I think he got these local guys involved—money talks. Sturkey comes from old Northeastern money, and he's got the people's money, too, since nukes are an energy provider."

"You need to be extra careful," I said. There was a long silence. I could hear the wind in the palms, always that relentless wind from the water. I'd always loved that sound. Right now I felt it was wearing me down like it did stone into sand.

"Don't worry, I'm steering clear of Fletch and the bunch," she said. "I gotta say, he looks awful. Kinda gray in the face."

"Tell Laura to let us know about Mary," Jackson interjected. "And to stay in touch."

Jackson and I lay down on the floor of the living room again, my head on his shoulder, each of us staring off into space in the dark. The gleam of the only traffic light in town was blinking yellow-off, yellow-off. I suddenly felt like I was drowning in the Gulf, swallowing fishy-tasting water and oil and runoff muck. I must have finally fallen into a deep sleep, because I woke up to daylight. As I sat up, I groaned. My back hurt, and my butt was stiffly asking me why in middle age, I'd sleep on a hard cold floor. I shivered, covered myself with the blanket and lay back down. I could hear Jackson talking to Daisy about flying kites out at Dad's. He was making coffee, and I heard the toaster spring up.

"Peanut butter," Daisy said. "Mama said it's better for you than butter. She's a health freak." I heard rummaging around, and then Daisy laughing softly. "It's got a face," she said. "Can I eat the eyes? They're raisins, right?" I'd never been able to get her to eat raisins. Ever. I pretended sleep, savoring the smell of toast and fresh coffee.

Soon, he had her out the door and in his car on the way to school. Last night's doom and gloom had left me temporarily. I could learn to live with this, I thought, finally getting up and pouring an already made cup of coffee.

I STOOD HOLDING A .38, wondering what I was going to wear to the party Saturday.

"This sucks," I said, then pulled the trigger. Jackson and I were standing at the forested corner of Dad's property, surrounded by pine trees and bear grasses. I'd canceled my appointments for the morning. All the sexiness I'd felt getting up that morning burned off. The shock of the sudden loud bang, the buck back against me as it fired.

"You're strong enough," he said. "Steady the arm. Don't think about the jolt you're going to get afterwards. Focus on the target. Think about the family you have to protect." I'd finally hit the target. He showed me how to put the safety on and how to carry the gun in the waist of my jeans.

"You sure that safety won't go off?" I said. "I've got valuables down in these pants."

CHAPTER 30

FRIDAY. A THICK FOG HAD MOVED IN, and Dock Street looked hazy and forlorn, the bait shop shut, restaurants on the dock street closed until tonight when the big Christmas costume party would occur. By now the word was out that Mary was near death. A second mysterious death, or near death on the island. People were clustered together inside warm places whispering their theories. I'd walk past the cafe, the restaurant, the post office, and people inside would look out, stop talking, and watch. The Christmas lights on the streets shone in broad daylight.

I focused on the party. Parties made sense. They had no depth, they cost a lot. But parties pushed away our gloom.

I'd kept the shop closed, but I was still busy, sweeping the floor, cleaning mirrors, brushes, rearranging shampoo and conditioner bottles. Mary's heart was beating more strongly, Madonna had reported. And more miraculous than the virgin birth, Madonna had also passed on to me that Mary was five months pregnant, and the fetus, it seemed, was thriving.

Since the news media had picked up on Mary's situation, she was protected by law enforcement 24-7 now. A guard hovered in the yellow halls of the hospital constantly. Who'd take care of that baby? I wondered. Whose baby was it? I turned on the radio to hear "Jingle Bell Rock" by Brenda Lee, which I couldn't help but sing along and dance to.

And I went about my life as women have done forever in the face of trouble: by keeping the small things as they'd always been. As the sun sank and people clamored to town for distraction, I changed my mind about closing the shop. Work connected us with the world. I opened the shop and stuck a sign out that said, "Free haircuts for all St. Annes Night party attendees." Laura breezed in for a spruce up before she headed back to Tallahassee to check on news of Mary for the paper and to pick up her guy friend.

"Give me something wild," she said, bouncing into the chair. "I've invited the reporter from the *News* to be my date tonight."

"Really?" I said. "Tell me about him." She wouldn't. She told me she'd introduce him tonight.

Her eyes were the round brown of a sunflower center, so I decided to choose a color opposite on the color wheel for her hair. I plaited a turquoise strip of ribbon into her hair and swooped one side of her hair close to her eye. The rest I swirled into a lazy updo, teasing the back for lift. The other side I pinned behind her ear. "Put on black eyeliner and a deep wine lipstick. Your nerdy glasses will just look naughty librarian," I advised. The phone rang.

Cooter, telling me he'd found Tay out on the road by Dad's property discharging explosives. "Let me talk to him, Cooter, please," I said, putting down the bobby pins I had in my mouth.

"What, Mom," Tay said, already on the defensive.

"Get back to the pit. Do *not*, I repeat, do *not* explode anything else today. Otherwise, Cooter will take you in. Jail, you hear me, JAIL!" My yell echoed around the hair salon. Laura gave me a shocked look.

Tay didn't argue. I supposed he understood since Cooter had picked him up. Then again, maybe not. It *was* Cooter.

"Friggin' frig!" I said, slamming the black retro phone down too hard on the counter. "He's exploding things out on the state road!" I said to Laura as she calmly put her earrings back in. What was there to say? 'Oh, it's okay—so he's a potential terrorist and jailbird—he's still your sweet son?' She squeezed my hand with her soft hand as she was leaving.

A tourist couple stopped by and wanted haircuts. They'd been traveling for months in an RV and finally were going to get civilized again, they said. I gave the guy the complete head shave, leaving the half an inch of silver fuzz he wanted, as he'd just pierced his ear. His soft hair was falling like fur all around me as I wondered—had Mary's depression finally gotten to her? Was that why she had yelled at me?

The hardest question came to me as stark as this customer's almost bald head. Did I do something to trigger Mary's self-destruction?

When the dude's hair was finished, I took the phone outside to catch what little sun I could, pacing the sidewalk and calling the hospital. Mary was stable, and still in a coma, the nurse's station informed me. The phone rang. It was Jackson.

"Are you calling to tell me you can't make it tonight?" I said. My ex had done that one plenty. I stared at the sidewalk crack.

"No," he said. "Calling to tell you what I found out about Mary's health history."

"Go ahead, but please don't let it be bad."

He asked if everything was okay, and I assured him it was. I would have a scheduled customer in just a few minutes.

"She's had three pregnancies that we know of, traced over twenty years. The first, an abortion, one born with a birth defect and died of SIDS at home in Cureall, and one miscarriage," Jackson said. "What was she doing in Cureall, anyway?" I could hear cop radio noise in the background. I remembered Mary saying to Daisy that she'd always wanted a little girl. And there was Fletch, who seemed to despise his own children, enough to kill one of them, or let the child die. Willing to kill the other one as an adult.

"Cureall's where she and Fletch have that little love nest of theirs. I have a feeling it wasn't SIDS. Fletch seems to like getting rid of kids," I said, running down the litany of Fletch's violence with even his own children. "Poor Mary." The line was silent.

"No wonder she was in a recovery place," Jackson said. "Or no wonder she had so many problems producing babies." A car from out of town drove past, then another. Things were picking up for the big night of events.

"Did she try suicide, or is she in the hospital because she was pregnant again, or because she was talking to me?" I said. "And did those babies not make it because of Fletch or because of the poison in her water?" My neck felt tight.

"LaRue, you can't blame yourself. She was given a high dose of Dilaudid and she took Percodan and drank alcohol with it."

"Okay," I said. "Can I call you back?" The tourist lady was patiently waiting for me, flipping through a magazine.

"That's okay, just concentrate on tonight," he said. "I'll come by around seven-thirty? Want me to pick the kids up at the pit?" He was too good to be true. But I didn't like depending on anyone but Madonna and Laura.

"Thanks for thinking of it, Jackson. Tay and Daisy are going to drive in together. He's got the van. But thanks a million," I said. The tourist lady with the now-shave-headed man was sitting down in the chair, anticipating.

Jackson continued. "Don't handle any of the food. No tea antidotes for medications. Don't bring a thing. Don't touch a thing. Someone could easily try to frame you or poison you. Now, do you have your thirty-eight?"

"Yes," I said. "It's tucked into the inside pocket of my camos."

"No food, no coffee, no tea antidotes?" he said.

"No," I said, as I put the cape around the lady and snapped it at the neck. I'd take my scissors in case. I always had.

"Okay, then. We'll boogie till we drop," he said. "Forget your troubles."

"Right," I said. "I wish you were right about that." I hung up the phone.

Next, the lady wanted *her* head shaved. I talked her into leaving an inch and bleaching it white blonde. After an hour, they both left twinnish and happy. They tipped well, and I needed a nap. I closed up shop, clomped upstairs and got into the bathtub, and then went straight to bed.

"SO WHAT D'YA THINK, Mom?" Tay said that afternoon late as he walked into the apartment, Daisy right behind. He'd driven back from their grand-dad's. He was grinning broadly.

He wore a long-sleeved red T-shirt with a black skull in the center, black pants, and a Santa hat. The T-shirt was spray painted white along the edges to look like Santa's fur. He'd let the fuzz grow on his chin and had spray painted it white. He'd made his hair look like dreadlocks. One side of his face was painted white, the other black.

"Check this out," he said, turning around. On the back of the T-shirt, it said, *Consume me.* "Ha, get it? Consumer holiday?"

"Isn't it yucky, Mom?" Daisy said. She was dressed in a red velveteen dress, a tawny braid running down her back.

"Hmm, what should I say to a Santa who likes cannibals?" I said. "You look hideous? Sorry, dude, I don't think any kiddies will be leaving you any cookies and milk tonight. No explosives at the party, okay?" I pointed at him and put a cookie at his mouth. "Eat and shut up."

"Don't worry, Mom," he said. "I'm saving the explosives for more important things." I ignored that comment.

I wore a faux Indian leather jacket from the sixties and tied a scarf in my hair. I had far too much to think about to spend energy on a costume.

"Did your Grandma Happy braid your hair?" I said to Daisy.

"Yep, good, huh? She gave me a potion, too, to give you. She said you'd need it tonight." Daisy handed another Tupperware container full of what looked like the same tea as before.

"Oh, hungry crawling Jesus!" I said, slamming it down on the counter. That was the last thing I needed Jackson to know about.

"Mother, where do you get these colloquialisms?" Tay said, like a sociologist.

"Is Mama cussing?" Daisy asked him. I ignored them both, shoved the tea into the refrigerator and headed out in the Saturn to Mac's reception hall.

I pulled into the lot, which held only three other cars. A vaporous and chilled night. The place was lit up with white lights trimming the walls and a blue mirror at the end of the hall where Mac had collapsed at the wedding weeks ago now. At the other end, the tables for food and drink. At every corner of the room, punch tables had been set up. At the end away from the blue mirror, the punch with rum sat, separated from the plain punch. The bowl smelled sweetly of rum drink, and the room smelled of eucalyptus.

The moon had a bright white cast and reflected like a luminous ribbon in the Intracoastal Waterway. Sprangle Island loomed its shadowy silhouette beyond. I thought of the graveyard on that island with remains of bodies long abandoned and left with the moss, no-see-ums, and sound of the tide. I shivered, pulling my scarf closer.

Randy Dilburn met me at the door and we headed towards the tables. He was dressed in a silk shirt. I commented on its softness, and he said, "It's old.

Really old."

"Looks to me like you take good care of things," I said. He shrugged.

"Where's Tay?" he said.

"He and Daisy are walking over with Jackson." I saw his face visibly change.

"Oh, bringing the cops so you can't get arrested again, huh?" he said. "Good idea." He walked to a table and nibbled on some celery and dip, and then went to the glass window to check the view of the Gulf. What did he care? He hadn't called or made any contact since our kissing session.

Tay came trouncing in, kicking his leg high in a karate chop. He pretended to kick me in the belly, then chop my neck off with a "Ssssshhhhhhhooooooo-pow!"

"How charming," I said. "You can kill your mom in two moves. Where's Jackson? And Daisy?"

"Mom, I've been meaning to talk to you about Jackson," Tay said, tugging at his shirt, shifting from sneakered foot to sneakered foot. "You're not—he really likes you. He's like . . . uh, uh, he's like Aragorn in the Ring trilogy—you know, the Hobbit trilogy. He upholds the law without having an ego. He fights chaos without brutality."

"Well, just be sure not to mention the tea your Grandma Happy made, okay?" I said. Tay frowned.

"I brought the tea," he said, pulling it out from his gigantic backpack pocket. "Grandma Happy told me you had to have it. I didn't let Jackson see it."

"Oh, boy," I said. "Put it under the table, will you?" I pointed to the table of punch under the window that faced the Gulf.

In walked Jackson with Daisy. Jackson wore jeans, a black T-shirt, and vintage Dingo boots, which I immediately coveted. I glanced at Randy, who avoided my eyes while he roamed the room checking punch bowls. The lights went low, and the DJ put on Tom Waits.

Randy and Jackson somehow merged and started talking about music and wandered off together. It seemed they'd both played in bands when they'd been younger. Daisy ran up to me and said, "Mama, I want some chips."

"Where do you put all that food?" Taylor said, grabbing some potato chips himself. We all three stood by the window looking out at the Gulf and the moon and the island beyond.

"They say the ghosts of all the people who died in that flood nearly a hundred years ago come back this time of year," I said, pointing to Sprangle Island in the short distance across the water. "Do you all miss Trina?"

"Mom, stop being so weird," Tay said.

"Mommy, are they gonna get me?" Daisy said.

"I was just kidding around," I said. "I was just wondering if you were thinking about her, Tay. And Daisy, I shouldn't have brought it up." She did have a propensity to fret over possibilities. Failure as a mom number 3,862.

"I don't think Trina would haunt me, us," Tay said. "Mom, I need to get something to eat. I'm really hungry," Tay said, holding his flat, skinny stomach. I followed him to a real food table.

"Get food, of course," I said, "but please, tell me—you don't take this voodoo stuff seriously, do you? You wouldn't get addicted to cough medicine. You wouldn't do satanic rituals where cannibalism was practiced, would you? Or use violence to—"

"What are you talking about?" he said as he turned to me like *Have you lost your mind?* He frowned, his mouth stuffed with grapes. "Take a chill pill, Mom," he burbled.

"Tay, my man," Randy yelled out across the room. Tay walked across the room to him. "What are you, anyway? The Jackie Chan of St. Annes?" They huddled and then began to show each other Tae Bo moves.

Daisy went to meet her friends who had a makeup kit and were gathering in the corner to indulge in putting on too much blue eye shadow and painting their nails glittery silver.

Madonna made her appearance. Pearls and a black spaghetti-strap dress. She sashayed over to the punch bowl. All the men's eyes followed her. Jackson literally followed her.

"Think that stinker Fletch or his bro Cooter will show up?" she said, grabbing a scoop of guac and chips.

"If I know those brothers, they will *not* be sitting in ICU with a woman in a coma with a St. Annes party going," I said. "They're crude enough to come here with no thought that it might be tacky when they ought to be in mourning and at the hospital."

Jackson cleared his throat. "What we need," he said, shoving his hands into his back pockets, "is to find out what Trina actually had on Fletch. Or on the ECOL group." He and I sat in cold folding chairs behind one of the tables, our backs to the Gulf. "You don't go murdering people because they find out you're illegally building subdivisions that will eventually send sewage into the rivers." He lowered his voice. "Mac was chased out of Mexico for it, probably, but it was called a mistrial. There's got to be more."

He grabbed, then crunched on a carrot stick. "That's the missing link at this point. It's one thing to have bad bookkeeping, it's yet another to kill someone. There has to be more than she could prove." He ruminated, chewing, then said, "You know, the county commissioners protect this stuff and give the

CEOs of land developments a lot of clout. It would be hard to get in there and accuse them of criminal acts."

He grabbed a handful of roasted nuts now. "Something else. For someone to hire a thug with a silencer on a boat, to threaten the son, too. I think I'm going to have to go see that son, Preston Edwards. Or pull it out of Fletch and Cooter somehow." The room was filling up. "By the way, I've still got tests running, and the hair samples and fingerprints from Mary's trailer."

Madonna pulled Jackson away and introduced him to the owner of the Hook Wreck. She deposited Jackson there so he wouldn't be playing detective all night and getting me worked up. Then she walked over to Randy and blatantly laid a big kiss on his cheek. Even I was shocked. And jealous. Why? God, was I *that* greedy? I turned to the punch bowl and looked out on the moonlit water. The reception hall got louder. Jimmy Buffet, the renewed Gulf coast hero, for having a huge concert in Alabama and riffing on BP's huge blunders, played on the stereo in the background.

I felt Madonna next to me. "Coming to give me a smacker now?" I said.

"That's it," Madonna said. "It's the cologne on the boat. Randy was on that boat. Smells great. He says it's called 'Solo.' Moreover—I know you intellectuals like words like that—moreover, guess what? It's rare, a very rare scent. He got it on his way back from Africa when he stopped in Spain. They make it exclusively in this Spanish city, Valencia. Don't even sell it here. Therefore, as you intellectuals like to say, for anyone else to be wearing it would be out of the question." I kissed her on the cheek. So my guess was right. But what did it mean?

"You're the best," I said. The room had gotten warm with people.

"You're not getting fresh with me, are you, Rue?" she joked.

"I'm just feeling desperate and vulnerable," I said. "Stupid, anxious, crazy, exhausted, sorry for myself. What an ass." She bumped me with her hip.

"Let's dance," she said, pulling my arm. Motown Tunes were playing now, and we soon had a big line dance going.

Then, to my surprise, in lumbered a big man dressed as a silvery Neptune. His deep, loud voice gave him away. Mac Duncan. The kids were squealing. *It's a monster! No, it's God!* I went back to the punch bowls, refilling them, as I was ironically chosen to be responsible for the food tables, and looking to see if Jackson was watching. He was deep in conversation with the Hook Wreck guy. The spiked punch was going fast. Some younger tourists from down the road came in and started to disco. Tay's hip-hop/grunge crowd was bouncing around in a circle. In the corner, Fletch stood with Cooter. They had their hands in their pockets. Daisy had gotten Neptune to play limbo with the kids. He held the broom while they all lined up and bent backwards under the stick as it crept lower and lower.

"Where's your cop? The date for the night?" Randy said with sarcasm. Jackson, he meant. He was digging at me. He knew Jackson was talking to the Hook Wreck guy.

"I don't know," I said, waving my hand. "And it's not a date. And he's an investigator. I'm not in charge of anything tonight. He's out there somewhere, I suppose." He gave my stupid costume a once-over.

"Poor mixed up little wampum girl in a Pakistani scarf," Randy said. "Which kind of Indian are you? Nothing is turning out right these days, is it? Come dance with the lawyer who wears old silk shirts, but who's not quite cool enough to own Dingo boots."

"I guess nobody ever told you how to ask a girl to dance? Or were you actually asking me to step outside and settle this?" I said, yanking the dumb scarf off my head.

He grinned. "I'm just teasing you. Laura told me you really could be in danger. She told me about the county commission's cover up. I'm pissed beyond pissed now. I knew the sewage and those neighborhoods with bad septic issues were causing the problems, I just didn't know how to get the information."

"Yeah," I said. "What some people—you grew up here, too—what're they thinking?"

Smokey Robinson was singing a slow heartbreaker. Out of the corner of my eye, I saw Cooter and Fletch head outside. Randy began to slow dance with me. I felt reckless and was fighting off guilt over Jackson's seeing us. Almost everyone was stepping off the dance floor to cool down. I was anything but cooling down. Randy must have been feeling the same thing, because he pulled me closer. Randy and I stood almost eye to eye.

When the fast music started up again, we sauntered over to get something to drink—unspiked punch. "What do you think Trina really had on them? It's one thing to know the books are bad, and yet another to prove someone's doing illegal building and hiding it," I said to Randy. "Laura used her wiles to get the paperwork this past week, but that's Laura. What would Trina have had on him?"

"I don't know, LaRue, or I'd have told you," he said. "Maybe it had something to do with her son. The one who disappeared on the fishing trip."

He looked around the room and grabbed a sandwich. "Still no sign of your cop, homegirl. Guess you'll have to put up with me." I tried to avoid eye contact, messing about with the sandwiches and punch. Randy took off his shoes and shoved them under the table.

Cooter and Fletch had come back in and looked for all the world like the redneck mafia, standing in that corner. I felt my boot for my .38. Hard as a rock. Now, suddenly, I knew what Trina had discovered.

Jackson was dancing with Madonna. The room had begun to get steamy, and the music was turned up loud. Nelly was wailing, *It's getting hot in here, So take off all your clothes*, a ridiculous song, but so danceable. I watched three older couples get up, all dressed as parts of a turkey dinner, and shake it as I wormed my way towards Jackson. I came up behind him and leaned in close to his ear and said loudly, "I figured out what she had. What Trina had. I'll bet I know where it is, too. I have an idea who might have poisoned Mac, too."

"Can it wait till the end of this dance?" he said twisting a strange hip dance. Madonna waved me away. Lots of costumed people were creating a mass on the dance floor. Santas were dancing with reindeer and sexy elves or Christmas trees.

"Give it a rest!" she shouted over the music, swinging her hair around. Tay and his gang were in the corner doing a parody of *with a little bit a ah ah*.

I moved back to the punch bowl area where big Neptune Mac, Fletch, and Randy were having a bit of an uneasy conversation, not making eye contact, arms folded over their chests, shouting over the music about weather. Where was Laura?

Someone gestured to me to come over to get my phone. Where was Laura? "Hello?" I said, stopping up my other ear to hear.

"Hey, it's me!" Laura said. She sounded close, but I could hear highway noise.

"Weird." I walked out into the cold night. "Those invisible vibes in the universe. I thought of you and the phone rang. I was just worrying—where are you? Are you okay?"

"Yeah, I'm fine. Mary's come out of the coma," Laura said. "She wants to talk to you. She's got some interesting things to tell you, I might add."

"When? Tonight?" I said, looking back into the room, noticing how many of the grunge kids had worn Santa caps, but smeared their mouths with what seemed like blood.

"As soon as you can get here," she said. "Maybe tomorrow, first thing? She's pretty tired. In and out, you know. But definitely out of the coma."

"Thank god," I said. "So, you're not coming to the party?"

"I'm sorry, LaRue, we're too tired tonight," she said.

"We," I said. Things must be going well in Gainesville, I guessed.

"We. Tell ya later," she answered. I wasn't going to get any more from her tonight.

"Do *not* tell anyone about Mary's recovery, understand? Tell no one but Jackson. Only you know this. Only you," Laura said.

"Okay," I said, looking through the window into the reception hall and across the dance floor, as if they could hear the conversation. I walked back inside, phone still to my ear. The song had finished and there was a momentary lull before the next began. Which was why I heard Mac.

"Argh, Shiver me—" Neptune-gone-Captain-Bly said, then he coughed. Not a normal cough, a wheezing, throat-holding cough. He coughed again, holding his stomach this time. Neptune crashed to the floor.

"Oh, my god, Laura, Mac has fainted. I'm gonna have to go. Will call you back when I can, okay? Mary—I won't say anything. I'll call you back."

Madonna knelt next to him. "Mac! What is it?"

"That punch! That!" he said, pointing to his punch glass.

I couldn't move. This again? And in the back of my mind, I was wondering, factoring. Mary was awake and wanted to talk to *me*—not Fletch, not Mac, not Cooter.

Then Jackson darted over to Mac in his cop way, picked up the cup, and sniffed. He glanced at me for a split second. Then back to Mac. Then he said something to Madonna and walked over to me. Meanwhile, Cooter had ambled over to the table where I'd been standing all night and scooped up the Tupperware container sitting under the table.

"This belong to you, Miss LaRue?" he said. I nodded feebly. He was on his cell phone.

"You had nothing to do with this, right?" Jackson said.

"Of course not!" I said. "Are you joking with me?" I must have looked wild-eyed.

"Did you bring this tea here?" Jackson said. I felt the eyes of the party on me. The DJ's music had stopped.

"No! I left it in the fridge at home!" I said. "Tay brought it at Grandma's instructions."

Jackson cleared his throat and began to yell. "Did you have anything to do with any of the making of this punch tonight?" he said. His voice was getting louder.

I looked down at the carpet. "NO. I'm not saying anything else." I was standing in the middle of the room, staring at the floor.

I looked up. His green-brown eyes appeared so disappointed, so hurt. "I didn't bring the tea! I didn't know anything like this would happen again! Why would I have invited you?"

He seemed furious. His voice was vacillating from very loud to deep. "Listen up," he shouted. "Get over—get over in the corner so I can talk to you! Now! I need to call the poison unit again and have Mac taken to Memorial. No one will believe this happened, especially while I was here. But what I really can't believe—" he stopped and walked away, swearing under his breath.

I was furious. My kids had suddenly appeared behind me. "What's going on, Mama?" Daisy said. "Is Mr. Mac sick again?"

"Get your stuff now, both of you, please. Now." I gulped back the shake in my voice. The redneck mafia was gathered around Mac. Everyone in the place had heard Jackson yell at me. But maybe Randy wouldn't think me a pariah and a murderer, maybe he didn't care what things Jackson yelled. I headed out the door to catch Randy as he left.

Madonna stood outside smoking a cigarette. "Fucking idiot," she said. "Doesn't he know better than to drink poison?"

"Madonna, call me tomorrow morning first thing on my cell," I said. "Laura called. I have to do some things now. Please, don't ask me any questions about it. I'm not allowed to say anything."

She nodded. "Where you three going?" she asked.

"With Randy. I'm not going home, or anywhere where Jackson or Cooter or Fletch or anyone else can find me. Call me in the morning. Please."

CHAPTER 31

OUTSIDE, the wind was spitting wet and riding chill from the north. The fog rolled like unsettled specters under the streetlights. The hundred-year-old oaks by the cove sighed heavily while the palms made a whoooo sound. Daisy clung to me, and Tay was silent behind me. The moon was still rising in the sky, more copper now.

"So why can't you drive yourself home?" Randy asked. He leaned on his car, one leg crossed over the other, his hand on the driver's door.

"I don't want to go home, Randy," I said. "Okay? Cooter just found the tea. He thinks I tried for a second time to poison Mac. The state cop just yelled at me, and I don't want to go home right now."

I knew what I wanted from Randy. His eyes had gone cold when he glanced at me, but then he looked from Taylor to Daisy, and he shrugged. "Okay. Everybody get in."

"Mom, I guess I shouldn't have brought the tea," Taylor said, heaving his big backpack into the car. "I'm sorry, but Grandma —"

"Don't worry, honey. I didn't poison Mac. This is much bigger than herbal tea," I said, hugging him to me in the back seat. Meanwhile, Daisy had climbed into the front.

"I like your car, Mr. Randy," she said. "It's clean. Our car is never clean. Mr. Randy's car smells good, too. Mama's smells like a chicken coop."

"Wonder why that is, Daisy-eat-anything-and-drop-everything-in-the car," Tay said with sarcasm.

"Wanna drive?" Randy said to Daisy.

"I don't think so, not tonight. It's actually a very dark night," she said in an adult way.

The wind pushed the car a little sideways as we headed out. Randy had decided to hug the Gulf tonight, maybe to keep us from being spotted. Our town had a complex set of city blocks that allowed people to sneak around to get to different islands off the main island.

"Okay, where do you want to go, LaRue?" he said. "What do you have in mind?"

"Live Oak Island," I said. "Trina's house. I'm looking for something. I want to show you."

"Okay," he said, no change of tone. He turned right at Gulf Drive, and we headed to Trina's house.

Stepping out of the car, I found Trina and Fletch's place dark. Blacker than the interior of the car, and surrounded by water oaks with no streetlights near-by. Only the moon lit anything. It required a minute or two of eye adjustment. I wondered where Fletch was staying lately with Trina dead and Mary in the hospital.

"I'm sitting here in the car with the kids," Randy said. "Better take this," he said, rummaging around in the glove compartment and handing me a small flashlight. I could smell the briny water in the near distance. I crept toe-to-heel like Grandma, padding over the dirt and decaying leaves of their yard, using the flashlight to check for night animals. As soon as I was out of sight from the car, I touched the .38 in my boot. I pulled the key I'd stolen from under the statue, unlocked the back door, and tiptoed in. I quickly turned on Trina's computer.

"Where would you put it, where?" I said aloud. Then I thought carefully about where Preston would have looked. I turned off the computer and head-ed to the back. If you wanted to keep something from your husband, where would you put it? In a safe. Under something. In a closet where he wouldn't think to look.

The carpeting in the house muffled all sound. Too quiet. I wanted out. Did Preston have the key? Where would another one be? If she went for a boat ride on her last day alive, she'd have left her purse home. Beside her bed. I found it under the bed, her keychain, and a tiny key that had a taped message on it that said, "recipes." What man would think to look for incriminating evidence in a recipe box? I raced back to the study piled neatly with large boxes of files and fished around in the closets with the flashlight. Nothing. Finally, I gave in and turned on a small light that sat atop the desk in the room. Then I spied a metal file box big enough to hold a box of folders and opened it. Way at the back, a lean recipe box under some empty file folders. Please, I whispered. My hands were trembling. The key worked.

Out sprang a bundle of letters, some pretty old, the paper brittle and browning.

I took in a breath and began to scan. One from Preston, one from Mary, one from an attorney in Mexico City, others from locals—Mr. Colbert, Mrs. Colton, who lived in the swamps and had died of leukemia. Sadly, their two death certificates. Lots of letters smashed into this recipe box.

"Mom," I heard faintly from the window facing the road. Daisy shouting from Randy's hybrid, right outside the window where I was working. She must have seen me turn on the small light. "I want to go now. It's too scary here."

"Mom, come on!" Tay said. "You're—come on!"

I snatched up the whole box and key and contents, locked the door, and fled down the back stairs. Everyone was complaining when I got in the car. *It's cold, it's late, you could get arrested, what are you doing? Have you lost your mind?*

"Shut up, goddamn it!" I said. The three of them went silent. "I found hardcore evidence here. This is the stuff she never got to use on Fletch or Mac. She had an appointment with Mac on her books the day she died."

Randy started the car up, wheeled slowly down the block, turned at the U and headed back towards Gulf Drive. I went on, waving the box in the air.

"This was what she had on those guys." I was a little breathless. "Sorry kids, I guess I should be sheltering you here, but this is the gruesome truth. The day Trina died, she went to Mac's office to tell him what dirty business she knew he and Fletch were into, and he behaved as friendly as ever. I expect Mac got in her car with her and rode with her to the house."

The moon was a high shiny dime in the sky now, and Randy, a cool blue-black silhouette driving silently, finished his U-turn and headed back out towards town.

"Trina and Mac had a cup of coffee or something. Mac promised her something—that he'd clean up the site, something to keep her quiet." I wondered if Randy had been listening to my theory, as his silhouette finally nodded. "Mac dropped a mild tranquilizer in Trina's tea and offered to take her out on the boat, pretending he'd show her something. She agreed—she was tranquilized, after all."

"Mama, I don't understand," Daisy moaned.

"Shh!" Tay said. "Be quiet for the first time in your life!" He smacked her with the palm of his hand and she stifled a wail. I turned around and gave him a look, then turned back around, ignored them and continued.

"Preston was also on board at the invitation of Mac, and Fletch, and the thug. Trina went to sleep. They threatened Preston, knocked him out, and cut her throat. Then dumped them at the funeral home. Madonna and I went on Mac's boat and found the knife. Jackson had it checked out. It matched Trina's blood type."

There Randy sat, emotionless, calm, driving to his place. Why had he been on the boat the same night I had been, looking for something? For what? "Okay, now what?" Randy said. He turned and looked at me.

"One more favor, please?" I said. "Take me down to the real estate office, but down the cove side so people won't notice I'm breaking in."

Daisy started to whimper. "Mama, I'm scared. What if you get caught? What if—"

"Shut up, Daisy," Tay said, putting one arm around her. Now he understood what had been going on.

"Tay, don't strangle her, all right?" I said. He sat back. "Change places with her, how about it?"

"Don't you want me to go with you?" Tay said.

"Okay," I agreed. "Let Daisy sit back here for now." We stopped the car at the corner of Gulf Drive, and they swapped places. Daisy curled up into me. It gave me comfort, too. I gave instructions to Tay. "You can't speak unless it's an emergency, and don't touch anything. Just be the lookout, okay? No arguing with me." He nodded.

"You have a key to this place, too?" Randy said. "Perhaps I should change my locks? Or is it my boat you want?" I chose to ignore him, especially since I'd stolen his ECOL file and my fingerprints were still on it. The pines were whipping around on Gulf Drive, their shadows in the sky looking like the hair of untamable women.

"Randy, if anyone comes, drive off. Regardless, drive off," I said.

"Mama—" Daisy said. Everyone shushed her. *It'll be fine, Don't worry, It's just a precaution,* we were all saying to her. By the time we got to the highway, only eight blocks from the real estate office, she was blubbering. I asked Randy to pull the car over, and I took her outside and picked her up, smelled her little-girl smell, and held her tight.

"Daisy, you're my precious girl." I smoothed her silky hair. "I do not want you to get into any trouble. Nobody's going to get hurt, okay? In case the police come by, it's better for everyone if you weren't there. The law doesn't like having little kids involved. They could take you away from me, and I don't want that to happen. If anything happens, you can go with Mr. Randy. He will take you out to Grandad's, okay?" I was rocking her against me, humming Humpty Dumpty. Even though it was one of those scary songs, it always had comforted her as a baby. Daisy was about a third of my weight, but I had so much adrenalin going, I didn't feel it. "Please trust me. It's going to be fine." She stopped crying, and I put her back in the car next to me. Her braid had strands wisping all about her face and neck now.

We headed for the back side of the real estate office where the cedars and palms grew tall on Fishhouse Cove, and the moon shone huge and orange over the water. Tay and I got into the back door. He watched each window and door. After I found the file, we headed straight out again.

"What in the hell now?" Randy said.

"Please take me to your house," I said. "We can sort through this at your place tonight, and then I can call Jackson. The kids can sleep on your floor in the other bedroom with me where it's soft and carpeted. I just can't go home now. I live too close to town. Please. No one will know I am at your place."

"Okay," Randy said. "First you want a ride, then my house, and next, I'm sure you'll need the boat to escape to where? The Caymans?"

THE CLOSER WE GOT to Randy's house, the more I wondered if this was the place we should have come to. Laura's was the last house along the airstrip neighborhood that was lit. No one seemed to be home. Life was not evident out here at all. The wind was blowing trees almost sideways on the tiny peninsula.

In my hand I held my daughter's hand. The letters of people deceased and those still alive who'd suffered from Fletch's and Mac's deadly hands sat in my lap. The water and its nitrates and bacteria and the aftermath in their bodies had probably slowly killed these unknowing victims. Low clouds raced over the coppery moon. Nothing but nature's darkness and a moon that saw too much.

"Mommy, why are we going to Mr. Randy's? I just want to go home," Daisy said sleepily.

"We'll be there in just a minute, sweetheart. It's quieter out here. Be patient," I said. Tay swung around to yell something at his sister, his faux dreads rising up like palms in the wind. I shook my head *no*. He turned around and let out an exasperated spit of air.

Once inside, we all let down with growling sighs and began to warm and to settle. Randy offered Daisy a big T-shirt. I saturated a washcloth in hot water, cooled it a bit, and wiped her face with it. Randy made us hot tea. He and Tay sat in front of the big glass doors facing the deck and the Gulf, watching the ocean crashing in hard, the sagging moon's reflection surfing to shore. It was a spring tide, an extremely high tide with the full moon.

I lay down with Daisy on the floor of the bedroom where Randy had dropped a couple of sleeping bags for us. "Why are we here?" she said, using Tay's backpack for a pillow.

"I thought we'd be safer," I said. "Somebody has tried to poison Mr. Mac again. Some people think I did it, and they might come around to bother us at our house tonight. They don't know we're here. We'll go home tomorrow. I almost forgot—tomorrow's Fish Day at Grandpa's! Maybe you can catch a fish, and we can have it for dinner!"

She sat up. "Can I use the orange squiggly lure you and Grandpa always fight over?"

"Hmmm, maybe, if you're a really good girl. Now lie down and try to relax. Remember how I taught you to take deep breaths to relax? Try that now, okay?" She took five deep breaths, then was quiet. Within five minutes, she was breathing steadily, deeply, asleep.

I came out to the living room, and Randy poured hot tea. Tay was looking at me quizzically, his black and white face smeared now. My impulse was to say, Look at your face! But I curbed it. "Come help us look through this stuff,"

I said. He sat down. Then he said, "I'm tired. I'm going to go keep Daisy company." I nodded and held my arms up for a hug.

"Don't you want to take off your . . . face mask?" I said. He shook his head somberly. "I can sleep like this." He wandered off down the hallway.

Randy and I began to open each letter, reading them to ourselves. Outside the wind was whooshing through the pines, and the waves boomed in the distance against the coastline.

"Did you hear that?" I said. "I thought I heard a car drive up and the engine go off."

"No, it's the weather. And you've got the Gulf so close, you hear all kinds of things," he said. "The house creaks, you know. You get used to it," he said.

"God, listen to this," I said. "It's from Edwards, written years after his brother drowned, to his mom: 'I haven't wanted to write this letter, because I know it would anguish you more. You had to give me up, and I understand that. I know you know he let my brother drown. Now, years later I'll tell you the story . . .' Blah blah . . . 'thought I was asleep in the lower deck . . .' so forth . . . 'Jay was only five, and was walking on the edge of the boat and slipped and fell into the Gulf. I heard him come up gasping, then back down again . . . he came up again, and I heard, "Help me!" I thought Fletch would go in after him, but he didn't, just watched my baby brother go under, left him there. I was too traumatized to do anything. I've always felt guilty about this. Later, when I pretended to wake up, I looked him in the eyes . . . flat as paper dolls, watching me now.' " I laid the letter down and took a deep breath.

"Yep. They're bad," Randy said, shaking his head slowly. He had swollen eyes and a deep crease between his brows. He needed a hair trim, or maybe just a shave. I was antsy. Loose strings of hair hung down his neck in the back. "I just read a letter Mr. Colbert wrote to Trina about nitrates and the invasive bacteria in the waterways, about the infections that assist tumor growth in animals and people, about the deals ECOL was making out on the state road." He threw the letter down and sat back. "Colbert had done some research into these septic tanks and runoff. He went to Mac's office with a list of a hundred ways people get sick living near this kind of waste. Mr. Colbert was in the last stages of cancer then. He showed Mac what his neighborhoods without proper septic had begotten. A wasted, blue-lipped man."

"I'm not sure what goes through these guys' heads," I said.

"They don't think," Randy said. "They stopped thinking sometime long ago."

I thought I could hear brush moving outside. The strong wind had the palms clattering away. I touched the side of my boot. Randy didn't notice, intently reading the next letter. I should probably drink some Kava tea, one of

Grandma's specialties.

I read again. "Oh, my god. Mary *did* write Trina. 'I know how you must feel, Mrs. Lutz. My little baby Adam, even if he did have a defect, was mine, and didn't deserve to die. He was mine. I left that day to get him some extra small diapers, and I came back and Fletch told me the baby had died and that Mac, who'd just moved to town, had called the morgue to have him taken away. I didn't even get to say goodbye. . . .'

"Oh, my god, why didn't she *tell* somebody?" I said.

Randy said. "No wonder she drank so much. No wonder she—"

"Yes," came a voice from the kitchen, "that's why she did it, that and the other miscarriages."

In walked Neptune, or Mac dressed as Neptune, rather, silver beard missing. He had his own .38 in his hand. The kitchen was dark except for the incandescent bulb over the stove.

"Put that away," Randy demanded, standing up. "LaRue's kids are asleep in the back." My blood went to ice. I slowly reached down to my ankle as if to scratch, tapped my boot, then stood.

Mac's silvered hair shone yellow under the bulb. Such pretty hair. Such a waste. What a strange thing to think. He was smirking, looking handsome, but now it took on a sinister quality I'd avoided noticing before. I wished to hell Randy hadn't mentioned my kids.

"I thought you'd been poisoned," I said from the living room, next to the dining table. Mac pulled the barrel of the gun to the ceiling, then pointed it back down aiming at my chest.

"I'm not an idiot, my dear enterprising Indian girl," he said. "I figured out some antidotes of my own in case you or Randy or Madonna or Laura, or one of you little sneaks was trying to poison me."

"You goddamn son of a bitch," I said.

"Now, don't be cursing like that in front of the children, LaRue," he said. "You don't want to be waking them up right now. They'll find your bodies eventually, lying in the bottom on that boat out there, which happened because of a big argument between star-crossed lovers. Now get moving," he said. "To the sliding glass door."

"Did you try to kill Mary?" I said. I didn't move my legs. "She knew, didn't she? She knew Fletch killed her baby, the one with the birth defect, and that you disposed of the body. You knew she was pregnant again, and again and again, and this time, she might spill the beans on you two. And whoever might get sick and die from your projects, from the poison that spills into the water. You know damn well nitrates in the water can cause spontaneous abortions, cancers, respiratory and skin problems, all out there in the swamps and the rivers. You knew Mary and Trina had talked just before you killed Trina." I stood still so he wouldn't shoot immediately, bringing the kids out of the room.

Mac stood with a thin smile, unfazed. I should have shut up, but I didn't. "Mary threatened you, didn't she? She knew there was hard evidence of the burials. She was going to try to put a stop to ECOL, she was going to try to frame you and Fletch for the murders." I hoped my questions would deflect him from concentrating next on my children.

"Curiosity, curiosity," he said, wagging the gun. Then he pointed it at the glass doors.

I kept talking to stall him, hoping Randy would think of some way to distract him so I could reach down into my boot. He'd be as dead as I was, I decided. "We found the knife you or someone used to kill Trina," I said. "On your boat. It's been turned in as evidence." He smirked. I ignored him and went on. "Fletch has had Preston Edwards terrified since he was a boy. You're a terrorist. An environmental terrorist."

He gave me a faux surprised look. "Why LaRue, after all the business I've given you over the years. What kind of thanks is that?"

"Okay, Mac," Randy said. "You can have all these letters. It's too late. You don't need to kill us. Enough have died already."

"My dear boy, after all the business I've given *you*. That day in my office, when you showed up to remind me of the ways you hysterical environmentalists think everything is killing you all," he mocked. "Weeping over your wife dying of cancer in the hospital." He laughed.

Why hadn't I noticed this about Mac before? I imagined him in a straight jacket, pacing padded walls saying, *you hysterical environmentalists.*

"Mac, what are you going to do? You're wearing a silver Neptune outfit," Randy reasoned. "You'll be easy to spot. They'll be able to pick you out, of course, anywhere."

"Oh, no," he said. "It's all worked out. I have connections in Veracruz, and from there I have a little retirement gig worked out in Mexico. Right on the ocean. A surfer's haven. Low maintenance, affordable for someone from the States." He laughed again and pointed us towards the sliding glass door.

"What about Mary?" I said, as we opened the door to a strong wind. "The law found hairs in the trailer that they can identify. They've done an analysis and they'll figure out you OD'd her." We were walking across the deck now, Randy frowning and staring down as he stepped beside me in front of Mac.

"They won't figure out anything but that your hair was also there, LaRue," Mac said. "And I'm tired of listening to you ramble. Now walk. To the boat." I glanced back towards the house for a split second. I said the most earnest prayer of my life.

Outside, the wind moaned, cutting cold around us. The Gulf waves were crashing onshore, like muffled explosions. Mac gave commands. "First go around the front of the house and stand by my car. Not behind it, beside it where I can see you. If you two are going to shoot each other, we need two guns." He laughed that deep heh heh heh that slowed my blood.

He fished around in the trunk with one hand, the gun in the other. The moon illuminated the front yard for a second out of the cloud cover, then disappeared again. I realized I would really miss everything. The beach, the lantana, the monarch butterflies in the fall winging all the way across the Gulf in pairs to Mexico. Wild irises in late spring. How the fish gather at the surface when the mosquitoes hover there in summer.

I thought I detected movement in the second bedroom where the kids were sleeping. Mac was muttering and chuckling to himself.

Randy moved slowly towards me, eyeing Mac, then whispered in my ear. "I'll try to hit him when we get to the boat. Or push him in. You run. Get the kids, and take off—the keys are on the dining room table."

"But what about—" I said.

"What are you two lovers quarreling about now?" Mac said. He pulled up out of the trunk with a gun in each hand like some kind of gun-slinging cowboy he'd seen on a scratched-up Western. "Now move! Down to the boat!"

I walked without feeling my feet, one step at a time across the sandy lot, trying to think of how to reach for the gun in my shoe. The sand squeaked under our feet, muffled by ocean.

Suddenly I saw movement by the water on the other side of the house, ghostly walking towards the Gulf. Two figures, one tall and slim as a young pine, the other two-thirds that size looking like a T-shirt with small legs. Good god. They both carried something. The box of letters? What? I could not accept what I saw.

CHAPTER 32

AS WE APPROACHED THE DOCK, Mac told us to climb down into the boat one at a time, Randy first. Mac had the gun pointed at my skull. The boat rocked like a washing machine sloshing. Slowly Randy stepped down into the tottering boat, the wind and waves high. The moon appeared from behind clouds, and I saw the box of medications in the boat just next to the throttle on the deck.

"Why's that there?" I asked Randy softly as I stepped down into the boat. I squinted to scan the stacks and saw a big bottle of Percodan. I was going to die, sure, but the betrayal hit me like falling face first in the water. Why hadn't I noticed this earlier? It was Randy who'd tried to poison Mac.

"Stop talking now, you two!" Mac said as he stepped in, aiming both guns again at me, steadying himself and walking backwards towards the motor. The metal tip of the barrel was six feet away. I stood at the throttle starboard side. Even though I was already dead, I was pissed off at Randy, the poisoner. Across from me and closer to Mac stood Randy. "LaRue, you move over to the middle farther from the wheel. Randy, you stand—"

Suddenly a loud clap like thunder exploded on the port side of the boat five feet from where Randy and Mac stood. The two of them fell to the deck of the boat, and a giant cloud of smoke pushed right into us. The wind was blowing just that direction. We coughed, the smoke completely fogging the boat. I could barely see, and my eyes stung shut. Then the black smoke began to lift.

"Hey!" Mac said, scrambling for the guns that had slid starboard side and back towards the motor. I barely made out his silver Neptune arms waving smoke away from his eyes. Then he was rubbing his eyes, coughing. Randy swooped towards me in one motion, grabbed me around the waist and heaved me up onto the dock where I fell. "Run!" he said, jumping nearly on top of me. Mac was still struggling to see and to grab the gun. I scrambled to my feet on the dock, tearing towards the house. I stopped only for a second to grab the gun from my shoe, and I screamed, "Daisy! Taylor!" Then I was running headlong, the house in front of me. Randy had veered towards the car. I slid the glass door open and snatched the keys. The kids were outside, but I checked the bedroom anyway. Rumpled sleeping bags and no kids. The gun shook in my hands. I ran outside to hear an explosion from the boat.

Its force was so strong, a reverberating kaboom, that I fell down on Randy's driveway not far from the docked boat. "Daisy! Taylor!" I screamed, scrambling up, looking around. A bloodcurdling scream went up, a deep horrible animal sound. I ran for Randy's car, calling the kids, kneeling behind it.

Randy ran over beside me, breathing hard. "Tay bombed the gas tank open. Mac's burning." Then we heard a splash. He must have thrown himself into the water.

"Daisy! Taylor!" I screamed again. Randy and I both stood up. The fire blew up into the fast-moving fierce air, taking on a life of its own in the strong wind. I could hear myself sobbing, unharmed, but where the hell were my kids? The air around us suddenly felt desert hot. I heard a whoosh as the pine branch hanging above the boat caught fire.

"Mom!" Daisy yelled. She peered out from behind Mac's truck in the road.

"Over here," Taylor followed up, his voice coming from the same place. "Behind Mr. Mac's truck!" I put the safety back on. I've never run so fast. They stood together panting behind the truck, both with eyes wide. I grabbed them both by the shoulders and held them hard to my chest. Taylor had gotten rid of his mask.

"Oh, my god," I said, my whole body shaking.

"It's okay, Mom," Tay said. Then his eyes grew round, soft. "Where'd you get that gun?" He was looking over his shoulder at the .38 shaking in my hand, the safety still on. I shoved the gun back into my boot.

Then I heard the whining of a fire truck. "Oh, my god," I said.

"Mom, is Mr. Mac going to live?" Tay asked. Daisy started to cry quietly.

"I don't know. But sounds like help is coming." We stood huddled, panting, trembling, watching the fire truck's lights flying towards us from town. Several volunteers jumped off, talking, and then shouting, headed down to the boat with large hoses. Randy ran out and said to them, "There's a burning man in the water!"

"What were you doing?" I said to the kids as I turned, leaned back on the car and slid down to sit on the ground, still gasping. "You two. At the water."

"I was just trying to scare Mr. Mac," Tay said, standing and shrugging. "He had gotten really scary, like a bipolar or something. I didn't mean to set anybody on fire. Mom, do you think he's crazy?"

I nodded and tried a frozen smile. "You could say that." I wrapped my arms around Daisy, who had crawled into my lap.

"Is he dying?" Tay said, trying to look at the scene. "Am I a murderer?"

"Don't move," I said, grabbing his arm and pulling him down. "Sit. He's a murderer. He killed Trina, and he tried to kill Mary. No telling who else. Stay here. The firemen can handle this. They're used to saving people who are burned."

We all three sat, our breath coming slower, listening to the roar and the shouts of firemen, something plunging into the water.

"Taylor is so smart!" Daisy finally said. "He gave me the smoke bomb that Grandma taught him how to make."

I turned to Taylor. "Grandma was teaching you this when you were out at the pit?" I said.

"Yeah," said Daisy, "and he taught me how to use it, too!"

"Daisy, you're smart, too," I said. "Brave. But damn it, this is too dangerous."

"See, it was a decoy," Tay said excitedly, standing up again. "Mac looked the wrong way while you guys got off the boat, and then I threw the flammable bomb—just to scare him—to keep him from following you. I didn't mean to hit the gas tank." He sounded regretful.

I shook my head, breathing a little hard still. I pulled him back down and put my arms around them both.

"It's okay, Mom," Daisy said in a most grownup voice, like the voice that had said, "Actually, it's a very dark night" just hours ago.

"So you called the cops?" I said to Tay.

"Of course. Your cell phone was sitting on the desk in the bedroom. Jackson's number was on your speed dial, so I called him. He must have called the fire department, 'cause he knows Cooter's not worth a damn."

"Daisy," Tay said. "Good job with the decoy."

"Thanks, kids. I'm sure you know you saved my life. And Mr. Randy's." They said nothing, just looked at each other. Then a high five. The fire truck took off again to get Mac to town, I expected. The helicopter would take him to Tallahassee Memorial's burn unit. "But you know, I've been so worried about you, Tay. Your alarm systems, your knife at school, your skull shirts." I pointed at his shirt. "Revenge is not a good thing. People just keep trying to get revenge. It causes—"

"Mom!" Daisy suddenly said. "Chill out, will ya?" I sat back, leaning my head on Mac's car tire. We all three sat for another minute shivering, the wind roaring, the hoses hissing.

When we walked back to the house, there was Jackson. He stood in the kitchen and relief washed over his face as the three of us piled in, scraggly, through the sliding glass doors. An ambulance whined in the distance. Another cop with Jackson held his ear to a phone, calling to make sure the emergency Memorial Hospital helicopter had been launched from Tallahassee to pick Mac up.

Jackson's face was serious. "Good work, Tay," he said, meeting us in the living room, slapping Tay on the back. "You all okay?" He glanced from smudged face to smudged face. Nobody said anything. "Everybody okay?" We all mumbled yes. "Let's all sit down, shall we?" he said, inviting us to the floor. We stood numb.

"Mac's got burns all over his body," he said. "But he'll survive. He jumped into the Gulf quickly enough. And he'll have a long prison sentence waiting on him when he gets out of the hospital. I've got the knife with his fingerprints, and, as it turns out, his hair in the trailer. Fletch's fingerprints were on the glass and the narcotic bottle. He'd started Mary drinking early and put the drugs in her first drink that morning." He paused to see if I was watching. "And Mary. Mary is doing a Lazarus, rising from near death. She's been talking from the ICU bed. To Laura. Seems she's suspicious of Fletch's having killed a couple of kids along the way, too."

"So where's Fletch?" I said.

"In St. Annes County lock-up," he said. "Along with Tiffany, who admitted to forging narcotic prescriptions and the death certificate for Mac."

"Finally," Randy said, hands in his back pockets. I hadn't seen him come in from the back of the house. I sat down on the floor and dragged the kids with me. I wanted them next to me. Then, exhausted, we all lay down flat on the floor.

"You're in big trouble," Jackson said to me, with his eyes taking the tricky shape they did when I wasn't sure if he was kidding or not. He pointed at me. "For making punch, for having the tea antidote, for—"

"I explained that to you before," I said, sharp, if weary. "I never did anything wrong in the first place. And I didn't bring the tea."

"Sorry, Mom," Tay said. "Mom told me to leave the potion at home. My Grandma told me Mom needed it, and no matter what Mom said, I should take it anyway."

"Take this box of letters, too," I said, too tired to argue.

"Good work," Jackson said, paging through the letters. "These should help. With the ECOL situation, too. Unfortunate that Mac and Fletch had to get arrested for two human murders alone. Yep, you finally gathered some real evidence," Jackson said. Always the joker.

"The knife?" I said, in no mood for banter.

Jackson ignored me. "How about that. Good work." I remained lying down. The kids were yawning as they sat up.

"I think that's what Trina finally threatened him with," I said, pointing to the letters. "And Mary—I think Mary was coming to her senses before the poisoning. Both women were scared enough not to say anything. All these years. I think Trina was afraid Fletch and the redneck mafia would go after her living son, Preston."

"Well, after all this work I ought to at least rate a dinner with you," he suggested. He glanced at Randy, who was standing by the glass doors, hardly seeming engaged, hands in his pockets. "Or breakfast. Especially since we were so rudely interrupted at the party."

Coral curves of clouds were now beginning to light up the gray sky as the sun began to show its rays over the horizon. Like commas, or fish hooks, or curls on a girl's head.

"Let's do it. Breakfast. Make it now," I said to Jackson, glancing at Randy. "Or almost now. And you have to be willing to have these two along," I said, pulling the kids in towards me. "If they stay awake long enough. But first I need to have a talk with my lawyer friend here. In private."

Randy turned around and looked at me guiltily, and said, "Okay, where to?" I pointed to the hallway. I wasn't going to get out of visible range of my kids.

We stood in the hall. I was too tired for subtlety. "I saw the Percodan in your boat. Right?"

"Right," he said. His arms were folded in front of him.

"And the night, the very night I was first accused of poisoning Mac, which you had done, never meaning to frame me, you brought a big pretty fern to sit on the outside of my apartment with a note that said that Mac deserved it, right?" I said. "You got the hibiscus you planted out front at the same time."

"LaRue, I wasn't trying to kill him," Randy said. "I was trying to scare him, to terrify him. I wanted him really worried about all the things he was doing."

"Right. And you spoke to my son about revenge. How to get revenge on people who had done bad things to other people. You told Tay that Mac and Fletch had not liked Trina," I said. "I don't like you teaching revenge to my kid."

"Nobody ever thought about me in this whole thing," Randy said. He looked beat, defeated. He no longer looked cute. "My wife died of ovarian cancer. Do you have any idea what it's like to watch someone die slowly of cancer? Then one of my best friends died because of those men and what they were doing, and nobody was doing anything about it," he said, his whispering voice rising.

"I'm sorry. I really am. But encouraging revenge—he's my son," I said. "He's at a vulnerable age. He's been in trouble at school, bringing his knife, and talking about security systems, accidentally blowing out the Main Street lights. Next thing you know— It's got to—"

"Mom," Tay said from the room beyond us, "are you giving Mr. Randy a hard time?"

"It's okay, Tay," Randy said. He turned back to me. "I'm sorry if I messed up your life. I really am. These deaths—it can make you nuts." He ran his hand through his hair. He did have urgent eyes, and he was raised by a particular Southern church set of parents. He was an emotional basket case, and I was too busy and too fragile.

"Randy, there are women all over the island who would love to go out with you," I said. "If you want to find love again, you have to throw the past to the fickle Gulf wind. She'd want you to go on. Forgive, and open yourself up." I was sounding like a rabid preacher. Maybe that was the language he heard.

He didn't say anything. He was looking at the floor.

"Look, I care about you a lot, but I have to tell Jackson it was you who poisoned the coffee, it was you who poisoned the punch. Unless you are ready to do it yourself."

"Mommy," Daisy said, "are you still back there?"

"Okay, I'll do it," Randy said. I sighed and headed back down the hallway to my kids and my date. Randy asked the other cop if the two of them could speak outside on the deck. As soon as the sliding glass door closed on them, I saw that Randy began talking.

THE SKY'S BACKGROUND eased from grayish to lavender. Then the coral began to disappear, and the lavender began to fill in the sky over the green-black Gulf. I fell asleep with my kids on Randy's carpeted floor, Jackson hovering close by. When I woke up, Randy was gone. Jackson had called in the state forces. They'd whisked Randy away to get a statement. The sun stood brilliant in a powder-blue sky, and the wind had died. December. Christmas would be sneaking in, making St. Annes people exuberant. They'd be forgetting, for the moment, the past violent seasons on the Gulf.

We headed back to town, the four of us, the kids sleeping, draped over each other in the back seat of Jackson's car. I was trying to tune in some decent music on the radio, humming *You can't hurry love, No, you just have to wait.*

"So you're back in business, back in the good graces of your town," Jackson said. The sun was rising and trying to shine across the Gulf as we crossed from Randy's place back towards town.

"You sound like a medieval mayor, dude," I said, flipping off the radio. "You know, I'm beginning to realize that in the long run, business people like Mac aren't going to help. He did bring me business. But I'd rather have the steady income of the town and the few tourists who still come to see this old place. They got me through this period, you know? But I didn't need him to get by," I said. "I thought I did, but . . . I was wondering what would happen to my kids, my dad, everybody, if I ended up in jail."

"You know, I had this sneaking suspicion it was Randy dumping the drugs in drinks," he said. "He's one of those moody sulkers that women get sucked into liking." I squirmed in the seat.

"So how'd you figure out it was him, I mean 'he'?" I asked. A few fishermen's trucks and cars were parked at the fish place by the cove, and the sign blinked a blue "OPEN." I could smell the biscuits and bacon and suddenly felt extraordinarily hungry.

"Well, I never knew for sure, but after he was close and talking to you at the party last night, he made this smooth move of pretending to put his shoes under the table, and he pulled out a plastic bag from the left shoe. But you don't always go arresting people right away, especially when you've got so many interconnected people, events, and it's first-degree murder you're working." He looked at me sharply. "And you left with him, so I figured you'd beat him up good," he added.

"What? I had no idea he'd done it! You told me you didn't want me to leave! Made a huge angry scene about it. How embarrassing is that?"

"LaRue, you've got a long way to go if you're going to be a detective," he smirked. "Think about it from Randy's point of view. If LaRue is the prime suspect, then he can leave without worrying. Off scot-free."

"You let me go away with him, knowing he'd tried to poison Mac? Me and my two kids? He could have killed all of us!"

"Ha!" Jackson said. "Hardly. Two different kinds of explosives with a canny son and daughter. You had a gun, a cell phone, am I right? And you ended up putting one guy in the hospital, and one in jail? I think you all handled it okay."

Despite wanting to smack him, I realized Jackson had a point. I beamed. I belonged to my kids, and they were capable. We turned onto Main Street. This was our town. Dusty little boxes lined up along the Gulf coast or not, we belonged. Could we together defeat the huge corporations using our waters?

At least I could say I saw one of those schemes snuffed out. We drove right up to the front door and parked, something possible in a small town. There's so much to be said for that simple fact.

"I kind of like this detective thing," I said.

"Oh, no," he said, as we stopped in front of the cafe. "Please tell me you didn't just say that."

I could see Madonna and Laura through the window, reading the paper and eating. The smell of fresh bacon and eggs and biscuits danced in the air. I was just a Southern girl, too tall, with two demanding kids, a faithful retired dad who didn't know what to do with me, a nutty Indian grandmother, and here was a guy who liked me just fine. The kids roused when the car came to a halt, wiping their sleepy eyes.

"Let's go," Jackson said.

Jackson read my mind. "How do you account for your grandmother knowing when to send you tea?" he asked. I thought about how she knew the water was tainted, and that a tornado would hit Florida that day, that she knew to teach Tay how to use explosives a certain way, and lots of other things. We walked into the warm restaurant. The murmur rolled up at us, and people waved at us or gave us curious looks. Word had already gotten out.

"Now that's a mystery I can't solve," I said. "Maybe you should have a talk with the Little People who live in the trees."

HERE ARE SOME OTHER BOOKS
FROM PINEAPPLE PRESS ON RELATED TOPICS.

For a complete catalog, write to Pineapple Press,
P.O. Box 3889, Sarasota, Florida 34230-3889, or call (800) 746-3275.
Or visit our website at www.pineapplepress.com.

Secrets of San Blas by **Charles Farley.** First novel in the Secrets trilogy. Most towns have their secrets. In the 1930s, Port St. Joe on the Gulf in Florida's Panhandle has more than its share. Old Doc Berber, the town's only general practitioner, thought he knew all of the secrets, but a grisly murder out at the Cape San Blas Lighthouse drags him into a series of intrigues that even he can't diagnose.

Secrets of St. Vincent by **Charles Farley.** Second novel in the Secrets trilogy. Things are not always as serene as they seem in the little Florida Panhandle village of Port St. Joe. Bluesman Reggie Robinson has been wrongly arrested for the gruesome murder of Sheriff Byrd "Dog" Batson. Doc Berber and his best friend, Gator Mica, mount a quixotic search for the sheriff's savage killer on equally savage St. Vincent Island. If they survive the adventure, they'll return with the shocking secrets that will shatter the town's tranquility forever.

Secrets of St. Joe by **Charles Farley.** Third novel in the Secrets trilogy. Someone in the tiny village of Port St. Joe is trying to murder Doc Berber and everyone he loves. When the doctor foolishly sets out to track down the revenge-crazed killer, he is forced to confront the most shameful secrets of the town, the murderer, . . . and himself.

A Land Remembered by **Patrick Smith.** This best-selling novel tells the story of three generations of the MacIveys, a Florida family who battle the hardships of the frontier to rise from a dirt-poor Cracker life to the wealth and standing of real estate tycoons.

Conflict of Interest by **Terry Lewis.** Trial lawyer Ted Stevens fights his own battles, including his alcoholism and his pending divorce, as he fights for his client in a murder case. But it's the other suspect in the case who causes the conflict of interest. Ted must choose between concealing evidence that would be helpful to his client and revealing it, thereby becoming a suspect himself.

Privileged Information by **Terry Lewis.** Ted Stevens' partner, Paul Morganstein, is defending his late brother's best friend on a murder charge when he obtains privileged information leading him to conclude that his client committed another murder thirty years earlier. The victim? Paul's brother. Faced with numerous difficulties, Paul must decide if he will divulge privileged information.

Delusional by **Terry Lewis.** Ted Stevens' new client is a mental patient who is either a delusional, psychotic killer or an innocent man framed for the murder of his psychologist—or maybe both. Nathan Hart hears voices and believes that a secret organization known only as the Unit is out to get him. Is the Unit responsible for the murder of Dr. Aaron Rosenberg? Or is something more sinister afoot?

Doctored Evidence by **Michael Biehl.** A medical device fails and the patient dies on the operating table. Was it an accident—or murder? Smart and courageous hospital attorney Karen Hayes must find out: Her job and her life depend on it.

Lawyered to Death by **Michael Biehl.** Hospital attorney Karen Hayes is called to defend the hospital CEO against a claim of sexual harassment but soon finds she must also defend him against a murder charge. The trail of clues leads her into a further fight for her own life and that of her infant son.

Nursing a Grudge by **Michael Biehl.** An elderly nursing home resident, who was once an Olympic champion swimmer with a murky background in the German army, drowns in a lake behind the home. Does anyone know how it happened? Does anyone care? Hospital attorney Karen Hayes battles bureaucracy, listens to the geriatric residents ignored by the authorities, and risks her own life to find the truth.

My Brother Michael **by Janis Owens.** This novel tells the story of Myra Sims from Gabriel Catts' point of view. Gabriel recounts his lifelong love for his brother Michael's wife, Myra—whose own demons threaten to overwhelm all three of them.

Myra Sims **by Janis Owens.** In the sequel to My Brother Michael, we learn the story of Michael's wife, Myra, in her own flat Louisianan drawl as she evolves from voiceless victim to triumphant survivor. A rare literary opportunity to experience the same story from a different character's perspective.

Death in Bloodhound Red **by Virginia Lanier.** Jo Beth Sidden is a Georgia peach with an iron pit. She raises and trains bloodhounds for search-and-rescue missions in the Okefenokee Swamp. In an attempt to save a friend from ruin, she organizes an illegal operation that makes a credible alibi impossible just when she needs one most: She's indicted for attempted murder. If the victim dies, the charge will be murder one.

CPSIA information can be obtained at www.ICGtesting.com
Printed in the USA
BVOW03s2218190315

392425BV00004B/7/P